The Soulbane Illusion

A NOVEL

By Norman Jetmundsen, Jr.

BOOKS

Winchester, UK
New York, USA

For my Mother and Father,
Who gave me life and their hearts,

and

For my triplet sons,
Taylor, Nelson and Jonathan,
Who forever carry my heart

I Corinthians 13: 7–8

Copyright © 2003 O Books
46A West Street, Alresford, Hants SO24 9AU, U.K.
Tel: +44 (0) 1962 736880 Fax: +44 (0) 1962 736881
E-mail: office@johnhunt-publishing.com
www.johnhunt-publishing.com
www.o-books.net

U.S. office:
240 West 35th Street, Suite 500
New York, NY 10001
E-mail: obooks@aol.com

Text: © 2003 Norman Jetmundsen
Design: Jim Weaver Design

ISBN 1 903816 59 9

A CIP catalogue record for this book is available from the British Library.

Printed in Dubai, U.A.E. by Oriental Press.

"Fair is foul, and foul is fair."
—Shakespeare, *Macbeth, Act I, Scene I*

CONTENTS

PART II

PROLOGUE

THE RAIN from the menacing black storm clouds beat mercilessly on the unyielding stone of St. Michael's Mount this New Year's Eve. Despite the tempest's power, the torrent was drowned out by the crash of surf pounding the rocky island from which the ancient castle rose majestically, as the mighty sea battled the booming thunder to see who would reign supreme as the prince of murderous sounds on this bleak afternoon. The unforgiving, screeching wind chilled the air.

Inside the castle, seemingly at the end of the world on the barren, wintry Cornish coast, the rage of nature was muted. In the medieval Chevy Chase room, a group of about a dozen hooded figures in black gowns, faces hidden, sat at a long oak table, its extensive history etched in the uneven marks on its surface. Another dozen hooded figures stood around the table. The room was lit by flaming torches, and a blazing fire roared in the stone fireplace. Dark wooden beams arched over the room, accentuating the whiteness of the walls. The hooded figures conversed quietly among themselves.

The figure at the head of the table stood abruptly, his large frame giving him an imposing presence. The room quietened instantly and all heads turned toward their leader, who governed with unstated but unmistakable authority. "Does everyone understand their role in carrying out our stratagem?" he asked.

There was a murmur and all heads nodded their assent.

"Good," he continued. "Base Command has personally commissioned our vital work, so I need not remind you of the importance of our task."

An uncomfortable shifting movement rippled round the room. No one spoke.

"One further bit of advice. I can't emphasize strongly enough how important it is for you always to remember the need for subtlety. Don't bring attention to yourselves or your work. Instead, be diligent behind the scenes, careful not to draw notice. A quiet whisper is usually our most potent weapon. As you are well aware, we have altered our approach for this most important of projects, which we have named Operation Clootie. Our plan is to launch this final global stratagem one year from today."

The figure paused. The only sound was the crackling wood in the fireplace. He continued, "Each of you has been in place for many years, so by now you should be accepted and respected members of your communities, as disgusting as that may sound. Let me go over the basics one more time, so there'll be no mistakes." He paused. The hood moved from side to side, the face hidden in the dark cave-like opening. "While we can create the illusion of being one of these vile creatures by taking on human form – and each of you has assumed a specific human identity for a number of years – it is important at all times to remember you are not flesh and blood, but an illusion. You have all been thoroughly trained to employ the exact mannerisms and idioms for the person and nationality you're pretending to be. You also have to remember that these human bodies age and decay. Don't forget the importance of adding the touch of age to your looks: maybe a hint of gray, a few wrinkles, or the slight limp in your gait, perhaps the occasional health complaint, so you will fit in perfectly and raise no suspicions. Any questions?"

One member of the hooded convocation raised a hand tentatively, and when the leader nodded, the figure asked in a feminine voice, "When shall we next convene?"

"That has not yet been determined, but you'll be informed by the usual channels. Just be sure to travel conventionally, unobtrusively. Anything else?"

No one uttered a sound. "All right, we'll conclude our meeting in the usual manner. I arranged to have this place reserved for today only. The tide will come in soon, so you should not dally, but get along the causeway to the mainland. Once there, disperse quietly in the darkness and be on your way."

The leader gestured for the seated group to rise, and everyone at the table complied. The entire hooded group began a low, ethereal chant as they formed a large circle around the table. Tall candles burned on the table, their black smoke wafting upwards.

"Because of the tremendous importance of Operation Clootie, we have invited a special master to conduct our ceremony," the leader announced.

A figure in a scarlet gown and hood swept in as swiftly and silently as a whisper of wind.

"Morgana," the leader said, "we're ready for our Cimmerian communion."

The figure in red strode inside the circle of robed figures, raised death-white, bony hands toward the ceiling, and began the ancient incantation.

*   *   *

As the hooded congregation silently departed the castle, the leader grabbed the arm of one of them, saying in a quiet voice, "Stay behind, I want to have a special word with you." The figure nodded and stepped aside.

When the castle was deserted, save these two, the leader spoke in a whispered tone, "Soulbane, your report was a stupendous achievement. I see great potential for you. I have decided to give you some personal tutorials to fine-tune your fiendish skills. Is that satisfactory?"

"Perfectly."

"Any questions?"

"Just one. What about that damned Bryson?"

"Yes, I thought you might bring that unfortunate episode up. I have reviewed the situation carefully, and decided it was not your fault. I've made quite sure the Royal Hindness did not learn of Bryson's little discovery, especially given the disaster with Screwtape and Wormwood. It appears, however, that I was successful in stealing your reports back when I purloined the imbecile's computer, since he's never given any indication that he still has a copy. It's been so many years now that I believe it's safe for us to proceed. Ordinarily, of course, I would have banished you, but for the unfortunate misstep I had in that abominable homeless shelter. So, let's just say this entire debacle is our little secret. Understood?"

"Of course. But ... what about Bryson?"

"Since Slayspark failed so abominably and let the Enemy win the battle on Magdalen Tower, you and I will personally see to that cretin. Don't worry. I have plans to finish him once and for all. We have to be most careful, because the Enemy has been working his damnable magic to try and help the imbecile. Fortunately for us, Bryson appears to have turned a deaf ear to the Enemy. Besides, the war has only just begun – Bryson's on his way to becoming a successful professional, working his way up the ladder, as those loathsome creatures are wont to say, with all the attendant human stress in his life. So, I suspect our job of bringing him to his knees is already half accomplished. At any rate, he'll be vanquished when my plans for him are brought to fruition."

✻   ✻   ✻

It was almost dark as Soulbane left the castle. The rain and wind continued their relentless rage. Before long the rising sea would cover the causeway, transforming St. Michael's Mount once more into an island. He quickly removed his black robe and began walking on the cobblestone road away from the castle. He couldn't feel the water lapping up ankle-high on him, nor the bitterly cold wind.

Soulbane turned to study the imposing, dark outline of St.

Michael's Mount, astride the craggy pile. He had often wondered who Foulheart had disguised himself as in human life. He had some suspicions, but had never been able to confirm them. One day, he would learn more about Foulheart and his master plan to destroy the world through Operation Clootie, starting with the decadent western society. Foulheart had played everything secretively thus far, even with Soulbane. He knew that Foulheart was very impressed with his report on their Hindom's stratagems to destroy the western world and the Church, so he was confident of being suitably recognized when Operation Clootie was successfully concluded.

For now, however, he had other things on his mind. As he thought of Foulheart's remarks about Cade Bryson, Soulbane smiled.

PART

I

"In the middle of the journey of our life
I came to myself within a dark wood
where the straight way was lost."

–Dante, *Inferno, Canto I*

1

STANDING QUICKLY, Cade Bryson gripped the table tightly, digging his nails into the wood. He felt as if he was about to choke. Beads of sweat formed on his forehead. Adrenaline raced through his body, the product of something akin to sheer terror. Instinctively, to ward off his nervousness, he brushed the front of his thick blonde hair with his hand, while glancing quickly about the room. The dim light cast through the windows by the afternoon winter sun barely illuminated the dark-paneled, mahogany walls. A large, black-robed man entered the room commanding everyone's attention. Cade gulped hard, his knees shook.

"Has the jury reached a verdict?" the judge asked as he seated himself at the elevated wooden bench. A thin, middle-aged woman, with graying hair and round glasses, stood in the jury box amidst eleven other citizens of Atlanta, and said, "We have your Honor."

"What is your verdict?" the judge asked.

Cade's temples pounded, his tongue stuck to the roof of his parched mouth. This was the first major trial for which he had been given significant responsibility. It had lasted most of December up until today, January sixth. His firm's client had been sued for millions of dollars. Cade was close to being made a partner in the prestigious Atlanta law firm of Morris, Lodge, Gioia, Ledyard, and Walker. He knew the outcome of this trial would go a long way toward determining his future – a future for which he had worked so hard.

The woman glanced quickly at the parties to the case, then fixed her gaze on the judge. "We, the jury, find in favor of the defendant."

The judge asked, "Is your verdict unanimous?"

"It is, your Honor."

"Very well," the judge said, "this case is closed. I want to thank you jury members for your service."

As the judge continued to talk to the jury, Cade's senior partner, Harry Martin, grabbed his arm and squeezed it. Martin had olive skin, salt-and-pepper hair, and his trim physique hadn't changed a great deal since his days as a Marine helicopter pilot in Vietnam. Their client, Ralph Johnson, took turns shaking their hands vigorously.

Relief cascaded over Cade as his emotions, which had been bottled up during the month-long trial, were suddenly released. He paid no attention to the judge's remarks as he quietly accepted the congratulations of his trial team. His thoughts were interrupted when the judge rapped the bench with his gavel and stood. Everyone in the courtroom rose in response and remained quiet until the judge left the courtroom. The two attorneys for the plaintiffs came over with solemn expressions as they gave their obligatory handshakes and disingenuous congratulations.

While Cade and the trial team packed their briefcases, Johnson said, "Let me call the office with this great news. I expect you to be my guests at the Commerce Club for lunch."

Cade glanced at his watch to see that it was almost one in the afternoon. The jury had been out for several agonizing hours after the closing arguments first thing this morning. Cade had been up most of the night helping Martin prepare the closing. "Harry, do you mind if I skip lunch?" My daughter's birthday party is this afternoon."

Martin's face became more serious. "I think it's important you come to lunch. Johnson and his company are good clients. We've just won a big trial for them, and we need to celebrate with him. You'll have plenty of other birthdays later."

Cade felt the heat rise in his face, but he nodded and said nothing more. Maybe he could figure out a way to slip out and get to the party.

*   *   *

Everyone was in a celebratory mood as they enjoyed the expensive wine Johnson ordered at the downtown club, regaling one another with tales of different parts of the trial. Cade's gaze went from the group celebrating their trial to the tastefully furnished dining room. *Victory is sweet.* Johnson made sure the waiter kept the wineglasses full. As the group finally stood to leave, Cade realized the afternoon was quickly becoming dusk. He glanced at his watch and winced. It was much later than he thought. He'd have to hurry to make it to Sarah's party.

"Cade, let's meet around eleven tomorrow at the office to wrap things up." Martin puffed on a cigar as they stepped into the elevator. "You did a superb job, my boy."

"Thanks, Harry. I'll see you tomorrow," Cade replied as they exited the elevator of the building. He hurried to his car.

*   *   *

Cade maneuvered his six-foot-two body into his olive Land Rover, still euphoric, both from his courtroom victory and his share of the several bottles of wine they had consumed. He hadn't even bothered to call his wife, Rachael, about the victory. He wanted to surprise her by showing up at the party and telling her the good news. He'd missed sharing most of the Christmas holiday with his family due to the trial, and he was ready to make up for lost time. Cade smiled when he stared at his light blue eyes in the rearview mirror. Life was going his way. He'd fallen in love with Rachael Adams when they were students at Oxford, and they had been married in Merton College Chapel almost ten years ago. After graduating near the top of his class at Washington and Lee Law School, Cade clerked for Justice Howell on the Eleventh Circuit Court of Appeals, and then went to work with the law firm. He continued to shine there and was recognized as one of the top associates. He'd worked very hard to be made a partner, and out of his starting class of twenty-five associates, he was one of a handful still left at the firm. He was proud of his accomplishments. Cade knew that his father, a prominent lawyer in another large Atlanta firm, was equally proud of his son.

He could hardly wait to see his beloved daughter, Sarah, who turned seven today. She was a precious, bright girl with her mother's deep blue eyes and Cade's blonde hair. Rachael was a history professor at Emory. Her career was also blossoming.

As he turned onto Peachtree Street, Cade's heart sank. The late afternoon Atlanta traffic was at a virtual standstill. *So what else is new?* He thumped the steering wheel in frustration. He'd never make it to the party now. He decided instead to greet his family when they returned home.

Opening the front door of his house, Cade grasped the bouquet he'd bought on the way. At least he could take them out to dinner to celebrate Sarah's birthday and his trial.

"Rachael! Sarah! I'm home."

No one answered, and Cade quickly realized none of the usual whirl of activity was evident. He dashed up the stairs hoping to find his girls there, but no lights were on. He took off his jacket and tie, flung them on the bed, and walked downstairs.

Finding no messages for him, either on the refrigerator or their voicemail, he sat on the couch in the den, and turned on ESPN, popping open a can of beer. Having slept little during his trial, he soon began to doze.

He awakened with a jolt, to find a women's roller derby show on television. His watch showed it was almost four in the morning. He sat up groggily, rubbing his face. He wavered as he stood, realizing with some alarm that he'd never heard Rachael and Sarah come in. He bounded up the stairs and was relieved to see Sarah sound asleep in her bed, clutching her favorite stuffed rabbit, Flopsy. He kissed her gently on the cheek.

Cade tiptoed into his bedroom and quietly slipped into bed. He reached over to nudge Rachael, but her only response was to roll over with her back to him.

* * *

Cade awoke at the sound of something downstairs and saw that it was almost eight in the morning. He slipped on a bathrobe and went downstairs.

"Hi, Dad." Sarah stood at the front door dressed in her blue school uniform. Her blond hair was tied in a ponytail, and she grinned at her father.

"Hello, sweetheart," Cade said, hurrying to pick her up. "Listen, Sarah, I'm really sorry I missed your party."

"That's okay, Daddy." Sarah's smile left her. "I'm used to not having you around. You should see the cool presents I got."

Rachael came from the kitchen. "Come on, Sarah, we're almost late for school." She ignored Cade, except to give him an icy stare.

"Rachael ... good morning." Cade tried to sound cheerful. "I won my trial," he added, trying to gain favor.

"Jolly good for you," she replied coldly, her English accent sharpened by her anger, as she opened the front door. "There's cereal in the kitchen, and I have a faculty meeting this afternoon. Julie's mother is picking Sarah up to take her to ballet, and I'll get her from Julie's later."

With that she slammed the door, leaving Cade standing bewildered in the foyer. He walked into the kitchen and spied the bouquet stuffed into the trash can.

2

CADE ENTERED his law firm on the thirty-fourth floor, ready for the triumphal reception after his big victory. His secretary, Susan Phillips, greeted him with a smile and was the first to offer congratulations.

"I heard about your outstanding win. We're all excited for you." Susan was a bubbly legal secretary, in her mid-fifties. Today she wore a bright red sweater that enveloped her large physique and matched her naturally glowing cheeks. Her short, gray hair and thick glasses gave her a matronly appearance.

"Thanks, Susan," Cade replied. "Any messages?"

"A few, but they can wait. I really didn't expect to see you today."

"Well, you know Martin." Cade sighed. "He never heard of the notion of taking time off. I'm supposed to meet with him at eleven. Has Rachael called?"

"No."

Several lawyers stopped by Cade's office to offer their congratulations and listen to a brief rendition of the trial highlights. He was eager to tell them all about the trial, but they soon begged off until later, exiting to chase their billable hours.

Susan stuck her head in. "Didn't you say you were supposed to meet Mr. Martin at eleven?"

"Yes."

"Well, it's eleven fifteen now."

"Oh no! I'm on my way." Cade jumped up and rushed out to

Harry's office two floors up. He had no desire to be at work. He kept thinking of Rachael's frigid demeanor this morning. His mind went back to how he fell in love with Rachael, and how ecstatic he had been when she said yes to his proposal of marriage. They had a storybook wedding in Oxford. Cade's family and friends had come over, and as a wedding present, his parents had given them a honeymoon in Venice.

The greatest moment of his life had been the birth of Sarah Elizabeth, just as he started his third year of law school. But between law school, having a child, and being an overworked associate in a demanding, high-pressure law firm, not to mention Rachael's responsibilities with her teaching, Cade and Rachael now spent little time with each other. They were also heavily in debt, as Cade had insisted on living in an upscale neighborhood and joining a country club – all, he told Rachael, to help his career. It will all get better later, just be patient, he often told Rachael ... and himself.

Harry walked around his desk when Cade entered. "Cade, you did a splendid job." The two men shook hands and Harry grinned. Harry was the top litigator in the firm and the managing partner. He appeared to have taken a special liking to Cade. Harry's reputation as a hard-nosed, no nonsense, workaholic lawyer was right on target.

Harry continued, "I am very impressed with your style and judgment. You're a natural. One of the best young lawyers I've seen. Better than your father when he was younger – but don't tell him I said that."

Cade joined in with Harry's laughter.

A stern look crossed Harry's face, like a black cloud moving in front of the sun. "There's only one thing holding you back." Harry motioned for him to sit as he walked around his desk and stood behind his tall, hunter green, leather chair. Martin carried the air of a decisive military leader.

Cade gripped the armrests of the wooden captain's chair, but said nothing.

"You obviously work hard, but you still need to get your billable hours up."

"But I'm already working nights and weekends," protested Cade. "And I do have my family."

"Cade, listen, it's a new day in the legal profession. Clients are no longer loyal, and you've got to earn their respect and keep them happy. And, in this firm, you just have to put other things – even family – second sometimes."

Most times. Cade refrained from verbalizing his thought, wryly noting that Harry himself was divorced.

"We've got a big operation here – over three hundred lawyers. As a partner, you eat what you kill. Like it or not, we all live and die by the billable hour. You have all the talent in the world, you just need to be more creative in how you bill."

"By creative, do you mean pad my hours?" Cade felt the heat rising up his neck

Harry winked and gave him a patronizing smile. "I didn't say 'pad', I just said be creative, and make sure you write down *all* of your time. We've got a chance to make a lot of money, my boy, so let's take advantage of it."

Cade shifted in the chair, started to say something, but thought better of it.

"By the way," Harry's words interrupted Cade's thoughts. "I just got a call from a potential new client. A man named Zac Pickering, who owns a construction company in Washington, D.C. I'm flying up to meet with him next week. I think it would be a good idea if you came along."

"Sure," Cade muttered half-heartedly.

When he returned to his office, Cade flopped into his chair and stared out the window. He was already tired from the ordeal of the trial, and Harry's lecture on billing more hours had deflated him.

When his phone rang, he instinctively buzzed Susan to answer it, not wanting to talk to anyone.

A moment later, however, Susan's voice came over his intercom.

"It's your father."

He picked up the phone. "Hi Dad."

"Hello son. I heard about your big victory yesterday. I'm proud of you. Harry tells me you did a splendid job."

"Thanks. It's always good to win." Cade wondered if his father had checked on him with Harry. Deep down, he knew he wanted very much to live up to his father's high expectations of him.

"How about lunch today so you can tell me all about it?"

"Give me a rain check. I'm tired, and I need to get my feet back on the ground." Cade didn't mention that he was thinking of going to see Rachael to make up for his *faux pas* with Sarah's birthday.

After he hung up, Cade decided to drive over to Emory and try to catch Rachael. His calls to her office had only landed him in her voice mail, so he thought a surprise visit might be in order.

✳   ✳   ✳

Driving toward the Emory campus, he had a pit in his stomach as he thought about his unsettling conversation with Harry, as well as his less than pleasant good-bye from Rachael this morning. The sun and blue sky gave a false impression of warmth on this cold January day.

His thoughts took him back to the incredible events that had led to his romance with Rachael. He recalled vividly the quiet, snowy winter's solstice night at Magdalen College when he'd discovered the strange correspondence in the library that had started it all. He'd had no inkling that this seemingly innocuous find would lead him on the adventure of a lifetime. It was Rachael who had made the connection between these strange letters from Foulheart to Soulbane and C.S. Lewis's own discovery of Screwtape's letters to Wormwood. Cade had been incredulous, but when they showed his discovery to Reverend Brooke, an Anglican priest in the Cotswolds, it was the vicar who'd become really excited about it.

This had been only the beginning of his adventures, which had taken him to a beautiful Mediterranean island and a lovely mountain-top college in the United States, as he sought to find other clues to the existence of more reports from these devilish characters. Ultimately, Cade had made an astounding discovery of two reports detailing ...

A blaring car horn interrupted his thoughts, and he realized he'd drifted out of his lane. He swerved quickly and missed the oncoming car by inches. Deciding to gather his wits, he stopped at a sandwich shop to get some lunch for Rachael and himself.

Once he reached the Emory campus, Cade walked quickly to Rachael's office in the history department. He bounded up the stairs with the bag of lunch containing two curried chicken salad sandwiches, potato chips, and soft drinks. His heart rate quickened at the prospect of seeing Rachael. He knocked on her door, and opened it before she answered. He bounded in and simultaneously discovered an empty office. A quick glance at a small clock on the bookshelves informed Cade that Rachael would still be teaching her class.

He glanced around the tiny office, standard issue to a young faculty member. Floor to ceiling metal bookshelves lined the right-hand wall, and the gray metal desk positioned to the other side left a small passageway to the seat behind it. Two small windows gave a view over the campus.

He plopped into the chair, which creaked from the heavier than usual weight, and put his bag on the desk next to the darkened computer monitor. As he leaned back, a photograph on one of the shelves caught his eye, and he stood to examine it more closely. He instantly recognized the photo of Rachael and himself, their arms around one another, as they prepared to step into a gondola on their honeymoon in Venice. Her long, dark hair, blue eyes, and wide smile brought the scene to life. He thought back to the first time he'd ever seen Rachael on Guy Fawkes' night at a bonfire near the Trout Pub in Godstow. He'd immediately been taken with this beautiful stranger, and, later at the pub, Cade had been excited to have a chance to talk to her. Her intelligence and vivacity soon had him captivated.

"Can you believe it's been over ten years?"

Cade jumped at the soft English accent, and turned to see his wife standing in the doorway, her shapely figure outlined in the light from the hallway. He eyed her beige sweater blouse and dark green skirt, thinking that Rachael was still as beautiful and young looking as on their honeymoon. Her lovely smile, however, was missing.

"No, I really can't." He put the photograph back on the shelf. "I brought us some lunch."

Rachael dropped her books and notes on top of the desk. "Good, I'm famished." She opened the bag and pulled out the sandwiches, then sat in the metal chair with green plastic backing in front of the desk, usually reserved for students.

Cade returned to her chair, apprehensive about Rachael's obviously cool demeanor.

"Rachael, … listen … ."

"No, you listen, Cade," she interrupted with an angry tone, surprising him. "Sarah was crushed when you didn't show up at her party. I made excuses about your trial, but when Susan called in the afternoon looking for you, she told me about it. I just *knew* you'd surprise us and be at the party."

"I'm sorry." He rocked back and forth, the squeaking chair keeping time.

"You're always sorry, Cade. I'm tired of making excuses for you with Sarah."

They sat in silence for several minutes, and Cade felt his hands sweat. He wasn't sure what to say, and finally went with his old standby. "Rachael, well … I'm under a lot of pressure at the firm and all … ."

"I beginning not to care any more. With you it's always work this and work that. Sarah and I scarcely know you. I even heard one of Sarah's friends ask her the other day if you still live with us."

"I … it's not easy on me either," he said in a pleading tone. "Say, maybe we can take a trip somewhere … get away for a few days."

Rachael smiled slightly, relaxing her stern look. "I know things are tough, but it's about time you thought about your priorities."

"It's just that I've had these trials, and you know how important this is to my career ... ."

"Is your career so all important you'd sacrifice your family?"

"If you can believe it, Harry Martin just told me this morning that I need more billable hours."

"More hours!" exclaimed Rachael. "That's ridiculous. You already work seven days a week, and on top of that you devote time to the board of that homeless shelter, not to mention your State Bar Association and all the other things the firm wants you to do."

"I know. I guess I'm over-committed."

"That's the understatement of the year. And you've never even had time to do anything with those Soulbane reports like you promised Reverend Brooke, have you? "

He felt his face grow hot. "Well, not yet. But I was thinking maybe ... ."

"That's what I thought," she interrupted, gathering up her lecture notes. "Are the computer disks still in that bank vault?"

He looked down at the floor, her comment cutting him to the core. Before Cade could reply, Rachael shoved a half-eaten sandwich into the bag. "When you make a promise, Cade, it's serious business. You'd better think about the consequences of a trail of broken promises."

Cade felt his anger rising, but decided to nip his knee-jerk comment in the bud.

She stood. " I have to go and teach my tutorial. We'll talk about this later." She placed her hand on Cade's arm. "Cade, I love you, but ... you've got to decide what's really important to you, or one day you'll wake up and we'll be gone."

He squeezed her hand. "I'm doing all this for you – for us." He started to tell her he loved her, but the words stuck in his throat.

Rachael went out of her office. He heard her footsteps down the hall, and then her voice, "You can at least take me and Sarah out to dinner tonight."

"It's a deal." Cade yelled, forcing himself to sound upbeat, in stark contrast to what he was really feeling.

* * *

He was wiped out from his trials – both in the courtroom and at home. Having no inclination to return to the office, he instead decided to go to his health club for some much needed exercise. It didn't take long on the stair machine to work up a huge sweat. Weeks of late nights, fast food, and pots of coffee, not to mention the stress of the trial, had taken their toll. He was huffing quickly, cursing how easy it was to get out of shape.

After he finished his workout, Cade ambled around the club. He grinned when he saw his best friend, Eric Majors, stretching after a run. Eric was a trim five-foot eleven, with short, curly brown hair and brown eyes.

"Eric, what's up man?"

"Hey, Cade, how was your trial?"

"We won!"

"Excellent news. Tell me all about it."

Cade proceeded to tell about the trial in detail. He and Eric had quickly become friends during their first year of law school. He often marveled at how much they seemed to have in common. Eric was Sarah's godfather.

As Cade was talking, two young women in their mid-twenties came up. The one with bright red hair and light blue eyes spoke first. "Hi, Eric. How are ya'?"

"Great, Muffy, how about you?"

"Super."

"Oh, Muffy, this is my good friend, Cade Bryson. Cade, Muffy Dawson."

Cade smiled. "Nice to meet you." He couldn't help but glance over at the other girl, who had long auburn hair, olive skin, and big brown eyes. Her toned arms and legs were accentuated by her skin-tight workout clothes.

"Oh, excuse me," said Muffy. "This is my friend, Sherry Talbot."

"Nice to meet you," said Eric and Cade simultaneously, and they both laughed. Eric and Muffy started talking, so Cade spoke to Sherry. "Have you been in Atlanta long?"

"Oh, about three months," she replied, in a soft, raspy voice.

"Where do you work?" For some reason, Cade felt almost shy talking to her.

"I'm a sales rep for a pharmaceutical company. How about you?"

"I'm a lawyer."

"Yeah," Eric interrupted. "Cade just won a big trial."

"Wow! Really?" Muffy asked.

"That's right." Cade felt himself blushing, but he also loved the attention.

"Tell us about it." Sherry flashed a beautiful, bright smile.

Cade told them the basics.

Muffy said, "Congratulations. That's great. Eric, we'll see you around. We've got to get to our aerobics class."

Cade winked at Eric as the girls trotted off.

"So, is Muffy a friend of yours?" Cade playfully tapped Eric's arm.

"You might say that." Eric laughed. "I met her here several months ago, and, well, you can see why I'm interested."

"I sure can, you old dog. What about her friend, Sherry?"

"I've seen her once or twice, too. If I didn't know better, ole pal, I'd think you were interested in Sherry the way you gravitated over to her."

Cade felt his face flush and said quickly, "I've got to run. Missed Sarah's birthday yesterday, and speaking of dogs, I'm in the old doghouse myself today."

"Cade, as hard as you are having to work, I wouldn't worry about that. You'll have time with your family later, when things ease up."

Cade was happy to have his friend's understanding. "Are you ready to hit the showers?"

"Not quite. You go on ahead, and I'll catch up with you later."

Cade headed toward the locker room. As he passed the aerobics room, he paused and spotted Sherry's reflection in a long wall mirror, observing that her graceful movements seemed to mask the difficulty of the exercise.

3

CADE AND HARRY MARTIN got out of the taxi in Washington D.C. While Harry paid the taxi driver, Cade surveyed the white, marble ten storey office building on Pennsylvania Avenue with tall, dark green, reflective windows, where their potential new client, Zac Pickering, had his office. The building was in the middle of D.C. and within walking distance of various government buildings.

As they stepped into the building's elevator, Martin said, "I've done some checking up on Pickering. Looks like he's got a fairly big construction company that does work all over the country, including Atlanta. He's got connections, too, because his wife's father is a U.S. Senator. This is a good opportunity for us."

Cade acknowledged these comments with a nod, just as the elevator doors opened. Directly in front of them was a large door with a bronze sign entitled, 'Pickering Construction Company.'

"May I help you?" inquired a young, blonde-haired girl at the receptionist's desk. When Harry told her who they were and why they were there, she picked up the phone. "Miss Vaughn, the gentlemen that Mr. Pickering is expecting are here."

Cade glanced around at the well-appointed office lobby. The hardwood floors were adorned by a number of oriental rugs, while a trio of antique pieces of furniture added their ambience to the scene. On the walls were several large landscape paintings, one of which appeared to be a Constable.

A minute later, a stout, middle-aged woman came into the office lobby area. Her brown hair was pulled tightly into a knot at the back of her head, and she wore a dark blue business dress. She extended her hand and said in a husky voice, "Hello. I'm Mr. Pickering's executive assistant, Marge Vaughn. He's expecting you. Come with me."

Cade and Harry followed her through another door into a smaller room, with a desk, computer, and phone. On the desk was a nameplate that read Marjorie Vaughn. The woman walked past the desk, knocked on a door, and opened it without waiting for a reply.

"Mr. Martin and Mr. Bryson are here to see you."

Cade walked in behind Harry and saw a large man in a white shirt and loosened red and blue-striped tie rising from his burgundy leather seat. A large, mahogany credenza and bookcase loomed behind him. He was about six feet tall, with graying hair surrounding a bald crown, and a paunchy stomach that hung over his belt. His small, dark eyes almost appeared to be squinting. Immediately noticeable was a two-inch scar on the man's forehead.

"Gentlemen, come in. I'm Zac Pickering." He came around his desk and shook hands, as both men introduced themselves. When Cade shook the man's hand, he found Pickering's grip to be vise-like and, upon closer examination, saw that Pickering had broad shoulders and thick arms. Cade guessed he was about sixty.

Cade studied the bookcase behind Zac's huge, English partner's desk. It was filled with books and framed documents, along with numerous photographs. Two hardhats with Pickering Construction on them sat on the top shelf of the bookcase. Before Cade could study the contents of the bookcase, however, Pickering bid them sit down.

As he sat in the straight, upholstered chair in front of Pickering's desk, Cade glanced out the window to see a spectacular view of the Capitol dome.

"Mr. Pickering," Harry began.

"Please call me Zac," he replied as he returned to his desk chair. Pickering had a deep, gravelly voice. "I appreciate you taking time to come see me." Pickering held out a box of cigars, which both Harry and Cade declined. Pickering picked up a lit cigar from his desk and continued. "I've heard a lot about your law firm. We're in the construction business and have several projects in Atlanta. One of the owners is threatening to sue, so I'm looking for some good lawyers to help me there."

At this point, Harry straightened in his chair, tugged at his collar, and told Pickering all about their firm. It was a spiel Cade had heard so many times, he almost knew it by heart. Martin was a master salesman, which was why he was such a successful trial lawyer. Cade barely listened while Martin took Pickering through all the reasons his construction company should retain Morris, Lodge, Gioia, Ledyard, and Walker.

Instead, Cade focused on the bookcase. A picture of some football team leaned against a trophy, but he couldn't make out the team or the faces from this distance. Several pictures of individuals, including a photograph of a very striking woman with dark hair and tanned skin standing on the steps of the Parthenon, were scattered on different shelves. A large photograph of a sailboat with a colorful spinnaker was displayed prominently. High on one corner, almost hidden, was a picture of a younger Zac Pickering with his arm around a small, grinning boy holding up a catch of fish.

Pickering was leaning back, puffing on his cigar. He nodded several times during Harry's presentation. He was somewhat red-faced and it quickly became apparent that Pickering, like Martin, had a Type-A personality. He was no-nonsense and got directly to the point. Pickering and Martin seemed to be hitting it right off.

"Zac, we have an excellent team who will give you top-notch service. Cade here is one of our best young lawyers, and I know you'd enjoy working with him, too."

Zac sat forward and put down his cigar. "I'm quite impressed, Harry. I tell you what. Let me think about what you've told me during the afternoon. I'd like to discuss it with you further tonight. Dinner's on me."

4

ABOUT TEN DAYS LATER, Cade, Rachael, Sarah and Eric were at the Buckhead Diner for Sunday brunch. Eric had called earlier about going to brunch, and Cade convinced Rachael to skip church today, to which she'd reluctantly agreed. Cade was just finishing up his Eggs Benedict.

"Uncle Eric, why aren't you married?" asked Sarah innocently.

"Now, Sarah," Rachael said, giving her daughter a severe look. "You leave your godfather alone."

"It's okay." Eric smiled at Rachael. He turned to Sarah, who was sitting next to him. "I just haven't found anyone as wonderful as your mother."

"Always the charmer, you are," Rachael giggled.

"Eric, I'm sorry," Cade added.

"Don't mention it," laughed Eric. "I'm much more worried about whether you're going to pass the cheesecake."

Cade grinned and picked up the dessert plate. "At least we know where your priorities are."

"Uncle Eric, thanks for coming to lunch with us today." Sarah smiled and sat in his lap. "Dad never goes into the office on Sunday morning when you come to lunch."

Cade felt his face redden. He could almost feel Rachael's gaze on him. Anxious to change the subject, Cade said, "Eric, where's your next boondoggle trip?"

"We're not jealous, are we?" Eric smiled broadly.

"You bet he is," Rachael replied. "All of us are. You're the only friend we know whose job is to travel all over the world and get paid for it."

"Actually," said Eric, "week after next I'm off to Hawaii."

When Cade and Rachael groaned simultaneously, Eric added, "Well, you know, somebody has to make these sacrifices."

Cade stood and mockingly threw his napkin at Eric. "Sorry to break up this nice lunch, but I've got to get to the office."

"Not today," said Rachael, with noticeable irritation in her voice. "It's Sarah's ballet recital today, and you promised you'd go since you haven't been all year, and I have to go to introduce our guest lecturer at Emory this afternoon."

Cade felt a combination of guilt and anger, and lashed out more strongly than he intended. "Rachael, I have a client coming in. It's that guy that Harry and I went to see in D.C. a while ago. He's a brand new client and I've been assigned as his primary attorney. It's not like I want to be there on Sunday, but ... ."

Eric stood quickly, and in the same motion picked up Sarah and held her in his arms. "Now, you two never mind about Sarah. Uncle Eric will take her. I've been wanting to see you dance anyway." He winked at Sarah. "And besides, I owe you a trip to the ice cream shop, don't I?"

"Yes!" Sarah clapped excitedly.

"It's settled then," said Eric. "Come along little princess."

※   ※   ※

Cade and Rachael said little on the drive home.

"Cade," Rachael said finally, "what's happened to us?"

"What do you mean?"

"Don't pretend you haven't noticed ... . we used to talk all the time. We were so close. But now, we hardly ever talk. And when we do, it's almost like I'm an imposition."

"No, you're crazy," he said, much too quickly and defensively. "I love you and Sarah."

"I know you love Sarah, but it's just not the same between us." Rachael turned and faced away from him, but he could hear her sniffles.

Cade was relieved that they were arriving at their house. He never knew how to handle Rachael when she cried.

"Rachael, I … please don't … ." He glanced at his watch, a habit he had developed as a lawyer.

"Not now, Cade," Rachael replied in a harsh tone, leaving him in no doubt that she had seen him look at his watch. "I'm late and I can see you're worried about being late, too. Anyway, I don't want to discuss it right now."

Rachael got out of the car and marched quickly toward the front door. Cade started to get out of the car and go after her, but thought better of it. *Rachael just needs to calm down a bit. I'll make it up to her later.* He put the car in reverse as the front door to the house slammed resoundingly.

5

"CADE, HOW YA' DOING, buddy?" asked the voice on the other end of the phone.

"George, so good to hear from you," Cade replied, sitting back in his chair at work and propping his feet up on the desk. It was his old college friend, George Mason, and Cade welcomed an excuse this Monday morning to take his mind off work. His meeting with Zac Pickering lasted until about nine the previous night, and Rachael was very upset when he came home so late.

"How's Rachael?" George asked.

"Fine, fine." Cade didn't want to mention the tension at home. "Long time, no see," he added to avoid any awkward silence.

"That's why I'm calling. Listen, I want ya'll to come down for Mardi Gras. You've been promising for years to come … ever since college. Kim and I would love to see you and Rachael. So, how about it?"

"That does sound fun. I haven't been to Mobile in years. But, I've got a lot of work on my plate."

"Yeah, yeah, don't we all? Come on, Cade. Live a little. We'll have a blast."

"When is it?"

"In a couple of weeks. Mardi Gras day is February twenty-fifth, I think. I'm riding in a parade the night before, and there's a terrific ball afterwards. I promise you won't regret it if you come."

"Okay, George, let me talk to Rachael. I'll call you back in a couple of days."

"Great, but the answer better be yes."

He pondered the call and how he could even broach the subject with Rachael. He and George became good friends at The University of Virginia. They were fraternity brothers and roomed together one year. Cade was a groomsman in George's wedding. He hadn't seen his friend since George had stopped over in Atlanta for dinner several years ago on his way up to their class reunion at Virginia. Rachael had never really seemed to warm to George.

He stood and walked down the hall to the coffee pot. As he poured his fourth cup of the morning, he stretched and put these thoughts behind him, focusing instead on preparing for the deposition he had to take tomorrow.

⁕   ⁕   ⁕

That evening, Cade looked for an opportune time to tell Rachael about George's invitation. She was still fuming about yesterday. He had begun to get excited about going to Mardi Gras, but guessed Rachael would not be at all enthusiastic. Finally, as he was putting toothpaste on his brush, he said from the bathroom, "Rachael, ole George called this morning."

Rachael was sitting in bed reading a magazine. "Oh, really, and how is he?"

"He's fine. Say, he's invited us to come down to Mardi Gras in a couple of weeks. It'd be fun to do." He winced in the mirror as he waited for Rachael's reply.

"That's nice."

He sensed the frostiness in her voice. Nonetheless, he went on, "I was sort of hoping we could all go down there. I don't have any trials set then, and it would be a nice change of pace."

"Why don't you go on your own? I know you'd like to see George. I'm in the middle of term and Sarah's got school, and besides, … ."

"I know … you think George is rather immature."

"You said it, not me."

Cade came out of the bathroom and plopped into bed. He looked over at Rachael, who kept reading her magazine. Without looking up, she added, "I know you want to go, and Sarah and I would only slow you down. You go on and have fun with George. The break will do you good."

He started to protest, but decided against it. He was surprised at Rachael's willingness for him to go, but knew deep down problems existed with their relationship that neither of them wanted to talk about. He looked at Rachael: her dark hair and blue eyes were still beautiful, but... but what? Some of the magic was gone. The first couple of years of marriage during law school had been great. But now he had a killer workload. Sarah also put a big dent in their social schedule, and much of their free time revolved around ballet and birthday parties. Somehow, he had not been prepared for being so domestic, which was one reason he secretly envied Eric.

"Well, think about it," said Cade finally. He realized that for some reason he secretly hoped Rachael wouldn't come. Maybe a little breathing room would do them good.

*   *   *

Alone on the plane to Mobile the Saturday before Mardi Gras, Cade looked out the window to see Mobile Bay spread out before him. This deep south February day was warm and sunny, and dozens of sailboats moved gracefully out in the bay. As the plane banked, Cade spied the large, gray outline of the World War II battleship, U.S.S. Alabama. The plane landed a couple of minutes later.

"Cade, over here." Cade turned in the direction of the voice and saw George waving at him just down the hall in the Mobile airport. George, who was about six feet with short brown hair and gray eyes, was dressed in khaki pants, a red knit shirt, and leather sailing shoes.

"Hi George, it's great to see you." Cade smiled and extended his hand.

George shook it vigorously. "I'm so glad you came down. We'll have a blast at Mardi Gras. I'm sorry Rachael couldn't come."

"Yeah, so am I," Cade said without conviction. "She had a lot of work to do, since she's in the middle of the semester." Cade didn't mention the argument they'd had about this, and he was relieved to be away from Atlanta for a few days.

"Come on, buddy." George put his arm around Cade's shoulders. "I'll get the car and meet you out front to get your luggage. And, by the way, here's your official welcome to Mobile." George pulled out several strands of colored plastic beads and ceremoniously put them around Cade's neck. Cade grinned, and the two friends walked off down the hallway.

*　　*　　*

"Tell me more about this parade you're in," Cade said as they rode in George's red Mustang convertible.

"I'm in the IM's ... that's the Infant Mystics. They've been parading since 1869."

"I didn't realize Mardi Gras here was that old."

"Oh yes, believe it or not, Mobile has the oldest Mardi Gras, even older than New Orleans. It's a lot of fun. But didn't you tell me you've been here before?"

"Yes, once when I was in high school. My folks took us on the way to a seminar Dad had at the Grand Hotel in Point Clear."

"I'll be riding on the seventh float," added George. "Kim will take you to our favorite spot to watch, and I'll try and cover you up with throws."

"Will you being wearing a costume?"

"This year's theme is Ancient Myths and Legends. I'll be on a float that's supposed to be Stonehenge, and we'll all be dressed as Druids." George pulled into a driveway. "Here we are."

Cade looked up at a two-story, brown brick house with a columned porch and upstairs balcony. Two enormous oak trees enveloped the front yard, with long trails of gray Spanish moss dripping from the branches.

He saw a petite, blonde-haired girl standing on the upstairs balcony wearing a tennis outfit. "Hi, Cade. I'm so glad you're here," Kim waved and smiled, and Cade returned the wave. Cade often wondered how George managed to land Kim, who was so pretty and vivacious. He'd learned at their wedding that George was from a socially prominent family, and that Kim, who had grown up in a small town in Mississippi, was captivated by the allure of Mobile society and George's social status. Not that Kim was pretentious, she just loved the fun of the social whirl of which George was a part.

*   *   *

The next afternoon, the three of them were sitting in the Mason's den. Cade was still nursing a headache from his Saturday night with George and Kim. They had gone to the Mystics of Time parade with dragon floats, then off to see the coronation of the King and Queen of Mardi Gras, and finally on to more parties. Since Kim and George had no children, they wanted to stay out late and party. Cade, feeling the freedom of not having any responsibilities for wife or child, had willingly obliged. It had been about four in the morning when they finally arrived home.

"It's almost time for the Joe Cain party," said Kim. "Let's go."

"Who's Joe Cain?" Cade asked.

"He sort of revived Mardi Gras after the Civil War," responded George. "There wasn't a lot of gaiety then, and he dressed up as an Indian chief – Chief Slacabamorinico, I think it was – and paraded around the streets of old Mobile. That got people into the spirit of Mardi Gras again, after the 'recent unpleasantness,' and Mardi Gras resumed. Now, on the Sunday before Mardi Gras day, a people's parade goes through the streets downtown, followed by a huge picnic party. We're skipping the parade. Actually, we've probably already missed it. Anyway, it's the party that's really fun."

They drove downtown, into increasingly heavy traffic. Eventually, they found a place to park, and George and Kim took an ice chest and picnic basket out of the trunk.

"Here, let me carry that," said Cade, pointing toward the ice chest. Kim handed it to him and they walked on until they came to a huge crowd of people, with bluegrass music blasting in the air.

Kim waved at a group of people and headed toward them. George introduced Cade to the group as Kim spread out two blankets.

George handed Cade a beer after they sat down, and Kim gave him a plate of fried chicken and potato salad, which Cade devoured. They sat on the blankets for a good while, chatting and listening to bluegrass.

Cade's cell phone rang, which embarrassed him since he'd meant to turn it off. He leapt up and began walking away from his friends. He put a finger in one ear to hear over the noise.

"Cade, hello, it's just me." Cade immediately recognized Rachael's voice. Instead of being happy to hear from her, he felt annoyed by the interruption. Rachael always seemed to be calling him, as if she didn't trust him and was checking up on him.

"Oh, hi. How's Sarah?"

"Fine. Are you having fun?"

"Yes. We're having a great time. Sorry you're not here." Cade grimaced at his less than candid comment. They talked for several minutes about inconsequential matters, avoiding any real discussion about themselves.

When he turned the phone off, he was frustrated. He'd known Rachael long enough to recognize when she wasn't happy, and he resented her calling and making him feel guilty about coming to Mobile. He flopped down on the blanket and opened another beer.

6

B<small>Y THE TIME</small> Monday morning rolled around, Cade was beginning to worry about his stamina. He'd only been in Mobile two days and was already exhausted. And he had yet another parade and the IM Ball tonight. He sat in a chair on the brick patio in the backyard with a mug of coffee and the *Mobile Register*. Kim had errands to run and George had to go to his office for the morning, so he could enjoy a little peace and quiet. He called Rachael, but only got her voice mail at school and realized she was teaching now. He thought of Sarah and missed his little girl. Sarah would be at school, too, so there was no use in trying to call her. A hammock hung invitingly under a huge, sprawling oak tree in the backyard, and he was soon was dozing in the gentle breeze.

* * *

When Cade awoke, he was disoriented at first, staring up into the green leaves and brown branches, with flecks of blue sky peeking through. He rolled out of the hammock and went into the Mason's kitchen.

"Of all the rotten luck." George's face was pale, and he was slumped over the kitchen table.

"What's the matter, George?"

"I'm afraid I've come down with some type of bug. It's been going around the office, and I had desperately hoped to avoid it, especially during Mardi Gras."

"Are you sure it's not just a hangover?"

"Yeah, I'm sure. I felt fine this morning when I got up, but after being at the office about an hour, I felt it coming on." With that, he lurched from his chair and ran up the stairs. Cade heard him throwing up and cursing.

"George, are you okay?" Cade yelled from the bottom of the stairs. "Can I get you anything?"

"I just need to get in bed. When Kim gets back, ask her to come check on me."

*   *   *

Late in the afternoon, the sky was getting dark, as night approached and storm clouds rolled in from Mobile Bay. Cade stood in George's front yard, his hands on his waist, trying to catch his breath from a two-mile run. He thought ruefully how he used to run five miles easily and vowed to do a better job of staying fit.

When Cade walked into the den, George was lying on the sofa, under a blanket, his face pale as boiled scallops.

"Cade, I'm so sorry about tonight."

"Well, you can't help it. I still had fun the last two days with you and Kim."

"I know, but I really wanted to take you to the IM's."

They sat silently for a few minutes, while a soap opera droned on in the background. Cade sat on the floor away from George, wiping his sweaty forehead with a towel.

"Say, I have an idea," George said, even managing a weak grin.

"What's that?"

"Well ... I could get in trouble for this, but what the hell."

"What are you talking about?"

"I think you should ride the float in my place!"

"No way, George. I can't do that."

"Why not? No one will know ... not if you wear my costume. Besides, you don't need to stick around here and catch my bug." He sat up slightly, saying, "Kim, come here a minute."

Kim appeared from the kitchen. "Yes, George?"

"I just had a brilliant idea. Cade can take my place on the float. Get him my costume. We're almost the same size. You can take him downtown, and help him get on the float."

"That *will* be fun." Kim giggled and clapped her hands.

"But, George ..." started Cade.

"No buts about it. You'll have a good time and no one will be any the wiser. Just remember to keep your mask on at all times and don't talk too much. Tell people you have a cold, or laryngitis, or something."

*   *   *

A half-hour later, Cade found himself, black Druid costume and all, getting into the Mason's red Mustang. They rode downtown until they came upon a dozen brightly decorated Mardi Gras floats lined up on the street. Variously costumed characters were going to and fro, many carrying huge bags of candy and boxes of Moon Pies. The gaiety and frivolity in the air were tangible.

"Now, Cade," said Kim as she parked the car, "put on your hood and mask, and I'll walk you to George's float. I've timed it so that the parade is about to start, and you won't be out of place already wearing your mask. Just remember, for the next few hours your name is George Mason."

"Right," said Cade, getting excited. He pulled on his mask, which was a white skull on a black background, pulled the black hood over his head, and hopped out of the car. Kim popped the trunk, and Cade hauled out two large bags of candy to carry to the float.

As they walked, Kim said, "Call me later, and I'll come pick you up."

"No need to worry about that. I'll just take a cab."

"George, where ya' been?" asked a man already on the float. He had his gown on, but the hood was off and his mask was pulled on top of his head. The paper float was decorated to look like

Stonehenge. A number of people in similar Druid costumes were already on the float, dancing and yelling.

"Hi, Charlie," yelled Kim from behind. "George over did it last night at Joe Cain, and I let him take a little nap this afternoon." She laughed heartily. "By the way, he's a bit hoarse, so I doubt you'll get much chatter from him."

Cade waved to the man called Charlie and accepted his hand to pull Cade up on the float. Another man in blue jeans and a sweatshirt handed Cade the bags of candy.

"Here, have some of this." Charlie handed him a bottle of Jack Daniels. "You know, hair of the dog!" Charlie laughed loudly.

Cade nodded in assent and lifted his mask just enough to take a big swig. At that moment, a band struck up a rhythmic drumbeat, and the men on the float began rocking it from side to side. Cade took another big chug and handed the bottle back to Charlie. He was beginning to enjoy himself.

The band started marching, and the float lurched forward. Cade grabbed his stanchion and held on. Soon, the float turned a corner, and the cheers of the crowd became much louder. Cade looked up to find a sea of people, raising their hands in the air and yelling. The roar increased considerably, like the ocean surf during a storm. He couldn't distinguish any words, except an occasional, "Hey, mister," and "Moon Pie" from people close to the float when it came to a standstill. He reached into the bag, grabbed a handful of candy, and showered the crowd below the float. *This is fun.*

"Hey, Charlie, how about another swig," he whispered hoarsely. Charlie complied and Cade took another gulp of the amber liquid. With each taste, he felt better and better. He quickly passed through the first stage of drinking, the one that makes you a genius, and soon was at the second stage, of thinking he was the best looking guy in town. He had to resist the urge to tear off his mask.

The float wound its way around the streets of Mobile. The air was chilly and the sky overcast. The full moon occasionally peeped between the passing clouds, but otherwise illumination came from the streetlights and from the men walking beside the floats holding bright lights. Cade learned to join in the rocking and swaying of the float, although he quickly found himself running out of candy.

"You're not pacing yourself, George," yelled another costumed man below him on the float, who obviously saw that Cade's bags were emptying quickly. "We're not even halfway around yet."

"Oh well," Cade said, not really caring now. By now, he'd moved past being attractive, to being rich, and he was eager to share all his candy with the crowd. He was having the time of his life, and when he ran out of candy, he'd just enjoy the ride. And he did.

*   *   *

By the time the parade ended, Cade was well anaesthetized, thanks to Charlie's Jack Daniels. And the fun was just beginning. He stumbled off the float and followed everyone to the Mobile Civic Center for the ball. He had to remind himself continually that his name was George and that he must keep the mask on. Once inside, he found the cavernous ballroom floor. At the far end was a stage with a band playing loud rock music. Surrounding the stage were huge painted scenes reflecting the theme of Ancient Myths. The room was hung with long strands of gold, purple, and green serpentine. A number of people, the men in tails and the women in long evening dresses, were dancing and milling around. Some members of the IM's strutted or staggered around in their parade costumes. All around the perimeter of the circular room were round tables and chairs, where groups of people were sitting. Cade ambled around the ball, thankful his mask hid his identity. He followed a group of people out of the main ballroom to the circular walkway that went around the auditorium and tailed them into another room. Inside was an open bar and a long table filled with all types of food: chicken fingers, roast beef sandwiches, raw vegetables, chicken salad sandwiches, potato chips, cookies, and brownies. Cade thought he'd died and gone to heaven. He ordered a bourbon and water, and made no complaint when he was handed a bourbon and ice. He grabbed some food before wandering back inside the main ballroom.

He sat at a vacant table to finish his drink. His face was getting hot under the mask, but he dared not take it off. He had never seen so many elegantly attired women. He glanced up and did a double take – he was sure he'd just seen Sherry Talbot walk by in a most revealing, low-cut dress. Even in the semi-darkness, he could see how beautiful she was, with her auburn hair cascading over her bare shoulders. Standing to speak, he caught himself, remembering just in time that he was masquerading as someone else. He wondered who Sherry's date was, but she disappeared into the crowd. He sat again, but for the first time in a long time, he felt a surge of electricity going through him, and realized just how attracted to Sherry he was. Cade thought of Rachael and a pang of guilt came over him. He finished off his bourbon and went for another.

The crowd was thinning out. Cade decided to explore more, secretly hoping he'd run into Sherry. As he gulped another bourbon, he pictured her in that dress. With several more bourbons under his belt, he was at the stage of drunkenness of believing he was bulletproof, and if he kept going at this pace, he'd soon be at the 'invisible' stage. As he meandered around the auditorium, Cade saw several figures in identical Druid costumes go through a side door. Reckoning they were from his float and probably going to another bar, Cade followed. He watched as they crossed the street and went into a nearby antebellum house. *That's probably where the real party is.*

He saw them walk up the steps to the front door and heard one of them mutter "Bacchus" to the large, hooded figure standing at the door. Cade followed them up the stairs, and the figure nodded assent when he repeated the same word. Just as he entered, he saw the revelers disappear at the end of the long hallway that ran through the center of the house. Cade walked down the hallway and took a left, just as the group had done. He entered to find about thirty or so costumed figures standing around, but without any drinks or gaiety. All of them had on the same dark gowns, hoods, and masks. Cade stopped short and started to back out, hoping no one would notice him, when suddenly the door was shut behind him with a loud bang. He jumped instinctively. Immediately, everyone in the room became silent, and one of the figures stepped forward.

"Good. We don't have much time, so let's get on with it." The figure had a deep male voice, with an English accent, although the sound was distorted by the mask. Except for Rachael, Cade wasn't used to hearing such accents, and he eased into a back corner of the room, trying to be inconspicuous.

The next thing he heard, however, sent lightning bolts of fear throughout his body.

"You all know why we're here. I picked this Monday night for our meeting so that we wouldn't run any risk of being here on that horrid day of Ashes. Besides, Mardi Gras is one of my favorite times and these Druid costumes give us the perfect cover. I must say, I rather like these skull masks. We might use them in future meetings." The figure uttered a laugh, which was muffled by the mask.

Cade was dumbstruck and was certain his heartbeat sounded like a bass drum. That voice ... and those words ... *Oh, hell ... Oh, hell ... this can't be* ... . Cade had to stifle a scream and pinch his leg viciously under his costume to keep it from shaking. Sweat poured down his face under his mask. His hands were damp and clammy.

The figure continued, "My plans for Operation Clootie are proceeding nicely. All of you are following my instructions well. We're making inroads all over the western world now, and soon Our Royal Hindness will be victorious."

Cade thought he was going to faint. *It can't be possible ... no, it's impossible*. He silently leaned against the wall and eyed the door for an escape. A huge masked figure guarded the entrance.

"Our forays into western society and its institutions are working to perfection, if I might be permitted to use a curse word. Our work in the areas of education, technology, genetic engineering, medical ethics, cultural divisiveness and so many others ... just masterpieces."

Instead of truly being invisible – which he would have wished with all his heart – Cade was sober as ice now, and one hair from total panic. *This just can't be real.* Surely he was about to wake from this nightmare. His head was spinning violently, and as the figure droned on, Cade used every ounce of concentration to keep from screaming or shaking. He worried he was about to black out and took deep breaths trying to calm himself. If he fainted now, he'd almost certainly never awaken.

7

CADE was losing all focus. This just *had* to be a dream – it couldn't be possible that his worst nightmare – one that had haunted him for over ten years – had come true. His mind raced back to a night in Oxford – Guy Fawkes' night, to be exact – when he'd been involved in a late night chase with … . He just couldn't bring himself to think about that awful night. But the harder he tried to banish the memory, the more vivid it became.

He didn't know how much time passed as his mind spun with thousands of disjointed thoughts. He became aware of some type of discussion, with the leader asking for various reports from the masked figures. In order to try and get his mind off his rising panic, he forced himself to listen, as he quietly breathed deeply and leaned against the wall, desperately hoping he was inconspicuous.

"… and we have the most marvelous plan," one figure was saying. It was a feminine voice with an accent Cade couldn't identify. "We developed a delightfully diabolical virus that will wreck computers all over the world. It will take them ages to discover a solution and the whole event will be deliciously wonderful, as we bring the world to its knees, and then … ."

But the leader interrupted, moving to and fro quickly. "No, damn you, no! You idiot. Fool. That's not the way to succeed at all. Haven't you junior fiends learned *anything* in my tutorials? We don't want these mortals to wake up and realize their dependency on technology! Hell forbid, it might make them aware of the spiritual dimension of their lives, which technology helps to mask. The last thing we want is to send some virus, amusing as that might be, and force them to realize how dangerously dependent they have become on computers and machines. No, a thousand times no! Some of my colleagues have no doubt planted these moronic notions in your pea brain. I'm the genius who's figured out how to win this war. That's why my Operation Clootie will bring me great glory in our Hindom. Don't you cretins understand? Our job is to ease these mortals off to sleep, letting them quietly and gradually succumb to the hypnosis of computers and technology. We don't want some virus to send a cold shower their way! Scrap that ridiculous plan immediately, or I'll replace all of you imbeciles. We're on the verge of a great victory ... ." At that, the figure stopped in mid-sentence and uttered a bone-chilling shriek, followed by an eerie laugh.

Cade couldn't believe his ears. He eyed the doorway nervously, frantic to escape. He felt dizzy and nauseous. *If I throw up here, I'm a dead man!* He took more deep breaths and focused his eyes on the floor to stop the spinning, wishing he hadn't been so liberal with the bourbon. Nothing could be worse than this.

But no sooner did this thought pass through his mind, than it did get worse. Another costumed figure said, "We were told that some damned human moron got hold of a copy of Soulbane's Reports."

"Where did you hear that?" asked the large figure, with a raised, angry tone of voice.

"I ... I ... just heard ...," said the other, in a meeker tone than before.

"Well, forget it. Soulbane and I have everything under control regarding that bastard Bryson. We're certain he doesn't have the reports. Correct, Soulbane?" Another figure nodded in agreement.

Now Cade knew the worst dread of his life had come to pass. He thought of the shrill laugh reverberating in a dark cave on the other side of the world in Malta, and that same laugh echoing across the lawn of Trinity College, Oxford ... . He was trembling with fear. He knew that if he revealed himself – the very one who had made that astonishing discovery all those years ago – he was history.

The room became as quiet as a crypt. The leader stood motionless for several seconds. Cade eyed the huge figure guarding the door, considering whether he could push him aside and rush out. The leader finally said, "Bleakblab or Scruntchmouth will be in touch with you about our next meeting. We will soon go into the final phase of Operation Clootie, and destroy the Enemy once and for all. Now, leave quickly and blend back into the crowd. The Mardi Gras party will soon break up, so make sure you're not noticed. We'll forgo the usual incantations tonight. Be off."

The figure guarding the door opened it, and the group silently walked out. Cade kept his head down, watching only his feet shuffle out of the room. His racing heart forced him to take short, hot breaths, which were almost suffocating under the mask.

Once outside, the costumed figures quickly separated and went different ways. The sky was still overcast and a stiff breeze blew from Mobile Bay. He walked deliberately for a bit, when his heart skipped a beat. Was someone talking to him? Had he imagined it? He kept walking.

"You … you I say, you didn't identify yourself at the meeting," said a voice behind him, but he dared not turn around. He was nearing the auditorium, when a group of people came out and stumbled down the steps. He rushed up the steps behind them, pretending he hadn't heard the voice. Quickly walking around the outer perimeter, dodging numerous party-goers and costumed figures, he reached another exit. As soon as he was outside, he ran as fast as he could for several minutes, until he found a large oak tree. Ducking behind it, he tore off his costume and mask, leaving only his sweat-drenched flannel shirt and khaki pants. He quickly bundled everything up and resumed running.

He ran for he didn't know how long, until he found himself crossing a railroad track and approaching the Mobile Harbor. The full moon was peeking between the clouds, casting glittering sparkles on the river. The steady breeze brought a mixture of salty air from the Gulf of Mexico and the muddy smell of the Mobile Delta. He sat on a bench, then immediately screamed, leaping instantly to his feet, startled by the man sitting on the other end of the bench. The man didn't even flinch, however, and Cade laughed nervously, then almost hysterically, when he realized it was only a sculpture.

Two drunks with greasy beards and unkempt hair and clothes were standing at the railing by the harbor, sharing a bottle and cursing the world. The fear running through his veins had heightened all of his senses. His whole world had suddenly come crashing down in something his worse nightmare could never have anticipated. His head was spinning and his mind racing: to that cave in Malta those many years ago, where a strange voice had screamed in the dark ... to that night in Oxford, when he chased a phantom figure through the streets and up into the tower of St. Mary the Virgin Church. *It just can't be possible.* He'd put the past behind him, in some ways had even begun to forget, if that was possible. Cade glanced toward the night scene of old Mobile, his heart stricken with terror: as impossible as it was to believe, Foulheart had lurched unexpectedly and uninvited back into his life.

*   *   *

"Cade, are you all right?"

He found himself sitting up in bed, disoriented, his head pounding. There was a knock on the door, and he recognized Kim's voice, "Don't tell me you're sick, too."

Cade gathered his wits, and said, "Uh, no, Kim, I'm uh ... I'm fine. Just had a bit too much fun last night, I guess." He slowly began to recall the cop who'd chased him off the park bench near the river and hailed a cab for him. He'd finally got back to George's at about three in the morning.

"I've got a pot of coffee downstairs," added Kim. "I'm glad you didn't get George's bug."

"Thanks," he called out. "Let me get a quick shower, and I'll be down."

"See you in a jiffy." Kim's voice faded down the hallway.

Cade slipped out of bed and pulled back the curtains. The bright light almost blinded him, accentuating his hangover.

With the warm water cascading over him, like a flash of lightning, a picture of cloaked figures flashed in his mind, and he felt panicked. Had it all just been a bad dream? The events of the previous evening came back to him, fuzzy at first, and then in a rush, as if a train had suddenly appeared from a fog. Despite the soothing shower, he shivered involuntarily. Surely, his encounter with Foulheart and Soulbane at Mardi Gras was nothing but a nightmare? Yet, to his horror he began to find that, unlike a bad dream, the images became sharper and more distinct.

Hundreds of thoughts flashed through his brain. Had he really stumbled upon Foulheart here in Mobile? He tried to recall all that Foulheart had said last night: something about an Operation Clootie, and plans for another big meeting. He recalled the phrase, "horrid day of Ashes." That was the same phrase used in the correspondence he'd discovered those many years ago in Oxford. But worst of all was that *his* name had been mentioned. His whole body trembled. *What about this Operation Clootie? What is it? Shouldn't I do something? But what? Tell someone? Who?*

He thrust his head under the shower, as if to wash away the events, but like a guilty conscience, the fear would not wash off. The realization that his encounter last night had actually happened sent his mind reeling back many years.

After Cade had discovered the strange correspondence in the Magdalen library, through a series of bizarre adventures, he had gradually come to understand that the impossible had happened to him: he'd discovered reports from a junior devil named Soulbane to his superior, Foulheart, on a plot to destroy the western world and the church. The reports contained highly perceptive insights into the spiritual battle taking place in the world that few people recognized. These fiendish characters had apparently taken over where Screwtape and Wormwood left off. He had even stumbled into an encounter with Foulheart in a dark cave and later, in a night chase in Oxford, when Foulheart had stolen his computer containing a copy of the reports.

He shut off the shower, and while drying himself, resumed his reverie. Cade had never been able to uncover the mystery of the human persona that Foulheart had adopted: whom *did* he masquerade as? He had miraculously recovered the reports and now the computer disks containing them were in a safety deposit box in Atlanta. Although he had promised Reverend Brooke that he would publish the reports because of the value of disclosing what these devils were up to, it had now been over ten years, and he'd gradually let his promise fade into the past. After all these years, he had almost begun to convince himself that his encounters with a devil had been mere fantasy. His heart thumped rapidly as the implications of last night's discoveries multiplied in his mind.

"What was it they said?" Cade was talking to himself in the mirror. He saw himself smile weakly as he remembered the answer. "That's right – they think I don't have the reports." He high-fived himself in the mirror.

As he dressed, he began to relax slightly. Ironically, the devil's mention of him by name actually gave him some comfort: not only did no one know he had been in the room last night, but Foulheart had actually stated that they believed he did not have the reports! *No, I'll just keep it all under my hat.* The disk could just stay hidden away in the safety deposit box, and no one, especially Foulheart, would be any the wiser. And, he reasoned, no sense in getting involved in whatever this Clootie business was. No, it wasn't his concern. He sure didn't need to tell Rachael about last night – besides, she probably wouldn't believe it anyway. This was best kept as his little secret. *As Falstaff said, 'Discretion is the better part of valour.'*

As he headed downstairs following the smell of hot coffee, he breathed a sigh of relief at his rationalization.

Cade had made many miscalculations in his life – this would prove to be one of his worst.

8

"SENATOR, would you like a lift?" Zac Pickering asked, from the backseat of his black limo, which had just pulled up to the curb near the U.S. Capitol Building. The March afternoon was cold, but sunny. The man in the dark gray suit bent over, peered in at Zac, and slid inside the car without saying a word.

When Senator John Gage was settled, he reached over and shook hands with Zac. "What are we going to see today?"

"A little office project." Zac winked at the Senator, a short, stout man with a full head of thick, silver-gray hair. "Of course, I wonder if your constituents in Illinois would have any interest in seeing this building?"

"Let's not find out," Senator Gage replied, with no hint of amusement.

The limo made its way down the mall, past the Washington Monument, and on toward downtown D.C. Finally, the vehicle stopped in front of a construction site, and the two men got out.

"Here, Senator, you'll need this." Zac handed him a yellow hard hat.

As they walked toward the site, Zac watched the tower cranes taking steel beams from the ground to the tenth floor where men were at work welding. The nine floors of steel beams already in place, gave shape to the unfinished building.

"Remind me how long Pickering Construction has been in

business?" the Senator inquired in a loud voice, to be heard over the noisy screeching and grinding of heavy equipment.

"Let's see." Zac stroked his chin. "I started my company about twenty-four years ago. Hardly seems possible. Thanks to some of my more prudent investors, we've been quite successful." Zac patted the senator on the back.

The senator immediately glanced around, but no one was near them. Zac studied the site, thinking about his business. He'd been in construction all of his adult life, but his luck changed dramatically when he'd met Florence Rogers. Zac's good friend, then Congressional aide John Gage, had introduced Zac to the beautiful, sophisticated daughter of the Governor of Missouri. Zac set out to make her yet another conquest. Florence worked on Capitol Hill and proved to be quite a challenge. Before Zac realized it, he was engaged to Florence. Some years after Zac and Florence were married, Florence's father, Frank Rogers, was elected to the U.S. Senate. This had proved most fortunate for Zac. The two men hit it off, and the senator and various others, including John Gage, backed Zac when he started his own company. Over the years, Rogers and Gage had introduced Zac to a number of powerful people, some of whom had also become private investors in the company. The senators and their influential friends used their contacts to make sure plenty of lucrative projects were awarded to Zac's company.

Zac carefully worked out an unwritten arrangement with these men: they would send projects his way, or use their influence, legal or otherwise, to see that Zac was awarded major contracts. Zac, in turn, ensured that some of the profits made a circuitous route to campaign funds or certain Swiss bank accounts.

"Hi boss." A voice interrupted Zac's thoughts. He focused on his project manager, Buck Wright, walking up to them in a red flannel shirt and blue jeans.

"Hello, Buck," Zac replied. He didn't introduce the senator, however, and Buck didn't inquire as to his identity. Zac occasionally brought people to his sites but rarely introduced them. Over time his *good* managers learned not to ask.

"You want a tour of the project?" Buck inquired, spitting brown tobacco juice on the reddish clay ground.

"Not today. We only stopped for a quick visit. Everything okay?"

"Yep. We're actually ahead of schedule because of all the dry weather. We should top this baby out in about five weeks."

"Excellent," Zac said, grinning.

Zac's cell phone rang. "Yes?"

"Mr. Pickering?" It was Marge Vaughn.

"What's up?"

"Your wife is here and says you're going to the theater tonight."

"Oh, right." Zac glanced at his watch to see it was almost five. He'd forgotten his arrangement to go with Florence and her parents to dinner and the theater tonight. "Tell her I'm on the way." He knew he did not need to disappoint his father-in-law, who, like Zac, hated such evenings. The two men always commiserated with one another during such outings.

"Sorry, John, I promised my wife I'd go to the theater tonight."

"No problem. I need to get back to the office anyway."

"If you don't mind, I'll get my driver to drop me off at my office, and he can take you to The Hill."

As they rode, Zac found himself fidgeting with his hands. He had a lot on his plate, some of which he didn't want his investors to know about.

"I'll talk to you soon, John," said Zac, as he hurried out of the limo. The senator nodded. Zac shut the door, waved the driver on, and headed for his office. Marge was supposed to have gone for the day, but Zac knew by now he could count on her sticking around with Florence until he returned. She would also be taking good care of Florence. Zac was grateful for his secretary, who had been with him almost a year now. He had run through several secretaries, and then Marge was recommended to him. She proved to be excellent, but even more importantly, she had the invaluable judgement to know who in Washington to put through to Zac and to whom to make excuses. She was so good that he'd made her his executive assistant. Zac had come to rely heavily on her, and he paid her handsomely. Marge was one employee he didn't want to lose.

Zac walked into the reception area of Pickering Contractors on the eighth floor of the office building and immediately noticed that the door to his private office was open. Sure enough, Marge was sitting at her desk in the outer office typing on the computer. She looked up and nodded toward the sofa behind Zac. He turned to see his wife sitting on the sofa in the lobby, a glass in her hand. Zac hoped Marge had fixed her a stiff drink.

"Sorry, dear," said Zac with no real emotion. "I was taking Senator Gage to see one of our projects."

Florence looked up from her magazine and smiled. "You're lucky Marge knows to fix me a gin and tonic to take the edge off. I've had a busy day."

Zac smirked to himself. *Busy, hell, busy with tennis or bridge or gossip.* He looked at his wife, who was tall and slender, with tanned skin and short hair that was still dark brown, thanks to a weekly visit to her hairdresser. Florence flourished in Washington's social life. Zac glanced around the outer office, with its oriental rugs, paintings, and antique furniture, all thanks to Florence, or, rather, her decorator. A far cry from the trailer that had been his office for the first four years he'd been in business.

Zac forced a smile. "I'll just be a minute." He hurried into Marge's office, saying quietly to her, "Thank you." He went straight into his office and shut the door. *This is the last thing I want to be doing.* He knew Florence was irritated they were running late, and Zac purposefully took his time. He walked over to his corner office window that looked down Pennsylvania Avenue toward the Capitol. It was dark outside now, and the Dome shone in the spotlights. He hardly ever noticed the view anymore, unless some new client remarked about it. He looked at his reflection in the dark glass, his body lit by the overhead lights. He hardly recognized himself at first, almost expecting still to see the fit, muscular build of the young Zac, instead of the balding man with a paunch staring back at him. He looked over at the picture on his bookcase, displaying the Notre Dame football team on which he had been the starting fullback and second-team All-American. He squinted to see his face showing on the second row, and looked up one row for the face of their nose guard, John Gage. Next to that stood another framed photograph of his sailboat *Skoal* under full sail, including a multi-colored spinnaker, in the St. Francis Drake Passageway in the Virgin Islands. Zac's thoughts meandered to a mental picture he dared not display in a photograph in his office: a blonde woman standing on the bow, waving playfully at him.

He took out a key and unlocked the cabinet under the bookcase. He pushed aside some papers and reached in, feeling for the bottle. His hand touched a wooden box, which he knew contained the Colt revolver. His fingers moved on until they felt the large glass bottle and pulled out the Glen Livet. He opened it, poured a shot, and tossed it down.

He strolled into his private bathroom. While washing his face, he ran his fingers across the scar on his forehead, compliments of a University of Michigan linebacker. He swallowed two aspirin and swished some mouthwash to kill the smell of the Scotch. He straightened his tie and brushed down the graying hair on the sides of his head. He thought for the thousandth time that he needed to lose some weight.

As he came out of his office, Marge was putting away things on her desk and reaching for her purse.

"Thanks, Marge. I'll see you tomorrow. By the way, did you make that deposit?"

Marge turned at the outer door and nodded, confirming for Zac that she had made a deposit into one of the Swiss accounts.

"Good," he said smiling and walked into the lobby. "Well, dear, I'm ready."

Florence stood, revealing her elegant figure and attire. For a woman approaching fifty, she looked exceptionally good in her dark blue evening dress and high heels, with her bronzed skin accentuating her pearl necklace and earrings. Zac noticed her attractive physique, yet felt nothing but indifference. He had learned long ago, however, that one of his best talents was acting, and he thought he deserved an Oscar for the charade he carried on pretending to love his wife.

"We're late," was all she said as they reached the outer door to the office. He closed the door behind them and hurried to join his wife, who was walking swiftly down the hallway. *Soon, I'll have made enough money to end this pretense and move to the Caribbean.* This thought brought a huge smile to his face.

9

AFTER CADE returned from Mobile, he quickly became absorbed in his law practice, immersing himself in preparation for his next big trial. The impact of that frightening episode had dissipated considerably, and he no longer had nightmares about it. He'd decided not to mention the Mardi Gras events with Foulheart to anyone, even Rachael. He didn't want anything to interfere with his career, and he quickly rationalized the devils' meeting by telling himself he didn't want to get involved. The knowledge that Foulheart thought Cade did not have Soulbane's Reports gave Cade a great sense of security. As time passed, Cade quit worrying about it and threw himself even harder into his work.

In mid-April, his good friend Philip Preston talked Cade and Rachael into taking a weekend trip. Except for his trip to Mobile for Mardi Gras, Cade hadn't taken any time off this year. But now one of his big cases had just settled, giving him a little breathing room, and he was glad to get away for the weekend.

"What an incredible view!" Cade was standing on the wooden veranda of Philip's mountain cabin in Highlands, North Carolina. The deck literally hung over the edge of the mountainside, giving the sensation of being suspended in mid-air. He stared off at the view of mountains and valleys jutting out in long, succeeding waves until they were lost in the mist of the smoky, late afternoon clouds. Only the bluish-green mountain tops were visible. The scene was completed by a canopy of deep blue sky. Cade blew hot air on his hands, and zipped up his windbreaker to warm himself from the cool breeze.

"Yes, we love it here," Philip replied, as he prepared to put some steaks on the grill. Philip and Cade had been boyhood friends in Atlanta, and they went to college together at Virginia. Philip was tall, slim and lanky, with straight brown hair and brown eyes, and a boyish face that never seemed to age. His easy, outgoing manner helped make him a successful commercial real estate broker.

"How long have your parents had this place?"

"Let's see, Mom and Dad bought it about a year and a half ago. My family started coming to North Carolina years ago to an Episcopal Conference Center called Kanuga, near Hendersonville. In fact, we all still go back and spend a week there every year. My parents fell in love with the Carolina mountains, and looked all over this area for a retirement home. They plan to spend a lot of time here when Dad retires next year."

"How high up are we?" Cade looked at the stately mountains, blanketed with the light green color of early spring foliage. He inhaled the sweet, intoxicating mountain air.

"I think we're up a little over four thousand feet."

Cade looked in the window to see Philip's wife, Carol, and Rachael scrubbing potatoes, tossing salad, and talking. Carol was a petite girl with short, dark hair and matching charcoal eyes. Unlike Philip, she was rather shy and reserved. She was a talented photo-journalist whose work had been discovered by several national magazines. The Prestons, who married just after they graduated from college, had come to Cade's wedding in Oxford. Both Philip and Carol hit it off with Rachael, and the two couples had been close friends ever since. Carol was Sarah's godmother.

"Cade, didn't Rachael tell me you saw George Mason recently?"

"Yes. He invited me to Mardi Gras in Mobile."

"I haven't seen George in years. How's he doing?"

"Same ole George. He hasn't changed much since college. Fun-loving as always."

"How was Mardi Gras?"

"It was great." Cade felt a spike of fear run through him as he thought about his encounter in Mobile. He hadn't given Mardi Gras much thought these past weeks. He wondered if maybe he should tell Philip about the meeting, but thought he could never explain it – or all the other mind-boggling events of ten years before. Because he and Philip were such close friends, over the years Cade had really wanted to share his Oxford story with Philip, but had just never seemed to find the right time. Philip and Carol went to the same Episcopal church as the Brysons, and Philip was very involved there. Cade somehow made time to serve on the Finance Committee, but wasn't nearly as active as Philip. Philip often invited Cade to come to his weekly Bible study, but Cade just never seemed to have the time.

Cade continued, "In fact, don't tell anyone, but George got sick, so I secretly took his place on the float. It was a blast. I haven't had that much fun in a long time."

Before Cade could say any more, Carol showed up with two goblets of red wine. "Here, gentlemen. Some libations before our kingly feast." She smiled warmly.

Cade took the glass and sniffed the bouquet of the Cabernet he'd brought for the weekend. Sarah was staying with Cade's parents, and Carol's parents were taking care of their nine-year old twin boys. The four of them had taken a long hike in the morning and picnicked near a waterfall, which had been exhilarating for Cade. As he sipped the wine and smelled the steaks cooking, he finally relaxed. The setting sun cast a pink-orange glow on the top of the white clouds that had settled into the valleys just below the peaks of the mountains.

*   *   *

"That was a wonderful dessert," Philip said, as the four of them finished the trifle Rachael had prepared from her mother's family recipe. They were in the large main room of the cabin, sitting on the floor made of old, wide pine lumber. The dark log walls were illuminated by the fire in the stone fireplace, which also kept the evening chill at bay.

Carol stood. "Rachael and I are going into town before it gets too late and do some window shopping. Care to join us?"

Philip looked over at Cade and winked. "No thanks. You two go on, and Cade and I'll do the dishes."

"That's a deal." Carol bent over and kissed her husband on the cheek.

The two men made short work of the dishes. Philip poured the remainder of the Cabernet into their glasses. "Grab a sweater, and I'll meet you on the deck."

Cade complied and went outside. He leaned against the wooden railing. The night sky was filled with thousands of stars, and a gentle breeze filled the air with the aroma of mountain flowers. A serenade was provided by competing choruses of frogs and crickets. It had been a long while since he'd last found the time to gaze at the Milky Way.

"I can see why you and Carol love this place," Cade said when Philip joined him.

"I'm just glad we finally talked you into coming to Highlands with us."

"It's easy to lose track of time up here." Cade marveled at the fact that almost no lights were visible at night from the cabin, and he felt as if time stood still up here in the midst of these serene, peaceful mountains. He wondered if maybe this was the time to talk to Philip about his encounter with the devils. Now that so much time had passed, he was almost too embarrassed to mention it. And yet, he knew he could trust Philip, and that, of all people, Philip wouldn't think he was crazy. Maybe it *was* time to say something.

Philip interrupted Cade's thoughts when he leaned on the rail next to Cade and cleared his throat. "Is everything all right with you and Rachael?"

"Yes, everything's fine. Why do you ask?"

"I don't know. It's just that there seems to be a strain on you two when you're together. Carol actually mentioned it first, I guess sort of woman's intuition. You're such close friends of ours that we've been kind of worried."

Cade felt his defensiveness throw up a shield. As he considered how to respond, Philip continued, "You seem to work all the time. Look how long it took to get you up here for a weekend. I just want to be sure you take time to smell the roses."

"Listen, Philip, I'm doing what I think is best for my family. I know I'm working hard, but soon I'll be able to take more time off. I'm coming up for partner at the end of the year. Things will get better then."

"I'm glad to hear it. But Sarah is already almost ... ."

"Don't bring Sarah into this. You know I love her more than anything in the world. Nothing is more important to me than my daughter." Cade felt increasingly frustrated, as if Philip was backing him into a corner. He turned toward Philip and blurted out, "Did Rachael put you up to this?"

Philip avoided his gaze and looked off into the distance. "No, ... well, she did say something to Carol several months ago, and we ... ."

"I appreciate your concern, but we're doing fine." Cade no longer gave any thought to confiding in Philip about his encounter in Mobile. He finished his wine and yawned. "I think I'll call it a night. I'm pretty beat. See you in the morning."

He hurried away to the guest bedroom. He didn't feel like talking to anyone, not Philip and especially not Rachael. He quickly undressed, crawled into bed, and pulled the down comforter up to his chin. Lying in the soft, warm bed surrounded by the cool, fresh mountain air, Cade wasn't sure if he was more angry at his friend for prying, or more embarrassed at how close to the mark Philip had come. He turned off the bedside lamp. An owl near the open window hooted into the night air.

10

"Zac, you want another drink?" Gail was standing in the cabin of Zac's thirty-six foot sailboat.

"Sure, why not?" He was sitting in the stern holding the wheel. He stared at Gail, in white shorts and turquoise bikini top, her tanned skin contrasted by long, straight, bleached-blonde hair. He glanced up at the sails, full in the moderate Caribbean breeze. The *Skoal* was in a broad reach back to St. Lucia, and Zac smiled as he surveyed the truly idyllic scene: a blue sky outlining the sails, as the bow gently plowed through the azure sea topped by white caps. This warm April in the Caribbean was a far cry from the rainy and unseasonably cold weather he'd left in D.C. He first met Gail when she was working at a cocktail party in Washington, D.C. several years ago. She had no money, and Zac had worked out a most satisfying arrangement with her. It didn't hurt that he was wealthy enough to take her places she'd only dreamed of – not to mention that he helped maintain her little cocaine habit. He looked off to starboard to see his landmark, the peaks of the pyramid-like twin Pitons, directing him into the harbor.

"Your manhattan, captain." Gail laughed as she held out the glass.

Zac grabbed her wrist as she bent over to hand him the drink, and she kissed him passionately. The boat abruptly leapt up as it hit a wave, and the drink spilled on both of them, disrupting their kiss.

"Here, take the helm and steer just to left of the mountains. I need to trim the sails a bit. We'll be in the harbor soon."

Zac trimmed the genoa jib, untied a halyard and dropped the mainsail. He quickly fastened the boom to the backstay and furled the large sail around the boom, making it fast with the mainsheet. The boat slowed with the loss of the mainsail and gently bobbed in the waves.

Just then his ship-to-shore radio squawked. He picked up the mike.

"Skoal, here. Over."

A scratchy voice with a deep Southern drawl came over. "Mr. Pickering?"

"Yes, who's this?"

"It's Bryson, sir. Cade Bryson."

Pickering's heart rate rose as he wondered why his lawyer was calling him in the Caribbean.

"Yes, Bryson, what the hell is it?" Zac did not like this unwarranted intrusion.

"Sorry to bother you, but your secretary told me how to contact you. Just thought you should know the owner of your mall project in Atlanta sued your company yesterday."

"Dammit. Are you serious?"

"I hate to bring you bad news. But Harry Martin and I are already working on it. Don't worry, we've got everything under control for now."

They talked for several minutes, and Zac agreed to call Bryson when he returned to D.C. in three days.

"I'll take her now." He had just come out of the cabin, having taken a big swig from the bottle of bourbon before he came back on deck. He stood in the stern, holding the wheel. He put his arm around Gail, his mind a million miles away thinking about the new lawsuit in Atlanta. As they entered the harbor, he saw a young couple in a small motorboat, laughing and opening a bottle of something that appeared to be champagne.

"More honeymooners," laughed Zac, pointing to the couple.

At that comment, however, Gail stopped smiling and turned to face the bow. The couple in the boat were giggling, and the man had a camera taking pictures of the woman as she raised her glass in the air, as if making a toast.

As the *Skoal* glided past the young couple, the man waved and pointed the camera toward Zac, who returned the wave and even managed a smile.

11

SEVERAL MONTHS had passed since the weekend in Highlands. After Philip's observations, Cade, if anything, had thrown himself even more furiously into work, not wanting to admit to himself he and Rachael had any problems. He was even more bound and determined to prove himself to everyone by making partner.

Cade glanced up from his computer screen, blinked and rubbed his eyes. It was almost ten at night, and he'd lost track of time working on his brief due to the Eleventh Circuit Court of Appeals next week. He was frustrated because he'd been at a meeting of the board of a homeless shelter that had lasted three hours. His entire afternoon shot, he had rushed back to the office to work on his brief. He stood and stretched, wondering why he hadn't heard from Rachael. She often called Cade, especially when he worked late. He had long ago become annoyed with Rachael's seeming insecurity in always checking on him.

He picked up the phone to call her, but thought better of it in case she was asleep. He turned his computer off and recorded his billable hours for the day.

He paused before writing down his time. What had Harry said to him? "… you just need to be more creative in how you bill." *It would be so easy to add a few extra hours. No one would ever know. A few extra hours here and there could really add up.*

Cade started to do just that, then stopped and threw his pen on the desk. "I'll know," he said in a loud whisper. He picked up the pen and wrote down accurately the time he had spent working on the brief. *Guess I'll just have to work harder*. He flipped off the office light.

* * *

When he pulled into his driveway and parked, Cade grabbed his jacket from the backseat and glanced at his house to check for any sign of activity. The absence of lights gave him the answer. This July was about as hot as Cade could remember, and Atlanta was stifling even now at ten thirty in the evening. The air, thick and warm, was filled with sounds of the cicada chorus seeming to announce his arrival. He rubbed his temples as he walked toward the front door.

He switched on the light in the kitchen, hoping that Rachael had left him something to eat. She was usually good about leaving some leftovers on the stove for him to reheat in the microwave, since he rarely ate dinner at home with Rachael and Sarah.

He was famished, but didn't see anything left out in the kitchen. When he opened the refrigerator, he spied several bowls and dishes with food in them, and a bottle of champagne, which was highly unusual. He took a beer along with some chicken salad in a plastic container to make a sandwich. As he looked around for some bread, he noticed a box wrapped in shiny paper on the far counter and went to investigate. When he did, his heart stopped – on top was a card that said, "Happy Anniversary."

"Oh, no," he said out loud in a long, low sigh. "I can't believe it!" He hit the palm of his hand with his fist. Today was their anniversary, and he'd completely forgotten. And, not just any anniversary, it was their tenth. Then, to make matters worse, he looked into the dining room. The table was set with their wedding china, silver candlesticks, and a bouquet of red roses in the center. At the sight of the elaborate table setting, Cade recalled that Rachael had asked if he'd be home for dinner tonight, and he'd absent-mindedly said he would.

He rushed up the steps. He passed Sarah's room first, but she was not in her bed. Then, he also remembered, again too late, that

Rachael had said Sarah would be at Cade's parents' house tonight. Cade felt a pit in his stomach as the full impact of his blunder hit him. He walked quickly into his dark bedroom and turned on the bathroom light, which dimly illuminated the bedroom. Rachael appeared to be asleep, and when Cade got closer, he could see that mascara had run down her face.

He bent over and kissed her cheek, and said softly, "Rachael, I'm so sorry." She didn't budge. He slipped off his clothes and put on a bathrobe. He wasn't at all sleepy, so he went downstairs into his study. He usually liked to look at one or two of his books, or to work on his computer. Tonight, however, he sat in his desk chair and stared blankly around the room. Not only had he forgotten his anniversary, but he had no present to give Rachael in the morning. She had talked for years about wanting a pearl necklace on their tenth anniversary, and Cade had meant to surprise her with one. He buried his face in his hands, furious at his forgetfulness.

12

"Cade, I think we need some time apart." Rachael stared at her shaking hands. They were standing in the kitchen, late at night. Rachael had hardly spoken to him this past week since their anniversary. She was in a white bathrobe, her hair tied up with a band. Her eyes were bloodshot. Cade, as usual, had come home late, but this time he found only a peanut butter and jelly sandwich on the counter for his dinner.

"What ... what do you mean?" he stammered, stunned by his wife's words. He tugged at his tie, but it had long since been loosened. His white cotton shirt was wrinkled from the long day at the office.

"It's all too obvious. You clearly don't care for me like you used to ... I can see it in your eyes." Rachael looked up at him with an infinitely sad expression.

"But ... ."

"You *know* it's true. We haven't been close in a long while, and you're married to your law firm now. You never smile when you're around us. Tell me, where were you tonight?"

"At the office, as usual," Cade replied quickly, feeling his face glow with a bright red flush.

"Right, and I'm the Queen of England," Rachael said in a harsh tone. "I can smell the booze on your breath, and Stephen Banks called two hours ago from the office looking for you."

Cade felt extreme embarrassment at being caught, and he noted the irony that this was actually one of the few times during his marriage that he'd gone out for drinks without at least telling Rachael. His defense mechanism shot a bolt of anger through his body, and he blurted out, "Dammit, Rachael, you're so ungrateful. I work my tail off for you and Sarah, and this is the thanks I get."

"You, it's always about you, isn't it?" Rachael's angry tone surprised Cade.

"What are you talking about?"

"You're so concerned about yourself. It's *your* job, *your* friends, *your* ... . "

"Wait a minute, Rachael."

"No, I'm tired of waiting. I left my country to be with you. I sacrificed my career for yours by teaching part-time. I've begged and pleaded with you to let us have more children and ... ." Rachael choked up and started crying.

Cade advanced to hug her, but she backed away, dabbing her eyes with the sleeves of her bathrobe.

"Everything I do – all my hard work – is for us."

"I wish I could believe that, but I can't go on like this anymore. It's been months since we made love ... ." Rachael's cheeks glowed with a blush. "You obviously don't find me attractive anymore, and I see how you eye other girls when we're out. Then, when you stayed at the office working late on our tenth anniversary, it suddenly struck me that I just don't care any more."

"Rachael, I still care very much." Cade found himself calling upon all his skills of advocacy and realized he was not speaking from his heart.

"Listen, I have next semester off to work on my dissertation, and Mum is getting older. Let me take Sarah and go to England for a while. You can work, and we'll see what it's like to be apart. That way, you won't have to explain anything to anyone ... I know how *precious* your reputation is to you," she added, her sarcastic tone as pleasing to hear as a fingernail scratching a chalkboard.

Cade's anger almost overwhelmed him, but he caught himself. "I don't want to be away from Sarah that long … ." He immediately knew he'd said the wrong thing, and quickly added, "I mean … ."

"I *know* what you mean. You care for Sarah, but not for me." Rachael started crying again.

"I meant both of you," he said, unconvincingly. "Let's just let things calm down. We don't have to decide anything tonight." He put his arms around Rachael, and this time she didn't back off, but her arms remained at her side. Deep down, Cade did not find himself wanting to stop her from going home to England. Instead, something whispered to him that a few months in Atlanta by himself might not be all bad. He was coming up for partner soon, and would be working hard anyway. He'd been away from Rachael and Sarah before – for weeks at a time on business – so, maybe this wouldn't be so bad after all. The break might do them both good.

Rachael stepped back after a few moments and wiped her eyes with the sleeve of her bathrobe. "I'm too tired to talk any more about it tonight. It's for the best. We'll just see how the autumn goes with Sarah and me in England, then, if … if you don't love me anymore … ," her voice cracked. She ran out of the kitchen and up the stairs.

Cade walked slowly into the den and sat, putting his face in his hands. He tried to think what was the best thing to say to Rachael. He went over to the bar and poured himself a glass of bourbon. As he sipped it, Cade thought back to the glorious July afternoon ten years ago when he and Rachael had been married in Merton College Chapel. On that day of exquisite sun and blue sky, Rachael looked radiant, and he was very much in love. He remembered how his parents had been resistant at first when he told them he was getting married to an English girl they'd never met, and how they had tried to talk him out of it, saying that's not why they sent him to Oxford. But when they flew to England and met Rachael, she had won them over. Their honeymoon trip to Venice was idyllic. Their first years of married life had been fun, so what happened? Cade had trouble pinpointing anything specific. No, it had been gradual: the grind of law school, the grueling years of long hours as an associate for a major Atlanta law firm, the responsibility of a child, an over-committed and hectic lifestyle. Over time, he and Rachael had simply spent less and less time with each other, less and less time talking, less and less time sharing.

Rachael became pregnant unexpectedly after they had been married less than two years. Cade had not been ready for children, and he had resented this intrusion. He loved Sarah with all his heart, but law school had been made harder, and the addition of a baby had practically ended their social life and put a real strain on their meager budget. He resented the time he had to spend away from his law practice, when Sarah was sick or had a party, and Rachael wasn't able to take care of it because of her university workload. Cade realized he also resented Rachael's career as a college professor, even though he welcomed the additional income. He kept telling himself that one day he'd make partner and have a great income, and then they could relax. So far, however, that had been nothing but a pipe dream. Plus, he had visions of a bigger house in Atlanta, and the initiation fee at the country club had set him back a bundle.

Maybe it would be good if Rachael and Sarah went to England this fall. A little freedom seemed rather enticing, especially after the row they'd just had. He decided that he'd make just enough of a fuss so as not to let on how relieved he was to have Rachael and Sarah gone for a few months. Cade smiled, downed the rest of his bourbon, went upstairs and crept into bed. He didn't bother to say goodnight or even to give Rachael a gentle caress as he used to do. He was soon drifting off to sleep.

*   *   *

"Daddy, why aren't you coming with us?" Sarah asked at the Delta terminal in Hartsfield Airport. It was early September, and Cade had taken Rachael and Sarah to the airport for their flight to England.

"Honey, I have to stay and work. You and Mommy are going to

visit Nana for a while. You'll have a wonderful time."

"But Daddy, I'll miss you." Sarah's eyes filled with tears. Cade felt a great lump in his throat.

"I'll miss you, too, sweetheart." Cade's eyes were blurring.

"We'd better get on the plane," said Rachael. She looked at Cade with sad eyes and picked up her carry-on bag. He leaned over and kissed her on the cheek, but Rachael didn't smile. Instead, she busied herself with her luggage and took Sarah by the hand. As they neared the entrance to the gangway, Sarah turned around and waved with one hand, while in the other she held her favorite stuffed bunny rabbit. Without thinking, he ran and picked her up, holding her tight.

"Sarah, you be good and mind Mommy," he said, trying to sound cheerful. "Rachael, call me when you get in and let me know you're safe."

Rachael nodded, but said nothing. She dabbed her eyes with a handkerchief and grabbed Sarah's hand again. Mother and daughter ambled down the gangplank toward the plane. He stood waiting expectantly, but neither turned around again, and they soon disappeared into the aircraft.

He went over to the window and watched until the plane taxied, sped down the runway, and took off, disappearing into the sky at dusk.

Cade thought of returning to the office, but quickly decided that he would have plenty of time to work in the coming months. He also thought about calling Philip, but when he recalled his discussion with Philip that night in Highlands, he was too embarrassed to call his friend. No, it was time to have a drink and apply a quick anaesthetic to his heart and emotions. As he got into his car at the airport, he instead called Eric from his cell phone. He only got Eric's voice mail at home and left a message telling Eric to meet him for a drink around eight. As Cade drove back to town, he struggled to force the image of Sarah waving good-bye from his mind.

His reverie was shattered when he realized he was just about to crash into the car in front of him. His wheels screeched when he slammed on his brakes. His Land Rover skidded sideways, narrowly missing the car in front of him. Cars behind him honked impatiently, as Cade regained control and continued down the highway.

His heart was pounding from the near miss, and he decided he really needed a drink now – no several drinks. He drove quickly now straight to the bar and lucked into a parking spot near the door. He tugged at his tie to loosen it while shutting his car door. He looked at his reflection in the window and brushed his hair briskly with his hand.

As his eyes adjusted to the dim light inside the bar, Cade spied Brad Smith, a lawyer he knew in town. It had been a while, Cade realized, since he'd roamed bars alone. Even if Rachael wasn't with him, he usually came with Eric or some buddy from work. Cade even found himself thinking that he missed bar hopping and felt a sense of relief that his family was gone.

"Cade, how are you?" said Brad, extending his hand. Brad was a bit shorter than Cade, with short, dark hair.

He was grateful to Brad for calling him over. He'd had a few cases with Brad and liked him well enough. Mainly though, he didn't want to look awkward going into a bar alone, especially if someone he knew were to see him. Cade was glad that Brad's greeting made it appear as if he was looking for him.

They exchanged pleasantries, and Cade ordered a drink. As they talked, Cade glanced around the bar, to see if he knew anyone else. He saw a group of attractive girls flirting with some guys and felt a pang of envy, reminding him that he was well out of touch with the night scene in Atlanta.

He was just about to call it a night, when the front door opened and in strolled Eric with a group of people. Cade recognized all of them from the gym, and his heart skipped a beat when he saw Sherry among them.

"Cade, what are you doing out and about, old man?" Eric asked, laughing.

Cade smiled, yet felt some embarrassment.

"Hi Eric, so you got my message?" Cade replied.

"Message? What message? We were all at the gym and decided to come over for a quick drink." He leaned over and said quietly, "Where's Rachael?"

"Oh, yes, Rachael," Cade whispered hesitantly. "Well, actually, I need to talk to you sometime. She's gone to England for the fall, with Sarah." Cade was still very emotional about saying good-bye, and he wasn't ready to talk about it yet. He downed his drink and ordered another.

"Lucky for her. Cade, you know Sherry and Muffy, and this is Fred Thames and Sheila Brock."

"Nice to meet all of you," he replied, as he followed the group to an empty table. Cade took the last seat, next to Sherry. The group ordered a round of drinks. Cade took several large gulps of his bourbon. He began to relax and enjoy talking to Sherry. Finally, he glanced at his watch to see it was almost midnight, and he quietly paid the bill for the table.

"Some of us have to work tomorrow." Cade stood.

"Won't you have one more?" asked Sheila.

"Not tonight, thanks. I really do have to get to work early. Maybe some other time."

Sherry reached out and touched his arm. "Don't work too hard. It was good talking to you, and I hope to see you again soon."

Cade wondered if she had winked, but decided it was his imagination. He gave a quick wave, and turned to say, "Hey, Eric, give me a call tomorrow."

Eric nodded. "Sure thing old buddy. You'll be a bachelor like me for a while, and we'll have a great time checking out the bars together." Cade gave a brief wave, but made no other reply.

As he drove home, he felt a strong rush of two conflicting rivers of emotion colliding in him: incredible sadness and yet also a sense of freedom.

13

L AUREN ST. JOHN sat at her desk in the third-floor office of the laboratory in Oxford. She had been working on a problem with her research for many hours and lost track of time. It was an overcast afternoon in early October, and she glanced out of her window at a huge maple tree adorned in bright yellow leaves.

"Dr. St. John, can I speak to you a minute?"

Lauren spun around in her chair to face the open door. Standing in the doorway, dressed in a white lab coat, was a large man with a shaved head.

"Of course, Dr. Elliott, please come in."

Dr. Christopher Elliott entered and shut the door behind him, as he habitually did whenever he came to see her. They both worked in an Oxford laboratory studying infectious diseases, and Dr. Elliott was not just her boss, he was one of the few people in the world who knew Lauren's true role at the lab.

Elliott stood behind the wooden guest chair, his forehead furrowed, and declined Lauren's gesture to be seated. Resting his hands on top of the chair, he said in a low voice, "I'm afraid we may have a problem."

Lauren sat forward, her right elbow resting on her desk, while she tapped her chin with her right index finger. Almost unconsciously, she raised her left hand to tuck her short, strawberry blonde hair behind her ear.

"The Prime Minister has been contacted through diplomatic

channels about a potential new strain of Ebola that has been discovered in Africa. Apparently, he is concerned it could reach Europe. I've arranged for you to give a public lecture at a medical meeting in Rome in about three weeks to give you a cover for going there. While you are in Rome, you will meet secretly with the Americans and representatives of principal European countries to discuss this development."

"What else do you know?" Lauren shifted uncomfortably in her chair.

"Not much else, I'm afraid, at least at the moment. This has been given highest priority by Number 10, so it's obviously of major concern."

"All right. I'll make the necessary arrangements, so let me know any other details as soon as possible."

"Right." He started for the door, then turned. "By the way, how is your work going on your special project?"

"It's a bit puzzling right now. I've had the strangest results in the lab. Can't quite work out what to make of it."

As Dr. Elliott reached the door, Lauren said, "Are you going to at least tell me the subject of my lecture in Rome?"

"What? Give you advance warning and spoil all the fun?" Dr. Elliott laughed heartily and opened the door. Just as he exited, he stuck his head back in. "I know you'll be brilliant as usual."

Lauren wadded up a piece of paper and threw it at him, but Elliott dodged it and disappeared.

Lauren sat back in her chair, rubbing her eyes. How had she ever managed to get herself into this job in the first place? She shoved away the image of the hospital emergency room that popped into her head, and turned to face her computer screen again, still puzzling over her latest lab results. She was tired from a long day of getting nowhere in her research.

When the phone rang, she picked it up quickly. "Hello, Dr. St. John speaking."

"Oh, Lauren, you sound so official." It was the voice of Lauren's friend, Mary York, who was a don at Magdalen College. She and Mary had been college classmates at Balliol and friends ever since.

"Hi Mary. It's been a long day."

"I wanted to confirm we're on for dinner tonight at Magdalen."

"Absolutely, I've been looking forward to it all day."

"Good. Meet me at Magdalen about seven. Oh, and I've just learned a former student of mine, Rachael Bryson, is here this autumn working on her dissertation. She'll be joining us as well."

After chatting a few more minutes, the women hung up.

Thinking about the pleasant evening ahead of her, Lauren stood, stretched, and attacked her problem with renewed vigor.

It was time to take some new measurements. Lauren walked down the hall past the laboratory near her office, until she came to an elevator. To summon it, she keyed in the security code known by only a very few people. It took her to a deep-level basement. Once there, she placed her hand on a sensor, which read her handprints. As a metal door slid open with a whoosh, a computer voice said in a monotone, "Welcome, Dr. St. John."

Lauren entered into a secure dressing room to put on her 'moon suit,' as she called it. She carefully placed the bubble over her head, secured it tightly, and checked her oxygen supply. She wrinkled her nose as she noticed her reflection in the thick plastic visor. Her hair was hidden under the helmet, but she saw her green eyes and pale complexion in the image.

Not bad, for a forty-something woman, she thought to herself, and almost laughed out loud at her vanity. People often remarked to her about her dry wit. Lauren went to the next security point, ready to enter a room that only a few people in Oxford, and only a handful of senior government officials London, even knew existed. Lauren St. John, medical doctor and researcher, had long-since given up trying to understand the odd curves in the road of her life that brought her into this world of secrecy.

14

"CAN I HELP YOU?" asked the porter at the Magdalen College Lodge when Lauren entered the narrow room at the entrance to the college that evening.

"Yes, my name is Lauren St. John, and I'm meeting Professor York for dinner."

"Right you are," the porter replied. "She told me you were coming. I'll take you there." He escorted Lauren to the front courtyard, paved in stones with criss-crossing walks. It was already dark on this cool, early October evening. She glanced up to her right to see Magdalen Tower rising high above the west front of the Chapel and bathed in soft floodlights. An unseasonable fog was beginning to thicken, adding a halo effect to the lights around Magdalen. The top of the tower was obscured by the mist. They entered the passageway, passing the entrance to Magdalen Chapel on the right. The tower clock sounded, announcing that it was seven, as they walked on to the Fellows Smoking Room.

"Oh, Lauren, good to see you." Mary York came forward to greet Lauren when she entered the room. Mary was a short, petite woman. Her dark hair, streaked with gray, was pulled back in a bun, and she wore thick glasses. She was a professor of history and had written a highly acclaimed book on the Reformation in England.

"Hello Mary," replied Lauren, smiling. "It's so nice of you to invite me to dinner." Lauren was genuinely glad to see her friend.

Although they both lived in Oxford, they rarely saw each other. Mary was married to an architect, and they had two children. Lauren had never married.

"My pleasure. Care for a sherry?"

"Yes please." Lauren accepted the offered glass.

Wooden tables of various shapes were placed around the room, as well as a number of burgundy leather chairs. Waist high light oak linenfold panelling went around the room, and numerous beautiful paintings hung on the white walls above.

At that moment, Mary glanced over Lauren's shoulder and smiled again, saying, "Rachael, lovely to see you."

Lauren turned around to see a beautiful, tall, dark-haired woman entering the room. She had bright blue eyes and a vibrant smile. The woman extended her hand to Mary. "I'm so grateful for your invitation, Dr. York."

"Allow me to introduce you," Mary said, gesturing to Rachael and Lauren.

"Dr. Lauren St. John, meet Rachael Bryson, one of my former students and one of my best."

Rachael extended her hand. "Pleased to meet you doctor. Do you teach here at Magdalen with Professor York?"

Lauren and Mary smiled at this comment, and Mary said, "Actually, Lauren is a medical doctor, and she's engaged in research here in Oxford."

"And how do you two know each other?" inquired Rachael. Lauren thought how poised and elegant Rachael was.

"We were classmates at Balliol," replied the professor. "And do call me Mary."

Lauren scanned the room, already well filled with fellows and their guests engaged in pre-dinner banter, and Mary motioned toward some unoccupied chairs, where the three women sat to sip their sherry and chat. Lauren learned that Rachael was a history professor in the States, and that she was married to an American named Cade Bryson. They had one daughter, Sarah, who was seven.

Mary had been one of Rachael's tutors at Merton, and the two had become friends. Rachael was in Oxford this term to complete research for her doctorate thesis on the Elizabethan era.

"Rachael, where are you staying while you're here?" Lauren asked.

"My mother now lives in Lower Slaughter, so we're staying with her."

"Really! That's where I live. What's your mother's name?"

"Bridgett … Bridgett Adams. Do you know her?"

"I'm afraid not," Lauren replied. "I'm sorry I haven't met her, but I don't spend a lot of time at home. I seem either to be at the lab or traveling somewhere."

"Mother hasn't lived there very long. She's recently moved from Tintagel, so I'm not surprised you haven't met her yet."

"As I recall," interjected Mary, "your mother is quite a seamstress."

"That's right," Rachael replied, with a smile. "I'm biased, of course, but I think she makes wonderful dresses."

"I'll certainly have to go and see her." Lauren laughed.

A tall, handsome gentleman with dark brown hair and horn-rimmed glasses, dressed in a dark suit, approached the three women. He was accompanied by a large, older man with white hair and a white beard.

"Mary," said the first man, "it's nice to have you and your guests here this evening."

Mary extended her hand saying, "Good evening, Dr. Pearigen."

He continued, "Allow me to introduce my guest, Owen McCrady."

"Of course – I know Bodley's Librarian quite well. How are you Owen?"

"Very well, Dr York," he replied graciously, but with a mischievous smile.

"President Pearigen, please meet my friends, Dr. Lauren St. John, who is a medical researcher here in Oxford, and Rachael Bryson, a former student who is over here working on her thesis. Dr. Nigel Pearigen is the President of Magdalen, and Dr. McCrady heads our magnificent Bodleian Library."

As everyone exchanged pleasantries, the Senior Common Room butler spoke quietly to Pearigen, who nodded.

"Do excuse me," Pearigen said. "It's time for dinner." He walked off as McCrady bowed slightly. Lauren heard some shuffling movements and noted that the fellows and guests were following the president out of a door at the end of the smoking room. The fellows each began to put on black academic gowns as they exited. The group walked outside onto the wooden walkway along the top of the fifteenth-century Cloisters. Lauren looked down into the quadrangle, a lovely and peaceful spot that time seemed unable to invade. The queue of people went inside a hall through a door from the walkway and stood behind the wooden chairs at the long High Table, graced by silver candelabra, until everyone had arrived at their seats. Mary showed Lauren and Rachael to theirs, and positioned herself between her two guests.

Lauren took in the scene from the view of the elevated platform supporting the High Table: the linenwood paneling and the large portraits hung around the impressive hall, with it's magnificent timber ceiling and an exquisitely carved oak buttery screen at the far end. Although now electric, the small yellow lights lined up along the three long rows of tables in the hall were reminiscent of bygone days when candles had been the only light. It was easy to imagine similar dinners in this great hall hundreds of years earlier, with fires roaring in the huge fireplace. Everyone remained standing while the Latin blessing was recited by President Pearigen, "*Benedictus benedicat, per Jesum Christum, Dominum nostrum. Amen.*"

Lauren and Mary caught up on old times, and then Lauren listened while Mary and Rachael talked about Rachael's research. Lauren saw Rachael's eyes light up when the conversation turned to her daughter. She sipped her glass of claret and closed her eyes to savour the aromas of the meal.

When the meal was finished, everyone at High Table stood once again, as President Pearigen recited the benediction, *"Benedicto benedicatur, per Jesum Christum, Dominum nostrum. Amen."*

After dinner, the three women gathered with a few of the fellows for port and fruit in the Senior Common Room downstairs in Cloisters behind the Chapel. The walls were brown square paneling from floor to ceiling, and a beautiful red, blue and green oriental rug in nested geometrical patterns, covered much of the wooden floor. Lauren observed with fascination the rare eighteenth-century mahogany port railway. It consisted of a slanted plank with three wooden tracks mounted on brass that carried two circular decanter holders on brass wheels. The chairs were arranged in a semi-circle before the fireplace, with small dessert tables beside the chairs. The fellows passed the port and other dessert wines to one another by moving the holders along the tracks with cords connected through runners, so that the decanters could be passed almost silently with the assistance of gravity.

Owen McCrady sat between Lauren and Rachael, and he was utterly charming. He discussed a wide range of subjects, as well as his work at the Bodleian. He seemed to know a great deal about medicine and music, two subjects of particular interest to Lauren, and he also talked at length with Rachael about her history research and about her family. He invited Lauren and Rachael to come for a tour of the Bodleian sometime.

After about an hour and a half-hour of savoring the exquisite wines, fruit, and chocolates, and enjoying the wide-ranging conversation among the fellows and guests, Mary escorted Lauren and Rachael to the front gate, where they bid one another farewell. The fog was now so thick, it was difficult to see more than a few yards.

When Lauren and Rachael stepped onto the sidewalk, Lauren said, "Rachael, it was very nice to meet you. I hope we shall see each other again soon."

"I'd like that very much."

"Can I give you a lift?"

"Thanks, but I have my mother's car. Please look us up in Lower Slaughter sometime. I'd love you to meet Sarah and my mother."

"I'll be sure to," replied Lauren as she shook hands with Rachael.

The two women parted, with Lauren walking toward Magdalen Bridge and Rachael heading up the High toward Queens. Lauren had enjoyed her evening with Mary and Rachael, but she envied these women, who appeared to have everything going for them.

*   *   *

Lauren found herself sitting bolt upright, her forehead damp. Disoriented in the dark, she was mired in the wasteland between dream and reality, but in this instance she wanted reality. As she became more alert, reality won and she reached for her bedside lamp, banishing the ghosts of her dream.

She said out loud to herself, "Bloody hell, Lauren, can't you get over this? It's ages in the past."

Lauren shook involuntarily and got out of bed. She wrapped a bathrobe over her nightshirt, walked into the kitchen, and fumbled in the darkness for the light switch. The small clock by the stove said one thirty-six. The night was still and the house quiet.

Lauren made some hot chocolate and sat at the small table. She watched the thin curls of steam drifting from the cup. These nightmares had never left her, not in all these years. Would she ever forget? Lauren hated these lonely late-night vigils, and God knows she'd had plenty of them.

In her loneliness and fear, Lauren's thoughts ran to Ian Chadwick. He had intrigued her since the day they met. Just when Lauren had virtually given up hope of ever finding a companion, Ian had walked into her life. She recalled the first time they met at the lab, when Ian was introduced to her. *That was what, about eight months ago now?* She was walking down the hallway and had seen a tall, dark-haired man, with high cheekbones, a strong chin, and fathomless dark eyes. She had read that some women literally swooned upon meeting Lord Byron, but had never believed it until her meeting with Ian.

Lauren was so deeply shy when it came to men, that she hid her insecurity with a biting sarcasm. After meeting Ian and giving him a dose of her best acid, Lauren figured that would be the last she would see of him. But several days later, he came round to her office and asked her to join him at a quartet recital in Oxford the next evening. They hit it off that evening and had seen a good deal of each other since then.

She wondered where their relationship was going. She had noticed, lately – or at least, thought she had noticed – that Ian seemed more preoccupied than usual. Lauren put that down to the stress of work, and also wondered if, perhaps, she wasn't rather insecure. After all, while he was not the only male who appeared to notice her, he was the only one who seemed genuinely interested in her research.

And yet, something was missing. But what? He was at the same time charming and mysterious, which held a magnetic attraction for Lauren. She had fallen deeply in love with Ian.

Lauren put her head in her arms and took several deep breaths. For a moment, the thought occurred to her that maybe she should pray. But she had long ago given up on such nonsense and quickly dismissed the thought. Finally, exhausted and tired of thinking, she shuffled back to bed and soon drifted off into a restless sleep.

A vague sense of something awoke her – the sun, streaming through the window. Lauren curled up under the covers, wishing she could sleep forever.

15

"*SALUT*," TOASTED IAN CHADWICK, touching his wineglass to Lauren's, producing a high-pitched ting.

Lauren glanced around the room at Brown's. The Oxford restaurant was packed as usual this cool late-October night. The dark wooden chairs, the off-white walls, and the tinkling piano all combined to produce the familiar Brown's atmosphere, evoking in her a warm and secure feeling.

"Ian, this is just what I needed today." Lauren looked at her companion and tapped the wood of the chair for good luck.

"Rough day?"

"You could say that," Lauren sighed. "I got some strange results in my lab experiment, and I just can't understand it."

"Want to talk about it?"

"No, not really. Let's talk about something else and enjoy the evening. At least what little time we have. My flight leaves early in the morning, so I'm driving to London tonight."

"Tell me again what exactly you're doing in Rome."

"Dr. Elliott asked me to give a paper on some of my research on infectious diseases to an international conference. I only wish you could go to Rome with me." Lauren didn't dare divulge the true nature of her trip, even to Ian. She wondered if he knew about her real work. She had only told him about her research on more common infectious diseases, but had never told him about her work for the British government.

"So do I." Ian's tone was less than convincing. Lauren thought Ian seemed distant and preoccupied again. She had learned to try and overlook his periodic dark moods, that seemed to come and go like the waxing and waning moon. Ian could be quite engaging, but he was an enigma as well. Nevertheless, Lauren had been married to her career for years, and for the first time in many years, she found herself giddily in love.

As they finished their after-dinner coffee, Ian stood. "I'd better walk you to your car, so you can get to London. It will be late enough as it is."

"I suppose you're right." Lauren was reluctant to end this intimate evening. Being with Ian was so absorbing, she rarely thought about time. She *was* due to leave from Heathrow very early in the morning, however, and needed to get into London to get some sleep.

"I'll see you when you return," Ian said, as he walked Lauren to her car.

"Can I give you a lift somewhere?" she asked, hoping for a few more moments together.

"Thanks. My car's not too far away, and I could use some fresh air."

Lauren hesitated, hoping Ian might say something more, but he shuffled his feet and appeared anxious to be off. She quickly kissed his cheek, got into her car, and waved as she drove off.

As she sped down the M-40 toward London in her Jaguar, Lauren went over in her mind the paper she would give in Rome. Although that was merely a pretext, she had to make sure it was a *bona fide* lecture. Suddenly, she gasped. In her rush to leave the lab and meet Ian for dinner, she had left her computer. Her entire presentation was on her laptop, not to mention special instructions from Dr. Elliott, and she had to have it. Lauren slapped her thigh in a gesture of frustration, but realized she had no choice but to go back to the lab, no matter how late that made her.

When she arrived at the lab, Lauren searched for her building key as she rushed up to the back door. As she expected, most of the building was dark, with only a few dim lights remaining on. She went up to the second floor and walked down the hallway. A bright light was coming at an angle out of one room: Ian's office. *He must have forgotten to turn his light off.* She stepped inside to extinguish it.

She'd never really been in Ian's office, despite the fact that they were in the same building. Although her office was on the third floor, she was so busy with her secret research that she spent most of her time in the underground lab. Plus, she did not want co-workers to know that she and Ian were seeing each other, so she avoided the second floor whenever possible.

Lauren glanced around the room. Books and papers were scattered around, but no personal touches warmed up the sterile, white-painted cinder block room. She heard a beep and saw that Ian's computer was on. She walked around, thinking to turn the computer off. On the screen was an email message. Not being able to help herself, she bent over and gazed at the screen.

She blinked and looked again. Rather than finding some message about research, she instead saw an oblique message, in English, but almost nonsensical. It talked about implementing Operation Clootie, with some vague reference about an upcoming meeting although no place was specified. The message was signed "Foulheart."

The name Foulheart rang some vague bell in Lauren's head, but she couldn't remember why. A noise down the hall jolted her. Someone was coming. Her heart skipped a beat, and she took a deep breath. What if someone found her lurking in Ian's office?

She looked around quickly, as the steps came nearer. She went to the door and peeked out. To her relief, she saw that it was the night cleaning crew coming down the hall. She took a deep breath, switched off the light, and slipped unnoticed out of Ian's office.

She went up to the third floor, listened to two new voicemail messages, then quickly retrieved her laptop and walked briskly back down to the second floor. She went around the man with the cleaning cart, nodded at him, and turned the corner. Ian's office light was on again, a thin line of yellow light coming from the cracked doorway. Thinking that the cleaning crew had failed to turn it off, she slowed to do so.

Before she reached the door, she jumped when the phone rang inside Ian's office. Who would be calling this late? Should she answer it? It was probably a wrong number. She didn't have time to ponder these questions long.

"Yes," said a voice from the office, startling Lauren. It was Ian. Lauren tiptoed near the doorway. She felt almost dirty snooping, but she was very curious. *What is Ian doing here?*

"No, no one is around ... Right ... I'm anxious to get going with Operation Clootie ... Yes ... ."

Lauren drew a deep breath, then worried that her gasp was audible. Who was Ian talking to this late at night? What was the meaning of the strange email? Lauren's temples were throbbing. Was this Operation Clootie some secret mission for the British Government?

Ian resumed talking. "Yes, I understand completely. I know what to do ... Right ... Yes, I'll be at our next meeting."

Meeting? Ian didn't mention anything about his going to a meeting. Lauren thought she was going to burst, and momentarily considered confronting him, but decided against it.

Ian said, "Same password? ... All right ... I'll see you then."

Ian apparently hung up the phone. She held her breath and heard him shuffling some papers. She was tip-toeing away when she heard the computer shutting off and Ian's chair creaking. She darted into the adjoining dark office. The light switch in Ian's office clicked, and his footsteps faded down the hall.

In total darkness, Lauren was shivering. She wasn't sure how long she needed to stay in the office, but wanted to make certain it was long enough for Ian to have left the building. Finally, she quietly opened the door and tiptoed into the hall. No one was there, and she walked quickly toward the exit. She was glad she had parked at the back, making it unlikely Ian had seen her car.

As Lauren drove to London, she puzzled over the strange events. *Why did Ian come back to the lab? What does the strange e-mail and phone conversation mean? Is he also engaged in secret research?* She felt guilty for snooping and convinced herself that Ian had really done nothing wrong. And besides, with the type of secret research going on in their lab, maybe all this was just precaution on Ian's part. He probably had a meeting that he couldn't tell Lauren about, just as she could not tell him why she was really going to Rome. *Hadn't he mentioned something about a password?* By the time she neared London, Lauren laughed at how ridiculous it was that she'd snooped on Ian's phone call and let her imagination run wild. After all, wasn't Lauren hiding the true nature of her work from Ian? Foulheart and Operation Clootie were probably just some code names dreamed up for yet another secret project in their lab.

✳   ✳   ✳

Lauren hopped out of the cab and quickly paid the driver. She turned, almost breathless, to look at the Roman Colosseum. It had a reddish orange hue in the setting sun, and appeared especially stunning against the clear blue sky. She only had a few hours off this afternoon and wanted to make the most of it, so she hurried inside. She also needed time to think about her secret meeting this morning with officials of other governments. They had expressed concerns over possible leaks of critical information about the new Ebola strain. Until more was known about this new strain and whether there was any effective anecdote, it would be disastrous if the news became public. The ensuing panic was potentially worse than the disease.

As Lauren toured the Colosseum, she referred often to her guide book about the rich history surrounding this place. She had been here before, but only in the summer when it was very hot and crowded. On this cold, October afternoon, she virtually had the place to herself. She walked high up in the Colosseum, paused, and peered down on the crumbling outlines of rows of seats and on the central arena. Her mind wandered, as she dreamed about the millennia gone by in this place.

"Lauren? Lauren, is that you?"

Lauren was startled and jumped. As she turned around, she gave a relieved laugh when she saw Mary York. "Why, Mary, what in the world are you doing here?"

"I'm here on a University tour of sites of ancient Roman history."

"Is your family with you?"

Unfortunately not. They're in school, so Dennis stayed with them. What are you doing in Rome?"

"I'm here for a conference on infectious diseases. I have to give … ."

"Mary, are you ready to leave?" said a voice behind them, interrupting Lauren. She turned and saw three people standing there.

"Oh yes," replied Mary. "Look, I've just bumped into an old friend. Let me introduce Dr. Lauren St. John. Lauren, this is Professor Anthony Miller from Harvard." Mary indicated a large, African-American man with short-cropped black hair.

"Pleased to meet you, professor," said Lauren.

"And you," the man replied.

"And this is Dr. Homer Blake from the Ashmolean Museum." Mary pointed to a short, mousy-looking man, with thick glasses and brown hair.

As they shook hands, Mary continued, "And you remember Owen McCrady, Bodley's Librarian."

Lauren turned to see a familiar large, red-faced gentleman with a snow-white beard and gray, Basset-hound eyes. "Of course I remember you, Dr. McCrady, and our charming conversation at Magdalen," said Lauren. "I must say I think you have the world's greatest job."

McCrady laughed jovially. "Thank you. I happen to agree with your assessment."

"Shall we be off?" Mary asked.

Professor Blake replied, "Yes, I'm afraid we're running behind schedule and the others are on their way back to the bus. Nice to meet you Dr. St. John."

"And you," Lauren replied.

Dr. Blake added, "Dr. St. John, we're having a cocktail fund raiser at the Ashmolean soon. Mary is one of our supporters. Do come along and join us for the evening."

"A splendid idea, Homer, " Mary said, smiling. "What a small world, Lauren. It's lovely to see you, as always."

"You too. Thanks again for dinner at Magdalen. We must get together more often." She gave her old friend a hug.

Lauren walked slowly toward the exit, then turned for one last look. The setting sun splashed the sky with pink and purple, while casting long shadows across the Colosseum.

16

"To Cade," said Eric, lifting his wineglass, after the waiter cleared their dinner plates.

"Here, here," echoed Philip lifting his glass and touching it to Cade's and Eric's.

"It's great of you guys to treat me on my birthday," said Cade. "Especially having steaks at Bone's!"

"What are friends for?" Philip retorted.

"There are none finer than the two of you." Cade had been feeling sorry for himself. His parents were on a trip to Bermuda and had not made it back in time for his early November birthday. He had not been thrilled at the prospect of spending his birthday alone and was glad when his friends called and invited him to dinner.

"Happy Birthday to you, Happy Birthday to you … ." Cade was surprised to hear singing behind him, and turned just in time to see the waiter bringing a cake with lit candles. Several others in the restaurant joined in, as did Philip and Eric, culminating in a round of applause at the end of the song.

"I can't believe you guys," Cade said in mock anger.

"Cut the cake, birthday boy," Philip chuckled.

Cade obliged as another waiter brought a bottle of champagne and three glasses. He handed the pieces of cake to his friends, but felt a lump in his throat. This was the first birthday he'd celebrated without Rachael since they had been married.

As if reading his mind, Philip asked, "Did you hear from Rachael and Sarah today?"

Cade nodded, taking a sip of champagne. "Yes, they called and woke me up this morning." After a scotch and water to start the evening, two bottles of wine, and now champagne, Cade was feeling sentimental, if not melancholy. He missed Sarah terribly and longed to see her. Although being away from Rachael and their arguing had been somewhat of a relief, he'd begun to miss her as well and to regret their less than cordial parting. He and Rachael hadn't really talked about when – or if – she and Sarah were coming back to Atlanta. Talking to them on the phone today had heightened his desire to see them. Cade wondered if he should go over to England, but the partnership vote was coming up soon, so he dared not go just now. He'd make it up to Rachael and Sarah later somehow.

"When do you plan to see them again?" Eric asked.

Cade, well under the influence of the alcohol by now, decided that it was time to confide in his two best friends. "Well guys, I guess I need to level with you." He paused, took a sip of champagne. "Rachael and I, well, we're sort of separated … I mean not just because she's in England."

Both Eric and Philip sat up straighter and eyed Cade, but said nothing. "Philip, I owe you an apology. That night in Highlands you were right about me and Rachael, and I guess you just hit too close to home."

"No apology necessary."

Cade continued, "I don't know what happened, really. Rachael and I seemed so perfect for each other. But, we've drifted apart, and, somewhere along the line we just seem to have lost the magic. We're almost like strangers now."

"Do you still love her?" Philip asked.

"I … I don't know. To be honest, when Rachael left for England, I was really hurt and down, but that didn't last. I got busy at work, and then, I sort of enjoyed my freedom. I miss them, especially Sarah, but, well, I don't know. I'm confused I guess."

"Have you told Rachael that?" Philip interjected.

"Not exactly. I just can't bring myself to. I … ." Cade felt a catch in his throat.

"How did you two fall in love in the first place?" Eric inquired. "I mean … I know you met in Oxford, but how did the relationship develop?"

"You'd never believe it if I told you." Cade was emboldened by the alcohol.

"Do tell us," Eric encouraged, pouring Cade more champagne.

"Well, you see … and you must first promise me you'll keep this a secret. Will you promise?"

"Of course," said Philip quickly, just as Eric raised his right hand as if being sworn in.

"What I'm about to tell you, well … no one knows except a few people. You see, I discovered some strange letters in Oxford, from two characters named Foulheart and Soulbane."

Eric and Philip gave him the most quizzical of expressions.

"Yeah, I know, it sounds crazy. I thought they were a joke. But, I'd just met Rachael, and she was intrigued by the letters. So, we took them to an old vicar in the Cotswolds named James Brooke. Well, to make a long story short, Brooke got excited and thought there might be something to the letters, too, because they referenced C. S. Lewis and Screwtape and Wormwood, and said something about some reports."

"Who are these characters you're talking about?" Eric asked.

"I must confess I thought the letters were a college prank. They were bizarre, but there was also something sinister about them."

"Oh, come on. You're pulling our legs," laughed Philip.

"I only wish I were," said Cade solemnly.

Philip and Eric stared at Cade with looks of disbelief. Cade wiped his forehead with his handkerchief. "Anyway, the letters contained some riddles, and we prayed, and suddenly strange coincidences happened. A friend out of the blue invited me to Malta, and I found a report from this character named Soulbane. But, even more astounding – and I know you won't believe me – in a cave there, I encountered a strange, chilling being who I think was a devil named Foulheart. You see, crazy as this sounds, I now believe these were two sinister characters who took over from Screwtape and Wormwood and prepared a report on the western world and the Church."

"Come on, come on," Eric said, with a look of incredulity. "This is wild talk. There's no such thing as devils. We all know that's just pure superstition."

Philip added, "It's getting late and we've also had a lot to drink. Be serious and quit joking."

"I wish it was a joke. No, Philip, I not only found a report in Malta, I later discovered another in Sewanee."

"I'm worried about you, man." Eric was staring at Cade. "All this talk about reports and devils. Why haven't you told us this before?"

"I guess I was too embarrassed."

"What did you do with these reports you say you found?" Philip inquired.

Cade looked intently at his friends. "Of course, I can't expect you to believe me. I know this sounds bizarre. I didn't really know what these reports were when I found them, so I typed them on my laptop and put them back so these characters, whoever they were, wouldn't know anyone had stumbled upon them. But they must have realised I'd seen them because this Foulheart fellow stole my computer and we had a chase all over Oxford one night. I'll never forget it as long as I live. It was on Guy Fawkes' night."

"Did you get the computer back?" Eric inquired.

"No, he got away with it. I thought I'd lost the reports for good. Then, a few days later, a friend returned the computer to me, with the reports still intact."

"Cade, that's incredible," said Philip. "Do you still have the reports?"

"Yes. I promised Reverend Brooke I'd publish them, but I got busy with law school and then work, and just sort of kept putting it off. Anyway, Rachael helped me with all this, and by the time I got the reports back, I was in love with her. We got married the next July, before I started law school at W & L that fall."

"Where are the reports now?" Eric emptied the bottle of champagne in their glasses.

"Oh, I've got a disk in a safe place. And, a backup disk is with a friend of mine in Oxford named Robert Thompson."

"Who is this Foulheart fellow?" Eric sipped his champagne.

"I have no idea. I never got a clear look at him. All I remember is this chilling laugh of his." Cade shuddered at the thought.

"What are you going to do with the reports?" Philip asked, as he motioned for the waiter to bring coffee.

"I'm not sure ... I feel guilty that I didn't follow up on my promise to publish them, and yet, in some ways, I'd just as soon forget about them and get on with my life."

"Can we see these reports sometime?" Eric inquired.

"Oh, sure, I guess so. I know I can trust the two of you to keep a secret."

"Is there anything we can do for you and Rachael?" asked Philip, returning to the initial topic of conversation.

Cade was beginning to get very tired. "I think I'd better go home now, it's getting late."

"I'll certainly keep you in my prayers. I'm worried about you." Philip's brow was furrowed. "I'm driving you home."

"That's not necessary," Cade said, his speech slurring.

"Don't argue. We'll get your car tomorrow."

As they stood, Eric said, "Let us know if we can do anything for you."

"Don't worry, I will. You're the two best friends I have. And, for now, please don't tell anyone about me and Rachael."

Both friends nodded solemnly in reply, as they walked out of the restaurant.

17

ZAC PICKERING walked out of the cocktail party onto the hotel balcony and surveyed Washington D.C. at night from the birds-eye view before him. The clear, moonless November sky was filled with stars. He took this view for granted, despite the awe-inspiring scene of the floodlit white stone monuments and buildings at night.

"Zac, can I speak to you a minute?" said a male voice, as someone tapped Zac's shoulder from behind.

Zac turned to see the large frame of his father-in-law, Senator Frank Rogers. Despite his age, and walking with a cane, Rogers was still an imposing figure. His piercing blue eyes seemed to telegraph his sharp intellect. "Sure, Senator. Mind if I freshen my drink first?"

"Not at all. In fact, I'll go with you."

The two men walked to the bar, had their glasses refilled, and returned to the balcony.

"Care for a cigar?" Rogers offered one when they reached the railing, away from the crowd.

"Thanks, but no. Florence has been nagging me to stop, and well … ."

"Say no more." The senator laughed. "My daughter has a lot of my wife in her."

Zac chuckled, wondering what the senator wanted to see him about.

"Beautiful view," remarked the senator. "That's something I've never gotten tired of, even after all these years in Congress." He lit a cigar and took a few puffs.

"It hardly seems possible you've been here this long," Zac said, just to keep the conversation rolling. Rogers was one of the most senior-ranking members in the U.S. Senate.

"You know, Zac, I rarely like to discuss business," he said, coughing slightly. "But, I'm nearing the end of my career, and, well … I want to be sure I have enough to have a nice retirement, if you know what I mean."

Zac knew precisely that the Senator was referring to Zac's special Swiss bank account.

"I … I understand. But, why are you … ."

Waving his arm in a sweeping motion as if he'd created the Washington skyline, the senator interrupted him, saying, "I've got a clean record with no hint of scandal, and I want to keep it that way. I've heard that … well, I'm not a man to mince words … I don't want this screwed up because you can't keep your pants zipped." He took another puff of the cigar, still staring off into space.

Zac felt his heart surge, and a current of fear shot through him. *How could he possibly know about Gail?* He tuned back in to what the senator was saying.

"Now, mind you, not that I've always been a saint myself, so I'm not here to preach. But, I'm giving you fair warning, if you're having an affair, it had better end now, and if you do anything – *anything* – to blow scandal my way, I'll have your nuts in a vise before you can even blink."

"I … how … but I'm not … ." Zac realized he was not helping himself with his stammering.

"Listen, Zac," said the senator, turning to face him directly, "I happen to like you and, well, Florence *is* my daughter, and I'd do anything for her. But my reputation is at stake, too, and you damn well better not screw it up. There's nothing more to be said. I'm not the one to cast the first stone, as they say. This is just a friendly little warning. The next time, I won't be so polite."

"I understand," Zac muttered. His heart sank. How could the senator know about his affair? Zac thought he'd been so careful, so discreet. He should have known not to underestimate one of the most powerful men in America.

"Now, let's go inside and enjoy the party." The senator put his arm around Zac's shoulder, like they were the oldest of friends.

When the two men came into the room, Florence waved at Zac and smiled. With her looks and aristocratic air, Florence stood out, even at a Washington cocktail party. She obviously enjoyed being married to a wealthy businessman, as well as being the daughter of a powerful senator. The Washington scene was just her cup of tea. Theirs was more a marriage of convenience now, or maybe really a symbiosis: she enjoyed his money and social status, and Zac profited by being married to the daughter of a senator. A perfect match, he smirked.

Gail, on the other hand, made Zac feel alive again for the first time in years. They had been so discreet. How in the world had the senator found out? As Zac stared at his wife with no real emotion, he wondered, would he ... could he ... give Gail up?

18

CADE YAWNED as he leaned on the exterior wall of The Tutwiler Hotel in Birmingham, Alabama and stretched his legs in preparation for an early morning run. He had arrived late the night before and faced a long day of depositions. It was foggy and chilly this early Wednesday morning. He'd only just recovered from his birthday dinner with Eric and Philip several days ago. Harry Martin had largely turned over Pickering Construction's case to Cade, which is what brought him to Birmingham. As he stretched, Cade recalled what Harry had said, "Cade, you're one of the most promising litigators I've seen, and your work has been superb. It's important now that you learn to take first chair on cases, which is what we'll expect you to do when you make partner. I have a lot of faith in you, so I'm going to let you take the lead in Pickering's case. I'll be available to consult with you, but I want to let you take the ball and run with it."

"Cade, is that you?" said a raspy, female voice, breaking Cade's reverie.

Cade turned around to see Sherry Talbot standing in the doorway of The Tutwiler. She was wearing yellow sweats, a long sleeve Hard Rock Cafe shirt, and her hair was tied in a ponytail. He could not have been more surprised than if Elvis were standing there.

"Oh, hi Sherry. What in the world are you doing here?"

"My company is having a sales meeting here."

"Are you getting ready to exercise?"

"Actually, I was about to take off on a run. How about you?"

"The same. Want to run together?" Cade felt a surge of excitement at the thought, and held his breath momentarily for Sherry's reply.

"I'd love to, if you promise to take it easy on me," Sherry replied, breaking into a broad smile. Her ponytail shook as she moved her head.

"Great, let's go," said Cade.

The two jogged slowly through the still quiet streets of downtown. The city was blanketed in a light fog, which gave off a diffused, pink glow from the sunrise.

"How far were you planning to go?" asked Cade.

"Oh, I thought about five miles."

"Perfect," said Cade, who was beginning to breathe harder. In Rachael's absence he had spent more time exercising, and he was in much better shape now that he'd been during his run in Mobile.

The fog began lifting as they ran up a steep hill on Twentieth Street. When they reached the top of the hill, Cade could see the statue of Vulcan staring down at him from atop Red Mountain.

The pace suited Cade just fine, and he had a nice chat with Sherry. Cade told her a little about the case he was working on, and he learned more about Sherry's pharmaceutical sales job. She was easy to talk to, and she seemed very attentive. He found he was quite enjoying this early morning run.

The run became much easier on their way back down the hill. As they neared the hotel, they passed a beautiful Norman-style brown stone church on the corner called the Cathedral Church of the Advent, where a statue of Christ stood in a niche in the wall with outstretched arms. Cade glanced away quickly.

"Well, Cade, that was great. Thanks for letting me tag along," said Sherry, when they stopped at the hotel. She continued to walk in circles, her hands on her hips.

"My pleasure." He was bent over and grimacing, as he fought to catch his breath. Sherry was in better shape than Cade anticipated.

As they walked toward the hotel lobby, Cade wondered how long she would be in town, and if he might see her again. He was hesitant to say anything, when as if reading his mind, she said, "How long are you here for?"

"Just until tomorrow, unfortunately. I have depositions today and tomorrow morning, and then I head back to Atlanta. How about you?"

"We're here for most of the week."

As they got on the elevator, Cade found himself saying, "I guess they have you tied up tonight, with meetings and all ... ."

"Actually, no. We have evenings free."

"Would you ... I mean ... if you don't have plans ... ."

"If you're asking if I'd like to have dinner, I'd love to. I don't really care to go out with the others, if you know what I mean, and it's no fun just getting room service."

"Good. I tell you what, I'll meet you in the lobby at eight, and we can go somewhere, if that sounds okay."

"Sure, I'll see you then," she said as she stepped off the elevator.

* * *

Cade paced in the lobby of The Tutwiler, glancing at his watch. It was ten minutes after eight, and Sherry wasn't there. Had she forgotten, or changed her mind? Should he call her room?

"Hi. Sorry I'm late."

Cade turned, and at first was baffled by the stranger looking at him. Then, he recognized Sherry, who had been transformed since their morning run. Her auburn hair, curled like small rolls of serpentine, cascaded to her shoulders. She was wearing a short, low-cut, black dress that appeared to have been painted on her. Cade couldn't help but notice her shapely, muscular legs and arms, and her smooth, olive skin.

"Oh, hi," said Cade, when he remembered to stop staring and start speaking. "No problem. My car's out front."

"Where are we going to dinner?"

"A place called Highlands Bar and Grill. It's a restaurant I try to get to when I'm in Birmingham."

* * *

"My meal was fabulous," Sherry said, sipping her Chardonnay after dinner.

"I'm glad you liked it." At that comment, he winced to himself. Under the table, he fingered his wedding ring, as he remembered that the last time he'd been here, it was with Rachael. Cade picked up his wineglass and took a large sip. He glanced around the restaurant, filled with people at the dozen or so white-clothed tables. The golden painted walls and dim lighting gave the room a warm ambience.

The waiter approached. "Would you care for dessert?"

"Sherry?"

"Oh, why not. After all, we did have a long run this morning. How about if we split something?"

"Splendid idea," said Cade, who turned to the waiter. "Just bring us your favorite dessert. Oh, and two glasses of port."

"Right you are, sir," the waiter replied and left.

* * *

When they arrived at the hotel, Sherry gave Cade her warmest smile. "Thanks for a wonderful evening."

"My pleasure," Cade replied, and he meant it. "Are you up for another run in the morning?"

"Oh Cade, I'd love to, but we have an early breakfast meeting. I'm sorry."

"That's fine, I understand." Cade nevertheless felt keen disappointment.

Just before the elevator doors closed, three ladies entered. Two were carrying large bags. One tall, regal looking woman was wearing a mink stole and held a small Pomeranian with orange and white fur. Except for the change in color, it was difficult to tell where the coat ended and the dog began.

"Now Winston, you behave yourself," the woman said to the

dog, who licked her hand. Another woman pushed the button for the top floor. The three ladies did not seem to have even noticed Cade and Sherry, there being no disruption in their conversation. Cade found himself pressed against Sherry and felt a surge of excitement run through him. It was an almost overpowering sensation, which he had not felt in several years. He felt the urge to put his arm around her, but resisted.

"Thanks again. I had a great time," said Sherry as she got off the elevator on her floor. She waved to Cade and tilted her head in a coy manner. "See you in Atlanta."

Cade caught himself staring at her, and quickly gave a wave before the doors closed. He continued up in the elevator, oblivious to the gossip of the three women.

19

L AUREN PULLED the car over when she saw Rachael standing in front of her mother's house. The sight of Rachael renewed a sense of envy and insecurity in Lauren. Yesterday evening at the Ashmolean Museum party, Owen McCrady had invited Rachael and Lauren to take a tour of the Bodleian this Friday morning. When they accepted, Lauren offered to drive them, and in addition, she had agreed to go with Rachael to visit some friends of the Brysons who lived in Iffley Village. But later in the evening, Ian and Rachael seemed to be getting on a bit too well for Lauren's liking. Now, she regretted getting into all this.

Rachael opened the passenger door and bent over, "Are you sure you have time to go with me?"

"Absolutely. I needed a day off work anyway. I'm excited about seeing the Bodleian, and your friends sound very nice." Lauren forced a smile.

Rachael sat in the car and turned to Lauren. "I know you'll enjoy meeting the Thompsons. It's such a dreadfully cold, dreary day, and I really appreciate you driving me there."

"You're very welcome. I'm sure it will be a treat for me too."

After they arrived in Oxford and parked, they walked into the stone courtyard of the old Bodleian, surrounded on all sides by the golden-stoned library buildings, with the bronze statue of William Herbert, Third Earl of Pembroke staring at them. They hastened through the front entrance and inquired at the desk for Dr. McCrady.

Shortly thereafter, Bodley's Librarian himself appeared. He was accompanied by the Harvard professor Lauren had met in Rome.

"So good to see you both," he said as he extended his hand to greet them. "This is Professor Anthony Miller of Harvard, who is here this term."

Miller smiled. "I hope you don't mind if I tag along with you on your tour?"

"Not at all. It's our pleasure," Lauren replied.

Gesturing to the three to follow him, McCrady said, "Let's start here at the Divinity Schools."

For the next couple of hours, McCrady took Miller, Lauren and Rachael on an extensive tour of the library, beginning with two fifteenth-century rooms: the Divinity School, with its elaborate stone fan-vaulted ceiling, and Duke Humfrey's Library, with its beautiful and ornate hand-painted ceiling. During the tour, he showed them some of the ancient, chained books and other rare manuscripts; and even took them through the underground tunnel under Broad Street, connecting the old library with a newer addition.

Lauren was utterly charmed by this gentile, intelligent, widely-read man. He conversed with her and Rachael about many different topics, and he was well versed enough in medicine and history to carry his own with both women. In addition, he inquired at length about Lauren's and Rachael's families, hobbies, and tastes in food, books, and clothes. Lauren began to understand how he had become the librarian of one of the most important libraries in the world. She thought McCrady was one of the most interesting people she'd ever met.

Just before they finished seeing the library, Miller begged off to finish some research. As the others concluded their tour in the main quadrangle of the old library, Rachael said, "Dr. McCrady, we'd love to take you to lunch to thank you for this wonderful tour."

"Ladies, there is nothing I'd like better, but I'm afraid pressing library business prevents me from accepting your kind invitation."

Lauren added, "I learned so much I never knew. Thanks for your kindness, and I hope we can repay you someday."

McCrady smiled. "Don't mention it. Truly, it was my pleasure. Rachael, I'd be delighted to meet Sarah sometime, and if your husband comes over, please bring him along as well."

"You're much too kind," Rachael replied.

"I should be off," he added quickly. "All the best to you both."

As McCrady disappeared into the library, Rachael turned to Lauren. "At least let me buy you lunch for driving today and agreeing to take me to see the Thompsons."

Lauren, although still somewhat upset at Rachael and Ian's lengthy conversation last evening, was mollified by the delightful morning tour. "That would be lovely. How about if we go across the street to The King's Arms?"

"Splendid idea," said Rachael, as they walked toward the exit. As they entered Catte Street, she added, "Don't you think Dr. McCrady is one of the most captivating people you've ever met?"

Lauren nodded. "Absolutely."

*   *   *

Over lunch, Rachael said, "Tell me about Ian."

Lauren's blood pressure shot up at this remark, but she took a deep breath and replied, "We work in the same lab, although we're on different projects."

"Is that how you met?"

"Yes, I was walking down the hall one day, and I saw this man – tall, dark, and handsome, just like a film star ... ." She laughed. "Anyway, he's about my age and not like anyone I've ever met. He's engaging and interesting and mysterious and ... ."

"*I know,*" interjected Rachael. "I can see why you're in love with him. He had me enchanted yesterday evening. I think I told him my life's story, and I hardly let him get a word in."

Lauren glanced down and said simply, "Thanks. He is quite special."

She felt another surge of jealousy as her thoughts returned to last evening. They had travelled together, since Rachael's mother's car was in the repair shop. Ian had come to the event as well, and he had been quite charming. *Too charming.* Later in the evening, Lauren had been in a long conversation with Mary and Homer Blake, the Director of the Ashmolean. She had looked over to see Rachael and Ian, alone in a corner, talking and laughing. Watching Ian pour on the charm to someone as striking as Rachael soon had Lauren's insecurity running riot. It had ruined the evening for her, and she barely spoke to Rachael on the way home. It was only because the two of them had already accepted McCrady's invitation to visit the library and she had also promised Rachael to take her to Iffley later in the afternoon that she was with her today.

After lunch, they returned to Lauren's car. "Tell me about your friends," Lauren asked as they drove over Magdalen Bridge, wishing to talk about something other than Ian.

"Well, let's see. Robert Thompson is probably in his eighties now. He was a porter at Magdalen when I first met him. He and Cade were friends. Robert's wife is Rose, and she's a dear. They have one son who still lives at home, named Clive. He's probably close to forty, and has Down's Syndrome.

As the car neared St. Mary's Church in Iffley, Rachael directed Lauren to the street they wanted. "There's the house … the one with the red door." Lauren parked the car, and they went to the door and knocked.

"Rachael, my dear, so lovely to see you again," said the elderly woman, plump and gray-haired, who opened the door. "Do come in. Such a dreary afternoon!"

Rachael stepped in and hugged the woman. "Rose, this is my friend, Lauren St. John. Lauren, this is Rose Thompson."

"Lovely to meet you," Rose said, smiling at Lauren. "The tea is ready, and Robert is dying to see you." She led them into the living room. The earth-tone colors of the furniture and numerous family photos, coupled with the glowing fire, made the room warm and inviting.

"Didn't you bring Sarah?" asked Rose. When Rachael shook her head, Rose added, "I hope you at least brought some pictures. You bring her next time."

Just as she spoke, a large man, with thick glasses and wispy gray hair, walked into the living room. He was slightly stooped, but said in a strong voice, "My dearest Rachael, let me look at you."

"Hello, Robert. You look well. This is my friend, Lauren St. John."

"Welcome to our home," he said, extending his hand to Lauren before putting a bear hug on Rachael. Lauren looked closely at Mr. Thompson. He seemed vaguely familiar, and she assumed she'd seen him around Oxford.

"Now, Robert, let these ladies sit and have some tea," said Rose.

"Yes, dear," he said, winking at his two guests.

Everyone sat as Rose poured tea and offered cucumber sandwiches, followed by shortbread. Lauren looked about the room, as Rachael and the Thompsons caught up with each other. Framed photographs were everywhere, and one that attracted her attention showed Rachael, radiant in a wedding dress, standing between Rose and Robert. A handsome, tall, blonde-haired man stood next to Rose, and Lauren surmised him to be Cade.

"Now, tell us all about Cade," said Robert. "He's naughty for not coming to England with you."

Rachael shifted in her chair. "Yes, well, he's working very hard these days. He's …" but Rachael stopped.

Lauren glanced at Rachael whose gaze appeared to be on the same wedding photo and realized Rachael was crying.

"Oh dear, oh dear, are you all right?" said Rose, a look of worry on her face.

"Yes … well, no." Rachael dabbed her eyes with a handkerchief. "I can't pretend to the two of you … things aren't going well for me and Cade. That's why I've been so long in coming to see you… ."

Her voice trailed off.

"Dear Rachael, we're so sorry." Rose had a pained expression on her face.

"Somehow it's just not the same between us. I don't really know what happened. Cade was so loving and wonderful for the first couple of years of marriage, and then … he just became more and more involved with his work."

Robert looked at Rachael. "And why did you come to England?"

Rachael appeared taken aback by that comment. "I … I just thought that Cade and I needed some space. And … ."

"So you came home to mother?" Robert shook his head in a disapproving manner.

"Robert! How dare you!" Rose gave him a stern look.

Rachael held a hand up to Rose. "No … Robert's right. In fact, I've been doing a lot of thinking lately. I kept blaming Cade and his work but, after being away from him, I can see now how I smothered him. You see, my Dad left Mum and me when I was about ten, and I've never really got over it. I called Cade all the time at work, to ask when he would be home. When he got home, often late, I'd interrogate him about where he'd been. I guess I had a deep insecurity I'd never even admitted to myself. Funny thing is, it was Sarah the other day who pointed it out. She made a comment about why wasn't I calling Dad all the time now like I used to. Her comment hit me like a ton of bricks. I *was* always calling Cade. No wonder it drove him away."

Lauren, stunned and embarrassed by Rachael's honesty, stood quickly. "Do you mind if I use the phone? I've got to check in with my lab."

Rose nodded. "Let me show you where it is." She led Lauren into the kitchen and returned to the living room. Lauren called her lab and found reasons to talk to several different people, which took her almost half-an-hour. By the time she returned to the living room, Rachael and the Thompsons were laughing, and Rachael was showing them pictures of Sarah.

"You really must bring her to see us," said Rose.

"Of course I will," Rachael replied. Nodding toward Lauren, she continued, "We'd best be off now. Lauren was kind enough to bring me, since Mum's car is at the garage."

Rose stood. "Lauren, please come back anytime. You're always welcome."

"Thanks very much," Lauren replied. "Please tell Clive hello. I do hope to meet him next time."

As they came to the front door, Robert kissed Rachael on the cheek. "Don't you worry dear. Things will work out for the best. We'll pray for you. God's watching out for you."

Rachael smiled. "I know He is. Thanks for everything. I'm dying for Sarah to meet you. I'm sorry I haven't come sooner." She gave him a hug.

"We love you very much, Rachael," said Rose. "You come anytime."

*   *   *

Lauren glanced over at Rachael as they drove toward the Cotswolds. Rachael was uncharacteristically quiet. Lauren decided not to ask any questions. One thing she was sure of, however, was that God, if he even existed, certainly did not care.

Lauren heard sniffles. "Rachael, are you all right?"

Rachael's response was to shake her head and begin to cry harder.

Lauren looked straight ahead, her thumbs tapping on the steering wheel. Until this afternoon, she had grown more and more envious of Rachael, who seemed to be on top of the world. She was taken aback by Rachael's candid revelation to the Thompsons.

"I'm sorry," said Rachael softly.

"We're almost at my house. Would you like to come in before you go home?"

"I ... I don't mean to burden you with my problems."

"Not at all." Lauren parked in front of her cottage.

"Thanks, Lauren," replied Rachael. She stopped crying, and a hint of a smile crossed her face.

"Please make yourself at home." Lauren pointed toward a burgundy upholstered chair as she continued toward the kitchen. "I'll be back in a jiffy." She was thankful the cottage was tidy.

She put water in the kettle, started the gas stove and turned up the heat in the chilly cottage. A few minutes later, she handed a mug of hot tea to Rachael and sat on the sofa across from her. Lauren sipped her tea and said, "I don't know you all that well, so forgive me if I'm intruding. But, if there's anything I can do to help … ."

Rachael stood and turned to look out the window. It was dark outside and a gentle rain was falling. "I'm so confused, Lauren. I thought coming here to visit Mum was the best thing to do. My relationship with Cade just hasn't seemed right lately, and I thought maybe some time apart would help. It was actually very selfish of me, and what Robert said today was painful, but pretty accurate. I guess I did 'run home to mother'. Oh, Lauren, I just don't know what to do. I haven't had anyone to talk to here, except for my mother, and it's hard for her to be objective."

"Tell me about Cade."

Rachael turned and looked at her. "We met in Oxford over ten years ago now. We were both students. He's American, fair haired and blue eyed, really good-looking. He was not only bright, but such a gentleman. I'd never met anyone quite like him. He had so much Southern charm, as they say in the States."

"Was it love at first sight?"

"Hardly," chuckled Rachael. "We didn't get along too well at first, but we worked on a project together and ended up falling in love. We got married at Merton Chapel on a gorgeous July afternoon."

"What sort of lawyer is he? I don't think you call them barristers and solicitors do you?"

"You're right. You would call him a barrister here. He's a trial lawyer and works for a posh Atlanta firm."

"Is he coming over here to see you and Sarah?"

"I … I … ."

"I didn't mean to pry," interjected Lauren quickly, seeing she had obviously touched a sore spot.

"No, it's just that Cade seems to be married to his work."

Lauren sat forward, holding her mug in both hands. "I'm truly sorry, Rachael. I had no idea you were unhappy." Lauren's prior feelings of envy for Rachael had vanished. She added, "Do you still love him?"

"Oh yes, very much. It's just that I don't think he loves me any longer." Rachael started to cry again. She sat in the chair and gave an audible sigh. "I don't have my life all together like you do, Lauren."

If you only knew. To hide her discomfort, Lauren got up and poured more tea for both of them.

Rachael went on, "I'm so confused. I don't know what to do. I've thought of Cade every single day and miss him so much. I don't know what I would do without him." Rachael paced in front of the window. "I don't know what I expected. I guess I thought Cade would dash over here after us, but we've been here two months now, and he still seems caught up in his work. It hurts so much to know he must not really miss us. And poor Sarah, she misses her daddy terribly."

Rachael became silent. Lauren didn't know what to say. Finally, instead of addressing Rachael's problem, she said, "You know Rachael, life is awfully complicated sometimes. Here I was thinking you were so lucky, and yet, you've been struggling. I can only tell you that I'm not nearly as ' together' as you think I am."

At that comment, Rachael stopped pacing and stared at her quizzically. "What do you mean?"

"I never talk about this, but I was once a doctor. I always thought I would be a musician. But after my father fell ill and died, when I was about thirteen, I decided I wanted to be a doctor. I worked hard through school and was single-minded, almost obsessed. I never allowed anyone to get close to me, because I was so focused on my career. One night, just as I was close to finishing my residency, a mother brought a sick girl to the emergency department. It had already been a long day, and I was exhausted. The girl had a mild fever and a few other symptoms like sore throat and headache. I was tired and in a hurry to leave the hospital. I reckoned it was just an upper respiratory infection. I sent them away with a prescription and forgot about it.

Lauren paused and Rachael smiled sympathetically, but said nothing.

Lauren continued, "The next day, as I was making my rounds, I noticed a commotion in A & E and saw the same mother there. She was crying. I went over to see why she was back. The girl was in distress – non-responsive, with an extremely high fever and low blood pressure. A senior doctor thought that the girl might have meningitis. As I was standing there, she just stopped breathing. I panicked. We tried to resuscitate her but it was no good. For the first time in a long time, I found myself praying. But it was all to no avail."

At this point, Lauren choked up and dabbed her eyes with her sleeve. "The little girl died ... and ... and ... we couldn't revive her." Now it was Lauren who couldn't talk.

"Oh, Lauren, I'm so very sorry."

After a few moments, Lauren continued, "There was an inquiry, and I had to go through quite an ordeal answering questions about my initial faulty diagnosis. In the end, they decided to slap me on the wrist because the initial presentation of symptoms wasn't clear-cut. I will never forget having to tell that mother about her daughter. *Ever*. It was the worst day of my life. After that, my heart wasn't in practising medicine any more. I went into a deep depression and, after some therapy, decided to leave medicine, even though my superiors tried to talk me out of it. I didn't know what I was going to do. That's when one of my medical professors called about studying infectious diseases. It was really a perfect fit for me, because after the little girl's death, I dedicated myself to my research. In a way, I became a workaholic as a means of penance, I think." Lauren wondered if she should tell Rachael what she really did, but decided against it.

"So," Rachael said after several minutes, "I guess there's a lot more to our lives than appears on the surface."

Lauren nodded her agreement. "Yes, I reckon all of us work hard at creating illusions to mask who we really are. Rachael, I'm afraid I haven't been much help to you."

"Oh, but you have. You listened. And, between you and Robert today, I've seen my situation in a totally different light. I should never have left Cade. I'm going to call him and see if there's any hope."

"What can I do for you?" Lauren asked.

"Just say a prayer for us."

"You know, Rachael, I don't think I've said any type of prayer since that dreadful day with the little girl. I guess her death convinced me God either isn't there or doesn't care. Either way, it's all the same."

"I understand," said Rachael with a compassionate smile. "I'll pray for both of us." Rachael glanced at her watch. "It's quite late. Mum and Sarah will be wondering where I am. Can I use your phone?"

After Rachael made the call, she picked up her coat. "Lauren, thanks for everything today."

"Don't mention it. Thanks for listening to me, too. I hadn't realized how much I needed to talk to someone about all that. It's so painful that I've buried it deep inside me."

Rachael paused at the front door. "You can talk to me anytime. I really appreciate your friendship."

The two women hugged, and Rachael left to walk to her mother's house.

After she closed the front door, Lauren went to her bedroom, lay on her bed, and cried uncontrollably. It had been a long time since she had let her wound come to the surface, and tonight she made no attempt to force it back down.

20

IT WAS MID-NOVEMBER, and a thunderstorm raged outside Zac's office. He sipped black coffee as he reviewed an early morning fax from Cade Bryson reporting on developments in the Atlanta lawsuit.

"Here's your mail." Zac looked up to see Marge Vaughn standing next to his desk, holding out several letters.

After Marge left, Zac's attention went to an unopened express mail package marked "Personal and Confidential." He tore open the envelope, dumped its contents on his desk, and involuntarily gasped, "Oh hell!" He pulled a handkerchief from his pocket, wiped the sweat on his forehead, and took a deep breath – staring at the photographs spread on his desk, incredulous at what lay before him. He grabbed a half-smoked cigar that had gone out and re-lit it with shaking hands. He read and re-read the note, trying to comprehend its meaning, but he was having difficulty concentrating.

His thoughts were interrupted by the buzzing of the intercom, and his secretary announcing, "Mr. Pickering, your wife is holding."

Zac felt a sharp pang of … of what? Conscience? Guilt? Worry? He forced himself to smile, however, and took on the personae of a wealthy, prominent businessman. After all, he *was* the president of Pickering Contractors, one of the largest construction companies in D.C., a prominent civic leader, friend of senators … .

"Hi, Doll, what's cooking?" he said, exhaling a huge cloud of smoke.

While they talked, Zac flipped through the photographs like they were a stack of cards. *Who sent these? How did they get them? What am I going to do now? Does Florence know about this?* If so, she didn't mention it on the phone. Instead, all she talked to Zac about was the garden tour she was going on this weekend.

When he hung up from his wife's call, Zac stuffed the pictures and note into the packet and locked them in his private cabinet behind his desk.

＊　　＊　　＊

"Hello," said Zac in a bored voice as he answered the phone. It was on a Saturday afternoon, and he'd just returned home from the golf course. He was sitting in an easy chair in his den, sipping Scotch and water. Florence was in Virginia on her garden tour. It was a perfect fall afternoon in Georgetown, and he absent-mindedly stared out the window at the water fountain in his back courtyard.

"Pickering?" said the voice.

"You got him."

"This is your favorite little Caribbean photographer."

Zac immediately recalled the packet he'd received. He stood, spilling his drink all over himself. "Who the hell are you? What do you want?"

"Nothing that a little blackmail won't solve," said the man, followed by a smug sounding laugh. "Did you read my note?"

"I ... I'll find out who you are and, ..."

"Listen!" exclaimed the stranger, in a sudden, harsh tone, "Don't waste my time with idle threats. If I send these pictures to the senator and the papers, you're finished."

"How ... how do you know about the senator?" Zac asked, more from surprise than actually expecting an answer.

"Well, what's your answer? I don't have all day."

"Actually, I ... I have a plan." Zac tried to sound confident. "I just need a little more time. I ... ."

"You're just about out of time. Here's the deal. You have until January first to get what I want. If you fail, this is one new year you'll be sorry to see."

"Okay, I understand." The line went dead. He immediately hit *69 to find out where the call had come from. When he dialed the number given, the phone was answered. The same voice said, in a tone of rage, "What the hell do you think you're doing? Don't screw with me or you're a dead man." And the connection went dead.

Zac's hands were shaking as he put the phone back on the receiver. He hurried over to his liquor cabinet and poured a straight Scotch, downing it in one swig.

* * *

It was the Tuesday before Thanksgiving, and Cade was trying hard to get several projects done so he could join his parents and sister in Charleston for a reunion with his mother's family. He had told his parents that Rachael had to go back to England to work on her doctorate. They had appeared sceptical and asked lots of questions, but seemed to accept his story. But his sister, Elizabeth, had guessed what was really happening, and laid into Cade for his workaholic ways and his blindness in letting Rachael go. For these reasons, Cade was reluctant to go to Charleston for the holiday, but his mother had given him an ultimatum, since her family had not had a reunion in many years.

Sitting in his office, Cade looked up from the deposition he was reading to see his secretary standing halfway in his doorway.

"There's a Mr. Pickering in the lobby to see you. Would you like me to go get him?"

"No, I'll go see him." Cade wondered why Zac was here, since they had no appointment. The clock sitting on his bookshelves showed eleven thirty.

"Hi, Cade," said Zac, who was standing in the lobby, looking out the window at the Atlanta skyline. It was a sunny day, with only a few white clouds in the sky.

"Hello, Zac. What brings you here?"

"Sorry I didn't call. I was in town and had some free time. Thought I'd stop by and see if I could take you to lunch. I'd like to talk to you about our lawsuit."

"Uh ... well ... ."

"I understand if you're too busy," Zac added quickly.

"Oh, no," lied Cade. Although he was very busy, he couldn't bring himself to say that to his new client. "I'd love to go to lunch. Let me get my jacket."

Cade noticed a young man standing behind Zac. He appeared to be in his early twenties and was dressed in khaki slacks and a green and blue striped shirt.

"Cade, this is Ken Bowman. He's one of our computer geeks," said Zac, playfully hitting the boy on the shoulder.

"Nice to meet you, Mr. Bryson." The young man extended his hand to Cade.

"Cade, I hate to impose," said Zac. "We have a meeting this afternoon, and Ken here needs to do some work preparing for our meeting. Could he use your office while we're at lunch?"

"Sure, no problem. Ken, come with me. Zac, I'll meet you back here in a couple of minutes."

*   *   *

As Cade rode the elevator up to his office after lunch, he swore silently. *This was par for the course. A very busy day, and that's the day an important new client shows up unexpectedly for lunch.* And to top it off, Zac hadn't even talked about business or their lawsuit, so Cade couldn't bill the time. Instead, Zac spent most of the time asking him about Oxford, and getting recommendations on restaurants in Atlanta. He'd asked Cade all about where he lived and about his family. Cade found his patience evaporating, as Zac appeared in no hurry to finish lunch.

He exited the elevator and strode quickly to his office, frustrated over the almost two-and-a-half hour lunch with Zac. When he arrived at his office, Bowman wasn't there.

"Say, Susan, what happened to the guy who was using my office?"

"I don't know. After you left for lunch, I heard him make a few phone calls. When I got back from lunch, he was gone."

"Okay." He sat down at his desk and checked his computer to see he had twelve new emails. He became even more agitated when he spied two new faxes also waiting for him, as well as his voicemail message light blinking. *The wonders of modern technology.*

21

"DR. LAUREN, you're so nice to take me here." Sarah smiled at Lauren.

"I thought you might like Alice's Shop. Lewis Carroll, who wrote Alice in Wonderland, was a fellow at Christ Church, just across the street from this shop." Lauren had volunteered to take care of Sarah for the weekend, so Rachael and her mother could go and visit Bridgett's elderly sister, Charlotte, in Bath. It was a cold, overcast, dreary afternoon, common for December. A sea of people scurried along the Oxford sidewalks doing their shopping. It was especially crowded this Friday afternoon with Christmas only a couple of weeks away.

"Where did your friend go?" Sarah asked, as she meandered around the shop, stopping to look at this and that.

"Ian went to get us a special treat. He'll be back in a minute."

"What's a dreamboat?"

Puzzled, Lauren replied, "That's a strange question. Why do you ask?"

"Oh, I heard Mommy say that Ian is a dreamboat, that's all."

"That just means he's handsome," replied Lauren, who was rather unnerved by this.

"Dr. Lauren, look at this tea set. And there's the Madhatter!" exclaimed Sarah. She seemed to bounce from item to item like a pinball.

"Would you like this Sarah?" Lauren pointed toward the Alice in Wonderland tea set.

"Oh, yes please. Oh *please*." Sarah looked up at Lauren with an expression that would melt any glacier, not that Lauren needed any prodding.

"All right, but only on one condition." Lauren put on a serious look.

"What?"

"That you invite me to the first tea party."

"Sure I will!" Sarah was now jumping up and down.

Just as they stepped on the sidewalk with their new purchase, Lauren spied Ian striding up with something in his hands.

"For you, my princess." Ian bowed to Sarah and handed her a piece of fudge. Sarah's face glowed, and she bit into it immediately.

"And for you, m'lady." Ian bowed to Lauren, likewise handing her one. Lauren smiled warmly.

"What would you like to do now, Sarah?" Lauren asked, as they stood outside the shop. She almost had to shout to be heard over the traffic.

The little girl scrunched up her face as if in deep thought. "Oh, I don't know … . Wait. I know, I know. Dr. Lauren, will you take me to see Daddy's college?"

"Haven't you been there before?"

"No, I keep asking Mommy, and she always says that someday she will. Please show it to me."

"Do you know the name of his college, Sarah?" Lauren asked, just to see how much Sarah knew.

"Oh, yes. It's called Magdalen, and Daddy says they have deer and a big tower."

"Right you are. Okay, let's go."

The three of them cut across St. Aldate's Street in front of Christ Church and walked up to High Street, eating their treats. The Carfax at the intersection of St. Aldate's, Queen, High and Cornmarket Streets was so jammed with people that everyone was virtually at a standstill. Ian picked Sarah up and put her on his shoulders.

"Wow. I'm the tallest person on the whole street," Sarah squealed, with obvious delight.

Ian put her down as they neared the entrance to Magdalen. They proceeded through the open doorway and into the first quad. The Magdalen clock tolled the quarter hour, and Sarah looked up at the tower. "That must be the biggest tower in the whole world. What do the bells ring for?"

"They ring every fifteen minutes to tell you what time it is," Lauren answered.

"I don't see any deer," added Sarah, looking confused.

Ian laughed. "Magdalen is a big college, Sarah, and there are lots of places you can't see from here. The deer are in the park at the back. Want to go see them?"

"Sure." She ran in the direction Ian pointed.

Lauren and Ian walked behind Sarah, who didn't stop running until she reached the deer park. Soon, all three stood by the fence watching the deer grazing silently, oblivious to their new audience. Lauren took in the peaceful setting, enjoying the contrast of this quiet park to the noisy city just outside the college walls.

"Can we go and pet the deer?" Sarah inquired.

"I'm afraid not," Lauren answered.

"What else is there to see?" Before anyone could say anything, Sarah skipped down the path toward Addison's Walk, her hair bouncing with each skip.

Lauren shrugged at Ian, and the two adults followed the girl once again. The three of them went past New Buildings and through the large, iron gates leading to Addison's Walk.

After they made the entire circuit around the meadow, Sarah yawned. "I'm tired. Can we please sit down?"

"Of course we can." Lauren smiled at the little girl. "Let's go back into the college, and we'll find a place to sit." They walked into the college and through a passageway into the Cloisters.

"Look!" Sarah was pointing. "You can see the tower from here."

Lauren stopped to see that Magdalen Tower was framed through one of the arched stone openings in Cloisters. They continued walking through the Cloister's passageway, when Sarah asked, "What's that sound?"

"That must be the boys' choir singing Evensong," Lauren replied.

"Where are they?"

"In the chapel just over there." Lauren pointed to the entrance to the chapel under the high, stone archway.

"Can we go and see?" Sarah looked up at Lauren with a pleading expression.

"Well, I don't …" started Lauren.

"Please, pretty please." Sarah tugged at her sleeve.

"All right, but you must be very quiet." Lauren put a finger to her mouth for emphasis. She recognized the music as Rutter's lovely hymn, *What Sweeter Music*, and she had an overwhelming urge to go in and listen. "Come on Ian, let's go in."

"You two go on." Ian stopped at the entrance to the Chapel. "I need to get back to the lab to finish some work."

"Surely not this late in the afternoon?" Lauren felt a strain in her voice.

"Yes, I'm afraid so," Ian replied, with an insistent tone. "You and Sarah run along. I'll catch up with you later."

"Are we doing anything tonight?" Lauren realized that she had assumed they were, even though she and Ian hadn't discussed plans for the weekend.

"I can't tonight, Lauren. I have to meet some friends later."

"Dr. Lauren, come on." Sarah grabbed Lauren's hand and pulled several times.

Lauren began to walk with Sarah into the antechapel and stopped to look at Ian. He smiled faintly, shrugged his shoulders, and walked away. She felt a jolt of rejection in her stomach.

Lauren and Sarah went through the antechapel and eased silently into the chapel itself. Several people were scattered around on the tiered rows of dark wooden seats, and the choir was seated on the right-hand side near the front, dressed in bright red robes. The lights in the small, cylindrical glass lamps in the pews appeared almost like candles. She motioned to Sarah to go into the first opening on the left, just as the choir finished singing the Rutter hymn.

A priest in a black cassock and white surplice with a black tippet stood and read from a prayer book. It had been a long time since Lauren had attended an Evensong service, or any other service for that matter, except for an occasional wedding or funeral. *At least the music is lovely, even if it is accompanied by meaningless rituals.* She stared at the candles on the altar, and at the painting of Christ holding a cross on his shoulder. She had believed, once, but not since that night when He abandoned her. Her mind leapt to Ian's sudden departure, which puzzled and worried her. He was such a mysterious person, despite his great charm.

Sarah placed her hand in Lauren's and smiled, her childlike innocence radiating all that is right with the world. Lauren closed her eyes as the choir sang another hymn that she recognized, Sir Benjamin Britten's *A Hymn to the Virgin*. The melody stirred emotions in her she had not felt in a long time and transported her to days gone by, when a teenage Lauren sang in her church choir. At that time, Lauren dreamed of being a professional musician. Music was her true love and passion, not medicine. As the hymn filled the chapel, for the first time in ages a sense of peace enveloped her.

At the end of the service, Sarah and Lauren quietly departed. When they reached the Magdalen front quad, Sarah smiled. "Thanks, Dr. Lauren. I like being in God's house."

Lauren patted Sarah on the head, thinking about the naivety of the young girl. Meanwhile, the beautiful and haunting melodies from Evensong echoed in her head.

22

CADE WAS JUBILANT as he walked into the crowded and noisy bar. He had just come from the courthouse after winning his first big trial as lead lawyer for Pickering Construction. It took his eyes a few moments to adjust to the dim light. Small, colored lights were strung around the bar, in keeping with the Christmas season. Cade could hardly believe it was already mid-December, and he was more than ready to celebrate on this Friday evening.

At a tap on his shoulder, he turned to find a beaming Zac Pickering holding out a victory cigar, which Cade accepted. Jim Turner, the associate who worked on the trial, also accepted one.

Putting his arm around Cade's shoulders, Zac said, "Cade and Jim, I owe you both a drink. Come on." The three of them walked together up to the bar.

Several other lawyers from the firm stopped by the bar, and Cade enjoyed this chance to revel in his court victory. He was on top of the world. Zac ordered another round of drinks for everyone. Soon Cade felt the alcohol's influence, enhancing the moment with its unique blend of euphoria and bonhomie.

"Hey, man, congratulations." Cade felt a slap on the back and turned to find Eric. "How did you find out?" Cade yelled to be heard above the noise.

"I called you a while ago, and your secretary told me the jury came back with a defense verdict. She said she heard someone say they were meeting you here."

Cade and Eric exchanged a high five.

The door to the bar opened and in walked Harry Martin. He strode over to Cade, and the two shook hands. "Cade, I just got in from Chicago and heard the news. Wanted to come over and congratulate you personally. Great work. Come by and see me Monday, and let me hear all about it."

"Thanks ..." said Cade, but Harry was already halfway out the door. " ... Harry," Cade finished. He motioned for the waitress and ordered another bourbon.

"Your drink, sir," said a female voice behind Cade. He turned to get the drink from the waitress and was stunned to see Sherry Talbot in a slinky, hunter green velvet dress, holding his drink.

"Sherry ... what are you doing here?"

"A group of us came here after work, and I bumped into Eric. He told me about your big win, so I thought I'd come offer my congratulations."

"Well, ... thanks. Can I buy you a drink?"

"I don't know ... I'd probably better ... ."

"Oh, come on." Cade held her wrist. "Just one?"

"You talked me into it." She moved her head coyly to the side, her hair tossing gently on her shoulder.

Cade obtained a drink for Sherry, and Eric joined them.

"Cade, I've got to go," said Eric, after he had spoken to Cade and Sherry for a few minutes. "Let's grab lunch next week and catch up."

"Sure." Cade shook hands with his friend.

The other lawyers began to leave. Zac walked up to Cade. "This is a great day for Pickering Construction. I appreciate your hard work. I'll be in touch soon."

"Thanks, Zac." Between the noisy bar and the drinks, Cade could hardly focus on what his client was saying.

Zac patted him on the back and ambled out of the bar, puffing on his cigar.

Soon Cade found that just he and Sherry were left sitting alone at a table. By now, he had no cares. He stared at her, thinking how beautiful she was. Sherry glanced up at him, appeared embarrassed, and looked away.

Finally, he said, "I guess we'd better go. I'll see you to your car."

"That would be nice." Sherry stood, touching Cade's arm gently.

"Good to see you again, Cade," Sherry said when they reached her car.

"And you." Cade wondered if his words sounded slurred. "Say, maybe I should follow you home." He paused, put his hand on the car to steady himself, then added, "Just to make sure you get there safely."

"Oh no, Cade, you don't have to do that. I'm fine."

"Okay." Cade heard the disappointment in his voice and wondered whether Sherry noticed it too. "Well, I guess I'll ... ." He stopped in mid-sentence.

"What's the matter?"

"I just remembered. I rode over here with another lawyer."

"Then hop in and I'll take you to your car. Where is it?"

"It's ... it's at the office."

They got in Sherry's car. Cade rubbed his eyes to see if that would eliminate the fuzziness in his vision.

"Cade, are you all right?"

"Yes, why do you ask?"

"You just look so tired, and you keep squinting."

"It's been a long week – the trial and all." Cade realized he'd had far too much to drink, but didn't want to admit it.

"I tell you what. My place is near here. Let me take you there and make sure you're okay. I don't think you should drive right now."

"Are you sure?" Cade didn't even think about what he was saying. He looked over at Sherry. Her dress had inched up when she sat in the car, and he eyed her shapely legs.

They drove a few minutes, and Sherry pulled into a parking deck.

"Can you make it?" she asked when the car was parked.

"Yeah, sure." He opened the door, stumbled, and almost fell. He stood quickly. Sherry didn't give any indication she had noticed.

They walked across the enclosed, concrete lot and through a door into a small lobby. Sherry hit the elevator button, and the doors soon opened.

After they got off on Sherry's floor, Cade walked alongside her down the hallway, noting that this was an upmarket condo building. He had to concentrate on walking straight, feeling rather as if he was on a ship.

He heard keys jingling and watched Sherry open a door. As she entered, Sherry turned on a lamp. Cade walked in behind her, looking over the elegantly furnished apartment. Colorful, modern paintings hung on the walls, and the leather furniture and oriental rugs were well coordinated.

"Let me make you some coffee." She walked toward the kitchen.

"Thanks. Could I have some water, too?"

Sherry stopped at a cabinet just outside the kitchen, opened the door and fiddled with something. The condo was soon filled with the soft strains of a jazz saxophone. Cade spied a balcony and went out onto it. Taking several deep breaths hoping this would clear his head, he stared at the panoramic view of Downtown Atlanta, with its lights like thousands of fireflies. It was raining gently, and the yellow-orange light from the street lamps nine stories below made the raindrops look like tiny sparks as they passed by. The soft rainfall, accompanied by the music, gave him a feeling of serenity.

"Cheers," said Sherry from behind, and he turned to see her holding a glass of water.

Cade bowed in mock humility and took the glass. He thought she looked sensuous as she stood there in her bare feet, the soft light from the room highlighting her figure. Without thinking about what he was doing, Cade found himself moving toward her. He hesitated. She took the glass from him and set it on the railing.

"Care to dance?" she said softly.

Without replying, Cade put his arms around her, and she nuzzled her head on his chest. He felt his heart pounding. He pulled her tighter, and they began the slow lovers' ritual of movement. The gentle rain continued to fall. Sherry's perfume filled his nostrils, and her hair felt like satin. He stopped his slow turn, stepped back slightly, and looked into Sherry's eyes. She smiled and wrinkled her nose playfully. She took his hand and led him inside, as if leading a small child. They walked into her bedroom, where she turned on another small lamp.

"Let me slip into something more comfortable," she whispered in his ear, squeezing his hand.

Cade nodded and sat on the edge of the bed, electricity running through his veins. He grabbed the knot of his loosened tie. His arm flung down as he almost tore it off, and his hand hit the bedside table, causing a tiny clang. Cade glanced down at the cause of the noise: his gold wedding band, sparkling in the soft light from the lamp. He felt a pang of conscience somewhere deep within, but slowly tugged on the ring. It held fast for an instant, then, as he twisted it, the ring did his bidding and came off. He placed it on the table, out of sight behind the lamp.

He stood and restlessly paced, listening to Sherry sing quietly to herself in the bathroom – the Marilyn Monroe song 'I wanna be loved by you'. Filled with anticipation, he wandered over to the bathroom, and glanced through the half-opened door. He stopped and stared … motionless … breathless. Involuntarily, he leaned forward to look again, then stepped back. He pinched his thigh to prove this was not just a dream. He couldn't move. He couldn't breathe.

Suddenly, his survival instincts took over. Stunned by the most shocking sight he'd ever seen, Cade turned and ran.

23

"DON'T GO! Please, don't go!" Lauren was awakened by her own screams. She was surrounded by darkness, but quickly discerned that she was in her bed. The image of the pale girl lying on the table remained vivid before her, as if she was staring at a photograph. A strange noise added to her fright. Was it the ghost of the girl?

There it was again, a crying sound. Lauren's heart pounded with fear. She twisted on her side and turned on the bedside lamp, hoping this was all part of the nightmare.

"Mommy! Mommy!" cried the voice. Lauren leapt out of bed, simultaneously remembering that little Sarah was spending the weekend with her. She hurried into the guestroom and the dim light from her bedroom was enough for her to see the gray outline of Sarah sitting up in bed. Lauren heard the little girl's sobs.

"Everything's all right," said Lauren, in her calmest doctor voice. "You're having a bad dream."

Sarah cried louder. "I heard someone screaming, and it scared me."

Lauren pulled the child close, as much for her own comfort as Sarah's. Tears formed in her eyes. *No, Sarah, it wasn't you who had the nightmare.* She hugged Sarah tightly, and for the first time in many years, thought of her own mother holding her as a little girl.

After a few moments, Sarah stopped crying, and the cottage became quiet. Lauren leaned back slightly and looked at the little girl. "Are you okay now, sweetie?"

"I'm scared. I want Mommy." Sarah hugged her more tightly. "And I miss Daddy. I don't think he loves me any more."

"Of course he does," said Lauren softly. She gently laid Sarah back down in the bed, pulled the covers up to her chin, and stroked her head.

Lauren stood quietly after she thought Sarah had fallen asleep, but the girl's head came up slightly. "Please don't leave. I like having you here with me."

"I'll come straight back." Lauren patted Sarah on the head and left the room.

She returned shortly with a flute and began to play Debussy's *Reverie*.

"That sounds nice." Sarah curled up in a fetal position. A moment later, Sarah sat halfway up. "I don't have Flopsy."

Lauren looked around and saw the stuffed bunny had fallen on the floor. She picked it up and nudged it into the girl's arms, then tucked them both under the covers.

Sarah smiled. "Thank you, Dr. Lauren. Will you please keep playing?"

"Of course I will." Lauren resumed her tune, until Sarah had fallen asleep.

As Lauren stumbled back to bed, she pondered her recurring nightmare. Would she ever get over it? Would she ever forgive herself?

* * *

Cade was running down the road, which glistened from the streetlights reflecting the damp pavement. He had no concept of time. The gentle rain had soaked through his clothes, but he barely noticed. The clop, clop of his leather shoes echoed off the pavement, disrupting the stillness of the evening. His lungs burned, but he didn't care. He wanted … he wanted to be dead.

He ran furiously, aimlessly. What had he done? How had his life become so shipwrecked? Finally, he stopped in the middle of the street, bent over, huffing, his hands on his waist. Surely this could not be happening! He shut his eyes tightly, trying to erase the image in his head.

At the sound of a car horn, Cade jumped to the side of the street, startled. He just avoided a taxi speeding by. The driver gave Cade the finger, yelled something he couldn't understand, but knew was less than complimentary.

Cade stumbled over to the sidewalk and tried to gather his bearings. How long had he been running? Where was he? He looked at the corner street signs and discovered he was actually near his house. He must have run this way instinctively. A huge maple tree stood on the corner, and Cade, feeling faint, leaned against it. He took deep breaths and stared up into its leafless branches. The rain continued its gentle descent.

He could not banish the image that flashed in his mind constantly – the sight that struck fear in his heart.

"Come on, Cade, get hold of yourself," he said out loud. The maple gave no response. He turned and slapped his hand against the trunk, hoping … hoping for what? The image remained, an uninvited and unwelcome houseguest in his mind.

Cade turned and walked toward his home. The rain came down harder, but he did not pick up his pace. He trudged along with shoulders slumped and unsteady gate, as if his destination was the gates of hell. And, maybe it was.

He unlocked the front door and went instinctively toward the alarm to disarm it, only to realize it wasn't beeping. He must have forgotten to set it in the morning, probably due to his nervousness over the closing argument he would soon give. He locked the front door and turned on the alarm. The methodical "beep, beep" of the alarm began as it engaged. He plodded upstairs, his wet hands fumbling with the buttons of his soaked, white cotton shirt. When he came to the bedroom, he turned on his bedside lamp and tossed his wet clothes into a pile on the floor. He dried his hair with a towel and grabbed his bathrobe from the hanger inside the bathroom door. With head pounding and hands shaking, he reached for the mirrored cabinet to find some aspirin. Suddenly nauseous and gagging, he grasped a glass, filling it with water. As he took a swig, Cade stared in the mirror. He had been avoiding the mirror. He didn't want to face himself. What he saw were deep circles under his eyes, and wet, disheveled hair. Shame was written all over his pale face.

He couldn't stand the sight, so he quickly choked down the aspirin and walked toward his bed. As he sat on the side of the bed, he saw the message light flashing on the telephone. The red digits on the alarm clock read two thirty-seven. He was going to ignore the message light and turn off the bedside lamp, but instead hit the message retrieve button.

After a few moments, Rachael's voice came on: "Hi, it's me. I miss you so much ... Sarah and I both do ... I ... I love you Cade ... ."

There was a pause in the message, and he heard sniffles. He glanced down during this brief silence and had yet another shock. On his left hand was a tiny, white ring: the telltale mark where his wedding ring should have been. *Oh my God! I left it at the condo!* Cade's stomach tightened and he felt a cascading disgust envelope him.

Rachael was speaking again, "... anyway, the reason I called is first to say I'm truly sorry that I ran off to England and left you. I realized after something Sarah said that I must always have acted like I didn't trust you ... I guess I have a lot of insecurity. And, I've thought a lot about the wedding vows I took. I meant them, Cade. I'm sorry if I seemed to smother you; I don't know if I did anything else wrong, or where we went wrong, but I love you, and I want to stay married... ."

Cade felt as guilty and dirty as he'd ever felt in his life.

"But if you don't want to be married, I won't stand in your way. I love you, but I can't live like this. I've been miserable every day since I left you, and I can't go on ... ." There was another brief pause, "I'm so sorry for everything ... I love you so much, ... I ... ." She began to cry again, and the message stopped.

Cade closed his eyes tightly and groaned. He slid to the floor, hunched over, pounding his fists on the floor.

Frozen in his mind was a sight he'd give anything to erase: when he had peered through the crack of Sherry's bathroom door, he had seen Sherry standing there, her back to him, wearing a pale blue satin nightgown. And then ... and then ... he glanced toward the mirror she was facing. At first, the impossibility of the sight didn't register. Then the full force of his recollection slammed into him: as he stared at her face in the mirror, before his very eyes, the reflection became that of Marilyn Monroe, blonde-haired and ruby lipped, as the image smiled coyly and blew itself a kiss. Then, in another instant before Cade's shock even registered, he found himself staring at Vivien Leigh as a resplendent Scarlett O'Hara. Cade had pinched himself and looked again, only to see Sherry's image once more, with her long, auburn hair and big brown eyes. Immediately, he vividly recalled the night in Oxford when Foulheart had transformed his appearance to that of Robert Thompson. Without another thought, he'd panicked and run out of her apartment as fast as he could.

WuuH. WuuH. WuuH.

Cade's head jerked up. He was lying on the floor next to his bed. The lamp was still on. *What in the world?* He was groggy, and his head pounded.

WuuH. WuuH. WuuH. The loud wail wouldn't stop.

Cade panicked when he realized it was his security system alarm. Someone must be trying to break into his house! He stood and looked around. He didn't have a gun. He rushed to the phone, then remembered that the police would be automatically notified. He grabbed an old baseball bat he kept in his closet, and went to the top of the stairs.

The entire house was dark, except for the dim light in his bedroom. A noise downstairs startled him. He started to yell, but thought better of it. His heart was racing, and the bat slipped in his sweaty palms.

Not able to stand there doing nothing, he hurried down the dark steps, two and three at a time. His bare feet made no sound on the carpeted stairs. He heard another noise and stopped near the bottom of the stairway – it sounded like it came from his study. The door to the study was shut, but a thin ray of light shone under it. He tiptoed to the door and stopped to listen. Gripping the door handle with one hand and raising the bat with the other, he flung open the door, screaming, "Help, police!" The entire room was torn apart as if a cyclone had just blown through. Across the room, the window stood open. He rushed to it, but could see no one. Then, it dawned on him – whoever had been in here was already inside when he came home. *Who was here? What were they looking for?* He felt violated knowing some stranger had not only broken into his house, but had actually been inside while he was there. He looked at all of his books thrown around on the floor, his desk drawers open, and papers spilled everywhere. The bat slipped out of his grip and banged to the floor.

He became aware of blue lights circling outside in the darkness and also that the alarm was still going off. He ran over to the box and disengaged the alarm. He ran upstairs to get his bathrobe, and went barefooted to the front door to greet the police, thinking, *this is literally the night from hell.*

24

"DR. LAUREN, wake up. It's time to go to church."

"What?" said Lauren sleepily. She rolled over to see Sarah shaking her.

"I said, it's time for church. Come on. I'm an angel in the Christmas play today."

Lauren groaned. Her momentary confusion was dispelled when she remembered that Rachael had told her about Sarah being in the church play. Lauren had agreed to take Sarah to church, even though she felt a bit uncomfortable about it. By now, Sarah had taken hold of her hand and was pulling on her.

"All right, all right," Lauren attempted to smile as she sat up in her bed, rubbing her eyes.

"Hurry, or we'll be late." Lauren saw that Sarah was already dressed in a white robe with a silver halo around her head.

*   *   *

As Lauren walked toward St. Mary's Church, she glanced around nervously. The tall spire rose above the trees. Sarah grabbed her hand, and towed Lauren up the path. As they reached the entrance, Sarah said, "I have to go around to the back for our nativity. Will you please sit up close so you can see me?"

"Of course I will. You'll be wonderful, Sarah. Off you go then."

After she sat in a pew near the front, Lauren stared at the altar, with two lit candles and a wooden cross. Above the altar were stained glass depictions of the Virgin Mary. Childhood memories of going to church with her parents filled her thoughts.

The congregation of about eighty or so rose for the processional, and the choir paraded in after the crucifer. Lauren remembered walking into church many times as a teenage member of the choir. As the priest passed by, she recognized him as someone she'd seen around the village. She knew his name was David Cooper and thought how handsome he looked, with his thick, wavy brown hair, just slightly graying on the edges. He was smiling broadly as he walked up the aisle, singing loudly and well off-key.

Lauren sat as the service began, deciding she just had to grin and bear it for Sarah's sake. Shortly after the opening hymn ended, the children came out and set up the nativity scene. They looked so angelic in their costumes, their faces glowing as they stared out into the congregation looking for their parents. Lauren felt a pang of longing and regret that she had no child of her own. Another, older priest read the narrative of the nativity as the children acted out the scenes. She glanced at Sarah when the angels came out, and Sarah gave her a small wave. Lauren smiled to herself. *Christmas*. Her mind flooded with warm memories of childhood Christmases as she watched the play.

When the nativity was completed, the congregation clapped. Then the shepherds, Mary, Joseph, the wise men and the angels joined their parents in the pews. A beaming Sarah sat next to Lauren, who hugged the girl saying, "You were wonderful."

Reverend Cooper went to the altar and began the communion service. Lauren didn't bother to take out a prayer book. She became aware that Sarah was tapping her and looked over to see Sarah – and everyone else – standing for a hymn. Lauren had been so lost in thought she was the only one in the church still sitting.

After that, Reverend Cooper went into the pulpit. He opened by saying he was going to talk about the meaning of Christmas and the Incarnation. *Sermons are so boring*. She paid attention, however, because he was such an attractive man, and his smile radiated from the pulpit. She decided he must be about her age. He actually seemed excited about church. *How interesting – and unusual.*

He spoke about the "word made flesh," which Lauren had heard before, and about what the Incarnation really meant. To her surprise, Lauren found herself actually listening.

Cooper said, "Let me read you something from C. S. Lewis. You've heard me quote him many times in the past. Here's what he wrote in a book called *Miracles*:

'The central miracle asserted by Christians is the Incarnation. They say that God became Man… . If the thing happened, it was the central event in the history of the Earth – the very thing that the whole story has been about … .'

The vicar looked up and took a sip of water. "But this story is not just about some cute little baby in a stable, sleeping in a cow trough. It's also about the Creator of this universe, dying on the Cross, so that you and I might truly know forgiveness. And yet, even that's not the end of the story, because this same Jesus rose from the grave three days later, to show us that God is love and that eternal life is fact, not fantasy."

"God is love." The words echoed in Lauren's head. *But how? How could He have let that little girl die? How could He have ignored my prayers that night? How? How? How?*

Reverend Cooper was concluding, "So, dear friends, the message of Christmas is hope. Despite all the bad in this world – all the evil and sin and death – Christmas means God loves us and we have hope. And that, my friends, is good news."

When the sermon was finished, Lauren sat motionless. It was as if the priest had just read her mind and addressed some of her deepest thoughts – and fears. Since her recent visit to Magdalen Chapel, something had been stirring in the deep recesses of her soul: a restlessness for something she could not yet name.

When it was time for communion, members of the congregation began to walk up the center aisle and kneel at the altar rail.

"Dr. Lauren, aren't you coming?"

Sarah was already standing in the aisle, beckoning to her. Sarah smiled and tilted her head, causing her halo to sparkle in the church lights. Lauren hesitated, wondering whether to go to the altar. She stood and walked with Sarah toward the front, looking at the floor to avoid eye contact with anyone.

When they came to the altar, Lauren and Sarah knelt at the rail. The vicar progressed along the rail, speaking and putting a small piece of bread in each hand. As he neared them, Lauren could hear the words, "The body of our Lord Jesus Christ, which was given for you, preserve your body and soul unto everlasting life." When he came to Sarah, he put his hand on her head and blessed her. Lauren had intended to refuse the bread, but when the priest came to her, he smiled and seemed to look deeply into her eyes, compassion speaking from his own eyes. Lauren cupped her hands, and he pressed a small piece of brown bread into them with his large hands. An inner calm came over her as she silently ate the bread.

The elderly priest followed with a silver chalice. He bent over and offered her the cup of wine, saying, "The blood of our Lord Jesus Christ, which was shed for you." Lauren couldn't even remember the last time she had taken communion. But the words of the sermon struck a chord deep inside, a chord long forgotten and neglected. *Forgiveness. Hope Are they really possible?*

*   *   *

"Mommy, Dr. Lauren took me to Daddy's college," yelled Sarah, as she ran down the path in front of Lauren's house. Rachael was standing at the gate, her arms wide open.

Lauren walked behind, carrying Sarah's overnight bag.

Rachael stooped to welcome her daughter. "Hello, darling. I missed you. Did you behave yourself?"

"She was a perfect angel," Lauren said, smiling. "Literally and figuratively. She was a beautiful angel in the play this morning. I hope you'll let her stay with me again sometime."

Sarah tugged at Rachael's sleeve. "And, Dr. Lauren bought me an Alice in Wonderland tea set."

"You shouldn't have. Thank you so much for taking care of Sarah." Rachael stood and took the bag. "Was everything really all right?"

"Yes, she was well behaved. And, I got to play mother, which was … ." Her words trailed off. Lauren added quickly, "Won't you come in for a cup of tea?"

Rachael shook her head no. "I've got some errands to run. I can't thank you enough. Mum and I were really glad we went to see Aunt Charlotte. She's not in good health, and she's my mother's only sibling."

Sarah was skipping down the path. "It was truly a pleasure. Rachael, I … Sarah asked me to take her to Magdalen. She talked a lot about her father, and I just thought I should tell you."

"Thanks," said Rachael, softly. "I was wrong to take Sarah away from Cade and bring her here for so long. I guess … ."

"Listen, Rachael, I'm not saying it to pry into your personal business," interjected Lauren.

"I know." Rachael looked directly at Lauren. "Thanks so much for your help." Sarah returned and was bending near the ground, apparently showing something to Flopsy. Rachael looked over toward her daughter. "Sarah, come along. Your grandmother is anxious to see you."

Lauren waved as Rachael and Sarah left. "Now Sarah, remember your promise?"

Sarah turned around. "I will."

"What's that?" Lauren heard Rachael ask Sarah, as mother and daughter strolled down the path.

"I promised to invite Dr. Lauren to my first tea party." Rachael looked over her shoulder at Lauren and smiled.

"Oh, Lauren," said Rachael, walking quickly back toward her. "Are you going to be here all week?"

"Yes. Why do you ask?"

"I'm going to take Sarah on a sight-seeing trip this week. I've been promising her all autumn, so we're going to see Salisbury,

Stonehenge and London. She's been wanting to see the Tower of London and the Crown Jewels. Would you mind just checking in on my mother while we're gone?"

"Not a bit. Have a lovely time."

"Thanks. I'll make it up to you somehow."

"Don't mention it." Lauren gave a brief wave.

"Bye-bye Dr. Lauren." Sarah was holding Flopsy up in her hand.

"Good-bye, Sarah, and thanks for a wonderful weekend." As she walked into her cottage, Lauren thought about comforting the little girl late at night, and felt a void in her own life. She longed for a sense of security, a sense of fulfilment. To the outside world, Lauren appeared as a bright, witty, attractive, medical researcher. Behind the veneer, however, she felt like a piece of driftwood floating aimlessly on the sea.

*   *   *

Cade threw open the suitcase on his bed and began to pack. The Sunday evening news droned on the television, but he paid little attention. He hadn't slept after the alarm episode. Once the police left, he'd spent the early Saturday morning hours cleaning up the study, and most of the rest of the day working with Susan Phillips and Jim Turner trying to get his cases in order and make sure they would handle any deadlines. Cade brought Jim up to speed on his cases, so that Jim could cover for him until he returned.

Ever since leaving Sherry's condominium, Cade's fear had increased. He was panicked about Rachael. He had tried to call on Saturday and Sunday, but got no answer, which only heightened his worry. He had to make sure his wife and daughter were safe.

The first flight he could get on short notice was on Monday afternoon. He fidgeted constantly, still shaken by the horrifying events of Friday night.

He glanced over at a photograph on his dresser of Rachael and Sarah wearing white linen dresses and holding hands, with bright sand dunes, brown sea oats, and the bluish-green Gulf of Mexico in the background. He resumed packing with increased vigor.

*   *   *

Zac sat in the co-pilot's seat of his company's Lear Jet. The pilot was getting take-off instructions from the tower at Charlie Brown airport. Normally, he would observe the take-off procedures, because of his interest in flying. He particularly enjoyed these night flights, when the weather was clear, studying the different colored landing lights that outlined the runway and directed the planes. Tonight, however, he was preoccupied. "You mean you didn't find anything?" he yelled over the cell phone.

The hoarse male voice on the other end of the line continued, "Like I said, I went all over his study, man, and there were no computer disks anywhere."

"Are you damn sure you were thorough?"

"Listen, man, I tore the place to hell, and they ain't there. Besides, I almost got caught. He come home while I was there, but he must've been drunk or something. I heard him stumbling around, talking to himself. He's a weird dude, man. Talking out loud about his soul or something. Gave me the creeps. Anyway, the jerk turned on his alarm, and I had to sit there waiting for him to go to sleep. When I tried to get out, the alarm went off. I only just got out of there before he came downstairs."

"Are you sure you left no clues, fingerprints or anything?"

"Yeah, I'm sure."

Zac turned off the cell phone. "Damn it!" he shouted. "What the hell do I do now?" The pilot had headphones on and was talking to the tower. He appeared oblivious to Zac's ranting.

Zac stared out the window. He was nearing the end of his rope. He had until January first to prevent his sailing trip photos from reaching the wrong hands. On top of that, his start-up Internet business was in real trouble. He'd almost depleted the Swiss bank accounts thinking that he'd make so much money on his Internet venture, he'd have enough to replenish the account, make his investors happy, and be able to retire to his sailboat. He was running out of options and time. He'd be ruined, and that was one scenario he could not accept, no matter what it took.

He was forced to come up with another plan. He hadn't gotten where he was by being short-sighted. He tapped the pilot on the arm, and when the man lifted his earphones, Zac yelled, "We've got a change in plans. We're staying here." The pilot shrugged his shoulders and began to inform the tower of the change.

Zac smiled at the thought of his foolproof backup plan. *You little twerp, you're toast now.*

25

FIRST THING Monday morning, Cade drove straight to his bank. He walked through the teller lobby and went downstairs to the basement. Retrieving the key from his pocket, he handed it to the solemn woman sitting at the desk near the vault holding safety deposit boxes.

"What's your box number?" she said in a monotone voice, without looking up.

"Oh, it's 1954," he replied.

The woman took the key from him and walked into the vault. He followed her, brushing lint off the front of his navy blazer. She opened a large, thick, metallic door marked number 1954 with two keys, and handed Cade's key back to him.

"Thanks," he said. The woman nodded and returned to her desk.

He pulled out the heavy drawer and set it on the counter. He rifled quickly through the contents, pulling out a few coins, several pieces of antique silver, and several legal documents, including, he noted wryly, his wedding certificate. He didn't bother with any of these items, however, but instead kept searching until he found a brown envelope, with thick tape over the seal, and no marking on the outside.

Cade needed no reminder of the contents of this envelope. It contained something so incredible, that he often wondered if it had all been a dream. But now that he knew Foulheart or his cronies were after him, the reality of it all rang crystal clear, and he desperately wanted to get to his family. He figured he should keep the invaluable contents of the envelope with him.

He pulled out a pocket knife, cut the tape, and breathed a sigh of relief: The disk was still there – the disk that contained the reports of … .

"Excuse me, sir," said the bank woman, interrupting his thoughts. He instinctively gripped the envelope tightly.

He looked up at her, puzzled by the interruption. She was handing him a piece of paper. "I forgot to have you sign the log."

He complied, handed it back to her, and replaced the other items in the box. As he put the disk in his jacket pocket, he grimaced. He'd made a promise many years ago to publish these reports and had failed to do so. The promise was not forgotten – though he had tried hard to forget. God knows he had tried.

Walking out of the bank, he found himself wishing he'd never picked up those first letters. He was in possession of perhaps the most important information anyone in the world could possess, and yet he'd done nothing with it all these years.

He could not know that his regret would, very shortly, be multiplied a thousand-fold.

*   *   *

Cade went from the bank to his office to make sure everything was under control before he left for England that afternoon. He was anxious to be off and make sure his family was safe.

Cade stuck his head round his secretary's office. "Hi, Susan."

"Good morning, Cade," she replied cheerfully.

"Thanks again for your help this weekend."

"No problem. I'm glad you're taking a little time off. You deserve it."

Cade walked into his office, opened his briefcase, and loaded it with items for his trip. He started to put the disk into the briefcase, and hesitated. He wondered if maybe he should copy the disk just in case, since this was the only one he had.

Jim Turner walked into his office. "Bon voyage, Cade. I'll take care of things while you're gone, so don't worry."

"Thanks, Jim. I really appreciate your help." Cade instinctively put the disk into the inside pocket of his navy wool blazer.

"Anytime. I've got to run and take a deposition in a little while. Have a great trip."

The two men shook hands, and Jim walked out.

Cade went into Susan's office. She was busy typing dictation and at first appeared not to notice. She looked up and took the earphones out of her ears. "Are you off?"

"Just about. As soon as I get my laptop. I think I've got everything I need for the trip. I've got to run home and finish packing. Now, you have the number at Rachael's mom's, where I'll be staying, and you won't let on to Rachael I'm coming?" He was worried that he'd been unable to reach Rachael by phone over the weekend, but had decided now just to surprise her and Sarah and not unduly alarm them. He had thought constantly about what to say to Rachael, and the episode with Sherry still made him almost physically ill.

" No." Susan laughed. "Now, don't you worry, we'll take care of things here."

"Okay." Cade was a bit embarrassed at his excessive worrying.

"Just bring me a souvenir," she said.

"You bet. I guess I'd ... ."

"Cade, can I see you a minute?" Cade turned around to find Harry Martin standing behind him and winced. He'd hoped to get away without anyone knowing, but especially Harry.

"Yeah, sure Harry." Anxious to get to the airport, Cade nevertheless motioned Harry toward his office. Harry seemed rather irritated and more abrupt than usual this morning.

They walked into Cade's office, and Harry shut the door.

"It looks like you're packed up. Where are you going?" Harry exhibited no hint of warmth.

"Actually, I ... I'm on my way to England to see Rachael and Sarah."

"England!" said Harry, almost shouting.

Cade was startled. "Yeah, well, I ... ."

"Listen, Cade, I don't have time to beat around the bush." Harry was standing in front of Cade's desk. Cade started to sit in his chair, but instead stood behind it and the desk, watching Harry pace as if he were a tiger in a cage.

"I've just had a visit with Zac Pickering, and ... ."

"Zac?" interjected Cade. "He's still in Atlanta? But I thought ... ."

"Yes, he was just in my office. Seems he's got some serious charges to make against you."

Cade felt his face burn crimson, and his heart rate soared. "Charges, what kind of charges?"

"Well, according to him, you've tried to steal some of his copyrights."

Cade felt fear, then anger. "Copyrights, but that's ridiculous, Harry. I never dreamed of such. What does he claim I did?"

"He says he talked to you about some sensitive Internet business ventures, and that he's just recently discovered you registered some of his Internet businesses under your name."

"But that's impossible." Cade was as dumbfounded as if Harry had just said the moon was actually made of green cheese.

"That's what I thought," said Harry. "But, he has some documents, and they do appear to back up his story."

"This is the most absurd thing I've ever heard, Harry. There must be some mistake, or is this a joke?"

"No joke." Harry was standing at Cade's window, staring at the Atlanta skyline. "Now listen, Zac Pickering is an important and powerful man, Cade. He has lots of influence. All I can say is, there'd better not be a shred of truth to this."

"Harry, you know me. Do you have any doubts?"

Harry looked at the floor and loosened his tie. "We have to get to the bottom of this right away."

Cade could see that Harry was not giving Cade his unqualified support. "Listen, there's nothing to this. I don't know what Pickering is up to, but ... ."

"Cade, my job is to protect this law firm. Now, I'm not for a minute accusing you of anything."

Cade smirked, because that's exactly what Harry was doing.

"You just forget any trips right now, until we sort this out."

"But, I ... my family ..." stuttered Cade. His stomach was in knots. He *had* to get to England right away.

"No buts about it. I've told you that sometimes your family comes second, and this is one of them. Now, be reasonable, and ... ."

"No, Harry!" Cade was surprised at the forcefulness in his voice. "My family is very important to me. I can't just abandon them." He knew these words were hypocritical, given his actions in neglecting his family for so long.

"Let me put it to you straight, Cade. I'm managing partner of this firm, and it's a helluva responsibility. You're just one fish in this sea, mister. Now, I've already called our computer department, and they're checking out what Pickering says. In the meantime, you stay close or else ... ."

"Or else what?" Cade's blood was boiling.

"Or else you're finished, that's what," said Harry. He turned and left Cade's office, walking briskly away.

Cade dropped into his chair, his frenzied thoughts rushing together like several converging rivers. *Zac Pickering? Copyright violations? What's this all about?* He tried to concentrate, but couldn't. He spotted the itinerary that his travel agency had faxed to him. Should he cancel his trip? How could he defend himself? Then, the startling image in the mirror flashed in his mind like a blinding spotlight. His heart raced. He just *had* to see Rachael and Sarah.

He didn't hesitate a moment longer. He grabbed his laptop and thrust it into his briefcase, stuffed the itinerary in his coat pocket, and felt for his passport in his jacket. He picked up the phone and when Jim's voice mail came on, he said, "Listen, Jim, something's come up. I can't explain now. Knowing how the firm rumor mill operates, I suspect you're going to hear some things about me. They're not true. Trust me. I need you to take care of my cases until I get back. I may need some other help, too. Thanks, Jim." He replaced the phone and walked to Susan's office.

She stared at him wide-eyed, her face pale. He knew she had overheard the loud confrontation. "Listen, Susan, you just have to trust me. I don't know what's going on, but it's plain crazy. I can't explain now. I've got to get to England. I can't ask you to help, because I know you need this job." He paused and looked at her.

He was about to continue when she said. "Cade, I know you well enough to know you couldn't do anything dishonest. It isn't in your nature."

"Does that mean you'll help?"

She glanced around. "Aren't you late for your meeting outside the office?"

He didn't have to ask her meaning. Smiling, he gave her a thumbs-up. "You're the greatest." He picked up his briefcase and hurried toward the elevator.

*   *   *

Cade rushed home to get his suitcase and drove straight to Hartsfield Airport. Due to his unscheduled meeting with Harry, he was cutting it close to make his flight. He got on his cell phone and made a call.

"Eric?"

"Oh, hi, Cade, how was your weekend?"

"Listen, Eric, I don't have time to explain. Some weird things are happening. I've decided to go to England. I'm on my way to the airport."

"What's going on?"

"I ... it's too crazy to go into right now. I've got to go get Rachael. Something strange happened ... but ... well, I'll tell you later. Listen, I'm in trouble at work. When I get to England, I may call you for help."

"Sure, you know you can count on me. But I wish I knew what this was all about."

"So do I. So do I. Listen, call Philip for me and just tell him I'm off to England. Oh, and please watch after the house. I've left the alarm on, if you'll get the mail and newspapers. I'll explain later. I've got to go. See you."

"Okay, well ... ."

"And Eric, thanks for being a good friend."

"Sure thing."

"Bye." Cade disconnected the line. Just as he was parking, his cell phone rang. He hesitated, but answered it.

"Hello."

"Cade, where are you?"

"Oh, hi, Dad. I was going to call you."

"I just got a call from Harry Martin. What kind of trouble are you in son?"

"Dad, I just can't explain right now."

"I want to help you son. Martin was vague, wanted me to call you. Said you might be leaving for England."

"Dad, you just have to trust me. Some client has made unfounded accusations against me that I don't understand. But, I have to go see Rachael. It's very important."

"Your mother will be concerned ... ."

"I know Dad. I'll explain everything soon. You've just got to trust me. Listen, I've got to go."

"But Cade, I ... ."

"I'll call you soon. Promise." This was getting more serious. Harry had actually called Cade's father, who was the managing partner of a rival Atlanta law firm. Pickering was obviously turning up the heat.

His cell phone rang again. Cade decided not to answer. What if it was Harry? At the insistent ring, however, he finally responded.

"Cade, it's Susan."

"What's up?"

"Just thought I should tell you that Mr. Martin was here a while ago asking for you. I told him you were out, and he asked where. He looked pretty mad."

"What did you tell him?"

"I ... he looked so agitated ... ."

"That's okay, I understand," said Cade with a sigh, figuring Susan told Harry where Cade was.

"I'm sorry ... I ... ."

"Listen, Susan, don't worry about it."

"Oh Cade, there is one thing though."

"What's that?"

"I told him I thought you weren't leaving until tomorrow. I just didn't tell him I was going by England time!"

"Great. Thanks Susan. I'm at the airport. I'll check in with you after I arrive."

"Have a good trip."

"Okay. See you soon." He turned off his cell phone, grabbed his bags, and hustled to the airport.

By the time Cade arrived at his gate, the plane was almost boarded. As he handed his ticket to the attendant, he heard a commotion behind him and looked down the hallway. About two hundred yards away, a tall, well-built man in blue jeans and black leather jacket was talking to an airport security guard. Cade recognized the man as one of his firm's litigation investigators, and it didn't take Sherlock Holmes to figure out what he was investigating at the Atlanta airport. Cade ran down the gangplank, praying he had not been seen yet. He heard someone yelling, and his heart stopped. He kept walking, without turning, acting as if he had heard nothing. To his great relief, as he was making his way down the aisle of the plane, he heard its doors being shut. He put his carry-on bag in the overhead compartment and settled in his window seat, exhausted and relieved.

* * *

After the plane was in the air, Cade pulled out his laptop and the disk. In his rush to get out of the office, he'd forgotten to make a copy of the disk, but figured he would do that later. He couldn't believe it had been so long since he'd looked at the Soulbane Reports. He felt more than a tinge of regret that he'd left them locked in a bank vault all this time. Reading Soulbane's report, it wasn't long before he was shifting in his seat with discomfort: it was as if Soulbane was holding a mirror up to Cade's life. When he came to the section on marriage, Cade could hardly bear reading it. These words from a devilish tempter, which he had discovered many years ago, were eerily prophetic of the breakdown in Cade's own marriage. He glanced down at his ringless finger and a shooting emotional pain seared his conscience. He closed his eyes and wondered if God – or Rachael – could ever forgive him. Could he ever forgive himself?

PART
II

"Turning and turning in the widening gyre
The falcon cannot hear the falconer;
Things fall apart; the centre cannot hold... ."
—W. B. Yeats, *The Second Coming*

26

AFTER HE ARRIVED at Gatwick, Cade gathered his luggage and boarded the next train to Oxford. It was an overcast, chilly day. He had been unable to sleep on the plane, even though he had slept little for several days. His pulse quickened as he viewed the English countryside once more, and as he anticipated his surprise reunion with Rachael and Sarah. He yawned and stretched out his legs.

A lurch of the train awakened him, and Cade glanced up to see the sign for Oxford station. He looked out the windows expectantly, hoping to see the tips of the Oxford spires, but the train was already in the station. He stepped onto the platform and took a deep breath, glad to be in this wonderful city again. He wished he had time to explore it, but he was most anxious to see his family. He took a taxi to a car rental place and hired a small car.

Driving out of Oxford toward the Cotswolds, he had to remind himself about staying on the other side of the road, but was pleased when this seemed to come quickly back to him. When he reached the countryside, he thought of the many trips he had made to the Cotswolds while he was a student at Oxford. He had made only two quick visits to England with Rachael since they'd been married, but they spent the time in London and Tintagel, and this was his first chance in over ten years to return to Oxford. He felt a sense of homecoming as the rolling hills and beautiful streams of the Cotswolds came into view. He also wanted to visit Robert Thompson, whom he'd not seen since his wedding, although they had spoken over the phone several times. Dozens of memories flooded his mind as he drove through the countryside.

He made his way to Lower Slaughter from memory. It was there that he had first met Reverend Brooke, and he and Rachael liked the village so much, they had recommended to Bridgett that she move there. Cade had not yet seen Bridgett's cottage, but Rachael described it as quaint and cozy.

Nestled in the Cotswolds, the tiny, picturesque village of Lower Slaughter, with its weather-worn, honey-stone cottages, came into view. It was truly an idyllic setting, especially with the River Eye flowing gently through the center of the village. Cade had fallen in love with it the first time Rachael brought him here, and he was thrilled when Rachael's mother decided to move there.

He turned onto the village main street and saw the smoke drifting from the chimneys of the stone cottages and quickly dissipating into the gray sky. The dreariness of the weather was offset by the colorful Christmas lights adorning many of the village houses. He glanced down to check the address and soon found the narrow street, with rows of small, centuries-old cottages on each side. Nearby, he also saw the tall, cone-shaped steeple of St. Mary's Church, where James had been the vicar.

His heart pounded as he pictured Rachael and Sarah. He could hardly wait another moment. He quickly spotted Bridgett's cottage and pulled up in front. It was a one-story stone cottage, with a mossy, weathered slate roof and a small yard behind a crumbling stone wall. Ivy covered much of the walls, and the blue, wooden flower boxes in the front windows were empty. A green wreath with a red velvet ribbon adorned the brown front door. The wooden gate creaked as he opened it, and he rushed to the door, not bothering to put on his coat. He knocked rapidly, breaking into a wide grin.

Bridgett opened the door, a surprised look on her face. Her dark, curly hair was streaked with gray, and the lines in her face more pronounced than when Cade had last seen her. But her blue eyes still flashed as brightly as ever, reminding him of Rachael.

"Cade! What in the world are you doing here?" She had a look of worry, not welcome, and this alarmed him.

"Hi, Bridgett, I wanted to surprise Rachael and Sarah. Are they here?"

"Oh... Cade forgive me, please come in." He gave her a quick kiss on the cheek as he came through the door. Bridgett continued, "I'm afraid they've taken my car on a bit of a holiday. They're due to return in time for Christmas. Unfortunately, I've just got a call that my sister, Charlotte, has fallen and broken her hip. I'm in the middle of packing to go to Bath and be with her. A neighbour's giving me a lift to Cheltenham and I'm getting the coach from there."

Cade glanced at his watch and saw it was almost one.

"I see." His disappointment dropped into his stomach like a rock. "I hope Aunt Charlotte is okay."

"Yes, so do I," Bridgett said in a terse voice. "Cade, I do apologize, but I have to finish packing." He was aware of an uncharacteristic coldness in her manner.

She pointed to a room off the living room where they were standing. " Rachael's room is just over there." For the first time, Cade observed the cottage interior. It was very tidy and clean, with a dark blue sofa, some small, red, blue and green area rugs on the hardwood floor, and a stone fireplace. There were knickknacks around the room, and Cade saw a photograph of Rachael and himself on their wedding day standing in front of Merton Chapel. Next to it was a photograph of Sarah taken on her last birthday.

"That's fine. You go on and pack. Can I help you with anything?"

"No thank you. Just make yourself at home."

"Well, I'd hoped to surprise them, but I guess I'll just call Rachael on her cell phone and let her know I'm here."

Bridgett stopped short of her bedroom and turned. "Actually, she forgot to take it with her. She called last night to see if she'd left it here, and I found it in her room."

"You talked to her last night? Where is she?" Cade didn't dare alarm her with his concerns.

"They were in Salisbury, but she wasn't sure where they were going next. She said she and Sarah were having a terrific time and to expect them back on Christmas Eve. Unfortunately, I didn't know about Charlotte until this morning, and I have no way to reach Rachael unless she calls again."

"Oh, well," was all Cade could mutter in response, unable to hide his disappointment.

He went to the car and gathered his luggage. Tossing his bags on top of the embroidered white bed cover, he went into the bathroom to wash his face. When he had freshened up, he walked into the living room. Bridgett was just coming out with two bags, and he said, "Here, let me help you with that."

She nodded, and he took them from her. "Can I give you a ride?"

"No need to bother. Deidre Smith said she'd take me."

"It's no bother at all. I'd be glad to drive you there."

Bridgett seemed hesitant, then said, "It *would* be nice not to make Deidre come out on such a cold day."

"It's settled then. Give her a call, and I'll get my coat."

As he rejoined Bridgett, she said, "This is one of the coldest Decembers I can remember. They're predicting it staying like this until after Christmas. Maybe even some snow."

"You know, I've never seen a white Christmas." Cade stopped quickly to zip up his coat.

The ride to Cheltenham was uneventful. The two made small talk, but Cade could sense a coolness in Bridgett's demeanour, and he didn't want to talk about how things were between him and Rachael. As they parked at the coach station, Bridgett said, "Please tell Rachael where I am. I hope to be back for Christmas, but I'll just have to see how Charlotte's doing."

"Of course. Please give Aunt Charlotte my best."

"I left Charlotte's phone number in the kitchen if you need me. There's a spare house key under the gray flower pot in the back yard."

He followed Bridgett onto the bus with her bags and stored them in the luggage rack. There were only a few people inside.

"Thank you. I'm sorry to be in such a rush."

"No problem. I'll watch your house and see you soon."

He waved to Bridgett as the bus pulled away, then walked briskly back to the car. He was already chilled to the bone in the icy wind and frustrated beyond words at his circumstances. He wondered what he would do until Rachael and Sarah returned.

After he returned to Lower Slaughter, he was too restless to sit in the cottage, so he walked to St. Mary's Church. The day was overcast and dreary, and the arctic blast added to the gloom. Entering the graveyard, he passed through the lych-gate, his mind flooded with memories and emotions. He envisioned the tall, thin Reverend Brooke, with his silver hair, gray eyes, and long, bony fingers, as if the vicar were standing in front of him. He recalled their joint astonishment as the mystery of Cade's chance discovery of the letters had unfolded, and Cade smiled as he thought of the leisurely walks he and James had taken in the surrounding countryside and around Oxford, while James gently enlightened him about the depth and wonder of the Christian faith. Cade shuddered with embarrassment at how he had neglected his faith these last years.

He walked around a huge yew tree that swayed gently, guarding the ancient graves arranged around it. He came to the tombstone of James S. Brooke, which stood silently next to that of his wife, Anne. His eyes blurred as he recalled the deep friendship he had developed with James. He mourned the loss of someone who had been friend, mentor, and counselor. Cade so wished he could talk to James now: James would understand his dilemma and somehow help him.

"James, I'm afraid I'm in a bit of a mess. I sure could use your help." Cade felt foolish for speaking out loud to a grave and became silent. After a few moments, he sighed and turned toward the church. He entered through the large wooden door, taking in the familiar stone walls, and the bright, deep ruby, blue, and yellow stained glass. The church was deserted and cold. He ruefully thought how little he had prayed lately, in fact, for years. His mind raced to the August night that he had climbed up the spiral stone stairway to the top of Magdalen Tower. That starry night he'd prayed for the first time in his life. Faith had seemed so very easy at first, as he began to read the Bible, and his relationship with Rachael had taken off. And, of course, the amazing events surrounding Cade's discovery of the Soulbane Reports. The thought of the reports jarred him – maybe it would have been better if he'd never found them. He thought of law school and practising law, and of his hectic life. What had happened to his faith? There had been no dramatic event to undermine it ... just a gradual ebbing, like an unreplenished fire burning lower and lower.

He ambled up the distinctive tiled aisle, knelt at the altar rail and prayed silently. What a wreck he'd made of his life ... his marriage ... everything. Was there any way out now? A thought popped into his head. Something Reverend Brooke had said to him years ago about prayer ... what was it? He couldn't remember exactly... something about coincidences. *Well what do I have to lose?* He closed his eyes and said quietly, "God, I've made rather a mess of things." The images of the changing faces in the mirror flashed through his mind, and he shivered. "Please God, please help me. I feel so lost." He stood and glanced at the altar and the alabaster reredos above the table depicting the crucifixion of Christ. The figure didn't say a word. Cade wondered if he'd done nothing more than pray to stone walls.

Dusk was steadily approaching as he walked out of the church and down the pathway. A tall, gaunt, older man was standing near the gate, an umbrella resting on his arm, over the sleeve of his tan coat. The man's silver hair was disheveled by the wind, and he appeared to be observing a small bird perched all alone on the bare limb of a nearby tree.

"Hello," the man said pleasantly, as Cade approached. The man had bright brown eyes.

"Hi, how are you?"

"That's a lovely accent. Are you a tourist?"

"Actually, no. I know … er, knew, someone buried here."

"And who is that? … Oh, pardon my rudeness. My name is Neville Sterling." He shook Cade's hand. His grip was remarkably firm.

"Nice to meet you. I'm Cade Bryson."

"Really?" Sterling said, arching his bushy eyebrows. He had deep, wrinkled lines etched in his face. "Ah, so you're here to visit James, are you?"

"But how did you know that?"

"My friend James told me all about you. You were like the son he never had."

"I'm afraid I don't remember him speaking of you." Cade immediately regretted the remark.

"Oh," said Neville, whose smile disappeared.

"I mean … Mr. Sterling … ."

"Don't give it a second thought. And, call me Neville. I'm not surprised James didn't mention me. He was a rather private person. Why, I bet he never told you he was a war hero, did he?"

"No, as a matter of fact, he didn't."

"Yes, that's just like James. He was a Spitfire pilot, a highly decorated one."

"Gosh, I never knew… ." Cade was taken aback not only by this revelation, but by James's humility in never mentioning it.

"What brings you to England?"

"My wife is English, and she and my daughter have been here this autumn. My mother-in-law recently moved here. I just flew over to surprise my family, but I was the one surprised." He laughed. "It seems they're off on a little holiday. So, I decided to come see James's old church and visit his grave."

"I hope you see your family soon." Neville leaned over and picked up a brown hat sitting on the stone wall. "It's getting a bit nippy with the sun setting."

Cade yawned, exhausted from the trials of the last few days. "Excuse me."

"You look like you could use some rest, young man."

"Yes, I'm pretty tired after my trip. Nice to meet you, Neville. Perhaps I'll see you around the village? I'd love to hear more about James's Spitfire days."

"I look forward to it."

Cade looked back as he walked away from the church. Neville pulled something from his coat pocket and tossed it in the direction of the bird, which swooped to the ground in pursuit of the morsel.

27

CADE ROLLED OVER in bed and looked at his watch. He shook it, astonished that it was almost noon. He was obviously exhausted from his trial, the episode with Sherry, and the flight to England. Sunlight shot through the narrow slit in the curtains, laying a thin, yellow path on top of his covers.

He eased out of bed and shuffled over to the window. It was a clear, sunny day, although an elderly couple walking down the sidewalk had frosty breath coming from their mouths. He shivered and quickly turned up the electric fire to warm his hands. Realizing he was famished, he shaved, showered and put on fresh clothes so he could go in search of a meal. For the first time in days, he felt almost rested.

He walked down to the tea-room in the Old Mill Museum and ordered a roast beef sandwich, potato salad, and coffee. As he sipped black coffee, he tried to start a novel he'd brought along, but had trouble concentrating. His mind was full of other matters.

"Mind if I join you?" said a male voice.

Cade looked up to see Neville smiling down at him.

"Not at all, please do." Cade gestured to the empty chair at the table.

"I was passing by and saw you come in here. Thought I'd say hello and have a cup of tea," Neville said as he sat in the chair.

"I'm glad for the company."

"Any luck in finding your wife and daughter?"

"I'm afraid not."

"I know you'll be glad to see them."

"You can say that again."

The two talked for a while about the weather and other minor matters. Cade took an immediate liking to Neville.

After about fifteen minutes, Neville stood to leave. "Do you happen to have a car here?"

"Yes, do you need a lift somewhere?"

"Not today, thanks. I seem to recall that James told me you're interested in C. S. Lewis."

"That's right."

"There's a lecture at the Bodleian tomorrow by a noted Lewis scholar, a Professor Periwinkle. Apparently, some Lewis society is over here for the holidays, and they've arranged the lecture. I wondered if you have any interest in going?"

"Sure. I don't really have anything else to do until I locate Rachael, and I'd love to go back into Oxford."

"The lecture is at half ten. What do you say if I meet you at St. Mary's at about quarter past nine?"

"Sounds great."

"Jolly good. All the best." Neville gave a brief wave, and he was out the door.

*   *   *

The next day, Cade and Neville drove into Oxford and made their way to the Bodleian. They found that the lecture was going to be in the old Divinity School. They arrived just as it was about to begin, and quickly took seats toward the back.

"Ladies and Gentlemen … " began a man, who stood and turned to the audience of about forty people. He was tall and portly, with a reddish face, thick white hair and a trim white beard. He was dressed in a brown tweed jacket, blue tie, and gray slacks, with half-moon glasses that hung on his prominent nose, accentuating his large, sad, gray eyes. A silver chain, presumably attached to a watch, protruded from his coat pocket.

"Who's that?" whispered Cade to Neville.

"That's Bodley's Librarian, Owen McCrady."

"... and so, it is with distinct pleasure," continued the man, "that I welcome you to the Bodleian. And now, without further ado, I give you Professor Periwinkle."

There was a smattering of polite applause, as a man sitting on the front row stood. He was short and very thin, with a dark green coat, and blue and white striped bow tie. Cade thought he must be in his mid-forties. With his horn-rimmed glasses, he certainly looked the part of a professor. Cade glanced up to marvel at the exquisite vaulted ceiling of golden stone in this fifteenth century room.

"Good morning," Periwinkle began in a crisp, Australian accent. "Mr. Lewis was a man of formidable intellect and keen insight. He was not only a prolific writer and extraordinarily well read, but he was one of the greatest apologists of the Christian faith in the twentieth century."

Cade shuffled in his seat, and stole a glance at Neville, who appeared to be concentrating on the professor. Cade's mind wandered to his various troubles. *It will only be a matter of time until I hear from Harry Martin. Where can Rachael and Sarah be? I wonder when I'll see them?*

"... and the imagination of Mr. Lewis is no more keenly seen than in his invention of that unique diabolical figure, Screwtape."

Cade sat up straight, his attention riveted to Periwinkle. *Invention? If he only knew what I knew.* He listened intently as Periwinkle talked about *The Screwtape Letters*, explaining how they conveyed much about the Christian faith under the guise of fiction.

Fiction? Cade laughed to himself, thinking of his own adventures. His stomach tightened as he realized he'd blown a golden opportunity to tell others about Soulbane and Foulheart. *I wonder who they are?* "And in conclusion, let me just say that C. S. Lewis's works will endure. When others are long forgotten, his writings will remain fresh and profound for readers yet unborn. Thank you."

Loud applause echoed around the room.

Mr. McCrady stood and turned to the audience. "Professor Periwinkle is happy to stay and answer questions if you wish to come and talk to him. Also, we have arranged for you to have a tour of our Library. If you'll meet at the gift shop in fifteen minutes, a guide will take you around."

Everyone stood, and several went toward the front to talk to Professor Periwinkle.

"Cade ... Cade Bryson?" said a female voice.

Cade turned and saw a short woman with black hair and thick glasses smiling at him. He didn't have a clue who she was, but he smiled and said, "Yes, that's me."

"Hello. I'm Mary York. I'm a friend of Rachael's and ... ."

"Oh, yes, Dr. York. I remember you. You came to our wedding, didn't you?"

"Yes, I did. I'm flattered that you remember."

"Please meet my friend, Neville Sterling."

"It's a pleasure, Dr. York." Neville extended his hand.

"Very nice to meet you, Mr. Sterling." She turned to Cade. "So you're over here visiting Rachael?"

"That was the idea, but when I arrived two days ago I learned that she and Sarah have gone on a little holiday."

"Now that you mention it, Rachael told me she wanted to take Sarah on a trip."

"So you've seen Rachael since she's been here?"

"Yes, several times. She was one of my favourite students."

"You're at Merton, aren't you?"

"Actually, I'm at Magdalen now."

"Really? That was my college."

"Yes, I know. I hope you'll come and see us."

"I will. Say, did Rachael happen to tell you where she was going?"

"Let me see, ... I recall she said she wanted to go to Salisbury and Stonehenge, and then into London. Sarah wanted to see the Crown Jewels."

"Hello, Professor York. How are you today?" Owen McCrady had walked over to them.

"Good morning, Mr. McCrady. I'm well. Do you know these gentlemen?" she asked, nodding toward Cade and Neville.

"No, I don't think I've had the pleasure. I'm Owen McCrady." He extended his hand and shook both of theirs.

"I'm Neville Sterling." Neville paused, and the two men appeared to recognize each other, but McCrady said, "Pleased to meet you Mr. Sterling."

Cade stepped forward and shook hands with McCrady. "Hello, sir, I'm Cade Bryson."

McCrady tilted his head and eyed Cade. "You must be Rachael's husband."

"Why, yes. But how did you know that?" Cade was somewhat taken aback by this unexpected comment.

"I met her with Professor York at Magdalen one evening. You're a lucky man, Mr. Bryson. Your wife is absolutely charming."

This comment only served to pour coals on Cade's longing to be with her again.

Before he could reply, Periwinkle walked up and McCrady continued, "Have all of you met the Professor?" Everyone introduced themselves.

"I enjoyed your talk," Cade said as they shook hands.

"Are you familiar with C. S. Lewis's works?" The professor's face had an air of smugness about it.

"Actually, I am. I've read a number of his books, and I have a special interest in *The Screwtape Letters.*"

"Is that so?" interjected McCrady.

Cade nodded in assent, as Periwinkle said, "Yes, Screwtape is a marvelous and ingenious work. It exemplifies Lewis's vivid imagination, to create such fictitious characters."

"What makes you think they're fictitious?" Cade blurted out, before he had a chance to think. Everyone stared at him and, for an awkward moment, no one said anything.

Periwinkle laughed. "Oh yes, a bit of American humor, I see. Of course, no one *actually* believes in the existence of angels and devils now, do they?"

McCrady laughed heartily at this comment. Cade joined in half-heartedly.

Neville appeared to notice that Cade was flustered. "Well, Professor Periwinkle, one never knows. The Book of Hebrews says that people have entertained strangers unaware that they are angels."

Everyone smiled at this comment, and McCrady said, "Well, if you see any, we could certainly use a few angels around the Bodleian." This broke the group up with laughter. "If I can do anything for you while you're here, just let me know," added McCrady, as he walked off, accompanied by Professor Periwinkle. "Dr. York, it's always good to see you."

"And you," Mary replied.

"He's a wonderful man and a real asset to the library," she added when McCrady was out of earshot.

"Where does the title Bodley's Librarian come from?" Neville asked.

"Sir Thomas Bodley re-founded the library in 1602, and ever since, the prestigious position of head librarian has been known as Bodley's Librarian. Cade ... Mr. Sterling, it's nice to see you. I'm afraid I have to run. Hope to see you around."

Cade gave a brief wave. "Thanks for saying hello, Mary. And, if I don't see you before then, have a Merry Christmas."

"Merry Christmas to you, too. Give Rachael my best." Mary York walked out of the Divinity School.

"How about some lunch?" asked Neville after a few moments.

"Sounds great. Where?"

"The Turf?"

"You read my mind." Cade gave Neville a friendly pat on the back as they walked toward the exit.

28

AFTER LUNCH, Neville and Cade parted ways. Neville was staying in Oxford for the night and had offered to accompany Cade to the Tower of London the next day so that together they might have a better chance of finding Rachael and Sarah. Cade agreed to pick him up in Oxford and was glad Neville didn't ask him to explain why he was considering such a wild goose-chase. He was willing to do almost anything to see if he could find them, and he couldn't just sit in Bridgett's cottage any longer.

Cade went from the Turf past the Bodleian. As he walked along Catte Street toward the Radcliffe Camera, he paused in the square and eyed the tall steeple of St. Mary the Virgin, recalling his harrowing chase up into the steeple on that long ago night. He buttoned his overcoat and resumed walking to High Street. He had arranged to visit Robert and Rose Thompson later in the afternoon.

Heading down the High, he saw Magdalen tower looming ahead. That sight brought another rush of memories of those years spent as a student at Magdalen. Peering at the summit of the tower, he recalled the peaceful August evening he'd stood on the roof and prayed. That night, he'd certainly never envisioned how rocky his life's journey would become. In many ways, he'd virtually abandoned his faith. Not by conscious decision so much as an imperceptibly increasing negligence that carried him further away from God. Just the type of steps C. S. Lewis had written about, he mused with chagrin.

Because it was the Christmas break, Oxford was much quieter than usual. He quickened his pace toward Magdalen, wondering if anyone at the college would remember him. He went through the gate and looked into the windows of the lodge. The porter waved, and Cade recognized Mr. Henry, a thin, wiry man, who always seemed to be in a hurry. Cade returned the wave and went into the lodge.

"Good afternoon, Mr. Bryson," said the porter immediately. It was good to be remembered.

"Hello, Mr. Henry, and how are you?"

"Very well, thanks, but quite busy." Cade had to stifle a laugh.

"Mind if I walk around a bit?"

"Not at all. Old members are welcome anytime."

Cade was not used to being called an old member. "By the way, could I borrow an access card to look around the library?"

"Certainly. Here, take this one."

"Thanks. I'll return it on my way out."

Standing in the front quad, Cade took a deep breath of December air, which burned his lungs, and exhaled it like a smoking dragon. Before he returned to Oxford this week, his Magdalen days had become a remote, dream-like chapter from his past. Now that he was here, however, the years melted away and it seemed as though he'd never left. He walked first to the right and opened the door to the chapel. Inside the antechapel, he studied the stark black and white stained glass, and then entered the main chapel. The long wooden tiered benches on each side brought back memories of Evensong services. He paused for a few moments, then left the chapel to resume his tour. The college was virtually deserted. He walked around the ancient Cloister Quad and up the steps to see the empty dining hall before continuing around the Cloisters and toward New Buildings, walking past C. S. Lewis's old rooms. As if on cue, the Magdalen Tower clock began its timeless toll. Each new view or sound evoked more memories.

Passing under the giant plane tree, where Rachael had first

confessed her love to him, he thought of Zeke, James's beloved golden retriever, but most of all, he thought of Rachael. Suffocating guilt and shame swept over him. He desperately wanted to see her. It had taken the shock of his life to awaken him to the true love of his life. He berated himself for the false gods he had somehow worshipped: money, prestige, work, success, social status ... . But worst of all, the god of self.

He thought about the Soulbane Reports he'd read again on the plane to England. He had fallen prey to the stratagems that Soulbane had gleefully reported on. How? He had even been warned, yet ignored them. Now, the consequences were crashing down on him. Yes, he thought optimistically, he would put his marriage back in order and publish the reports. Then the shocking episode with Sherry flashed in his mind, and his optimism vanished.

At the thought of the reports, Cade walked briskly toward the library, putting aside for the moment his regrets for past failures. He entered the library and quickly went up the stairs. He had the place to himself; the dreary afternoon cast a pall of gloom around the room. He turned on some lights and immediately relived the night when, upon returning from the Turf, he had discovered the strange correspondence that had started it all. He walked quickly to *the* spot where he'd first found the letters and where, a year later, he had found another one, in which Foulheart had gloated over stealing Cade's computer.

He scoured the shelves for some sign of more correspondence, but found nothing. The muffled sound of the Magdalen Tower clock reminded him it was time for him to head to Iffley for his visit with the Thompsons. He took one last glance around the library and returned to the porter's lodge.

* * *

"Cade, how lovely to see you," said Rose Thompson when she opened the door. She was wearing a plain, dark blue dress, and was wiping her hands with a kitchen towel. A delightful aroma of baking filled the house.

Cade smiled and gave her a hug. "And you, Rose. It's been a long time, but I've thought of you often."

"Robert has been so looking forward to seeing you, Cade." A picture flashed in Cade's mind of Robert Thompson, the porter at Magdalen who had befriended him. He thought of Robert's broad, reddish face and tremendous smile, and his effervescent spirit. He recalled the many walks and bike rides the two had taken together, and although Mr Thompson was in his seventies when Cade was a student, he had clearly kept himself fit.

"Robert is pottering out in the garden, restless as always. He just went out there, so go and bring him in from this dreadful cold weather. I'll have tea ready in a jiffy."

Cade walked through the house just behind Rose, savouring the cozy living room with its brown cloth sofa and pictures, where he'd spent many happy hours on previous visits. He was eager to see his dear friend again.

As they came to the kitchen, Rose said, "I hope you're hungry."

"You know how much I love your cooking." Cade delighted in the warm, heavenly smell of roast beef and fresh baked bread.

"I've got some scones baking," she added, confirming what Cade's nose had led him to hope.

"You know they're my favorite. Say, where's Clive?" He recalled the first time they met in the Thompson's garden. Clive had been about thirty, with bright red hair and freckles. He possessed a delightful, simple innocence, and Cade quickly grew very fond of him, as did everyone else.

"He's working at Magdalen now and really enjoys it. The students like him, I think. He should be here later. He'll be very excited to see you, Cade. Now, you run along to the garden."

As he reached the door to the garden, Cade remembered that the last time he'd been here was the night before his wedding, when the Thompsons had hosted a beautiful party for their friends and families. It had been one of those dreamy English July evenings, with clear blue skies, a soft gentle breeze, and later a full moon –

right out of some fairy tale romance. He and Rachael had been blissfully happy that night. Cade could still taste Robert's special Pimm's punch. Today, the garden was in its winter mode, with little color other than a few holly bushes with red berries.

Cade quickly opened the door and had to conceal a gasp as he stepped into the garden. His vision of the robust Robert Thompson was shattered by the sight of a thinner, paler figure, his head covered by a hat, throwing breadcrumbs to two small birds.

"Robert!" He walked briskly toward his friend. The old man turned, and a great smile broke across his face. In a surprisingly strong voice, he said, "My dear friend … I never thought I'd see you again." The two men embraced. "It's wonderful to see you!" Robert said in an excited tone as he leaned back, staring at Cade.

"And you. How are you?"

"The better for seeing you. Bless you, Cade."

Cade eyed his friend. Although the body was frailer, he saw that Robert's eyes still twinkled with warmth and life.

Robert said, "We have a lot of catching up to do. How is Rachael? And Sarah? We've had such lovely visits from them. Sarah is a beautiful little girl – and so intelligent."

At the mention of Rachael and Sarah, Cade felt his face redden with embarrassment. He decided this was not the time to go into all that. Instead, he replied simply, "They're fine. I'll bring them next time."

"All the better." Robert winked and laughed. "Here, let's go inside and warm up."

The two sat in the living room near the fire and talked about what they had been doing for the past ten years. In a few minutes, Rose brought them a pot of tea and some shortbread. Outside, a bare branch brushed against the front window, as the chilling north wind flung winter into every crevice of the cottage.

After a good while of catching up, Robert asked, "And tell me, whatever happened with those reports you found?"

"Actually, I … I never did anything with them." Cade looked

down and shuffled his feet. "I guess between law school and my work and family, I just never got around to it."

"Oh, I see. Well, I still have that computer disk you asked me to keep. Do you want it back?"

"No, you keep it for now. I've actually been thinking lately about publishing them."

Robert took the teapot back to the kitchen, and Cade stood to stretch. He wandered over to the mantel and saw the familiar picture of Mr. Thompson and C. S. Lewis standing together near Addison's Walk.

His thoughts were interrupted when Robert came in with more tea and told him the latest news from Magdalen. The old man finally said, "I don't mean to pry, but how are things with Rachael?"

Cade looked out the window, avoiding Robert's gaze.

"Actually, things aren't going too well. I ... I haven't paid much attention to her lately, and we seem to have drifted apart."

Cade looked at his friend, expecting the worst. Instead, Robert was nodding with a knowing look. "Marriage is hard ... maybe the hardest thing you'll ever do. But, it's a wonderful thing. And Rachael loves you very much."

He felt a lump in his throat and was about to speak, when the front door flew open. A figure in a heavy coat, gloves, and a wool cap entered the room.

"Hello son. Come in and warm up."

Cade gave him a bear hug. "Hello, Clive, it's good to see you." Clive had put on weight, but still had bright red hair and a mischievous grin.

Clive's face took on a puzzled look. "Hi Cade. I didn't think you'd be back this soon."

"What do you mean?" Cade replied. Robert Thompson's smile disappeared. He had already confided that Clive seemed more confused lately.

"You know, you were just here yesterday," Clive said in a matter-of-fact tone.

"Let me get you a cup of tea." Robert had a grave look on his face as he poured a cup for his son.

"You didn't seem yourself yesterday," Clive continued. "I thought maybe you weren't feeling well."

"What do you mean?" Cade was both perplexed and alarmed.

"You just weren't very friendly and didn't even ask about Papa and Mother. All you wanted was your computer thing."

"What computer thing?" Cade was trying not to yell now.

"You know, that little computer disk you asked Papa to keep for you."

Cade stood, his heart racing. "Clive, don't kid with me."

"I'm *not* kidding." Clive had a pout on his face and turned red.

"What did you do with the disk?" Cade was becoming quite concerned.

"You remember ... I got it from the drawer in Papa's room and gave it to you."

"And you say this was yesterday?" Robert looked intently at his son.

"Yes ... yes."

"But why didn't you say anything to me when I got home?" asked Robert.

"Because ... Cade said to keep it a secret. He said he wanted to come back and surprise you later."

Cade turned to Robert. "Maybe you better check for the disk." Robert nodded and went off to do just that.

"Clive, are you sure it was me?" Cade paced in front of the fireplace.

"Of course I am. But you weren't very nice to me yesterday."

"I'm sorry," replied Cade, wondering what else he should say.

Robert returned, and his pale face gave the dreaded answer. He looked at Cade with wide eyes and just shook his head. Finally, he whispered, "It was there several days ago, but it's gone now."

Cade sat on the sofa, his face in his hands. *First Sherry. And now this.*

*   *   *

Driving back to the Cotswolds that night, Cade thought of many things: Reverend Brooke, the Thompsons, the reports, the mirror, the missing disk, and Rachael. He was on the verge of total panic. He just *had* to find his wife and daughter. But how?

29

A S SHE DROVE to work on Thursday morning, Lauren's mind was a thousand miles away. She had not slept much for the last week. The abrupt way in which Ian had left her and Sarah at Magdalen had been bothering her. She had also felt a strange restlessness at the Evensong service there, and had been challenged by Reverend Cooper's sermon. All of this combined to make her uneasy and pensive.

She believed she was in love with Ian, and yet she really knew little about him. At first, his mysterious ways had attracted her to him. His dark, handsome physique and intriguing manner captivated her, and she was flattered by the attention he paid her. As time passed, however, some aspects of the relationship seemed increasingly odd: he'd never invited her to his place, and often seemed to disappear for days on end, with little explanation other than it involved his research. Their relationship really hadn't progressed, and Lauren realized that her infatuation had created an illusion about their romance.

When she got out of her car at the lab, she quickly put on her overcoat, stung by the bitterly cold wind that whisked through the leafless trees. The dark clouds hung like huge gray balloons low in the sky.

"Good morning, Dr. St. John," said the receptionist as Lauren entered.

Lauren nodded, but said nothing, her mind preoccupied. She

stuffed her gloves into the pocket of her overcoat and unbuttoned it, without removing it.

"Oh, Dr. St. John," said the receptionist, waving her hand to catch Lauren's attention, "Dr. Elliott said he needs to see you immediately."

Lauren nodded and headed toward her boss's office, wondering why he wanted to see her. His door was shut when she arrived, but he called loudly for her to enter when she knocked.

"Ah, Lauren," he said with a hint of urgency.

"What is it?"

"Please sit down." As Lauren did so, he walked over and shut the door. Taking off his reading glasses, he continued, "I have something confidential to discuss with you." Lauren shifted in her chair.

"We've had a suspicion that some of our confidential research has been leaked. Special Branch have been looking into this. I'm not going to beat around the bush. We suspect it's Ian Chadwick."

Lauren gasped loudly.

"We know you have been seeing Dr. Chadwick."

"Well, I … yes." Lauren looked down, shocked, wondering if she was about to be accused of something.

"Let me be frank. We're deeply concerned about Chadwick." Lauren felt sick to her stomach. "Is it possible you inadvertently passed on information to him?"

Lauren tucked her hair behind her ear, as she racked her brain.

"I can't think of anything. Are you sure it's Ian?"

"We're not positive, but several odd incidents point towards him." He proceeded to fill her in on some of their suspicions and asked her to assist them in their investigation of Chadwick.

After she left Dr. Elliott's office, she stopped in the hallway, dumbfounded. Despite her better judgement, Lauren marched straight to Ian's office. The door, as usual, was shut. She stopped outside and hesitated, then knocked. No one answered. She tried the door and it opened.

The lights were off, and the office was dim in the gray morning light. Lauren flipped on the lights and walked in. She searched his desk, wondering where Ian was now. She saw no calendar or appointment book. In fact, his office appeared to have been stripped bare. Just as she was about to give up, she spied something crumpled up on the floor, where it had apparently missed the trash bin next to it. She bent over, picked it up, and unraveled it. She put her hand to her mouth. It was a photograph of Rachael! Immediately, Lauren heard Sarah's voice resounding in her head, "What's a dreamboat?"

Lauren stared at the photograph, unable to move. *Is it possible that Rachael and Ian are having an affair? Are they some sort of spies? Impossible! Or is it?* Now that Lauren thought about it, it had been odd how she and Rachael had met and strangely coincidental that she was living in the same village. Wrapped inside the photograph was a yellow piece of paper with a scribbled note, "Meet R at Tower of London, 3:00 p.m. Thursday."

That's today. Lauren glanced at her watch. She looked around for more indications of any liaison between the two, but saw nothing. Lauren stepped hurriedly out of the room and bounded up the stairs to her office. Her mind was a kaleidoscope of thoughts. She hung her coat on the door and sat in her desk chair, trying to catch her breath, and angrily threw the photograph and note against the wall.

Leaning her head back, she closed her eyes and sighed. She quickly dialed the front desk receptionist and asked, "Yes, is Ian Chadwick in the building today?"

"Let me check. One moment please."

Lauren became aware that she was tapping her fingers vigorously on the desk, and self-consciously made a fist to stop.

"No, Dr. St. John, we show him as being out today."

"Do you know where he is?" Her tone was more emphatic than she wished.

"I'm afraid not. Is there any message?"

"No ... no thanks." Lauren absentmindedly put down the phone. She jumped to her feet. Without another thought, she grabbed her coat and walked out of her office. When she came to the front desk, she said quickly, "I just remembered a meeting in London this afternoon. I'll be gone the rest of the day."

"Right. Thank you, Dr. St. John." The receptionist jotted something with a pencil.

Lauren almost ran to her car, not bothering to put on her coat. She tossed it in the back and jammed the car into reverse. As she drove down the M-40 to London, her heart raced. Her stomach was in knots. What would she see if she went to the Tower of London this afternoon? Had Rachael betrayed her? A wave of shame came over her, which she tried to ignore. Were Ian and Rachael spies? Lovers? Both? Should she call Dr. Elliott? Instead of searching for an answer, however, she merely sped up.

*   *   *

"It's good of you to take me with you," said Neville as they drove in Cade's rental car toward London.

"I was glad to have a chance to get out and do something. I don't like waiting around for my wife and daughter, and I appreciate having some company." Cade wondered if he should tell Neville the true reason he wanted to try and find Rachael and Sarah. After the revelation by Clive yesterday, he was stricken with fear for their safety, and he was frustrated that he had no way to reach them.

"I don't get around much these days, and I've been telling myself I'd like to go to the RAF Memorial one more time." He was looking out the side window. Cade had agreed to take Neville to the RAF Memorial near Runnymede on their way to London.

"I've never been there," replied Cade. "I'm interested in seeing it. And, I appreciate your willingness to go with me to the Tower of London to see if we might get lucky and surprise my family."

The two rode in silence for a while, then Cade said, "Neville, you've never mentioned a family."

Neville stroked his chin. "I never had one. It just never worked out."

When Neville didn't elaborate, Cade changed the subject. "Tell me more about James Brooke and his Spitfire days."

Neville appeared to brighten. "James was an extraordinary man, Cade. In his younger days, he was quite the athlete, especially cricket and rugby. Then, the War came along, and he volunteered for the RAF. He became a Spitfire pilot and was one of the best – and among the most highly decorated."

"James never mentioned any of that." Cade was amazed to learn this about his old friend.

"I'm not surprised. He was like that. A most talented individual, and yet truly humble. That's why he made such a wonderful priest."

"What did you think of Professor Periwinkle's lecture?"

"I thought it was quite good, at least until he said that part about needing a vivid imagination to believe in devils." Neville laughed heartily. "As I'm sure you know Cade, we might quote Hamlet to the Professor, 'There are more things in heaven and earth, Horatio, than are dreamt of in your philosophy.'"

"Actually, I'm glad you mentioned that. I ... I have something to tell you. I hope you won't think this is crazy." He was so desperate, he'd decided he had to tell someone, and Neville was the only logical choice.

"No, what?" Neville turned his head toward Cade, a look of concern on his face.

Cade proceeded to tell Neville a brief summary of his entire adventures, from the initial discovery of Foulheart's letters to the strange conversation with Clive the prior afternoon. Neville nodded his head several times while he spoke, but said nothing. Cade omitted the story about Sherry, however, much too embarrassed to mention it.

When he finished, Neville said, "Cade, this is a serious matter. You've got something very valuable, and obviously this Foulheart fellow wants it back. Do you still have your disk?"

"Yes."

"Good. You need to keep it in a safe place. Let me give this some more thought."

Cade was about to ask Neville something else, when he saw the sign to the RAF Memorial and turned off. A sign noted that the memorial "bears the names of twenty thousand who gave their lives for freedom."

As the two men walked through the entrance, Cade stopped in the open, grass courtyard to admire the beauty of the memorial. Around the courtyard were white stone arched columns, with arched windows behind. Neville walked on quietly ahead of Cade. He stepped through one of the open archways and slowly shuffled along one of the walls. His hand occasionally ran over the wall itself.

Cade walked up for a closer inspection. The place was silent save the wind, and deserted, but for the two men. Cade's fingers stung from the cold. He was about to say something, but didn't when he saw that Neville was tracing his fingers over names inscribed on the memorial. For the first time, Cade saw the names: thousands and thousands of names. His heart thumped. Everywhere he looked there were names: but these were not just sterile names inscribed in stone – these represented sons, and fathers, and friends, and brothers, and husbands. Oddly, it was not Churchill's words, but Lincoln's Gettysburg Address that came to his mind: 'We cannot dedicate, we cannot consecrate, we cannot hallow this ground. The brave men, living and dead, who struggled here have consecrated it far beyond our poor power to add or detract.' Cade thought of his own shallow and selfish life of these past years as he faced this memorial to such courage. He vowed to himself right then that he would change his life for the better. More of Lincoln's words flooded his mind, '... that from these honored dead we take increased devotion to that cause for which they gave the last full measure of devotion ... .'

Cade felt as if he were one inch tall, in the face of the courage and sacrifice of these men "for God and Country." A lump caught in his throat. He silently stepped forward to get a closer look at the names, names of strangers for whom he nevertheless mourned. He stole a glance at Neville, who was standing several feet away, transfixed, staring at the wall. Tears streamed down his face, yet he made no attempt either to hide them or wipe them away. Cade stood silently in the cold, in awe of this most sacred of moments, before continuing his survey of the memorial. He spied an inscription etched in the north window of the memorial. Winged angels were engraved on either side of the words he read silently:

If I climb up into Heaven, Thou art there;
If I go to Hell, Thou art there also.
If I take the wings of the morning
And remain in the uttermost parts of the sea,
Even there also shall Thy hand lead me;
And Thy right hand shall hold me.

The inscription noted it was from the 139th Psalm. The wind whispered around the memorial: was it repeating the names? Or, maybe the wind spoke immortal words – of bravery, sacrifice, and honor. Cade felt both shame and resolve as he stood silently before the names of these valiant men. Out of the corner of his eye, he saw a movement and turned to see Neville standing stiffly at attention before the memorial, his hair lifted by the breeze. Abruptly, Neville raised his hand ... and saluted.

30

LAUREN WAS in an emotional tug of war. She almost hated herself for foolishly driving all the way to London to look for Ian and Rachael, and yet, she couldn't stop herself any more than she could cease breathing. It was early afternoon when she arrived. She wanted to get to the Tower of London in time to find a place to look for them without being seen. She parked near Tower Hill, jumped out of the car and locked the door. She was oblivious to the bitter cold, the heavy traffic, and the other pedestrians as she walked toward the Tower.

She stopped in a small shop and bought a coffee and a sandwich. Back on the sidewalk, she sipped the coffee, savoring the warm liquid, as its smoky heat was quickly obliterated by the stiff breeze. Glancing at her watch, she found it was already after two. Near the entrance through Middle Tower, she stopped momentarily to survey the ancient fortress, whose mute stone walls kept many of history's secrets.

The Tower appeared almost deserted this bleak, December afternoon, and Lauren wondered where she could observe any visitors and yet not be conspicuous. Just as she passed under Byward Tower, Lauren saw two men come around the corner walking toward her. One was a tall, thin older man in a topcoat, with silver hair, walking beside a tall, younger man, in a blue down jacket, with thick blonde hair and blue eyes. The younger man seemed somehow familiar, but she couldn't figure out why. A

Yeoman Warder standing nearby and these two were the only tourists evident in the tower. As they walked past her, she heard the older man say, "I'm sorry we didn't find them." And then, they were past her. Lauren glanced at Traitor's Gate and walked into the main courtyard. She spied off to the left the spot where Anne Boleyn and others were beheaded, and the White Tower in the center of the courtyard. *Where can I go?* She finally decided to go up onto the wall walkway near the Wakefield and Bloody Towers, which would give her a view of the courtyard, but allow her to remain almost hidden from view. Two black ravens flew down and perched on a stone wall near her, as she found a place from which to mount her vigil.

Lauren continually glanced at her watch, which suddenly seemed to be going at half-speed. Although her hands were almost numb in the biting cold, she didn't dare go inside and give up her vantage spot. About five minutes to three, she drew a deep breath when she saw two figures come into the courtyard: a tall, dark haired woman in a dark blue coat, holding hands with a little girl, wearing pink mittens and a pink wool cap. Lauren instinctively ducked behind the turret. Even from this distance, she recognized Rachael and Sarah. Rachael was gesturing toward the Waterloo Barracks that house the Crown Jewels. They walked into the middle of the courtyard and sat on a bench. A few minutes later, Rachael stood and waved, and Lauren looked over to see Ian striding quickly into the courtyard, his long dark hair bouncing as he walked. Lauren stared down at them, her heart thumping. Ian walked up, kissed Rachael on the cheek, and picked up Sarah. Lauren was dumbstruck. Was it possible this woman whom she'd come to count as a friend had betrayed her? Had the man she loved betrayed her as well? She stood, breathless, her heart pounding, as the three of them walked toward the barracks. Ian gestured to a Beefeater, who walked over to them. The Beefeater took Sarah by the hand and began walking. Ian and Rachael followed behind.

Lauren had seen enough. Her disbelief turned to fury.

"May I assist you?" said someone behind Lauren. She turned to see another Beefeater standing there.

Taking a deep breath, and desperate to follow Rachael and Ian, she replied, "Oh, no, I was just walking around."

"Please, allow me to give you a personal tour. As you can see, it's very quiet today."

"Thank you, but I really must go. I'd love to some other time."

"As you wish, madam." The warder tipped his hat, smiled, and walked away.

Lauren turned and looked into the courtyard. It was deserted. She hurried down the steps two at a time. Not a soul was to be seen anywhere when she reached the courtyard. The only sound was the wind whipping through the trees, and the ravens squawking above. She shivered at the stark, wintry scene inside this fortress of blood. Marching toward the barracks, she stopped dead in her tracks. *What would I say to them? How can I explain my presence?*

Lauren was sick to her stomach. Had Ian, the first man she had ever truly fallen in love with, been stolen away by Rachael? Suddenly, all Lauren wanted was to be far away from London. Without a moment's hesitation, she turned and rushed out of the Tower. She wanted to blame the cold wind for her watery eyes, but she knew better.

It wasn't long after she set off before she was stuck in rush hour traffic. Lauren banged her hands on the wheel, but the traffic didn't move. She picked up the cell phone to call Dr. Elliott, but put it down. What in the world would she say to him? How could she explain this? Life was once again caving in on her. She screamed at the top of her lungs, but no one in the cars around her seemed to notice.

*   *   *

Cade dropped Neville off near St. Mary's and drove to Bridgett's house. It was dark and still bitterly cold, although the wind had finally died down. The clouds had dispersed and thousands of twinkling stars shone in the clear winter sky. Tired and depressed, he rushed inside the cottage, set a fire, and put on the kettle for tea. It had been a long shot to go to the Tower of London hoping to run into Rachael and Sarah. Cade and Neville had walked around in the cold for over an hour. The Tower had been virtually deserted and, finally, they'd given up.

He sat near the fire warming his hands. When the phone rang, Cade sprang to it, certain that Rachael was calling.

"Hello," he answered cheerfully.

"Cade is that you? It's Martin here," said the voice, and Cade's heart sank.

"Yes, Harry," Cade replied, irritated.

"Listen, Bryson, I don't know what the hell's going on, but you damn well better give me some answers. I told you to stay here, and now I find you've gone to England. Zac Pickering is breathing down my neck, threatening legal action. And, he says he going to the Bar Association with a grievance against you and the firm."

Cade knew he had to be dreaming. This couldn't be happening.

Martin continued, "I had our computer department do an internal check, and they've confirmed what Pickering says."

"What?" Cade almost yelled into the phone. "That's impossible!"

"Impossible? All I know is that your computer was used to register the exact proprietary names Pickering accused you of stealing."

"I can't believe it. Harry, I'm telling you it's not true. You believe me don't you? You know I wouldn't do something that stupid."

There was a long, excruciating silence that said more to Cade than a million words and, after a cough, Martin said, "Well, there's another – a bigger – problem."

"What's that?"

"It's the little bag of cocaine we found hidden in your credenza."

""But that's ... that's ... ." Cade *was* screaming now.

"Listen. My job is to protect this firm. I want your ass back over here pronto, or else I'll have no choice but to have you arrested."

"But, Harry, I'm innocent. And, I have my family to consider … ."

"To hell with your family. The firm's reputation is on the line. Now, listen closely … ."

"No, Harry, you listen," said Cade angrily. "My family comes first, and then I'll be back to defend my integrity. Bye, Harry."

"Dammit, Bryson, you'd better … ."

"So long, Harry." Cade slammed down the phone. He became aware of a loud, screeching whistle from the kettle. His mind raced with myriad thoughts while pouring the steaming water into the teapot.

He picked up the phone and dialed. When Jim Turner answered, he said, "Jim, this is Cade."

"Hey, man, what in the world is going on? There are a lot of rumors swirling around here."

"I'm not surprised. Listen, Jim, you just have to trust me. They're not true. I need to ask a favor – as a friend, not as a lawyer. Now, if you don't think you can help me, I understand …"

"You don't need to explain. If you hadn't taken me under your wing when I started here, I'd probably still be floundering. Now, what can I do for you?"

"I need some information on someone."

"Shoot."

"Zac Pickering."

"What!" exclaimed Turner loudly over the phone.

"I know, Jim. It sounds crazy. You know Pickering's a bigwig, married to a senator's daughter. For some reason I can't figure out, he's trying to frame me. Can you do some checking – off the record, of course – and see what you can find out?"

"No problem."

"Jim, I won't forget this."

"Don't mention it. Just bring me a bottle of good Scotch when you return."

Cade needed to make one more phone call. He tried Eric first, but got a voice mail saying Eric was out of town. He left a message, then called Philip.

When Philip answered, Cade stammered breathlessly, "Hey, this is Cade. Listen, I don't have a lot of time to explain. I'm in deep trouble.

"What is it? What can I do?"

"I don't know. I just need to talk." Cade proceeded to tell Philip the events that had transpired with Harry and Pickering just before he left for England and about Harry's phone call.

" ... . We've known each other a long time, Philip. You know I wouldn't steal some Internet names, much less do coke."

"I know. What do you want me to do?"

"I ... I just can't call Dad. Not yet anyway. Will you check on him? You're almost like a son to him. Just let him know that, no matter what he hears from Harry Martin, it's not true."

"Cade, you know I'll do anything for you..." After a pause, Philip cleared his throat. "but I'm not the one who needs to talk to your Dad."

Cade's stomach tightened. He knew in his heart Philip was right, but he dreaded the thought of calling his father.

Philip continued, "After all, he *is* your father. You've got to level with him. You're in over your head and mine. Your Dad will know what to do. You have to trust him, Cade."

"You're right," Cade replied dejectedly. One reason he liked Philip so much was he'd always admired his friend's common sense and good judgement. "Okay. I guess I'd better call him."

"It's really for the best. Tell your father if there's anything I can do, to let me know. Hang in there. Everything's going to work out. You're in my prayers"

After they hung up, Cade slumped down into a chair. His world was crumbling all around him. He threw a log on the fire and stared at the blaze. He'd rather do almost anything than call his father. Cade had spent his whole life trying to live up to his father's expectations, and now he was in the middle of a raging tempest. The last thing he wanted to do was to let his father know he was a failure. Nevertheless, he took a deep breath and dialed the number.

An hour and a half later, Cade put down the phone and drew a deep breath of relief. He walked over to the fireplace to warm himself, only to discover the fire was nothing but a few dying embers. He reflected on his talk with his father. He'd told his dad everything, the letters, the reports, Malta, Sewanee, Mardi Gras, Zac, Harry and, yes, even Sherry. Then, he'd braced himself for the inevitable tirade.

To Cade's surprise, however, his father was supportive and non-judgmental. His only rebuke was to ask why Cade hadn't confided in him long before. Son and father both cried as they realized the wall that they'd built between them. His father promised to do everything he could to help his son, even to the point of offering to come to England. Cade teared up again as he recalled the conversation.

He jumped when the phone rang again. He grabbed at it, assuming it was his father calling back.

"Hello," he said expectantly.

"Bryson?" queried a gravelly male voice Cade didn't immediately recognize.

"Speaking."

"This is Zac Pickering."

"What the hell ..." began Cade, his anger rising.

"Cut the crap and listen. All I want is the disks."

"What ... what disks?" replied Cade, profoundly confused.

"You know, the disks that have those reports you found."

"What ... how?" Cade, the dimmest light beginning to dawn on him, was still bemused.

"Listen. All I know is you've got some disks someone wants very badly. My ass is on the line and I need them."

"You mean all this is because of you?" Cade said, sarcasm spewing out.

"That's right, Sherlock, I'm in deep trouble, and your disks are my way out."

"But ... but ..." Cade's mind was racing. "What did you say to Harry Martin about me?"

"Oh, that," laughed Zac. "You remember that day I showed up at lunchtime?"

"Yeah," said Cade, barely above a whisper.

"While we were eating lunch, my colleague, who you so conveniently allowed to use your office, did a search on your computer. He couldn't find anything that looked like these reports I'm supposed to find, so we went to Plan B."

"You ... set me up? Listen, you little...." yelled Cade.

"Now, now, sticks and stones, ..." Zac replied in a patronizing tone.

"You'll never be able to prove anything." Cade was pacing back and forth.

"Do you know who I am son? I'll squash you. Don't mess with me, Bryson. Now listen, we can make this hard or we can make this easy."

"Talk," said Cade, breathing hard to control his anger and panic. Zac's little charade was becoming all too clear to Cade, and he wondered if his legal career was ruined. Harry Martin had told him how powerful Zac Pickering was.

"Just give me those disks, and I'll tell Martin it was all an honest mistake."

"If I give them to you, how can I trust you to keep your end of the bargain?"

"You can't, but if you don't give them to me, you're toast."

"How did you find me here anyway?"

"Oh, I just told Martin he'd better tell me how to contact you or else I'd take the firm down, too. Martin was only too happy to oblige."

Cade grimaced and pounded his fist on the table.

"Now, when can I get those disks?"

"But why do you want them?"

"I don't have time to explain, Bryson. I'm up to my ass in alligators, and someone wants your disks bad enough to blackmail me. I need them, pronto!"

"Are you the one who broke into my house?"

"After we couldn't find anything on your computer, that was the next logical place to look. The idiot told me he couldn't find them there either. I knew you were at the bar that night celebrating our victory. From the look of things with that brunette bombshell you were talking to, I didn't think you'd be home anytime soon."

"Why me?" said Cade, not really meaning to ask that out loud.

"Guess it's just your lucky day."

"Well, Zac, as you know, I'm in England, and I don't have the disks with me," he lied, trying to buy time to think.

"You've got until December thirty-one to get them to me." Zac's voice was rising. "I don't care how you do that, but if I don't have the disks by then, it's curtains for you."

"Right," said Cade softly, dejectedly. He dropped the phone on the floor and slowly bent over to pick it up. After these calls, he wondered if he should even put it back on the hook, and opted not to. He couldn't stand any more calls like those. He'd talk to his father later, after he got his wits together.

He slumped into a nearby chair, unable to believe what he'd just heard. He'd been set up and blackmailed. All for the disk he'd ignored all these years, while he worked so hard on getting ahead in the world. Cade laughed derisively at himself, all too aware of the irony of his situation.

His head was spinning from the phone calls. He tried to sit and contemplate his dilemma, but couldn't. He saw his career and his family going down the tubes, and he could think of no way out. He couldn't believe how Pickering had set him up. How could he defend himself? He had a new appreciation for persons unjustly accused, especially those powerless to defend themselves.

Edgar's words in *King Lear* popped into his head, "The worst is not so long as we can say, 'This is the worst.'" *Well, at least it can't get any worse than this.* Cade would soon regret this naive assumption.

31

N O LONGER ABLE to sit still, Cade grabbed his coat and rushed out the door, with no destination in mind. The cold air hit him like a blast of ice water. He took a deep, burning breath and exhaled slowly, watching the frosty breath reflecting in the street lamp's yellow glow.

He struck out purposefully, yet aimlessly.

The loud blast of a car horn shattered his thoughts, and Cade instinctively dove to the side of the street. He skidded across the pavement, just missing being hit by the fast-moving car. The car screeched to a halt just past him. The driver's side window came down, and a female voice screamed, " Moron! You could've been killed. Does Christmas really make you that suicidal?"

Cade lay on the street, face down, stunned by his close call and by the screaming woman. He turned over slowly, and could only see a dark figure inside the car. The door opened, and the woman, less anger in her voice, said, "Are … are you hurt?"

Cade responded after a moment's hesitation, "I don't think so. Just a bit dazed."

"Here, I'm a doctor. Let me have a look."

Cade sat up shakily. The yellow light from a street lamp illuminated the Jaguar that had almost hit him. Cade saw the outline of someone hastily getting out of the car.

Cade struggled haltingly to his feet. "I'm okay. Really."

By now the woman was standing right in front of him. She was tall, with straight hair that was halfway to her shoulders, although in the dim light he couldn't tell the color. Her face bore a look of alarm and concern.

"You're obviously not from around here. Are you sure you're all right?"

"Yes, quite sure, thank you. You gave me quite a scare."

"You weren't the only one! I thought I'd hit you when I saw you lying on the ground."

He managed a weak laugh. "I'm okay, really. Let me introduce myself. I'm Cade Bryson, and you're right, I'm not from around here." He was thankful to still be alive, much less unhurt.

A puzzled look seemed to cross the woman's face, and she stared, her mouth open. Finally, she said, "You're not ... you're not married to Rachael are you?"

"Well, yes, but how did you know?"

"I, ..." stammered the woman, who looked away, not meeting Cade's gaze. "My name is Lauren. Lauren St. John."

"Sorry to meet you like this, Lauren. Here, let's get off the street." The two of them were standing alone in the middle of the road, with her car running, the driver's door wide open.

"Right. Good idea."

"Say, you wouldn't happen to know where I could find Rachael, would you?"

"Actually ... I might," Lauren said in halting words. He sensed something wrong in her tone, which sent fear running through his veins.

"Would you like to come in my mother-in-law's cottage?" Cade was curious why she seemed so hesitant to talk about Rachael and his alarm increased.

"No thank you. I'd best be on my way."

"Is something wrong?"

"No," said Lauren, in almost a shout. "I mean ... "

Cade searched her face for a clue to her strange behavior, wondering what she was thinking.

She suddenly burst into tears, mystifying Cade. He didn't know what to do. Finally, he said, "What's wrong? I shouldn't have been wandering in the street. It's not your fault."

Lauren nodded her head, sniffling. She accepted his offer of a handkerchief and wiped her eyes.

"I think you'd better come in for a minute." He parked her car on the side of the street and took her by the arm. Lauren said nothing, but didn't resist. He led her to Bridgett's and, once inside, flung his coat on the kitchen counter. He noticed Lauren staring at it.

The two made small talk while Cade rekindled the fire. He looked at this attractive woman who'd almost run him over. Her eyelids were red and swollen, as if she had been crying for a long time, and her light green eyes were bloodshot. Her creamy complexion was smeared by eye makeup that ran down her cheeks. She nervously tucked her golden red hair behind her ear several times as they spoke, and her hands trembled slightly.

Cade handed her a mug of hot tea and sat across from her near the fire. She smiled, but it appeared forced. "Thanks."

"Are you sure everything's all right?" Cade was still baffled by her strange behavior.

Lauren gazed down at her mug. She tucked her hair behind her left ear again. Finally, she looked up. "I don't know how to say this to you. I don't even know you."

"Go ahead." He reached across and patted her arm to reassure her. "I've heard it all today anyway."

She tilted her head quizzically, "Well, … I …I believe that Rachael is having an affair with my boyfriend."

"What!" He jumped up from the chair, dropping his mug of tea on the floor. "That's impossible, not Rachael." Cade's temples were pounding.

"I certainly didn't intend to tell you. But I guess I'm pretty upset just now. I saw them … today … ."

"Where?" asked Cade, aware that his voice was raised and high pitched.

"At the Tower of London."

"But I was there today. I never saw Rachael."

"You were there?" She looked over at his coat. "Now I remember. I saw you."

"You saw me?"

"Yes, as I was coming in, you were leaving with an older man."

Cade sat, dumbfounded, staring at her. Finally, he said hoarsely, "Tell me what happened."

Lauren proceeded to tell him about meeting Rachael and their growing friendship. She also told him about Ian, and Sarah's question about him being a "dreamboat." She concluded with her discovery this morning of Rachael's picture in Ian's office, and her own trip to the Tower of London. He sat mute, unable to comprehend what he was hearing. *Not Rachael. Not my Rachael.*

"I was so upset, I guess I wasn't paying attention a while ago when I almost ran you over. I'm sorry, truly sorry."

"No, I'm the one who's sorry. Listen, I just don't know what to think about all this. I … I mean, I just can't believe it."

"Nor can I," said Lauren softly. Cade thought how intensely sad she looked.

He sat in silence for a long while, almost oblivious to Lauren. He thought he was prepared for anything, but he wasn't prepared for this.

She stood and brushed the wrinkles in her plaid skirt. "Listen, I need to go and you need time to think. I'd appreciate it if you wouldn't say anything just yet … about me spying on them. Not until we can both collect our thoughts."

"Let me drive you home," Cade said when he'd walked her to the car.

"Thanks, but I'm literally a stone's throw away." Lauren pointed in the direction of her house. "I'm sorry to meet you under these circumstances."

"Yeah, me too." Cade looked down, shuffling his feet.

She smiled weakly at Cade and patted his arm sympathetically.

As Lauren drove off, Cade groaned loudly, standing in the middle of the street. A dog barked somewhere nearby, and he began walking. He was totally crushed. He walked for a good while, mindless of the cold. Finally, however, his fingers stinging, he turned toward Bridgett's, when he looked up and saw the silhouette of the church steeple. Without making any conscious decision to do so, he walked into the church. It was almost completely dark, except for some dim lights up near the altar. He stuffed his hands into his pants pocket, hoping to warm them. The church was not heated, but still offered some relief from the biting cold.

He stood in front of the altar, near the communion rail, staring at the wooden cross placed on the communion table, in front of the pale, alabaster reredos of two figures on either side of the crucified Christ. His thoughts and emotions were a raging storm. He erupted, screaming at the top of his lungs, "Damn you, God! Don't you care at all? How could you let this happen?"

He spied a silver offering plate sitting on a nearby pew. He stooped over, picked it up, and hurled it, Frisbee-like, toward the altar. The plate crashed into the communion table and the metallic clang echoed throughout the church. The sound shocked Cade, and he gazed at the plate lying on the floor, then up at the carved figure of Christ on the cross, hovering over the altar.

The church was deathly still. "No," he whispered, "it isn't your fault, is it God? It's mine." As Cade reflected on this, the Soulbane Reports that he'd read on the plane flashed in his mind. He sat on the stone floor, put his head between his legs, and rocked back and forth.

Finally, he crawled over to the communion rail, knelt on the royal blue cushions and whispered, "God, I'm so sorry. I can't even think. Just help me, please, God." His hands gripped the wooden rail so tightly that his knuckles were white.

Neither God nor anyone else responded. He knelt in the silence, feeling as if he were nevertheless in the midst of a crashing waterfall. He looked up at the mute Christ figure and felt a combination of anger and despair. He was almost expecting the statue to speak. A red book lying on the floor at the end of the communion rail caught his attention. He struggled up, walked over and picked it up. The title read, *Holy Bible*. He sat in the first pew and quickly shuffled the pages, then closed the book with a thud. He stared at the lettering on the front. It had been a long time since he'd even bothered to open a Bible. He closed his eyes, and, on impulse, opened the Bible again. The book fell open at Psalms, and Cade focused on the beginning of Psalm 139:

> O LORD, thou hast searched me and known me! Thou knowest when I sit down and when I rise up; thou discernest my thoughts from afar. Thou searchest out my path and my lying down, and art acquainted with all my ways. Even before a word is on my tongue, lo, O LORD, thou knowest it altogether. Thou dost beset me behind and before, and layest thy hand upon me. Such knowledge is too wonderful for me; it is high, I cannot attain it.

He glanced up from the book toward the altar, his spine tingling as he recalled the recent visit to Runnymede Memorial, when he'd seen the inscription from this very Psalm. He considered the enormity of what he'd just read and sighed deeply. A noise from the rear of the church startled him. His heart skipped a beat. He leapt up and turned around.

"Who's there?" He squinted but it was too dark to see anything. He ran down the aisle to the door and flung it open, but saw no one. If anyone had been there, they had vanished in the dark and cold. He heard a rustling sound and stepped into the graveyard. The large yew tree rustled in the gentle wind. Maybe that's what he'd heard all along, he tried to tell himself.

The full moon cast a silver glow everywhere. Cade maneuvered around the gravestones in the eerie, pale light and dark shadows. He found Reverend Brooke's grave and stood in silence for several minutes, his lower lip quivering. Finally, he said shakily, "James,

I've really blown it. I let you down. I let Rachael down. I let everyone down. James, if only you were here to help me."

The tombstone, gray and shadowy in the moonlight, offered no consolation. He turned and walked away, the yew tree whispering its secrets as he trudged down the pathway.

32

CADE WALKED SLOWLY toward the cottage, in a stupor. He wanted to crawl in a hole and hide forever. He concentrated on literally putting one foot in front of the other. The bright moon illuminated the entire village.

He was as mentally, emotionally, and physically exhausted as he'd ever been in his life. The shock of Lauren's words reverberated in the deepest reaches of his heart. His regret over the way he had ignored his most precious earthly treasures knew no bounds. He was ready to make amends. *But is it too late?*

He sat wearily in a large, soft chair in Bridgett's living room, tilted his head back, closed his eyes, and took a deep breath. He was too weary and heartsick to worry about Harry Martin and Zac Pickering. But then, as with all bad dreams, Lauren's words intruded like cymbals, "I believe that Rachael is having an affair with my boyfriend." The fear of losing Rachael to someone else engulfed him.

His head resounded with the metallic clang of the offering plate he'd thrown at the altar.

Then, the Christ figure on the St. Mary's altar spoke to him, so softly he couldn't make out the words. He held up a mirror to the statue, but it's reflection was a black, hooded figure. Fleeting images of shattered mirrors and gold rings came and went.

Clang! Clang! His head jerked up. He was disoriented and thought he heard the collection plate hitting something again.

Ring. Ring. A noise was interrupting his dreams. The phone? He struggled up from the chair and stumbled toward it. The clock on the wall in Bridgett's kitchen read twelve forty-five. The dark windows confirmed it was still night.

Confused by being awakened from a dead, exhausted sleep, without thinking he picked up the phone sitting on the counter.

"Hello," he said hoarsely. The line was dead.

Ring. Ring. There it was again. More awake, he realized it was the doorbell. The doorbell? *But who would be here at this time of night? Could Lauren have come back?*

"Mother?" said the soft, female voice, when Cade reached the door. He was instantly alert as he recognized Rachael's voice.

He grabbed the door knob, ready to tear the hinges off, and yanked it open. What he saw stunned him. A virtual stranger was staring blankly at him. Rachael's hair was disheveled, her face pale, and her eyes red and puffy, with mascara streaked down her face.

"Rachael, what's happened?" Cade said in high-pitched tones, wondering if he was still dreaming.

Her eyes grew wide, but she remained motionless, like a mannequin.

"Rachael!" Cade's alarm was growing by the moment.

"Cade … what are … ?" Rachael said, softly, dreamily. She stared blankly ahead. Her face was uncharacteristically expressionless.

He stepped out and enclosed his wife in his arms. "I love you so much… ."

Rachael put her head against Cade's chest and sobbed. After a few moments, he held her at arm's length, looking questioningly into her tear-filled, reddened eyes and noticed for the first time that Rachael was holding Flopsy. Cade's alarm turned to terror. "Rachael, where's Sarah?"

At the mention of Sarah, Rachael lost any semblance of composure. He put his arm around her and virtually carried her inside. He sat her on the sofa and knelt in front of his wife. He shook her shoulders gently. "Rachael, talk to me. What's happened?

Where's Sarah?"

"She's … Sarah's been kidnapped." Rachael forced out the words between sobs.

"Kidnapped! That's impossible." Cade screamed, leaping to his feet. "How? When?"

Rachael was crying uncontrollably. She seemed to calm down somewhat as Cade became more and more agitated. She looked up at Cade and said in a whisper, "This afternoon, at the Tower of London."

"Who did it?" Cade's shock was turning to anger. "What did the police say?"

"I haven't gone to the police." She stared at the floor.

"What!" Cade was now pacing feverishly – hoping – praying – this was still part of a nightmare. "But Rachael, we *have* to call the police." With that, Cade started toward the phone in the kitchen.

"Wait!" Rachael's voice for the first time was strong, and the change in tone startled Cade, who stopped in his tracks and stared at her. "There's more," she said in a quieter tone.

He walked over and sat on the sofa beside her, taking her cold hands in his. A strange cloud came across her face. He was profoundly puzzled by Rachael's bizarre behavior.

Rachael looked up at him, intense sadness on her face. "I guess it really is over between us?"

He was dumbfounded. He looked into Rachael's eyes, and his heart melted. He'd never loved anyone like he did Rachael, and he'd never loved her more than at this instant. Yet the sparkle in her eyes that had caught his attention when they first met was vanquished, and replaced by … by indifference, Cade thought.

He felt her cold, soft fingers in his hand. Then, he suddenly understood and wanted to die. He instinctively looked down at their hands and lasered in on the finger where his wedding band had been from his wedding day until a week ago. He couldn't think what to say, but finally said, softly, "Rachael, no, it's not over. I love you more than anything in the world."

She looked blankly at him, with no warmth.

He squeezed her cold hands tightly. "Rachael, think. Where's Sarah? Why haven't you called the police?"

Cade felt his anger returning, knowing that he would personally kill anyone who did anything to harm his daughter. But nothing could have prepared him for what Rachael said next.

She looked at him, her eyes brimming with tears. "I ... I don't know how to say this ... but a devil kidnapped Sarah."

"A ... devil?" He repeated her word without comprehending it.

Rachael nodded. "He told me if I went to the police, I'd have no chance of ever seeing Sarah alive again. I've been trying to call Mother for hours, but the line was busy. That's why I came here. I thought something must have happened to her, too."

Cade remembered he'd taken the phone off the hook, and realized that's why the line was dead when he sleepily picked it up a few minutes before. He rushed over to put it on again. This all *had* to be a nightmare.

"Rachael, tell me *exactly* what happened." His emotions were swirling like a tornado, and he asked this question in an attempt to maintain some focus.

"Could you get me some water?" she asked.

Cade fetched her a glass, taking a big gulp himself before handing it to her. She took several sips. "We'd been having a wonderful holiday. I took Sarah to Salisbury, Bath, Stonehenge, and then London. I had met a woman here, who became a friend ... ."

"Do you mean Lauren?" Cade asked.

"Why yes. How did you know?" Rachael looked surprised.

"I met her tonight. But that doesn't matter now. Go on."

"Well, let's see.... Anyway, Lauren's boyfriend, a man named Ian Chadwick, called me before we left on our trip. He said he'd heard we were going to London, and that he was going to be there this week and had a friend who could give us a special tour of the Tower of London. I'd already been telling Sarah about the Tower, so that seemed like a wonderful thing to do."

Rachael began to take off her coat, and he quickly assisted her. He got up, stoked the fire and refilled her water glass. The clock now said one twenty-two.

When he sat again on the sofa, he took Rachael's hand and caressed it gently, looking into her eyes waiting to hear the rest of the story.

She cleared her throat. "We arrived at the Tower a few minutes early, and Ian showed up shortly after three. He introduced us to a Beefeater and said they would take us on a tour." Rachael began to cry again.

"It's okay, Rachael. Just tell me what happened." Cade felt a rising panic, as the enormity of this began to set in, but he couldn't let Rachael see his fear.

She resumed, "We ... we walked around. First, we went to see the Crown Jewels. Ian told me about the history of the place. I thought I knew a lot about the history of the Tower, but he seemed to know a great deal of detail I'd never heard before. I was impressed. At some point, I realized that the Beefeater and Sarah were not around. I called for Sarah, and Ian said I needn't bother, that Sarah was gone. I didn't understand at first. Then, he told me that he knew all about me – and Sarah – and you."

"Me?" Cade was incredulous.

"Yes. He said that they knew you'd found Soulbane's Reports... ."

"What! Rachael, tell me you're joking."

"If only I *were* joking ... . He ... he ... said that Sarah was somewhere safe, and that if I wanted to see her again, I'd better listen carefully. He told me that he wants your disks that contain the reports, and that he would meet me in four days at the New Globe Theatre in London at four in the afternoon to get them."

"Who is this Ian?"

"I ... I thought he was a friend of Lauren's, but ... ."

Cade spontaneously interjected, "Does that mean you're not having an affair with him?"

Rachael's head shot up, and she slapped him. He rubbed his

stinging cheek in shock. Rachael said, "Oh, Cade, I'm so sorry. I didn't mean it... ."

"No, Rachael, *I'm* the one who's sorry." He looked deeply into her eyes as he spoke. He knew he deserved it – and worse.

She whispered, "An affair? Whatever made you think something so preposterous?"

Before he could reply, Rachael said, "Oh, *now* I see. Lauren thought Ian and I were having an affair?"

Cade nodded.

She shook her head. "No Cade, I've always loved only you."

He put his arms around her and squeezed her tightly, as his own tears flowed freely. Finally, he kissed Rachael on the cheek and whispered in her ear, "Rachael, I'm so sorry for everything. I love you."

After a good while, he said quietly, "Please tell me what else happened."

"That's about it, really. He said he wanted the reports, and that I'd better not screw up. He said I'd better bring the disks, and that if I wanted to see Sarah alive, we'd better not dare keep a copy. He said if I called the police I'd never see Sarah again. I don't really remember much after that. He sort of disappeared around a corridor. I searched frantically all over the Tower for Sarah. She was nowhere to be seen. I wandered around for God knows how long. I kept trying to call Mum from a pay phone, but her line was always busy. Then, I really panicked thinking they had done something to Mum, too. I didn't know what to do, so I called your office from London, but only got your voice mail. I tried to call Mum one last time, but when the line was still busy, I rushed back. Where is my mother?" Rachael stood, a look of alarm on her face. "What are *you* doing here? Has something happened to her, too?" Hysteria was rising in Rachael's voice once again.

He stood and put his hands on her shoulders. "Your Aunt Charlotte fell and broke her hip. Your mother has gone to help her. It's a long story why I'm here. Let's just say I came to get you and

Sarah. I realized what a fool I've been. I got here several days ago and wanted to surprise you. But, tell me about this Ian character ... do you think he's Soulbane?"

"I've been thinking the same thing. He certainly seemed to know a lot about the reports you found." Rachael rubbed her eyes with her fists and yawned." Cade poured her a glass of sherry to calm her nerves. "Tell me again exactly what he said."

"He ... he said." Rachael choked up and took several sips.

She resumed, her voice a bit firmer. "He said that if I wanted Sarah back, I'd better get your disks with the Soulbane Reports. He told me he would meet me at the Globe Theatre on Monday afternoon at four. He ... he said that if I cooperated, I'd have Sarah back, but that I'd better not try anything foolish. No police, no tricks, just the disks. I tried to act like I didn't know what he was talking about, but he just said, 'Don't insult me. I know your husband has them. You'd better get them from the States and be here on Monday with all the copies of the disks, or you'll never see your daughter again.' Oh, Cade, what are we going to do?" Rachael sobbed in fits and starts.

His hands were shaking. For a while, neither he nor Rachael said anything. "I'll be right back." Cade went to the guest bedroom. He opened the dresser drawer and looked under his passport. There was the computer disk, marked "SBR." He closed his eyes and tried to focus his mind. "Lord, what do I do now?" he said quietly to himself. He thought about Zac's phone call. Had that just been hours ago? It seemed like ages ago now. His career was on the line, and if he gave the disk to Zac, he could possibly salvage his career. If he instead turned it over to whoever this Ian character was, his career, and all that he'd worked for, was probably over. Right now, Rachael knew nothing about the location of the disk. For all she knew, it was still in Atlanta. He stood in silence, holding the disk in his hands.

He returned to the living room and said quietly, "I have the disk here with me."

"You do?" Rachael's face seemed to relax ever so slightly.

"Yes. I've been thinking about them a lot lately and had decided I needed to make them public."

"Oh Cade, really? But why after all this time?"

He avoided answering her question. He wasn't ready yet to drop the Sherry bomb on Rachael. "I'm going to go to the Globe on Monday and get Sarah."

Rachael immediately leaned over and put her arms around his neck, whispering, "I love you so much darling."

"I love you, too." He fought back more tears.

"Rachael, you need some sleep. Don't worry. I'm going to end this with these characters once and for all."

"But what about publishing the reports?"

"That's not what's important now. You and Sarah are. Now, let me get something to calm your nerves, then off to bed you go." As he poured a sherry, he decided not to mention the disaster with Zac and Harry. Rachael was too emotionally fragile for any more bad news. She appeared to be about to collapse from exhaustion. After she sipped her sherry for a few minutes, her head began to droop forward. On impulse, he swooped Rachael into his arms, carried her limp body to the bedroom, laid her on the bed, and pulled the covers over her.

He closed the bedroom curtains, bent over and kissed his wife on the forehead. She was already asleep. He went into the living room and paced until dawn came to the quiet village. He wanted desperately to be doing something, but could think of nothing to do now. Faced with the terror of his daughter's kidnapping and his helplessness to act, Cade experienced a paralyzing dread unlike anything he'd ever known.

33

LAUREN SAT in her kitchen, trying to watch the BBC Saturday evening news. She had not slept well the previous two nights, unable to rid herself of the sight of Rachael's and Ian's betrayal of her friendship and love. She looked over at the small unlit Christmas tree standing in a corner in her living room next to the dark fireplace, and felt profound sadness. She had let herself begin to think that this Christmas with Ian was going to be magical, only to have her dreams shattered.

She jumped at the sound of the phone ringing, and although she had no intention to answer it, she finally surrendered to its insistent ring.

"Lauren?" said the voice. Instantly, Lauren felt her face grow hot as she recognized Rachael's voice.

"Yes," she replied, coldly and distantly, feeling the rising tide of anger inside her.

"I wonder if I might come and see you?"

"What the hell for?" Lauren replied, before she had time to think about what to say.

"I have something to explain to you. Cade told me that you were at the Tower on Thursday, and it's not at all what you think. In fact … ."

"Don't patronize me, Rachael." Lauren was unable to control her anger.

"Listen, Lauren, I don't know how to say this … . but it's Ian…"

Lauren grabbed the back of the chair she was standing behind, gripping it tightly to brace for Rachael's confession of her affair with Ian.

Rachael continued, "...he's kidnapped Sarah."

The words didn't register at first with Lauren, who was already thinking of her response to Rachael's confession. The words were so unexpected, that Lauren didn't comprehend them. She heard Rachael sobbing over the phone, and the awful meaning of the words filtered into Lauren's consciousness, as a new rain begins to trickle down a dry pathway.

"Rachael, is this some cruel joke?"

"If only it were," she replied softly. "Now, can Cade and I come over?"

"All right," said Lauren, unable to articulate anything more.

Lauren quickly picked up a few clothes lying about the living room and turned on a few more lights.

Shortly, a knock sounded at the door, and Lauren hurried to open it. She stared momentarily at Rachael, who appeared much more tired and pale than Lauren had ever seen her before. Cade was standing just behind her, his face half lit by the outdoor lamp. His broad shoulders were slumped, and the movement of his jaw indicated he was gritting his teeth. The cold wind rushed past her into the warm room.

Lauren forced a smile. "Please come in. I apologize for the mess. Cade, would you mind starting a fire? It's all ready to go." Lauren was still stunned by Rachael's startling revelation.

Cade knelt at the fireplace, touching a glowing match to the kindling. Rachael appeared listless standing beside him. "Could I offer you some tea or sherry?" Lauren inquired.

"I could use a sherry, if that's all right," Cade said between breaths as he blew on the infant fire.

"Certainly. Rachael?"

Rachael declined. Lauren busied herself with tea for herself and the sherry, while Cade and Rachael took seats near the fire. She returned with the drinks, as well as a plate of shortbread.

Lauren stood at the fireplace, staring at the Brysons, her mind totally confused over their visit and Rachael's strange phone call. Cade spoke first. "Lauren, I don't know where to begin. You're probably going to think we're crazy."

Lauren tucked her hair behind her ear and laughed nervously. "Not any more than the rest of us."

Cade continued. "All I know to do is to tell you the whole story. So let me start with a winter solstice evening eleven years ago."

"The winter solstice, but that's today," Lauren remarked.

"I hadn't even realized that," he replied. "So, let me take you back to that night and tell you my story."

Lauren didn't remember drinking her tea, as she listened to Cade's story about his strange discovery of letters in the Magdalen library, and the adventures he underwent trying to solve the mystery of the letters. He told about discovering two reports from a devil named Soulbane, who reported to someone named Foulheart. Cade briefly told about having them on disk, but never having published them. He finished with the story of Rachael and Ian at the Tower of London.

Lauren sat on the wooden stool by the fire, unable to move, as if gravity had increased tenfold. She wanted to disbelieve this impossible tale, and yet ... Hadn't there been something about Ian that didn't add up?

As if reading her mind, Cade added, "And that is our story, strange as it sounds. I know you find it difficult to believe, but I couldn't have made this up."

Lauren glanced at the fire, which was nothing but glowing embers. Before she could stand, however, Cade retrieved two more logs for the fire, producing fireworks of sparks and crackling as he tossed them on the embers. She didn't know what to say, so just to say something, anything, she asked, "Can ... can I get you anything?"

Both declined and looked at her, as if waiting for an answer.

Lauren shifted uncomfortably in her chair. "I'm afraid I'm rather at a loss for words. And yet, something in my head keeps saying that, somehow, this seems familiar. But I can't think or even imagine why." She felt as if she were in a dense fog. Cade's tale was too much for her to absorb.

Cade stretched, holding his hands before him, palms toward Lauren.

She stared at his hands, mesmerized. Her mind flashed back to a bizarre night in the hospital, and a long-dead memory tried to resurrect itself.

"Are you all right?" Rachael said, looking concerned.

Instead of replying, Lauren said, "Cade, where did you get that scar?"

He turned his palm and looked at it, as if he was seeing it for the first time. "Oh, that. Well, that's part of the story I left out to keep it short. You see, after I found these reports and typed them, a man stole my computer from my room in Magdalen. I saw him getting away and we had a chase through the streets of Oxford. He finally escaped by going over the wall at Trinity. I made the mistake of trying to climb up and cut my hand on the broken glass on top of the wall. That ended the chase."

"Who was the man?"

"I never knew for sure, but I think it was Foulheart."

"When was this?"

"I'll never forget it. It was Guy Fawkes' night just over ten years ago."

Lauren gasped and put her hand to her mouth.

"Lauren, what is it?" Rachael stood and walked toward her.

"I can't believe it." She felt the blood drain from her face.

"Believe what?" Cade stared at her.

Lauren let out a deep breath. "About that long ago, just before I stopped practising medicine, I was working in the Accident and Emergency department at the John Radcliffe Hospital. One night they brought a college student in with a deep gash on his hand. He was delirious, and kept muttering something about his soul and a foul heart. I had to sedate him before I could sew his hand up."

Cade moved closer to Lauren now, staring silently at her, his eyes wide.

Lauren continued, "I recall the night because his words were so strange, and yet he wasn't drunk. We sedated him and I sewed his hand up. He checked out the next day, but I wasn't on duty, so I never saw the chap again."

"Lauren, that was me." Cade showed her the scar on his palm. "I don't remember a lot about that evening. I fainted, and when I came to, I was being taken to the hospital. I thought I was being kidnapped by devils and when I arrived at the hospital, I truly thought that was the end."

Lauren ran her finger along the scar and looked up at him. "Yes, I must have been the doctor who stitched you up that night. I can't believe it."

"Nor I." Cade had a look of total amazement.

"But how did you get to the hospital?" Lauren inquired.

"Oh, a Magdalen scout, Robert Thompson, called for an ambulance and came with me."

Lauren shot a glance at Rachael and exclaimed, "I *knew* I'd seen Mr. Thompson before! I just knew it Rachael." Rachael shook her head, incredulity written all over her face.

*　　*　　*

Zac hurried into his office and turned on the light. No one was around on Saturday night, and with Christmas so near, he was not worried about anyone walking in on him. He took out a key hidden in his desk and unlocked a cabinet behind his desk. He grabbed the financial papers faxed yesterday from his Internet venture and spread them in front of him.

He studied the numbers, silently cursing. What was he going to do? He turned on his computer and studied a new e-mail from one of his partners in the venture with a gloomy update on business forecasts. Zac puffed hard on his cigar and re-read the papers, as if hoping they would read differently. He felt tiny beads of sweat forming on his forehead, and a slight pain in his chest, which he ignored.

Because Zac's construction company was a privately owned and operated company, the involvement of the senators was not public information. Over the years, the Swiss bank accounts set up by Zac had accumulated several million dollars. It had all been done in a way that no one could trace this money to his investors.

Unknown to these private investors, however, Zac had surreptitiously funneled large amounts of these funds from the Swiss account into his Internet venture. He had figured this venture was such a sure bet, that he would make enough both to replenish the accounts before anyone discovered his withdrawals and to retire comfortably. Zac envisioned he and Gail sailing the Caribbean together.

He read the email for the third time and grimaced. It stated that they had depleted all the seed money, and that because cash flow was virtually non-existent, more money was needed, especially given the poor prospects for any immediate turnaround in business. Zac had no more money. He had drawn down the Swiss account much further than he'd ever planned, and he had used a dangerous amount of Pickering Construction capital to boot. In a fit of anger, he rapped the computer screen, as if that might somehow alter the words displayed on it.

The papers he now had before him made it clear that he was on the verge of bankruptcy. On top of that, he was being blackmailed with the threat of his affair being made public. He only had one way out of that. He had to keep the photos from being released in order to buy time to get his finances in order. If the Caribbean photos were sent to the senator now, Zac was history.

"Dammit, Bryson, you'd better come through," he muttered, locking the papers in his cabinet.

34

O N MONDAY, Cade and Rachael sat quietly in the dining room of Bridgett Adams's cottage, neither eating the lunch Lauren had dropped off for them. The December cold spell was not letting up and the sky was filled with snow clouds. The forecast predicted bitter cold and snow on Christmas Eve. He finally broke the silence. "I'd better get on the road. I want to get to the Globe early."

"Cade, please be careful." Rachael was looking down at the mug of coffee she continually stirred, but didn't drink.

"I will. Just say a prayer, and I'll be home with Sarah in no time." Cade smiled to mask his fear as he stood.

"I love you, darling."

"I love you, too." Cade took her in his arms and kissed her.

As he drove down the M-40, he thought back to the morning after Rachael appeared at the cottage doorway. Cade was so distraught over his daughter's kidnapping, he'd been unable to sleep. Rachael had slept until morning, utterly exhausted, but had awakened screaming from a nightmare.

Later that day, Cade had, with great trepidation, painfully confessed to Rachael about his close call with Sherry, and about the Mardi Gras discovery of the devils' meeting. He was afraid what this would do to Rachael on top of Sarah's disappearance. Not surprisingly, his revelations stunned Rachael, and for a long while that day, Cade wondered if he was headed for a divorce.

Yet late in the afternoon, after she returned from a long walk by herself, Rachael said she still loved him and forgave him. Cade, overcome with emotion, wept in her arms. On Sunday afternoon, they'd taken a long drive around the Cotswolds, after spending some quiet time in prayer that morning. Neither had felt up to going to church. Sarah's plight remained hammering in their minds every moment, the strain of their anxiety making them both feel ill; and yet as they shared this burden they were drawn closer. Agonising for their child, the distance between them diminished and healing began.

Cade maneuvered around the London traffic, parking as close as he could to the New Globe Theatre. The car's clock told him the time approached four, which the advancing darkness confirmed. He glanced over at the computer disk lying on the front passenger seat next to Flopsy. He had considered making another copy of the disk, but decided that could be foolish. He simply couldn't risk these fiendish characters discovering he still had a disk and coming after his family again. The only thing he could focus on was getting his daughter back safely, even if it meant Zac Pickering carried out his plans to destroy Cade's career. He put on his gloves, picked up Flopsy and the disk, and walked swiftly toward the Globe, oblivious to the myriad sounds and smells of horns, brakes, and exhausts. His heart was racing, as he contemplated finally meeting Soulbane face-to-face. Rachael and Lauren had described Ian and now the image of his target was clear in his mind's eye.

Arriving at the Globe, he paused to think how best to proceed. Looking around the large foyer area with its shops and displays, he spotted the ticket booth for those wanting only the tour of the building. He walked up and asked for a ticket.

"I'm sorry sir, we're not doing tours at the moment – the theatre has been hired for a private function."

This was an obstacle Cade had not reckoned on. "But it's really important I get to see the theatre…. I've come a long way," he finished lamely, realising even as he said the words that they would not make any difference. Sure enough, the girl at the counter merely repeated her apology and suggested he come back tomorrow.

Feeling a rising panic, he mounted the stairs to the upper level of the foyer, thinking he might at least get some view of the theatre itself.

"How do they expect me to keep my side of the bargain if I can't even get in?" he raged silently to himself. Fighting down the panic, he forced himself to think. There must be a way in. His adversaries were too clever to let something like this de-rail their scheming. Back at ground floor level he noticed a board by the corporate hospitality desk: 'The New Globe welcomes Divine Comedy Productions.' As he continued to scan the foyer, something suddenly clicked in his mind and he turned to look again at the notice: Divine Comedy ... a name taken from Dante's Inferno ... with a sudden thump of adrenaline kicking him in the chest, he realised this was the clue he was meant to find. Not amused by this devilish sense of humor, he went over to the desk.

" Excuse me, I'm here to join the Divine Comedy Productions function. The name's Bryson."

The man at the desk scanned a list. "Bryson... yes, here we are, you are expected Mr. Bryson. I'll show you through."

With that, Cade was ushered down a passage, through a door marked 'Private', and found himself in the seemingly deserted auditorium.

Once inside, he walked to the center where the groundlings would have stood to watch the greatest plays ever written. He turned to gaze around the circular theatre, observing the tiers of balconies and wooden railings. There were no signs of Sarah or anyone else. The open sky above him was quickly becoming dark, and the fading sunlight cast long shadows in the theatre. His heart sank as a catch swelled in his throat.

Cade whirled around at a noise behind him. Standing on the stage was a tall figure half hidden in the shadows.

A polished British accent suddenly boomed, "Tomorrow, and tomorrow, and tomorrow, creeps in this petty pace from day to day, to the last syllable of recorded time; and all our yesterdays have lighted fools the way to dusty death. Out, out, brief candle! Life's but a walking shadow, a poor player that struts and frets his hour upon the stage, and then is heard no more: it is a tale told by an idiot, full of sound and fury, signifying nothing."

Cade rushed forward to the edge of the stage and gazed up. In the fading light, he saw the visage of a man with dark eyes and hair fitting the description of Ian. Cade's anger boiled, and he took a deep breath to calm himself. "Where's my daughter? Where's Sarah?"

The figure stepped forward. "I hadn't expected to see you Bryson. It's rather a surprise, actually, but I'm delighted you're here."

"Who are you?"

"My friends call me Ian. I'm sorry you and I have never had the pleasure of meeting before, but I've heard a lot about you. You've caused us a lot of trouble."

"Where's Sarah? I want to see her now!" Cade was screaming.

Behind the stage, he heard a high-pitched voice say, "Daddy. Daddy. Is that you?" At the sound of his daughter's sweet voice, Cade became delirious with relief. His heart simultaneously melted and exploded with love as he heard Sarah's voice.

"Sarah, yes, it's Daddy. Are you okay sweetheart?" Cade yelled, as he tried to jump up on the stage.

Ian walked over and stepped on Cade's hand. "Not so fast. Where are the disks?"

"It's here. There's only one disk. I guess you stole the other one from Robert Thompson. You'll get this one when I get Sarah."

"How do I know this isn't a trick? That you don't have other disks? If you deceive us Bryson, it's curtains for your daughter."

"I give you my word this is all I have." Desperation was creeping into his voice.

"Give me the disk. That's all I want. Then you can have this vile creature." Ian stood directly over Cade. "The disk. *Now!*" His voice was strong and firm, his tone impatient.

With trembling hands, Cade produced the disk from another pocket, held it up and tossed it on the stage. Ian bent over and picked it up.

Cade said, "It's okay, Sarah. You're safe with Daddy now." He pulled himself halfway up on the stage. Ian stepped forward and Cade felt a heavy blow to his face. He fell hard to the ground, dazed and bleeding.

His daughter was screaming, "Daddy! Daddy! Where are you?" He struggled to stand and looked around, but couldn't see her anywhere.

He was insane with anger. "Where's my daughter?" he screamed, flailing his arms wildly. Ian had disappeared into the shadows.

Cade was about to vault onto the stage in pursuit, when a different voice, with a familiar American accent said, "Hello, Cade."

Cade's mind went foggy, not comprehending this *non sequitur*. He looked up and saw another figure emerging from the shadows into the dying light. He staggered back as he stared at the face of Eric Majors.

Relief flowed through Cade. "Eric, what are you … . Quick, help me up. They've got Sarah." He was excited to see his best friend and figured Eric had talked to Philip and decided to come over to help him. Rachael must have told Eric to come here. He held his hand up for Eric to pull him on to the stage. Instead, Eric folded his arms and gave a shrieking laugh.

"You just don't get it, do you?"

"What?"

"Allow me to more fully introduce myself. I'm an author. My name is Soulbane."

"Yeah, right, and I'm Santa Claus. This is no time to joke, Eric." Cade was still holding his hand out to Eric.

"This is no joke you imbecile." Eric's voice was loud and sinister. He stared at Cade with a look of scorn.

"But that's crazy. You can't be … ."

"Enough!" screamed Eric. "You're such an utter fool."

"Where's Sarah?" Cade felt waves of panic sweeping over his body.

"Daddy, Daddy, where are you?" The voice was Sarah's, but it came from Eric – a perfect imitation of his daughter's voice.

At those words, Cade screamed and rushed the stage in a blind rage. Eric retreated toward the rear. Cade pulled himself up on the stage. He ran in the direction where Eric had disappeared. He came to a door where he thought the two fiends had gone, but found it locked. He pulled furiously on the unyielding door, yelling, "Eric, where's Sarah? Eric!" There was no reply.

He heard a rumble which, as it grew louder, Cade recognized as a wicked laugh. The voice of Eric echoed from somewhere far away. "Bryson, you fool. Do you think for a moment we fiends have any sense of what you mortals call honor or decency? How horrid. Thanks for giving me my reports back. Do you really think I'd be foolish enough to risk bringing that urchin here? Wait in Lower Slaughter to hear from me – and if you go to the police, you'll never see your daughter again." This was followed by a loud, sinister laugh that echoed and died out.

Cade was frantic. He jumped off the stage and ran out the door through which he'd first entered and back up the passage to the foyer, hoping to cut them off as they exited the theatre. It was totally dark outside, and a chilling wind stung his face. Clouds blanketed the moon. He gave no thought to anything except Sarah, and raced around the building as fast as he could. The only response was the whistling of the wind and the sound of the traffic.

Cade's lungs burned and his muscles screamed as he ran desperately around the Globe again. Nothing. He went to the bank of the Thames and looked up and down the river, but there was no sign of them. After about a half-hour, he realized it was futile to continue to search. The fiends had vanished. He sank down on his knees, put his face in his hands, and screamed, "God, don't you care? Please take anything from me – *anything* – but my little girl."

He pounded his fists on the ground in anger and frustration. He didn't know what to do now and felt as helpless as he'd ever felt. Finally, his anger overcame his grief, and he vowed silently to himself that he wouldn't give up – ever. He stumbled toward his car, his mind racing. As he neared the car, he saw a policeman walking down the sidewalk.

His first instinct was to rush over and report the kidnapping. But what in the world he would say? Here he was, an American in London holding a stuffed bunny rabbit, with a wild story about fiendish characters and devils' reports and kidnappings. He'd never be believed. More importantly, he recalled Eric's warning.

The policeman walked toward him, and Cade merely nodded while holding Flopsy behind his back. The policeman tipped his hat at Cade and walked on.

Cade could think of nothing to do. He was terrified and stunned. The shock of the encounter at The Globe was beyond his ability to cope. In his muddled state, he could think only of following Ian's orders and returning to Rachael.

*   *   *

The drive to Lower Slaughter took an eternity. Cade mulled over and over what to say to Rachael. How could he ever explain the shocking revelation about Eric? He couldn't even comprehend, much less digest, what had happened at the theatre that afternoon. His hands shook with rage and anger – and terror. He replayed every second of the afternoon, searching for clues. As he drove toward the Cotswolds, he looked up to see the clear, winter sky illuminated by a full moon. He became aware of a song playing softly on the car radio and turned up the volume. A choir was singing, "… *the hopes and fears of all the years are met in thee tonight.*" For the first time, he realized tomorrow was Christmas Eve. He pictured the Star of Bethlehem overlooking an obscure birth of a child two thousand years ago. Was it really possible that the Creator of the universe had become "the Word made flesh"? Cade said a silent, desperate prayer as he sped into the night void.

35

"O COME ALL YE FAITHFUL, *joyful and triumphant, O come ye, O come ye to Bethlehem ... .*"

Cade grabbed the radio playing on the small table in Bridgett's living room and threw it against the wall. It crashed loudly and the music instantly ceased. Rachael screamed and the Bible she was reading hit the floor with a thud.

"I just can't take this!" yelled Cade, his frustration at breaking point. It was the middle of the afternoon on Christmas Eve. Neither one of them had slept at all since Cade returned from London. That had been less than twenty-four hours ago, but to Cade it seemed as though a million years had crept by since then. He was in shock over the stunning revelation that the person he counted as his best friend was instead not only a demon, but his nemesis Soulbane. Cade felt totally helpless, which only exacerbated the situation. He and Rachael discussed whether to call the police, but decided that was a risk they couldn't take. Lauren had stopped by on her way to the lab, and upon hearing the staggering news, promised to brainstorm about a solution. They had several phone calls, and at each initial ring, Cade dashed over to answer, his hopes rising. And each time, it had been some neighbor calling to wish Bridgett a Merry Christmas. Bridgett had called to say that Aunt Charlotte was not doing at all well and she needed to stay on. Cade decided not to worry her yet about Sarah.

"Cade, why don't you take a walk?" Rachael said gently. "I'll stay by the phone."

"I just can't sit here. Maybe I should ride into London."

"What good would that do?" Rachael's voice had a tone of exasperation, and Cade knew not to add fuel to the fire.

"You're right. I think I will get some fresh air." With that, Cade walked over and picked up his coat and gloves. "I won't be gone too long."

Rachael nodded, but said nothing. Cade stroked her face as if trying to soothe the agony there, and had to admire her brave demeanor in the face of this tragedy.

Stepping outside, he felt a jolt from the cold wind. The leafless trees were swaying, and the dismal, cloudy day was already ebbing. The December cold front still showed no signs of letting up. Ordinarily, such a Christmas Eve would have conjured up romantic, magical feelings, but today he felt only numbness. He set out purposefully on his hike, feeling that he could walk a thousand miles if it brought him to Sarah. As he passed the church, he glanced at the huge yew tree dancing in the wind and stopped momentarily to look at the crumbling tombstones oblivious to the weather.

He walked hard until he was breathing heavily. The stiff wind blew occasional snowflakes in his face. He barely noticed the Christmas decorations in the stone houses of the village. The image of Eric on the stage at The Globe was relentless in its pursuit of his sanity.

Was that Sarah calling him now? Cade's heart skipped a beat, and he turned his head in every direction. In the front yard of a nearby cottage, three young children in coats and wool caps were chasing each other, yelling and laughing. His heart sank like a stone in water, and the sight of these children playing, oblivious to any evil in the world, intensified his anguish. He picked up a rock, threw it as hard as he could into the air, and turned away from the sight of the frolicking children. After a good while, he circled back toward the house. The dreary day was fast becoming night. As he neared the cottage, he saw Lauren's car out front. He wondered if perhaps Lauren had news for them and started running. Upon entering, he heard a familiar voice behind him. "Dear Cade, I'm so sorry."

He whirled around, surprised to see Robert Thompson. Robert continued talking before Cade could utter a word. "Rachael called and told us about Sarah. Your friend, Dr. St. John, was kind enough to come and get me. What can we do?"

"Nothing that I know of. Except pray," Cade replied, his mouth pulled tightly into a grimace. The sight of his old friend brought a lump to his throat, and Cade's words caught there.

Robert put his arm around Cade's shoulder. "We're here for you."

Cade hugged Robert tightly, whispering, "Bless you."

The two men walked into the other room, where Rachael and Lauren were talking in muted tones. Food and a pot of coffee were set on the kitchen table. It struck Cade that this was like an old Southern wake, where friends and family gathered with the bereaved. Nothing in the house hinted that Christmas Eve had arrived.

The friends sat together, making small talk. No one dared speculate on Sarah's fate. The doorbell rang, and when Cade opened the door, Neville was standing before him, a wrapped present under his arm.

"Merry Christmas," Neville said, smiling broadly.

"Oh, Neville," Cade replied dispiritedly.

"Is something wrong?"

"I'm afraid so." Cade stared at the ground. A gust of wind reminded him that Neville was still outside, and he added, "Neville, forgive me, please come in."

Before they went into the other room, Cade quickly whispered a brief summary of Sarah's kidnapping.

Neville's face showed intense sorrow and concern. After appearing to reflect on all this, he finally said in a whisper, "Cade, I'm sorry. I'll do anything I can."

"Let me introduce you to Rachael." The two men walked into the living room, and Robert Thompson rose to his feet.

"Everyone," said Cade loudly. The assembled group stopped talking and turned toward him. "I want you to meet my friend, Neville Sterling. He's been most kind to me since I've been here, and I've just told him our news."

Neville smiled faintly and took off his hat. He walked immediately up to Rachael, taking her hand. "You must be Rachael. Cade has told me all about you and Sarah. I'm so sorry. What can I do?"

Rachael, her face outlining the strain she was under, nevertheless managed a slight smile and said, "And Cade has told me about you, Neville. I'm sorry we're not in much of a Christmas spirit around here."

"That's quite understandable," Neville replied.

"Neville," said Cade, who was standing behind him, "allow me to introduce Dr. Lauren St. John and Robert Thompson."

Neville went over and shook their hands in the order of introduction. When he shook Robert's hand, he said, "Cade has told me about all your friendship. I'm so glad to meet you."

"The pleasure is mine," Robert replied.

"Please take off your coat and have a cup of coffee," Rachael said, already reaching to take Neville's coat.

"Well, I hadn't planned to stay, but under the circumstances, I'll accept your offer. I brought this little present for Sarah. Just put it away for later."

He handed the coat and present to Rachael, who took them to another room. Cade and Neville went into the kitchen, where Cade proceeded to tell him the entire story of the events at The Globe. Then they returned to the living room, both holding mugs of hot coffee.

"I wonder if I might be so bold as to offer a prayer?" Neville said after a moment.

"That would be most kind of you," Rachael replied.

Lauren stood, suddenly looking awkward. "Perhaps I should going."

"Please won't you stay for a bit longer," said Rachael, a sense of pleading in her voice.

"Well ... I ..."

"Please do stay," Neville said in a calm, yet authoritative, voice.

Lauren nodded her assent and sat. Neville moved to the center of the room. "I know you all are devastated now, as I am. I actually came over to meet Rachael and Sarah. I do know, however, that the Scriptures say not a sparrow falls but that God doesn't know and care, and I am confident He is with us now – and with Sarah. Therefore, let us pray."

When Neville finished, Cade looked up slowly. Neville had a serene look on his face, and Cade himself felt an inexplicable sense of relief, like a warm river, running through him. Rachael stood and hugged Neville. The small clock in the hallway struck four in the afternoon.

"I also came to invite you to join me at the Christmas Eve service tonight."

Cade said spontaneously, "I don't think we're up to it tonight. I mean ... ."

Unexpectedly, it was Lauren who said, "You know, Cade... Somehow, and don't ask me why, I think Neville's right. There is nothing we can do for Sarah sitting here. I'm not much of one to believe in God, but ... I saw how much Sarah liked being in church when we went together recently, and the service tonight might be just the thing for both of you. I'll stay here in case anything happens."

Cade stared at her, unsure what to make of this. Rachael added, "You're absolutely right, Lauren. I can't think of any better place to be tonight than in church."

"Excellent," said Neville. "The carols start at half ten, so I'll call for you a little before then."

"I'd love to come," said Robert, but I must get back to Rose and

Clive. Rose isn't well these days, and I promised Clive I'd take him to church tonight, just like we always do. It means so much to him."

Lauren stood. "Robert, I'll take you home now."

Everyone said their good-byes and departed.

Just as Cade and Rachael sat, the doorbell rang again.

"Who could that be?" He struggled to stand.

He opened the door to a uniformed delivery man holding an express envelope. "Package for you sir, sign here please." He thrust a form and pen in Cade's face.

"I hope this is a present you've been expecting," said the man. "We've put on a special effort to get as much delivered today as possible. I'm knackered!"

Cade signed, and the man handed him the envelope and rushed away.

"Thanks and Merry Christmas," said Cade, who felt no joy as he mouthed the words. Who had sent a package? Probably something for Bridgett.

He closed the door and saw the envelope was addressed to him, from Harry Martin. He hesitated, not wanting to view the contents.

"Who was it?"

"Oh, just some delivery man."

"What did he bring?"

Cade rejoined Rachael, and sat on the sofa with her. He tore open the package, and stared at the contents.

"What is it?"

He couldn't speak and simply handed her the letter from Harry, enclosing a copy of the charges that Zac had filed with the Georgia State Bar.

"Merry Christmas, Harry," Cade said with no amusement.

"Oh, Cade, I just can't believe this." Tears formed in Rachael's eyes for the thousandth time today.

He replied in a hoarse whisper, "I know."

Without a word, Rachael moved closer to Cade, put his head in her lap, and gently stroked his hair. He sighed deeply as he felt her tender fingers run through his hair. How had Cade been so blessed ever to find Rachael? How had he been so foolish to risk losing her? Would he ever see Sarah again?

He felt as if a searing sword was piercing his heart. He was at the end of his rope. A deep sense of despair enveloped him. As the last vestiges of daylight on this Christmas Eve trickled through the windows, Cade reckoned that the appearance of Marley's ghost would be about the only thing left to make the nightmare complete.

36

CADE LOOKED UP at the altar as he sat in church next to Rachael and Neville. Tall candles glowed from the communion table, and evergreen branches covered the columns and rafters, their fresh scent permeating the church.

He stood numbly as the choir sang the opening hymn, "*O Come, O Come Emmanuel and ransom captive Israel ... .*" This was without question the worst day of his entire life, with which no nightmare could ever have competed. The church was virtually full for the Christmas Eve service. Cade glanced at Rachael. She was holding Flopsy tightly to her chest, but wasn't singing. He grabbed her arm and squeezed it, and she leaned against him. He heard Neville's strong voice booming out the words beautifully. Cade didn't bother to open the hymnal and regretted even being at the service. He glanced often to the rear of the church, hoping to see Lauren coming in with news.

The choir, in their red cassocks and white surplices, processed in and took their places in the choir stalls. Two priests, similarly dressed, walked together at the end of the procession up into the chancel. One was a thin, older man, and the other was tall and well-built, in his forties with thick, brown hair, square jaw, and large nose. He looked more like a boxer than a priest, Cade thought.

The service for Holy Communion began, but Cade was only vaguely aware of the liturgy. He found himself begging and pleading with God, wanting to make some deal to get Sarah back. Like a hot brand burning his chest, he also felt hidden anger at himself for having dragged his family into this in the first place. As he gazed at the altar, the words of Psalm 139 from the RAF Memorial window flashed in his mind, and he closed his eyes and prayed harder.

After what seemed like an eternity, it was time for the sermon. Cade couldn't focus at all on the words of the older priest. He held Rachael's hand tightly, with Flopsy lying in her lap.

After the sermon, of which Cade could not have repeated five words, the communion service continued. At one point, he felt Neville's hand on his shoulder, and Cade looked up to see it was time for them to go forward for communion. He walked zombie-like to the altar rail to receive the bread and wine and returned mechanically to his seat. He felt nothing: no comfort, no solace – just emptiness. *Is this what belief in God is ultimately about? Is faith really nothing more than a cruel hoax?*

After everyone had been served the sacraments, the younger priest said, "Let us pray."

Everyone knelt, and the priest continued, saying, "Almighty and ever living God, we most heartily thank thee … ."

Cade gazed at the floor, his mind a zillion miles away. He pictured The Globe Theatre again, as clear in his mind as if he were still standing there. He tried to remember Sarah, but couldn't quite get a clear image of her, which added to his torment.

He heard sniffling and looked over to see Rachael crying hard. She whispered, "I'm sorry, but I can't help it." He put his arm around her.

Cade became aware of silence. *Why isn't there any music?* He looked up and saw the younger priest standing at the altar, facing the congregation. His pale face and open mouth made him appear as if he'd just seen a ghost. He stood stiffly, like someone standing on the bow of a ship, staring far off at the horizon. Cade realized no one was saying anything. The choir sat mute. He glanced over to see if Rachael was aware of this strange behavior, but she was kneeling, her eyes closed.

He heard a noise from the rear of the church, and simultaneously felt a draft of cold air from that direction. He instinctively turned around. At first he thought his eyes were deceiving him, but his heart raced in astonishment.

He touched Rachael's shoulder. "Rachael," Cade's voice cracked, "look behind us."

Rachael turned and immediately screamed, "Sarah! Sarah!"

A murmur arose throughout the church, like a distant roll of thunder becoming louder and louder. Cade ran down the aisle toward the figures standing in the back of the church, still in disbelief. He stopped a few feet from them, frozen. Before him stood Eric Majors, with Sarah cradled in his arms. Was she asleep or dead? Cade couldn't bear to know.

Rachael was now past him, screaming, "My baby! What's happened to my baby?"

People were standing up now, gawking. Pandemonium broke out, as events swirled around Cade.

"I think she's okay," Eric said quietly.

"But how … what … ?" Cade started, but nothing else would come out.

Lauren was standing behind Eric and yelled, "Everyone step back. Here, put her down."

Eric complied and laid Sarah on the stone floor. She moved slightly, but didn't open her eyes.

Lauren grabbed the girl's wrist, and put her ear near Sarah's mouth.

"Her breathing is fine," said Lauren, who touched the girl's head. "But she's got quite a fever."

Cade felt a rush of relief at these words. Without thinking, he stormed at Eric and punched him in the mouth. Eric fell to the floor. Cade jumped on him and tried to choke him. Someone grabbed Cade's arm in a vise-like grip and pulled him off. The younger priest towered over them. "I don't know what this is all about, but there'll be no fighting in this church." Cade winced from the pain of the grip.

"We need to get Sarah to my house. I have some medical supplies there." Lauren's voice was calm.

A woman came up and knelt by Lauren. "I'm a nurse."

"Good." Lauren looked up at the crowd of people around her. "Help me carry her," she said to no one in particular. A stunned silence engulfed the congregation, as they stared at this strange sight.

Cade bent down to pick up Sarah, when a woman screamed. Everyone turned in her direction, and Cade saw that Eric was now slumped over in a pew, his face ashen, almost wrinkled.

"Cade, I must talk with you. It's urgent." Eric spoke in a raspy voice.

"I don't give a ... ." Cade stopped short, realizing where he was.

"Sarah is fine, just exhausted. I must talk with you ... about Foulheart."

At the mention of Foulheart, Cade stood and stared at Eric, who appeared to be changing – he seemed somehow paler and thinner.

"I haven't much time. I must speak with you privately. It's of the utmost importance. Please take me to your cottage."

"I want nothing to do with you. I ... ."

"I *know* how you feel. I saved Sarah today for you. Just hear me out before it's too late."

"You saved ... ?" Cade began to ask.

Lauren interjected. "Cade, you take care of him. There's really nothing you can do for Sarah anyway." She motioned to the priest. "Can you carry Sarah for me?"

The priest was already bending down. "Of course, let's go." He picked up the limp little girl and walked out the church door followed by Rachael and Lauren.

Eric suddenly looked years older, and he appeared frail. Cade saw Neville standing nearby. "Here, Neville, can you help me?"

The two men stood on either side of Eric and supported him as the three walked out of the church. People made a path for them to exit. When they reached the door, Cade heard the older priest say, "Ladies and Gentlemen, please, let's all sing, *Silent Night.*"

Cade and Neville stepped into the bitterly cold, dark night. It was snowing hard, and a white blanket already covered the ground. As they walked down the pathway, Cade heard the words of *Silent Night* wafting through the air.

*   *   *

"Let's put her down here," Lauren said as they entered her cottage.

The priest and Lauren gently laid Sarah on the bed in Lauren's guestroom. Rachael and the nurse followed them.

Lauren retrieved her medical bag from the closet in her bedroom. She wondered when was the last time she'd even opened the bag. Because of the nature of her work at the lab, she always kept an array of medical supplies, just in case she ever needed them. As Lauren hurried back to the guestroom, she felt her heart pounding and her palms sweating. She looked down at the unconscious girl, and immediately the scene of the dying girl on the bed in hospital flashed before her eyes. She hesitated in opening the bag, and her hands were shaking. A rising fear threatened to paralyze her. What if she misdiagnosed the girl? She had a compelling urge to run.

Someone touched her arm gently, and Lauren turned to see Reverend Cooper smiling at her, his brown eyes looking directly into hers. He said softly, almost inaudibly, "I'm right here with you. You can do it."

Lauren looked away and felt like crying. She glanced again at Sarah. Time to act was running out. Sarah moaned softly and clinched her fists, but her eyes remained closed. *It's now or never.* In a rapid movement, Lauren tossed off her overcoat, opened the bag, and took out various instruments. She turned to the nurse, "We'll do a thorough examination."

The nurse nodded and stood beside Lauren.

"Is ... is she going to be all right?" Rachael asked softly, her voice trembling. She was standing near the head of the bed, stroking Sarah's head.

"I don't know," was all Lauren replied, as she began. "Rachael, will you get me some towels from the bathroom, and wet one of them with cold water?"

Rachael left immediately. Lauren looked up at David Cooper. "I don't know if I can do this. You might want to say a prayer."

"I already have," he said quietly.

Rachael rushed into the room with the towels and stood next to the vicar. The nurse put the wet towel on Sarah's forehead. Lauren was now virtually unaware of her surroundings, as she focused on Sarah. She noted the fever, the labored breathing. She recalled Sarah's loving embrace the last time they had been together. And, she remembered what Sarah had said to her that morning in church, "Dr. Lauren, I talk to God all the time. He's my friend."

Talk to Him now, Sarah. Please talk to Him now. Lauren wiped her forehead with the sleeve of her blouse and got to work.

37

NEVILLE AND CADE assisted Eric, who seemed to grow weaker by the moment, over to Bridgett's cottage and got him on to a bed. Neville propped pillows behind him so that Eric could sit up comfortably while Cade placed a blanket over him.

"It's okay," Eric said. "I'm not in any physical discomfort, as this isn't a real body, although the weakness is real. Mine is a spiritual pain."

Cade stood staring at the man he had learned so quickly to hate, trying to comprehend this mystery. He looked on in amazement as Eric's wrinkled skin turned yellowish and his hair almost gray.

"What's this all about?" Cade sensed his anger seething inside him. He wanted nothing more than to choke Eric to death. He wondered if this was yet one more devilish deception.

Eric held up his hand as if to silence Cade and looked directly at him.

"I know you hate me, Cade, and you have good reason. Just hear me out. I haven't much time. Before I saved Sarah this afternoon, I almost killed her."

"You what!" screamed Cade. He felt a knife in his heart at these words and momentarily stood mute in complete shock and amazement. Raising his arm, he lunged toward Eric. Neville grabbed Cade from behind and restrained him with surprising strength.

"Sit here," Neville commanded and steered Cade toward a chair.

Cade felt suddenly faint and did as Neville said. The images in his mind were like riding a roller coaster in a dense fog.

Eric looked at Neville. "Could you please find a priest?"

"Certainly." Neville put his hand on Cade's shoulder briefly and squeezed it, picked up his coat and went out. Cade heard the front door shut, jarring him back to the present. *This simply can't be happening.* He couldn't take his eyes off Eric, or whoever it was, lying before him.

Eric said in a soft voice. "You have every right to hate me. But, I haven't much time and it's crucial you listen to what I have to tell you. Where to begin? For hundreds of human years, I've been working to destroy the Enemy ... I mean, God. I was given the name Soulbane, and my job was to poison and kill human souls. It was a job I engaged in with great relish. Then C. S. Lewis stumbled upon letters from one of my superiors, named Screwtape, and, in many ways, that was the beginning of the end for me. Our Hindom was in an uproar when Lewis published those letters and showed you mortals so many of our subterfuges. After Screwtape and Wormwood were banished, I saw my chance to advance. Unscrupulous advancement and self-aggrandizement are the cornerstones of our Hindom. I was assigned by my direct superior, Foulheart, to carry out a study on the decadent western world and the Church. That's where you came in, when you discovered our correspondence in the Magdalen Library. When our work involves taking on human form, it brings with it all the inconvenience of having to operate materially, like corresponding through actual letters. That was Screwtape's undoing, and we thought we were taking sufficient precautions, until you stumbled upon our 'letter box'. At first, we didn't know you had discovered my reports, of course, but later Foulheart suspected you. He first focused on you when it was reported that one of my colleagues, Slayspark, had allowed you to convert to Christianity. Foulheart was furious. He began to suspect you might have found one of my reports – he never dreamed you had both. That's when Foulheart stole your computer, and we thought that was the end of it forever. Nevertheless, you had our attention. I was assigned to destroy you once and for all, and to make sure that you did not have any copies of the reports. If you had published my reports with the insights of our underworld, it would be disastrous to our battle plans designed to destroy mankind."

Cade felt feverish. "I need a drink. I'll be right back." He hurried out and got a glass of water. He also took a wet cloth and rubbed his head and neck, rushed back into the room and took his seat again.

Eric resumed immediately, in a weaker voice. "Anyway. I studied you well and knew everything about you: likes, dislikes, hopes, fears ... *everything*. Normally, of course, we work only in the spirit world: we're that little voice of discouragement, despair, and temptation. But, with you, we had to take more desperate measures to see if you had my reports. So, I took the form of Eric and made sure we met at law school. I knew just the illusions necessary to make you become a good friend. My goal was to destroy your soul any way that I could, by first ingratiating myself with you. It was working perfectly, especially when you made me Sarah's godfather."

Cade shook his head in disbelief. His rage was offset only by the sight of Eric, who was literally ageing right before Cade's eyes. Eric's hair was now almost completely gray. His face had assumed the appearance of a dried prune, his skin sallow and pale.

"I couldn't be too obvious, of course. And, you'll realize if you think about it how I always seemed to be around at just the right times, and yet, I was often gone, too. I had other business to tend to that I'll get to in a moment. You never mentioned my reports, so after a while, I decided that Foulheart had succeeded in stealing them, or else you'd never had them in the first place."

Cade's ears grew warm, as he thought of his broken promise to James Brooke to publish the reports.

"I meddled in your marriage, encouraging you to become a workaholic, subtly trying to drive a wedge into your relationship with Rachael, while pretending to be your best friend. Remember all the times I mentioned wanting to be wealthy, and pointing to others who seemed so materially successful? And all those wonderful trips I took, making sure to describe them to you in great detail? Envy and greed are powerful aphrodisiacs to you mortals. I must say, it worked beautifully. You slowly, gradually, made work and money your gods. You took on so many activities, you were overextended and burning out. You quit praying and reading the Bible, you spent more and more time at the office, you neglected your family. Finally, Rachael ran off to England, and I knew I was on the verge of destroying your marriage. But you made your own choices. All I did was to plant seeds and encourage you to take the wrong paths. I was never allowed to force you to do anything."

Cade shifted in his chair. He was glad no one else was in the room to hear this all-too-accurate assessment of his life.

"Then, at that dinner you confided in me and Philip that you *did* have my reports. Frankly, I was completely stunned. That changed everything. I *had* to get those reports back at all costs, and I was determined to finish you and your family off for good."

"Is Philip a … one of you, too?"

"Oh, no. He's a mortal. And, I might add, he was a real thorn in my side, always trying to get you to think about Christian things." Cade recalled the many times Philip had invited him to a Bible study or church function. Usually, Cade had an excuse why he couldn't go. He'd always told himself he would get around to it someday.

"Did one of you get the disk from the Thompsons?"

"Yes, that was me. After you told me he had a disk, we couldn't risk having any evidence of my reports. It was a real break when I took your form and found only Clive at home. He's such a kind and trusting soul, it was a piece of cake to get him to hand it over. We also threatened to blackmail Zac Pickering, to see if he could get the other disk for us. We were desperate and did everything we could to thwart you. We couldn't risk any reports being made public, especially after what Lewis had done with Screwtape's correspondence."

In a hoarse whisper, Cade asked, "Sherry?"

"Ah, Sherry. When I felt the time was right, I had my colleague Sherry introduced to you. That night at the bar after you took Rachael and Sarah to the airport, I did get your message but just pretended that we happened to show up. I wanted to be sure you didn't forget Sherry. And, of course, I always knew what you were doing, so I knew when to send Sherry to Birmingham. We knew just the right strings to pull with you. Sherry understood that to capture you, she had to be coy and flirtatious. She never came on too strong, always teasing you and tempting you, stringing you along. It almost worked. But why did you run that night?"

"I saw her in the bathroom: one minute she was Marilyn Monroe, the next Vivien Leigh. It literally scared the hell out of me."

"So *that's* how you knew.

"What about Muffy? Is she one of you, too?"

"Oh, no. She was just a nice human ornament to have along for the ride, while I worked on you."

"But if you're only an illusion of a human what's happening to you now?"

The door opened. Cade's head shot up. Neville came in, followed by the vicar and Lauren. His heart was in his throat. "How is Sarah?" He almost screamed.

Lauren smiled and said quietly, "Sarah's going to be okay. She's in a state of exhaustion and has a fever, but she's physically all right. I did a thorough check-up. There's nothing wrong with her a lot of sleep and fluids won't cure. She woke up a while ago and spoke, although she was still too sleepy to know where she was. She's asleep now and Rachael stayed with her. I came to check on your friend."

Cade felt as if Niagara Falls had just hit him with relief at these words. He stood and hugged Lauren tightly. He turned to the assembled group. "Eric's got some things to tell me ... us. I'll fill you in later. Just listen now."

Eric smiled faintly. "Slobglob, who you know as Ian, met Rachael and Sarah at the Tower of London."

Lauren gasped and shouted out, "What did you call Ian?"

Eric continued, "I don't have time to explain. Cade will tell you later. Now, where was I? Oh yes, the Tower. Ian diverted Rachael's attention while our Yeoman Warder colleague continued his tour with Sarah. I then came up to Sarah and surprised her. She was so happy to see her Uncle Eric that she never gave it a second thought. We just walked out of the Tower, and I told Sarah that we were going on a special adventure and her mother would come get her later. She was so trusting that she never suspected anything."

Cade sat rigid in the chair, staring at Eric.

"I was going to kill her on Christmas Eve and delivered to you to crush your hearts forever. I was on the way to a railway line to toss her under a train. Anyway, as we were waiting near the tracks, little Sarah took my hand, looked up at me, and said, 'Uncle Eric, I love you.' At that moment, something happened to me. I can't tell you exactly what. But, in an instant, my evil intent melted. I experienced something I'd never known before. It must be what you humans call love, and so does the Ene ... God. I looked at her, and there she was innocently trusting me and smiling at me. Her goodness and love somehow captivated me. The train was coming fast, and suddenly I no longer wanted to harm her. In fact, I wanted to protect her. It was an emotion I'd never had. It was as if I had been chained down and suddenly I could fly."

Cade looked around the room. Everyone's eyes were fixed on Eric. He continued, "At that moment, I picked her up and ran away as fast as I could. She thought it was fun, and never understood the danger she was in."

"What time was that?" Neville asked.

"It must have been about four o'clock, since that's when the train was due."

Neville looked at Cade and smiled. Cade recalled Neville's prayer in the living room at four the previous afternoon.

"I knew where to find you, so I came here. On the way, Sarah started crying and became feverish. I know nothing about you mortals physically, so I didn't know what to do. By the time we arrived at the cottage, she was asleep. You weren't here and that woman Sarah calls Dr. Lauren told me you were at church. So, I took Sarah there."

"But what's happening to you now?" Cade was baffled by Eric's rapid physical decay.

"We fiends are spiritual beings. We can take on human form, but that's just an illusion. When I turned from evil, and turned toward love ... toward God, I gave up my ability to maintain my illusion. What you see now is the reality, not the illusion."

"How do you mean?" Cade inquired.

"This shriveled, pallid appearance shows the consequences on my soul of my sin. Although I've turned to God and in His eyes my sins are forgiven, I still reflect the putrid nature of sin's effect on my soul. I also now face His judgement ... but, I accept that. Regret is a terrible form of judgement and punishment, don't you see?"

"How can a devil who's done so much evil for so long, how can you possibly face God's judgement?" Cade was puzzled.

"How can I possibly avoid it? I have much to account for at my judgement – like all of you and like Foulheart, too. You humans are so short-sighted." He was now speaking in fits and starts. "You underestimate what the Christ did on the cross. He voluntarily took all sin upon Himself and suffered an excruciating death. If only you mortals understood, really understood, God's grace!" At this, a tear ran down Eric's face. "Grace is not a license to sin, and God's righteous judgement is an awe-inspiring prospect for all. Yet, forgiveness is available for everyone – even demons – who truly repent and turn to God. I know you find this impossible to believe, given who I am ... or was ... but I'm truly eager to meet God face-to-face now. I now understand why our job as devils was so frustrating – although we tried to fool ourselves as to our significance. That's because nothing in the universe is beyond the love and grace of God. *Nothing.*"

There was a gasp from behind, and Cade whirled to see Lauren, her face ashen. Tears were rolling down her cheeks. She buried her head in her hands. Reverend Cooper went over and put an arm around her shoulders.

"Tell me," inquired Cade, "how could you be a godfather to Sarah and say at the Baptism that you renounce evil?"

Eric looked at Cade. "As I'm sure the vicar can tell you, many people confess with their lips what they don't truly believe in their heart. It was the same for me in the sense that they were only words that held no meaning for me. In fact, under my breath, I disavowed the whole ceremony."

"What is heaven like?" Cooper asked after a few moments.

"I've never seen it – except maybe glimpses. We were never allowed by our Royal Hindness to get near heaven, and now I understand why. I can only say it will surpass all mortals' expectations – it will be glorious. I long now to be in Paradise, just like the thief on the cross."

"You know the Bible?" Cooper inquired, looking perplexed.

"Of course. It's part of our training. Misrepresenting and misinterpreting the Scriptures are some of our most potent and effective weapons."

Cade noted that the vicar appeared mesmerized.

Eric extended a now frail, shaking hand. "Oh, Cade, I have something for you."

Eric clasped Cade's hand, and Cade felt something hard inside his palm. He knew without looking that it was his wedding band. He immediately slipped it on his finger.

Eric said in a weak voice, "You're a remarkable man. We did all we could to bring you down, to make you unfaithful to Rachael, and we failed."

Cade felt a flood of relief at those words.

"And Cade, you have the Crown Jewel of all jewels for a wife, treasure her always."

Eric looked over at the vicar. "It's almost time. Can you read me

... I think you call it the 'Ministry at the Time of Death?'"

David Cooper nodded, walked over to Eric's side, and opened his Book of Common Prayer. He motioned for all present to circle around the bed, and he read from the eighth chapter of Romans about the love of Christ.

After he had read more prayers, the vicar looked at Eric. "Repeat after me. 'Holy God, Father, Son, and Holy Spirit, I trust you, I believe in you, I love you.'"

Eric repeated the words, his face taking on a look of serenity.

Cooper continued with the Ministry through several more prayers and made the sign of the cross over Eric. As the vicar started to turn away, Eric reached out with a trembling hand and took Cooper's hand. "Thank you, vicar. You are truly a man of God. Now I can go in peace."

Eric had shriveled up to the point of being almost unrecognizable. His head lay on the pillow like a sack of flour, and he barely turned it. He glanced toward Lauren. "Sarah told me that you play the flute. Could you please play something for me now?" Lauren nodded and rushed out of the room.

He looked up at Cade. "I know this is unfair, but you're the only person now who can stop Foulheart."

"How?" Cade frowned.

"I am part of a group assembled by Foulheart. We've all taken on mortal forms and have been in place for years. We – I mean – they, will launch a new plan called Operation Clootie, on New Year's Eve in Paris."

Cade recalled hearing these strange words in Mobile. Eric continued. "The final instructions will be given then, which also includes disclosure of my reports."

"Where is this to take place? How could I do anything?" Cade looked around the room, noting the strained and astonished faces of the vicar and Neville.

"The meeting will take place at an address on a small street in Paris near Notre Dame. You remember the purple symbol you found on the stone in Sewanee?"

Cade nodded.

"That same symbol will be on the door. You can go dressed as me. You'll find my hooded gown and mask in the backseat of the black car parked near the church. When you get to the door, someone will be guarding the entrance. You must give him a password. The password is ... ."

"Bacchus?" interrupted Cade.

Eric's eyes grew wide, and he stared with a look of total amazement at Cade.

"But, how ... how could you possibly know that?"

"I was in Mobile and stumbled upon your meeting."

"You were there?" Eric looked incredulous. "You never cease to amaze me, Cade Bryson. Then you know what our assembly is like. Just mimic my voice if asked anything, but try to keep to the back and say nothing. It is imperative you get hold of Foulheart's plans and expose them. But let me warn you. It's very dangerous. If Foulheart discovers you, you'll be dead."

Eric sat up partially and leaned forward, his appearance now horrifically skeletal. "Hand me a piece of paper and I'll draw you a map." As Eric wrote on the paper, he continued, "If he does discover you, you have *one* possible chance. Do you have a tape recorder and Bible here?"

Cade nodded and went to get them.

When Cade returned, Eric handed him the paper and added, "In case you must confront Foulheart, I'm sending him a message. It might help you."

Eric spoke into the pocket recorder as Cade held it up to his mouth, his voice stronger than before. "Greetings, Foulheart, this is Soulbane." Eric continued to talk, then opened the Bible and read from it. After he stopped speaking, he nodded and Cade turned off the recorder.

Eric's appearance had become almost transparent, and wrinkled beyond recognition. Lauren returned, and moved over to examine him, but Eric said, "There's nothing you can do. Will you please just play your flute for me?"

Lauren nodded, put her flute to her lips, and began to play Debussy's *Reverie*. Eric's eyes closed, and he gave no sign of life.

When Lauren finished playing, his eyes opened slightly, and he motioned for Cade to come closer. He bent down, and Eric said in a whisper, "Please find it in your heart to forgive me. And, please give my godchild my love. Ironically, it's my wonderful new love for her that destroyed my evil spirit. I only wish I'd given in sooner. All this time trying to destroy souls and block God's grace, and now I finally realize it's the most beautiful thing in the universe, thanks to Sarah."

Cade reached down and touched Eric's arm. "Thanks for saving my daughter."

"One final request?" whispered Eric.

"What?" Cade inquired.

"Please take some ashes and scatter them in the cemetery here."

Cade nodded.

Eric's face contorted, then he smiled, his gaze already in another world.

"But, Eric, who is Foulheart?"

Eric lifted his head slightly and gasped, "I ... I never knew for sure. I think ... think Foulheart is ... Foulheart is ... ." And then he vanished.

Lauren threw back the blanket, but all that remained were Eric's empty clothes.

There was stunned silence in the room.

The vicar made the sign of the cross over the bed. "'Heavenly Father, into whose hands Jesus Christ commended his spirit at the last hour: into those same hands we now commend your servant Eric, that death may be for him the gate to life and to eternal fellowship with you, through Jesus Christ our Lord. Amen.'"

Cade stared at the empty bed. He looked at his watch and saw it was almost three on Christmas morning. David Cooper came over and put his hand on Cade's shoulder. "I'll help you with a funeral service."

Cade nodded, but said nothing. His shock at what they had just witnessed left him speechless and stunned.

Lauren spoke up. "Vicar, I'll take over here. You must want to get home to your family."

"I'm a widower actually – no family."

Cade thought he saw their eyes meet, but he was too tired to think about it. As if abruptly awakened from a deep sleep, he blurted out, "Sarah, where's Sarah?"

Lauren smiled with a look of compassion. "She's sleeping in my cottage now. Rachael and Mrs. Young, the nurse, are with her."

"I've got to see her." Cade rushed out of the room. He dashed out the front door and stopped, startled, at the idyllic scene – the moon cast its light over the sleeping village, covered with immaculate snow. Not wishing to delay even a moment longer, he ran toward Lauren's cottage.

When Cade arrived at the cottage, he grabbed at the door and flung it open. He stepped inside and heard a noise in an adjoining room. He hurried in that direction and saw a woman in a rocking chair by a bed gently swaying back and forth, the wooden floor creaking in time. She was reading a book, but looked up and smiled when Cade entered. He looked beyond her to see his wife and daughter curled up together asleep in the bed.

"Is … is she all right?" he whispered.

"Yes," came the quiet reply from the woman. "She's been resting for a good while. You must be her father."

Cade nodded and went to Sarah's bedside. He saw her sleeping peacefully and gently touched her warm, rosy cheeks. He bent over and kissed her on the forehead, saying quietly, "Thank you, God."

He whispered to the lady in the rocking chair, "You can go home now. Thank you for everything."

She nodded and stood.

He added, "And, a very Merry Christmas to you."

She smiled, picked up her coat and purse, and quietly left the room.

Cade sat in the rocking chair and stared at his wife and child. He was too numb to think and lost track of time.

He heard something and looked up. He'd dozed off. Light from the early morning sun was streaming into the room. He looked over at the bed.

Rachael's eyes opened, and she smiled at Cade. Without warning, he burst into tears of joy and relief.

Sarah sat up halfway in the bed rubbing her eyes with her fists. She yawned and said groggily, "Daddy, I was having the most wonderful dream. You and Mommy and I were playing on the beach and having the best time."

"I love you so much," Cade said hoarsely, wiping his eyes with his shirt sleeve. He went over to the bedside.

"I know, Daddy. You love me more than the whole wide world, that's what Uncle Eric told me last night."

"He's right, I ...," but no other words would come out.

Rachael sat up, her face radiant for the first time since he'd come to England. Cade sat on the side of the bed and put his arms around Sarah and Rachael, holding them tightly.

Sarah pulled back, saying, "It's Christmas Day, did Santa Claus find us?"

Cade and Rachael laughed together, then Cade looked at his wife, concerned when he realized that Santa Claus had been the last thing on their minds this Christmas. As Cade was wondering what to tell his daughter, Lauren walked in with several boxes wrapped in bright gold paper. "You bet he did, Sarah. I found these at your house near the fireplace."

"Goodie, I knew he'd find us." Sarah clapped her hands as Lauren put the presents on the table next to the bed.

Cade took Rachael's hand and kissed it. He looked at Sarah as she tore at the wrapping on one of the presents, knowing that he had just received his greatest Christmas gift ever.

38

CADE AND RACHAEL held hands as they walked toward the graveyard at St. Mary's. It was early afternoon the Sunday following Christmas. "I'm glad you finally told your father about all this when you called him before Christmas," Rachael said as they walked.

"Funny, isn't it," Cade replied. "All this time dreading talking to him, and he proves to be my staunchest ally, next to you." He squeezed her hand and continued. "As we learned with Sarah, there's nothing like the parent – child bond. Or grandparents, for that matter. When I called them Christmas Day, they were elated at the good news. They had been worried sick and Mom said that Dad was planning to get on a plane and come over here. I told her I appreciated it, but with Sarah's safe return, it wasn't necessary. Besides, I needed him to stay in the States and help me with the Pickering debacle."

"Have you heard any more from Harry?"

"Not yet, but it's only a matter of time. The only reason they've left me alone, I think, is because I put Dad on their backs."

Reverend Cooper, Lauren, and Neville were gathered among the tombstones when the Brysons arrived. The yew tree, outlined against the blue, cloudless sky, danced in the chilling breeze, shaking off the last vestiges of snow. The gravestones were capped with snow, like mountains in the summertime. Rachael clasped Cade's hand, as they stood silently near the graves of Anne and

James Brooke. On either side of them were Neville and Lauren, while Reverend Cooper stood in front of the group, holding a prayer book. The vicar spoke slowly, his surplice billowing in the wind, as he read from the Anglican Burial Service:

"'We commend unto thy hands of mercy, most merciful Father, the soul of this our brother Eric departed, and we commit his ashes to their resting place, earth to earth, ashes to ashes, dust to dust. And we beseech thine infinite goodness to give us grace to live in thy fear and love and to die in thy favour, that when the judgement shall come which thou hast committed to thy well-beloved Son, both this our brother and we may be found acceptable in thy sight. Grant this, O merciful Father, for the sake of Jesus Christ, our only Saviour, Mediator, and Advocate. Amen.'"

When he finished speaking, the vicar took the small urn sitting near James Brooke's headstone. It contained the ashes of Eric's clothes. He overturned the urn and dark ashes floated out, the swirling wind mixing them with snow falling from the yew tree. The black ashes and snowflakes circled together like long ribbons whirled in circles. Cade stared at the sight, until the moment passed, and the ashes were all scattered.

The group walked in silence to the vicarage. It was the first time Cade had been there since James Brooke's death. As he stepped inside, he recognized the study, but noted it was much different now. Instead of the chaos of books lying all about, and the piles of papers scattered on the desk, the room was neat and tidy, and more sparsely furnished.

"Let me make us some tea," said Cooper, as he walked toward the kitchen. "Please make yourselves comfortable."

"I'll help you," said Lauren, with a touch more eagerness in her voice than was necessary. The vicar turned, paused, then smiled.

"That would be very kind of you," he replied.

It had been several days since Eric vanished on Christmas morning. The group assembled in the vicarage had attended church in the morning and agreed to meet at the graveyard at half past two for a memorial service. Cade had also requested that the group convene a meeting to discuss Eric's mysterious final words about the Paris meeting. Rachael took a seat in a tall upholstered chair, and Cade stood behind her.

Neville was pulling out some of the vicar's books from the bookcase and thumbing through them. He turned toward Rachael. "How is Sarah?"

"Oh, she's quite well, thank you. My mother returned from Bath yesterday and is looking after her."

"What has Sarah said about all this?" Neville stroked his chin.

"Believe it or not, she thought Eric came all the way to England to surprise her and take her on holiday. She had no idea she was ever in any danger. She bounced back from her fever in no time."

"That's marvelous," Neville sat down in the chair at the Vicar's desk. "What have you told her about Eric?"

"We told Sarah that Uncle Eric was very sick and had gone to heaven, and she appears to have accepted it as only a child can."

Lauren walked in with a tray of biscuits, and David Cooper followed with a teapot and some mugs. Everyone sipped tea quietly for a few minutes. Cade stared out the window at the cross on top of the steeple, his mind still reeling from the events of these past weeks. Finally the vicar spoke, "We need to decide what we should do about Eric's deathbed revelation. If I hadn't been there myself, I'd have never believed this. Nevertheless, I find I have no choice but to believe. Let's review what we know. Cade has filled me in on these Soulbane Reports he discovered years ago, and briefly on the events of the last months. Now, we're down to this business about Foulheart, and some supposed clandestine meeting in Paris two days from now."

Cade interjected, "I just have to go."

"No," said Rachael in a loud voice, which seemed to startle everyone. "Cade, you've ... we've been through enough. Let's leave well enough alone and don't get involved any more."

"I can't Rachael," he replied. "I believe I was given a

responsibility for these reports and making them public. Maybe if I had done that in the first place, none of this would have happened. I know if I had paid attention to them, I would have made better choices in my own life. Someone has to stop Foulheart."

"But it's so dangerous," said Rachael in a pleading tone. "I just got you back. I don't want to lose you. And there's Sarah to consider. She needs her father."

Cade bent over and hugged Rachael. "I *have* to do this. I'll never be able to live with myself if I don't go."

Cooper walked to the center of the room and looked directly at Cade. "Let me go for you, Cade. I don't have a family, and, well … as a vicar, it's my duty to fight for Christ wherever I'm called."

Cade just shook his head no. "You're kind to offer, but this is my battle. I have to settle this with Foulheart, whoever he is, once and for all. Otherwise, Sarah and Rachael and I will never be rid of them. This is the only way. Besides, whatever this Operation Clootie is, Eric said it was essential Foulheart be stopped from executing it."

Neville added, "I'm afraid Cade's right. He's been thrust into the middle of this for some reason, even if we don't understand it. We must get him ready for this meeting. Cade, you'll need to practice wearing the hood and gown that Eric left for you, and you'll have to learn to respond to the name 'Soulbane.' I'll work with you on this tonight and tomorrow."

"Thanks," replied Cade. Rachael buried her face in her hands, but said nothing.

Lauren, who had been silent this entire time, said, "I guess I'm the outsider here. A week ago, I would have laughed at the thought of religion, at least of taking it seriously, much less angels and devils and all that. My whole world has been turned upside down by this. But, I must say, it seems to me like Cade shouldn't try this. You know the old saying, 'Discretion is the better part of valor.'"

"Lauren, I appreciate your concerns," interrupted Cade, who was stung by the last comment. This was the same phrase he'd used in Mobile to talk himself out of taking any action. He pictured the Runnymede Memorial with the twenty thousand inscribed names and knew what true courage was. "My mind is already made up. They've kidnapped my daughter once, and they might try something again if I don't stop them. Besides, Eric said it was essential that I stop this Operation Clootie."

Rachael stood. "David, could we at least all pray for Cade?"

"Certainly," he replied. Everyone stood and joined hands, and Reverend Cooper prayed for Cade and his upcoming journey to Paris.

*   *   *

"Cheers!" Cade raised his wineglass, but Rachael didn't respond. They were sitting at a table near a bright, orange fire crackling in the large stone fireplace at The Trout in Godstow. The old, rough-hewn wood and plaster walls of the ancient pub added to the atmosphere. Rachael hardly touched her meal. He looked at her blue eyes shining in the candlelight.

They had talked about everything at dinner – everything, that is, *except* Cade's trip to Paris in the morning.

"Rachael, I'm so blessed to have you," said Cade, putting down his wineglass. He reached over and took her hand. "Let's take a walk."

The two put on their coats and walked hand-in-hand out of The Trout. It was still very cold, but all the snow was gone. The stars shone brightly in the clear winter sky. They walked to the middle of the stone bridge. There was no hint of wind, and the night was silent, except for the water gushing under the bridge.

He turned and faced Rachael, gazing into her eyes. His throat tightened. "Rachael, I'm so very sorry for this mess. How can I ever make it up to you? I … ."

But Rachael put her finger over his mouth in a sign of silence and shook her head.

Cade teared up and embraced her. "I love you so much." He

kissed her passionately.

"Ahem," said a voice nearby.

Cade and Rachael looked up, startled, to see a man with a hat and overcoat, walking his English sheepdog.

"Sorry to bother you, but I was afraid Frisky might think you were a statue, and well, he might, you know ... ."

Cade and Rachael burst into laughter, and Rachael said, "Here, Frisky." She held out her hand, and the dog came over, sniffed it, and deigned to let her pet him on the head.

"Good night to you," said the man, doffing his hat. As he started to walk on, he patted Cade on the shoulder, and winked at him while nodding toward Rachael. "She's a lovely lass."

Cade looked at Rachael, in complete agreement. Rachael's face showed intense sadness. "Cade, please don't go tomorrow. Think of Sarah. You don't have to go. No one will ever know."

"*I will*," he said quietly, but emphatically. "It's something I have to do." His thoughts went to the words in the north window of the Runnymede Memorial. "I won't be alone," he whispered to her.

"You know I believe in you with all my heart, don't you?"

"Yes, and that's all that matters." Cade had originally intended to talk to Rachael about what to do if he didn't return from Paris, but he just couldn't bring himself to say anything during dinner about it. Now he knew it would only upset her. He quickly decided to keep all his concerns to himself. Neither of them acknowledged this might be their last night together – ever.

"You need to get some sleep," she said finally, and Cade detected a catch in her voice. They walked back over the bridge holding hands, the stars observing them from above.

39

IT WAS STILL DARK outside when Cade, who'd slept fitfully, finally slipped out of bed. He dressed quickly, hoping to let Rachael sleep. He picked up a small bag with a few things he'd packed for the trip, including Eric's gown. As he fumbled on the dresser for the car keys, he felt something else. He handled it with his fingers and discerned it was a small, wooden cross that Rachael had obviously put there for him. He put it in his pants pocket.

He walked softly into the other room and stared at his sleeping daughter. After a few minutes, he walked over and tucked the blanket around her. He spotted Flopsy, who'd fallen on the floor, and picked up the little rabbit, placing him next to Sarah's head. Was that a smile on her face? He kissed Sarah on the cheek, stood to go, bent over and kissed her again. He took one last look at the sleeping girl, drew a deep breath, and walked out.

As he reached the front door, he heard a whisper, "Cade."

Cade turned around to see Rachael outlined by the light from a lamp in their bedroom. She was standing in her nightgown, yawning. She ran over and put her arms around his neck. "Darling. I love you so very, very much."

He held his wife as tightly as he'd ever done and kissed her. "No matter what happens, please always remember that I love you and Sarah more than anything."

"I know," she whispered quietly.

"I have to go now." He forced himself to let go of their embrace.

He knew if he lingered any longer, his resolve to find Foulheart might vanish forever. He kissed Rachael on her forehead, squeezed her hand, and went out into the cold, dark morning. The village was peaceful, and he rubbed his hands together as he hurried to the car. He saw Rachael peeping through the front window. He wanted desperately to run to her – to forget this insane trip – but forced himself to wave quickly and get into the car.

He was about to drive off, when a tap on his window jolted him. He jerked his head to the side, but couldn't see anything because the window was frosted over. There was a movement on the outside of the window and gloved fingers appeared wiping the ice off the window. In a moment, Neville's face, illuminated by the street lamp, was peering in the porthole. Cade smiled and got out of the car.

"What are you doing here at his early hour?" He stared at Neville, who was holding a paper cup with a lid in one hand.

Neville laughed softly. "I thought you could use some hot coffee."

Cade gratefully took the cup. "Thanks, Neville. That's just what I needed."

There was a slight lightening of the morning's darkness, announcing the approaching dawn.

"Guess I'd better be going."

Neville put a hand on his shoulder. "Before you go, I'd like to say a prayer."

Cade nodded and bowed his head. Neville's hand remained on Cade's shoulder, as he said, "Heavenly Father, we ask for your protection and guidance for Cade. Watch over my friend this day and forevermore. Amen."

"Amen," repeated Cade softly. He set the cup on top of the car and embraced the older man. "Neville, I can't thank you enough."

Cade retrieved the cup and got back in the car.

"God's blessing be upon you, Cade." Neville bent over and smiled. "I have one other thing for your journey. I've marked a page for you to read later." He handed Cade a pocket-size New Testament.

"I'll read it when I get on the train." Cade returned the smile, trying to mask his nervousness.

"Oh, one last thing." Neville bent down so their faces were level. "Remember what Lewis quotes at the beginning of *The Screwtape Letters*?"

Cade nodded vaguely, not sure to what Neville was referring.

Neville pulled out a dog-eared copy of *The Screwtape Letters* from his coat pocket and read, "'The best way to drive out the devil, if he will not yield to texts of Scripture, is to jeer and flout him, for he cannot bear scorn.' That's from Luther. Then also, Lewis quotes from Sir Thomas More, 'The devil … the proude spirite … cannot endure to be mocked.'"

"Thanks, I'll remember that. Good-bye Neville."

"Do you know the derivation of the word 'good-bye'?"

"I'm afraid I don't. What is it?"

"God be with ye." Neville patted Cade's arm and shut the car door.

The sky was pink and orange, and the rising sun cast a pale light over the village as Cade drove down the street. He glanced into the rear-view mirror and saw Neville standing in the road watching him drive off. Suddenly, Neville raised one hand – and saluted.

* * *

On the train going through the Channel Tunnel, Cade recalled the training Neville had given him. They had gone over what Cade observed during the devils' meeting in Mobile, and Neville had drilled him on learning to respond to the name "Soulbane" and to mimic Eric's voice. He mouthed the "Bacchus" password several times, shivering when he recalled Eric's deathbed words about the consequences if Foulheart discovered Cade. Remembering the small *New Testament* that Neville had given him, he pulled it out. *What was it that Neville suggested I read?* He thumbed through the pages.

He came to a page with the corner turned down and saw it marked the sixth chapter of Ephesians. He read to himself:

"Put on the whole armour of God, so that you may be able to stand against the wiles of the devil. For our struggle is not against enemies of blood and flesh, but against the rulers, against the authorities, against the cosmic powers of this present darkness, against the spiritual forces of evil in the heavenly places."

When he finished reading the entire passage, Cade closed his eyes. As the train raced toward Paris in the long, dark tunnel, Cade wondered where this day's journey was going to end.

40

Z AC PICKERING sat at his desk, his head in his hands. This was not how he'd intended to spend New Year's Eve. He stared in disbelief at the documents in front of him and read them for the third time, as if hoping they would somehow magically say something else. They still read the same: a summons and complaint had been served on him a half hour before, naming him as the defendant in a divorce proceeding initiated by Florence.

He fumbled in his desk drawer for a key and unlocked the cabinet behind his desk. He took out the envelope he had mysteriously received several months before, containing pictures of his sailing trip with Gail in St. Lucia. *I thought I had until New Year's. How in the hell did Florence find out?* Zac had been so careful, so discreet. His mind raced back to the cocktail party where Senator Rogers had warned him not to do anything to damage the senator and his family. Surely he could somehow figure a way to finesse himself out of this. He smiled slightly. After all, he was a pro at such illusions. Or maybe he could take the rest of the money he hadn't squandered in the Internet venture and head for the Caribbean with Gail. That prospect lifted Zac's mood a little.

His thoughts were interrupted by Marge calling him on the intercom. "Mr. Pickering?"

"Yes," Zac said tersely.

"There's a reporter from *The Washington Post* on the line, insisting that she must talk to you."

"Marge, do the usual stall and tell her I'm not available."

"Right." When Marge hung up, Zac was at least grateful for such a good secretary, who seemed to know just how to handle every situation. *The Washington Post*? Had Florence's attorney leaked the divorce to the press? Probably. Why hadn't he heard from Bryson? He needed that disk. He'd made certain to put enough pressure on Bryson so that the lawyer would have no choice but to give Zac what he so desperately needed.

Zac was not accustomed to failure, and this was not the time to panic. He'd been in many tight places before, and he'd figure a way out of this yet. He lit a new cigar and savored the tobacco's aroma, as he blew circles of smoke into the air. He had been very careful to cover his – and the senator's – tracks. So well, in fact, that not even the senator would be able to figure out how Zac had screwed him and the other investors. At least, not until he was long gone. He smiled wryly.

The intercom buzzed again, and Marge said, "Excuse me, Mr. Pickering, but two FBI agents are here to see you."

At this, Zac's mind raced. The FBI? What were they doing here? They couldn't possibly know about his clandestine financial dealings, could they? *They can't prove a thing.*

Nevertheless, Zac felt rising panic and took several deep breaths.

"Mr. Pickering?" said Marge again, in a more insistent tone.

"Oh, yes. I'll see them in a minute." Zac stood and walked over to the window, staring at the white dome of the Capitol. Those FBI bastards weren't taking him down, not with what he had on his senator friends. He smiled at his reflection in the window and puffed on his cigar.

After a few moments, he hit his intercom button.

Marge answered promptly. "Yes?"

"Marge, send the gentlemen in now."

Zac tightened his tie and put the divorce papers in a desk drawer. He forged a big smile and rallied his psyche to put on yet one more sales job for these FBI agents. They most certainly would be bluffing, going on half-baked information. He smiled thinking about the documents he'd shredded and the information he'd deleted from his computer a couple of nights ago, when he learned that his entire investment in the Internet business was gone.

As the door opened, Zac stood, the epitome of confidence and bravado. In walked Marge and a tall, thin man, in a dark gray suit and blue tie. His gaunt, stern face did not indicate a man with a sense of humor.

The man strode right up to Zac and extended his hand. "Mr. Pickering, I'm Agent Parr."

He gripped the agent's hand tightly, still exuding as much confidence as he could muster. He took another puff on his cigar and gestured toward a chair. "Do have a seat, Mr. Parr, and tell me what I can do for you today." He looked up at Marge. "I thought you said there were two gentlemen here from the FBI."

Marge looked straight at Zac, no hint of a smile, and said in a monotone voice, "I said there were two FBI agents here – I never said there were two men."

He stood motionless, staring at Marge. As comprehension dawned on him, he sat back in his chair, with a loud sigh. His smile vanished, and for the first time in many years, Zac felt totally helpless.

41

CADE WALKED DOWN the left bank of the Seine, dodging the mass of people hurrying along the sidewalk. The Cathedral of Notre Dame dominated the scene, it's December mood darkened by the dreary day, yet still majestic in its towering presence. The air was chilly, and the low-hanging clouds brushed the tops of the cathedral's towers. The congested traffic filled the afternoon with horns and exhaust. For all the splendor of the fine city, he gave no thought to sightseeing. His one mission before dark on this New Year's Eve was to locate the door marking the entrance to the midnight meeting Eric told him about.

Cade tugged at his hat and adjusted his scarf to virtually cover his face, to avoid any chance of being recognized. He glanced about furtively, wondering if any of the people he was passing were here for the meeting.

He glanced at the rough map Eric had drawn and soon came upon the side street noted on the piece of paper. He marched down it purposefully, yet almost hoping he would not be able to find the place. Soon, however, just where Eric had drawn it, he saw an otherwise inconspicuous white door in the middle of a row of buildings, just like a dozen other doors along the street. But this one had a discreet purple mark on it, small enough to be seen only by those who would be looking, and identical to the symbol on the stone in Sewanee where he had discovered one of Soulbane's Reports. He noted the door and its position on the street, but kept walking swiftly so as not to draw attention to himself.

Street lights glowed, as this final day of the year was saying farewell to the light. He gripped the handle of his canvas bag tightly, trying to avoid hitting anyone with it as he walked down the sidewalk. He wondered if he would greet the new year.

Aware he still had a good number of hours to wait, Cade pondered what to do. He decided to walk back to Notre Dame and spend some time there. He turned around and took another street, to prevent the possibility of running into any familiar faces on this road.

As he entered through the large doors of Notre Dame, he paused in awe of its interior. The massive structure rose toward the heavens, and hundreds of small votive candles flickered just inside the door, adding small spots of light inside the cavernous darkness.

He walked about halfway down the center aisle, slipped into a chair on the side, and gazed up at the massive columns, the beautiful ceiling, and the ornate altar. He closed his eyes, letting the image sink into his mind.

Cade's head rolled sideways, and he jerked upright. No surprise, he mused, that the minimal sleep of recent days was catching up with him. Only a few people were milling around in the cathedral now. The increased darkness told him night had fallen. A movement on the side near a confessional booth caught his attention, and he turned his head in that direction. His heart leapt into his throat.

Just exiting one of the booths, dressed in a priest's black robe, Ian was moving rapidly toward the rear. Cade jumped up and started after him, then stopped abruptly. It would be disastrous if Ian saw him. He couldn't help himself, however, and took off after him. He walked quickly toward the shadows near the wall, in order to hide his face. He peered toward the rear just in time to see the robed figure exit through the doorway, hurried to the door, and stepped cautiously outside. The thousands of seasonal lights that adorned the city kept the winter darkness at bay. He looked to and fro, frantically trying to find Ian in the crowd around the cathedral, and spotted him walking rapidly away. Ian crossed the street, and Cade resumed the clandestine chase. After several blocks, the man stopped to look at a newsstand, and Cade came abruptly upon him. The man turned and seemed to stare directly at Cade, whose heart raced with panic, as he regretted his imprudence in following Ian. His fear, however, quickly turned to relief when he saw that the tall priest was not Ian after all. Cade looked at the ground and walked on past the stranger.

He looked all around him, aware of his surroundings for the first time since he exited Notre Dame. Paris was coming alive for the New Year's Eve festivities. The air had turned very cold after sunset, especially with a breeze drifting through the streets. He wrapped his scarf around his neck.

He needed to walk off his nervous energy and struck out with no destination in mind. Although he wasn't hungry, he decided he should eat something to give him energy and clarity of mind for what would most likely be a long night. He found a small café and ordered a sandwich and coffee. As he sat waiting, his fingers tapped on the table. He pulled the pocket *New Testament* from his coat pocket and re-read the passage in Ephesians, then thumbed through the pages absentmindedly. The waitress appeared with his meal. Cade put the book in his coat pocket and began eagerly to devour the sandwich, finding he was famished.

As he sipped a second cup of coffee, Cade planned the evening. Sometime around eleven-thirty, he would have to find a deserted place to put on the robe and hood. It would have to be near the meeting spot, so that he wouldn't have far to go. He recalled seeing an alleyway near the door and decided he could change there. He would put on the robe over his clothes, taking off his coat, gloves, and scarf. He had Eric's shoes, and fortunately they were close to his size. He would put the recorder in his pocket, and leave the bag where he could retrieve it later. If all went well, Cade would soon know Foulheart's Operation Clootie plans. After that, he reckoned another five or six hours would see him safely back in England. He took the last gulp of coffee and reached down to pick up his bag. He grabbed only air. He bent over and looked everywhere under the table – no bag. Cade's pulse raced. Had his bag been stolen? If so, his plan was finished before he'd even begun. He jumped up and frantically searched the café. Nothing. He shut his eyes to think, and couldn't remember taking the bag with him out of Notre Dame. He threw some money on the table and ran toward the cathedral.

When he reached the enormous doors, they were closed. He tugged on them, but they didn't budge. Frustration made him kick them as he thought of the disaster of not having Eric's gown, hood and mask to wear: without this apparel there would be no infiltration of the meeting. He ran around to the side, hoping to see another entrance and wondering if he should try knocking, finally sinking down on the steps, thinking that he had come all this way for nothing.

After a few minutes, he slapped his thigh and stood to walk away. Hearing a noise, he wheeled around and saw a priest coming out of a door. He rushed up to the man.

Cade said excitedly, "Excuse me, I think I left my bag inside. Can you let me in?"

The man turned and looked at Cade, wide-eyed. He shook his head, indicating he didn't understand a word Cade had just said. Cade's mind reeled back to his college French.

"Pardon moi, monsieur. Je … ." Cade paused, he couldn't think of the right words to tell the man he'd left his bag inside. He performed a pantomime routine in an attempt to fill in his lack of French, as the priest stared at him with obvious amusement and puzzlement.

Cade used his hands to make it look like he was carrying something, and pointed toward the cathedral. "Moi … le bag, … il gauche derrière."

The priest broke into an almost hysterical laugh, wrapping his arms around his ample belly. Cade was baffled, wondering what he had said. He began to lose hope and wondered how he would ever tell Neville and Rachael of his *faux pas* – some French he *did* know.

The man smiled at Cade and pulled out a key, turning toward the church. "Merci," Cade replied. The priest opened the door and motioned for Cade to enter. He nodded and ran to where he had been sitting. To his enormous relief, the bag was on the floor where he'd left it. He snatched it up and hurried out.

"Merci beaucoup," Cade said excitedly. The man broke into another hearty laugh. Cade pulled out some money, but the priest held up his palms in a gesture of refusal. Cade looked around, saw a receptacle for donations, and stuffed some Euros into the slot. The priest nodded his approval.

Cade grinned at the priest when they were outside, and the man touched him lightly on the shoulder saying in heavily accented English, "Okay, welcome." He locked the door, waved energetically to Cade, and walked off into the night.

The sidewalks of Paris were filled with people. The frivolity and gaiety in the air were tangible, as couples walked arm in arm, talking and laughing. Cade went over to a wall near the river and watched the boats passing by. He took a deep breath and nervously walked around the center of the city, to wile away the remaining hours. The butterflies were multiplying in his stomach, and he continually wiped sweat off his palms. He tried not to think about whether he would ever see another dawn. Thunder rumbled in the distance. The overcast sky reflected the numerous lights, giving the impression that Paris was under a dome.

Cade looked at his watch so often that he actually lost track of time because he paid no attention. He became aware of a bell sounding in the distance and realized it was eleven thirty. He needed to get close to the meeting place right away and change clothes. His heart pounded from fear and anticipation as he walked quickly toward the side street.

The thunder was louder now, and flashes of lightning off in the distance illuminated the threatening clouds. He reached the alleyway and was relieved to find it deserted. Off came his coat, gloves and scarf, all quickly bundled up. Next, he took off his running shoes and white socks and replaced them with Eric's black socks and black leather shoes. He had to tug hard to get the shoes on, and felt the discomfort of wearing shoes that were too tight. Out came Eric's black robe. It fit almost perfectly, covering everything but his hands and shoes. He put on a skull mask identical to the one he'd worn in Mobile and pulled the hood over his head, recalling the night he'd ridden on the Mardi Gras float in Mobile. He was grateful he'd had at least one experience with wearing a costume and mask.

He stuffed his clothes in the bag and hid it in a crevice formed by some missing bricks in a wall of the alleyway, then walked slowly toward the meeting place, feeling very queasy. He was already sweating, despite the cold. Just then he remembered he'd forgotten the recorder and hurried to retrieve it.

Cade had taken off his watch, but guessed it had to be close to midnight as he approached the door. Sure enough, a dark figure loomed large in the shadows by the door, the sight of whom caused him to stop instinctively. Reminding himself that he was now Soulbane, not Cade Bryson, he nodded solemnly at the figure, who returned the nod. Cade said in a low mumble, "Bacchus." The figure said nothing in reply, but merely opened the door and pointed the way in.

Adrenaline seemed to be rushing out of his pores, making him feel light-headed. Was he walking to his death? He momentarily hesitated, thinking he still had time to make a run for it. Then another hooded figure came in the door after him, and Cade lost his chance to leave. He saw movement ahead of him. A gowned figure stood at the end of the long hallway. Cade proceeded down the hallway, which was lit only by candles.

He reached a stairway that went down into a dark basement. He had to be careful not to stumble on the short, steep, wooden steps. At the bottom, a dancing orange light loomed in the room ahead of him. Directly across from him was a blazing fire, and a number of hooded figures were standing silently near the fireplace. Candles burned on a small, circular, wooden table in the center of the room. Shadows danced eerily on the wall, in step with the flickering flames of the fireplace. A few feeble, electric lights were on the wall, but they contributed little to banish the darkness.

A large figure standing in front of the fireplace nodded toward Cade, but said nothing, and Cade nodded in return. He felt conspicuous and was aware of his labored breathing, as he endeavored to fade into the back of the group. Another hooded figure came into the room and went up to the one near the fireplace, appearing to say something to him. A second figure entered the room and shut the door, which closed with a thud. A sliding metallic sound indicated the door had been bolted.

Cade jumped involuntarily and glanced nervously about the room. There appeared to be about thirty or so figures, all in the same black gowns, hoods and masks. His mind flashed back to the meeting in Mobile. He labored to breathe the dungeon-like, musty, damp air. Sweat poured down his neck and back.

The large figure stepped forward, and the group gathered around him. Cade kept toward the back of the group, his eyes darting around the dimly lit room at the circle of ominous beings. His terror climbed steeply as the realization of his plight sank in: he was now locked in a dark basement in the middle of the night in Paris with a group of devilish characters, who would certainly kill him if they discovered his identity. He felt the same panic as he had in Mobile and regretted his foolishness in pursuing these devils here. He suddenly longed to be with his family.

"This is a great day for our Hindom," said the figure. He had a masculine voice, with a British accent. He sounded vaguely familiar, but his words were muffled by the mask, and Cade could not place the voice. The man continued, "As the humans begin their new year, we launch Operation Clootie, which has been years in the planning. Each of you has been an integral part of this diabolical plot, and I'm ravenous at the prospects for the havoc the implementation of this stratagem will wreak."

Cade thought the room resounded with the pounding of his heart. Sweat continued to roll down his forehead, neck, and back, and his clothes clung to him. He clasped his hands together to control his emotions. He dared not move. These shadowy figures were barely visible in the dim light from the fire and candles. Smoke filled the room, and Cade wondered if he could keep from choking. He doubted he'd ever get out alive.

The figure continued, as he held up a large object. "This notebook you see contains the final report prepared by Soulbane on our numerous victories in the world and the Church. Where are you, Soulbane?"

Cade panicked and felt as if his insides were on fire as adrenaline shot through his veins. What should he do? What if he made the wrong signal? Yet, he *had* to do something. His mouth was as dry as sandpaper. Finally, Cade slowly raised his hand, and lowered it quickly.

"Excellent work, my fine fellow," said the figure, nodding toward Cade, as he resumed his speech. "I also have in here the entire details of Operation Clootie, which I have personally devised. This is the only copy because I trust no one in our Hindom. I intend to ensure that our Royal Hindness will know who to thank for this masterpiece that will result in the destruction of the souls of millions of these horrid mortals. Each of you have been in place for many years now, and I trust you've established yourselves as competent in the different jobs you are pretending to hold."

There were several nods among the hooded figures, and one of them raised a hand and said in a female voice with a French accent, "Foulheart?"

"Yes, Darkeye, what is it?"

Cade's body shook as he understood he was staring at Foulheart.

"Are we to be in contact with one another now?"

"Absolutely not! You are to carry on just as before. Now, let me finish. I intend to visit each of you personally in the coming weeks to make sure you understand your roles. No one but me shall know your human identity or your role in the operation. I alone am the mastermind and you'll take orders only from me." At that point, Foulheart made a hissing sound.

He continued, "Soulbane's reports set the agenda for our overall plan. When I visit you, I will provide you with a copy, so that you can see how your part fits into our overall stratagems. We are winning more and more battles daily, and now, with the launch of Operation Clootie, whereby each of you is to begin to bring your fiendish work to fruition, we will see the end of the damned Enemy's vile human creatures once and for all!"

There were wolf-like howls from several figures, and various other sounds of approval.

"Now," continued Foulheart, "I need not remind you how critical it is for you to maintain the utmost secrecy concerning our plans. Only Base Command is aware of Operation Clootie, and I want it to stay that way. Should any of you fail … ." He broke off with a high-pitched screech that reminded Cade of the heinous cackle he'd heard that night on top of St. Mary's steeple in Oxford. Chill bumps ran up and down his arms.

Foulheart ceased his howling laugh. "Let's just say, you'll regret that day forever."

Another figure in the circle raised a hand, and said in a male, Australian accent, "We heard a rumor that these reports had been stolen by some human imbecile."

Foulheart turned toward the man swiftly, as if in anger, but said in a calm voice, "I'm glad you mentioned that, Bleakblab. Yes, thanks to my intuition, I suspected an American moron had the reports, and it turned out he did … ."

Cade now felt sick to his stomach and woozy. He wondered if he was about to faint.

Foulheart was saying, " … but thanks to Slobglob, we got them back. And, in the process, we destroyed the mortal's little runt. Right, Soulbane?"

Cade was ready to rush up and strangle him at this comment, but somehow controlled his anger. He merely nodded twice quickly, as if very pleased.

There was a loud, booming noise, like distant cannon. The storm was hurtling closer.

"That's the last we'll ever hear from Bryson. He won't dare ever cross the imperial Foulheart again." Foulheart burst forth with a loud wail, followed by a most sinister laugh. Cade's hands were shaking violently, and he had to grasp his elbows under the sleeves of his robe, to keep from giving himself away. His emotions raged like the approaching tempest outside, as hate and fear collided inside him. He again considered attacking Foulheart right then, but a small, inner voice stilled him. That, he knew, would mean certain death.

Boom. Boom-boom! A sudden, loud noise, like a bass drum, sounded all around them. Cade's head jerked around immediately, but he quickly turned back to face Foulheart when he realized it was only thunder. The storm must be virtually on top of them.

Foulheart spoke again, in a moderate tone. "It's almost time to depart. I want all of you dispersed before dawn, and I want you to make your way home as quickly as possible. We will not fail. I will personally see to it that our Royal Hindness is made aware of your efforts on behalf of our Hindom."

Cade gritted his teeth and eyed the closed door. He was drenched in sweat. Was it possible he could make it out?

Foulheart said, "Gather round and let me conclude our meeting with an appropriate salute to our Royal Hindness."

The group formed a circle around the table in the center of the room. They were chanting in low, hushed tones an eerie melody that reminded Cade of some despairing requiem. The candles were burning low, as was the fire in the large hearth. Cade took his place in the circle on the far side of the room away from the door.

Foulheart raised his arms toward the ceiling. "O Great Master of the Universe ... ."

Another loud peal of thunder almost drowned out Foulheart. Cade hardly listened, his mind racing. He planned how he would follow the group out the door and, as quickly as possible, he would disappear down some side street, dump the gown, and be on his way.

A stiff shove in the back jolted him from his imaginary plans. The group was beginning to disband. In only a minute or so, he'd be up the stairs and could quickly disappear. The large figure who had been the guard pulled a latch and opened the basement door. A dim light came from the hallway. The group was silent as they shuffled out single file. Because of his position in the circle, Cade would be almost the last in line. There was nothing he could do about it. As he moved forward, he smiled under his mask. Soon, he'd be free and would figure some way to expose this operation based on what he'd heard tonight. He walked slowly toward the door and freedom. Only Foulheart and two other figures, remained behind him. Just as he reached the door, a voice behind him said quite distinctly, "Oh, Cade, just a minute."

It was Neville's voice!

Even as he whirled around, Cade knew he'd fallen for one of the oldest tricks in the book.

42

*B*OOM. *BOOM-BOOM-BOOM!* Multiple flashes of bright light were accompanied by a volley of cannon-like sounds. Zac Pickering stood in the doorway of his darkened office, watching the fireworks outside his window. The old year would soon pass and a new one would take its place. Zac was in no mood for either nostalgia or celebration, however, and he flipped the light switch. He was still in shock over his discovery that Marge was an FBI agent, and he knew the game was up. Despite all his bravado, all his influence, and even his high-powered lawyers, he had to acknowledge that this time, he was history. He had only been questioned and read his constitutionally-required *Miranda* rights by the agents. He had not been formally charged today, but that would occur shortly. He realized they needed him for more important targets on Capitol Hill.

He flipped on the lights and surveyed his impressive office, starting with the nameplate on his large mahogany desk that told all visitors not only his name, but also his title as president of the company. His various achievements were recorded in photographs, trophies, diplomas, and other memorabilia he had collected over the years. These many vestiges of his personal achievements gave him no satisfaction now. If anything, they poured salt on his wounds, because they reminded him of the illusion he had portrayed all these years: the "successful" man, all the while masking his deceits, his affairs, his personal failures.

Until this afternoon, Zac had always somehow made himself believe that he was invincible, that he was the sole 'master of his fate,' no matter what. His pride and ego had grown out of control, he told himself, while his compassion and humanity – things he had thought about often as an idealistic young man – had been shoved away by his ever-increasing greed for power and money.

Zac went over to his bookcase, eyeing the reminders of his past. He paused to study a photograph of a much younger Zac and Florence, standing on the steps of the crumbling Parthenon in Greece. He had been in love with Florence then. Now, the divorce petition sat on his desk. He unlocked the cabinet under his bookcase and grabbed the bottle of Scotch, thinking ironically that he was not here to toast the new year.

Outside, more fireworks sparkled over the white Washington buildings and monuments. Revelers in the street below were yelling and laughing. He poured a glass of the amber liquid and gulped it down. Reaching into the cabinet, his fingers touched a wooden box. He hesitantly pulled it out, slowly lifted the lid, and ran his fingers over the cold steel of the revolver.

Zac had always been a winner – in sports, in school, in business. He couldn't face failure. His lawyer had given him the halftime pep talk about all the wonderful defenses they could interpose, and how unlikely it was that he would ever be convicted of anything, much less serve jail time. But something was different this time – Zac was not up to this fight. No, the house of cards had come tumbling down, and he knew this time the game was over.

After the two agents left his office, Zac called Gail at the apartment he'd set up for her in Key West. He needed to talk to her about Florence's divorce proceedings, and hear her voice. Zac had been shocked when a male voice answered the phone. He hadn't even bothered to ask for Gail and slammed down the phone.

He lifted the revolver out of the box and held it up, as if seeing it for the first time. It felt comfortable in his hand. He grabbed the Scotch again, this time drinking straight from the bottle.

The warm feeling of alcohol crept through his blood. "You stupid bastard," he said loudly. He burst out laughing as he sat in his chair. He swiveled around, looking at his office, thinking of his life. A sequence of images flashed in his mind: his mother calling him to dinner as a young child, his first day of practice as a scared freshman on the Notre Dame football team, and his wedding day. He shut his eyes, as if to wish away the memories. He put the gun to his temple and spun the cylinder. Maybe a little game of Russian roulette was the way to go? Without any more thought, he pulled the trigger. *Click!* There was a sharp metallic sound, but no shot.

Zac was shocked by the sound, instantly alert as if awakened from a dream. He'd actually pulled the trigger. He realized how frighteningly close he'd come to death. It shook him to the core. He stood and wiped the sweat from his forehead. *But isn't this the honorable way out? Honor. That's a word I haven't thought of in a long time.*

He twirled the gun around a finger, as if almost enjoying the drama of this moment. He spied another photograph, almost hidden, on the top shelf of his bookcase. Another image flew through his mind, an image of a young boy saying, "Daddy, can we play one more time?"

He leapt from his chair and picked up the photograph – the one he generally avoided – and studied it. It showed a trim Zac standing next to a young boy, and father and son were grinning as they held up the fish they had just caught.

"Daniel," he whispered. His hands shook as he looked at the picture of his son. Zac had not spoken to Daniel in several years. There were the big arguments, the screaming, and then Daniel just walked out one day. Zac had planned Daniel's life so well, waiting for the day his son would take over the business. Instead, Daniel opted to become a college professor, and Zac had been unable to forgive his son for ruining his dreams.

As he looked at the photograph, it struck him that Daniel was probably close in age to another young man, a man Zac had tried to ruin, Cade Bryson. He held up the gun once more to his head, his finger on the trigger. He had sometimes wondered what he would think about during his last moments. Yet, no profound thoughts came to him, no great words of wisdom – only sadness and regret. The old song by Peggy Lee, "Is that all there is?" ran through his head.

His hand shook, while his finger caressed the trigger. He shut his eyes for a moment, and opened them again to look at the photograph of his son. He laid the gun back in the box and clamped the lid shut. Zac sat in his chair, buried his face in his arms, and wept.

43

CADE TURNED TO RUN – too late. The door had already been shut by the tallest of the three. He turned around to face Foulheart, his pulse throbbing with terror as he confronted his doom. He stared at the two hooded figures outlined against the dying embers in the fireplace. The taller figure joined his two hooded companions.

Cade's anger skyrocketed at Neville's deception in cultivating his friendship to lure him to Paris and death. He took a step forward. Foulheart immediately held up his hand. Cade halted.

"So, Neville, it was you all the time?" Cade clenched his fist.

Foulheart merely laughed.

"Lusty," said Foulheart, "why don't you make Mr. Bryson feel at home."

The smaller figure's hand raised up and removed the hood and mask. Cade stared incredulously, as Sherry smiled at him. "Hello, Cade. What a small world, seeing you here in Paris."

Unable to speak, Cade stood mute and confused.

Sherry continued in a cooing voice, "You didn't even say good-bye the last time we were together." She walked up to Cade, removed his hood and mask, and stroked his cheek lightly. "Pity, we could have made beautiful music together."

She laughed, and Cade brushed her hand away. Sherry's face took on an angry expression, but Foulheart said, "Now, Lusty. You had your chance with him. Leave us! He's all mine."

"With pleasure," she said. "Come on Slobglob."

The taller figure removed his hood, and Cade gasped as he recognized the dark figure he knew as Ian. His mind flashed back to the image of Ian standing on the stage at the Globe.

"'Parting is such sweet sorrow,'" Slobglob snarled.

"You jerk, I'll …" Cade stepped forward. Foulheart immediately jabbed a long, sharp metal poker at him, stopping him in his tracks.

Sherry gave one last flirting look at Cade and tugged on Ian's cloak. The two walked around him. He watched as she slid back the bolt on the door. Just as the door opened, a bright bolt of lightning flashed in the staircase. A second later, a blast of thunder followed. The door closed quickly, and there was a sliding noise. Cade figured the door was bolted on both sides.

He turned to face Foulheart, grateful at least that he could cool down a bit now that he was unmasked. He smelled the charred remains of wood in the fireplace and felt the creeping chill of the night air. The candles in the room were ebbing, flickering in the cross-current of air in the increasingly cold basement. The small, electric lights around the room were blinking, and Cade guessed the electrical storm was affecting them. He squinted to adjust his eyes to the dimming light.

"Well, well," said Foulheart, "so you thought you almost had us?" He burst forth again with his chilling laugh, reminding Cade of the laugh in the Malta cave when he'd first encountered Foulheart.

"The least you can do, Neville, Foulheart, whoever you are, is to face me in person." Cade had resigned himself to his fate, yet he almost felt a sense of peace, a strange calm, as he came face-to-face with death.

Foulheart nodded. "By all means." He raised his hands and removed the hood and mask. Cade stared into the face of Owen McCrady.

"But, I thought you were Neville." Cade was shaken by yet another shattered illusion, as he tried to comprehend that Bodley's Librarian was really Foulheart.

"Yes, I know. I recalled you being with that chap, Sterling, in the library for the lecture on that villain, Lewis. I suspected it was you here tonight, and I reckoned Sterling's voice would trick you into turning around. I must say, my little ruse worked quite nicely."

"How ... how did you know I was here and not Soulbane?"

"You almost fooled me, I'll give you that. When I acknowledged Soulbane's good work, you held up your hand, and I saw the scar. I knew Eric Majors had no scar, and I began to put two and two together. Who had a scar on their palm, I asked myself? Then, it hit me – that lovely chase you and I had through the streets of Oxford. Soulbane told me recently that you cut your hand on the wall at Trinity. Pity I didn't finish you off there and then." McCrady laughed loudly, and it reverberated around the room.

"Plus, the real Soulbane would have taken my acknowledgement of his reports as a chance to gloat among his fellow devils."

Cade rubbed the scar on his hand, remembering the night he had chased the illusive figure through the streets of Oxford, to retrieve his stolen computer. So, it had been Bodley's Librarian all along. No wonder McCrady had gone into the subterranean passage of the library. Cade grimaced at his failure to publish the reports, and now he'd lost that chance forever. He thought about how he had let so many inconsequential things in his life smother the truly important ones.

McCrady paced in front of the dying embers. "It would have been quite disastrous for us if you had escaped with knowledge of our operation." He tapped the notebook. "This contains the identities of the fiends I've had in place for many years, and the master plan I myself have devised to bring down the Enemy. It also has Soulbane's Reports. You see, I have the perfect cover as Bodley's Librarian. I can travel at will and place myself in almost every social and intellectual circle. Oxford is a marvelous place from which to run this operation. Of course, knowing what a weak and shallow individual you are, it's just as likely that, even if you had escaped tonight, you would never have done anything to stop us."

McCrady's shrill laugh accompanied this jab at Cade.

Cade winced at the verbal knife in his gut, but said nothing.

"It didn't take long for us to get you off the Enemy's pathway," McCrady continued. " I was furious at Slayspark for neglecting you and letting you have that unfortunate episode on top of Magdalen Tower. The damned Enemy was rejoicing over you that night, I understand. Well, He forgets that it's the one who laughs last that counts!" McCrady's voice was becoming increasingly loud and angry.

"I personally assigned Soulbane to take care of you."

Cade wanted to scream and shifted uncomfortably. His feet were in agony, pinched by Eric's too small shoes.

McCrady's voice lowered, "We worked little by little on you, whispering that you needed to study harder to get a good job, that you needed to work harder at your job to be successful, that you needed more money. It's such an easy illusion to foist on you foolish humans, who invariably chase after these mirages. Neglecting your family became almost second nature, and we encouraged you to think that it will be better later, if only you can get through the present struggles. Of course, there's always something to keep you imbeciles looking for something better in the future, and 'later' never comes. The Enemy programmed you like that, so that you would long for what He calls 'heaven.' You see, we generally take the things He considers 'good' and just subvert them subtly for our purposes. Sin is the greatest of all illusions: it promises so much – pleasure, power, possessions, prestige – but it never ultimately satisfies you humans, because the Enemy made you for spiritual purposes."

Cade knew he had only a few precious minutes to live. He was trapped in this room with the deadliest enemy he could have ever imagined. He breathed deeply and decided to keep Foulheart talking.

"So, what makes you think your plan, this so-called Operation Clootie, will be successful?"

McCrady smiled with obvious self-satisfaction, scratched his beard, and said, "Because I'm smarter than all my colleagues. For centuries, they have tried to defeat the Enemy. And, they've had some wonderful successes. But most of them foolishly tried a sledgehammer approach, such as war, massacre, or holocaust. While those are quite enjoyable spectacles for our Hindom, they have mixed results."

"How do you mean?" Cade was puzzled, but fascinated.

"Anytime we show our Underworld in some dramatic fashion, it reminds mortals of several things, like their own mortality, and the existence of sin and evil. It thus often makes them aware of the important spiritual battle going on all around them to which they generally pay no heed."

Cade thought of the passage in Ephesians that Neville had marked for him.

McCrady seemed oblivious to the storm. "All too often, such dramatic events send mortals scampering toward the Enemy for protection – which is the *last* thing we want – and the Ogre is always waiting for his prodigal children with open arms. His humility is absolutely disgusting."

"Then what are you doing differently?"

"I have an ingenious master plan." He tapped the large notebook on the table. I have placed loyal fiends all over the world in different positions of influence – in areas of medicine, law, government, technology, the media – the list is impressive. And, of course, within the Church!" At that Foulheart burst out laughing.

"My trusty underlings have been in place for many years and have gained the confidence of the people they live and work with. You've read Soulbane's Reports, so you actually have an excellent idea of our stratagems to defeat the Enemy and destroy souls. Now, here's where my genius comes into play. Subtlety is the key. We don't do anything dramatic that might wake you fools up. No, indeed, we just lull you to sleep."

"And how do you do that?" Cade wanted to keep Foulheart talking, and the latter was obviously enjoying the chance to boast.

"Just think about it. The last part of the twentieth century witnessed a wonderful, oh, what is the word in vogue with you humans these days? Oh, yes, dumbing-down. A dumbing-down of horrid things like morality and conscience. Western culture is so much more to our liking these days, not to mention the Church, which is a pitiful remnant of a once formidable army. A gentle dust of relativism has saturated society, and anything goes now. Concepts of sin and evil have, for the most part, disappeared. Belief in the Enemy is now passé. We're winning the ultimate spiritual battle, which is the only one that truly counts. My plan is simple: take the stratagems outlined in Soulbane's Reports, and patiently, quietly, implement them with the help of my tempters. The brilliant stroke I've employed is the subtlety of it all, so you humans will never know what hit you until it's too late."

McCrady began to shake as he shrieked with laughter. "You see, Screwtape had the same notion, but he made the mistake of letting his lunkhead nephew, Wormwood, bungle their plans by allowing C. S. Lewis to discover their correspondence. When our Royal Hindness banished them, I saw my opportunity. I would take up where Screwtape left off, only I'd follow up with an ingenious master stratagem to implement my schemes. With Screwtape out of the way, it was my big chance. You almost ruined it for me, but fortunately, you blew it by not making Soulbane's astute reports public."

Cade looked down at the ground, acutely feeling the agony of his missed opportunity.

McCrady went on, "When Operation Clootie is concluded, our Royal Hindness will see the brilliance of what I have devised, and I'll no doubt take my proper place at the foot of the table with him."

Then, looking straight at Cade with the most evil and menacing look Cade had ever seen, McCrady said, "And now, my fine fellow, it's the end of the road for you."

44

D ESPERATE TO KEEP Foulheart talking and preoccupied, Cade
asked, "How did you know I had the reports?"

"Oh, that. Yes, well, since no one else is about, I can tell you that
was my one and only error, ever. When I saw you in Sewanee and
you returned immediately to England, I suspected you might be on
to us. That's why I stole the computer from your room in Magdalen.
After I let those despicable creatures in the homeless shelter take
your computer from me, I naturally assumed that was the end of it.
I still had to make sure you hadn't kept a backup, which is why
Soulbane was assigned to you. It was absolutely essential to know if
you had the reports. After I saw what our Royal Hindness did to
Screwtape and Wormwood when Lewis published their letters, I
couldn't take a chance. You became my pet project. We knew your
likes and dislikes so well, that we had Soulbane take on this Majors
character. Of course, we knew you'd soon become fast friends. We
assumed that, if you had the reports, you would eventually spill the
beans. It frankly never dawned on me that you had your computer
returned to you. I just had to ensure you had no other copy."

McCrady paused and grunted. "But, when you never mentioned
anything about this to Soulbane, we'd long since decided you didn't
have them. Our sport became to destroy your marriage and,
ultimately, your soul. We placed Soulbane in an important role with
an international consulting company in Atlanta, where he could
keep an eye on you while also playing a major part in Operation

Clootie. Of course, all we do is prod – it's *you* who made all the choices." Foulheart sneered at Cade.

Cade wanted to feel angry, but it was shame that washed over him. He knew only too well how he had gradually walked away from God and Rachael ... and himself.

"But didn't God have any say in this?"

"Oh, He tried. How He tried. Each time we worked on you, your wife would gently try to pull you toward the Enemy. That wife of yours, by the way, is what the Enemy calls a true 'saint'. She proved to be a real obstacle to our plans for you. The Enemy was always there at your side, but you ignored Him."

Cade grimaced and wanted to kick himself for his blindness to Rachael's virtues.

Before he had much time to think about Rachael, McCrady continued, "Or, someone else, like that Neanderthal friend of yours, Preston, who Soulbane informed me kept trying to get you to come to his Bible study. But, you see, the reason the Enemy is losing the battle is that He still believes in free will." At that, McCrady hissed. "He thinks you humans bear some responsibility for your choices, and He gives you freedom to decide. Not that He abandons you ... quite the contrary. He's always at your side, day and night, which is our real challenge. No, Bryson, we just – how shall I put it? – 'encouraged' you to make certain choices, and over time it became easier and easier to get you to make the choices we wanted you to make. After a while, you became deaf to the Enemy's pleas."

It was becoming quite dim in the room. The candles had burned very low, and the fire was now nothing but a mass of dull orange embers.

"I must say, we had our work cut out for us with you."

At this, Cade felt self-satisfaction that he had somehow thwarted them.

Foulheart went on, "Not because of you, I might add. We've never really understood this prayer business that the Enemy utilizes. It's a damnable magic, I tell you. That awful wife of yours prays for you every day, as does that cretin Preston. They and others were able to prevent us from fully implementing our schemes for you because of their disgusting prayers. I still don't understand how the Enemy uses prayer, but it's a powerful spiritual magic."

Cade reflected with chagrin on his own pitiful prayer life.

"But, it's all to naught. Nothing can help you now." McCrady pointed the poker at Cade, playfully jabbing it at him.

"So, were Ian and Eric part of Operation Clootie?"

"But of course. Ian had access to information concerning all types of biological and bioterroism disasters that might prove useful to our cause. Eric, in addition to keeping an eye on you, was involved in efforts to accentuate and promote cultural differences and divisions. I might add, one of my greatest accomplishments is the bishop I have well-placed to help us water down the Enemy's doctrine and replace any hearty and bold Christian faith with an ineffective, relativistic, new age version. So far, it's worked stupendously." Foulheart howled with laughter, which echoed around the room.

"Do you have other copies of this plan?"

"Hell, no! Do you think I would dare trust anyone else in our Hindom with this? They would take credit for *my* work and *my* genius. I can't allow that. This is the sole copy. I trust no one. This is my big chance to get the Master's attention. I alone know how all the pieces of this elaborate diabolical puzzle fit together. When this operation is completed and the Enemy's troops are in a shambles, our Royal Hindness will no doubt make me his second-in-command."

McCrady seemed to be enjoying himself. "I'm almost sorry it's the end of the road for you, Bryson. You've been a nice challenge. But, now that you've stumbled upon our little secret, well ... ."

Cade felt the fear rising again. What was McCrady going to do with him?

"By the way, since you're here, what's happened to Soulbane?"

Cade smiled for the first time. At that moment, almost as if

Neville were standing next to him whispering in his ear, Neville's words came to Cade, " 'The devil … the proude spirite … cannot endure to be mocked.' "

Cade straightened his shoulders, fixed his eyes on McCrady, and said in a jeering and haughty tone, "Before I tell you about Soulbane, I have something else to tell you." He almost relished this moment. "I was in your meeting in Mobile."

"What? Impossible!" McCrady's eyes bulged in astonishment. Cade proceeded to describe the Mobile meeting in great detail. McCrady paced faster, his hands flailing.

"By the way, my daughter is quite safe and sound. Eric saved her life."

McGrady's face betrayed his shock, but before he could say anything, Cade continued, "And now, you asked about Soulbane? Soulbane … is dead."

McCrady's expression changed from shock to incredulity. He opened his mouth as if to speak, but nothing came out. He finally exclaimed, "You putrid liar! That's impossible. There's no way he can be … ."

"There *is* one way." Cade was relishing this repartee. "He … I prefer to call him Eric … turned to God."

McCrady stopped pacing and ranted, "You bastard. That's a lie."

Rubbing it in, Cade continued, "In fact, we prayed with him before he died, and gave him a Christian burial by spreading ashes in his memory in the graveyard next to Reverend Brooke."

McCrady stood near a tall wooden chair near the fireplace, stroking his beard. "No, you're lying. Soulbane is one of my ablest underlings." He advanced towards Cade. "Bryson, I've had enough. This is the end of the road… . "

At that moment, a loud crash of thunder sounded, and all the lights went out. The room was dark, save the faint glow from the dying fire. All but two of the candles had burned out. Cade knew this was his only chance. He stepped forward, grabbed the notebook from McCrady, and shoved the table into him. The bearded man fell, and Cade ran for the door.

He couldn't find the latch in the darkness. His mind raced as he tried to recall where he'd seen Sherry push the bolt. He heard McCrady getting to his feet, screaming, "Bryson, you're a dead man!"

Cade's fingers ran over the door, searching frantically for the latch. He felt something hard and metallic, and pulled it with all his might. There was a loud scraping as the latch lifted. The door creaked as it opened. He ran up the dark stairs as lightning flashed briefly. McCrady was screaming curses, and Cade heard his footsteps on the stairway.

He reached the top of the stairs, clutching the notebook. He could see nothing in the dark and froze, fearful of stumbling. A flash of lightning lit the hallway and showed him the way to the door. At the front door, he pulled hard, but it didn't budge. Frantic, he kicked the door hard and it flung open. He ran into the street. Another brilliant flash of lightning lit the entire street, followed by a loud boom of thunder. The rain came down in sheets. The street was deserted.

Cade dared not stop for his bag or to take off his gown. He guessed McCrady was right behind him, and his only chance was to get far enough away to find a hiding spot. Cade ran down the middle of the dark street and soon came upon the Seine. Notre Dame was illuminated by the next lightning flash, but it was hazy in the heavy downpour. As he ran, Cade realized that all of this part of Paris was completely dark. The storm had obviously knocked out the electricity in this area. Only a few car lights provided some meagre illumination.

He hurried across the street and turned around. McCrady, gown billowing, was pursuing. Cade ran down the sidewalk next to the Seine and across the bridge toward Notre Dame, his lungs burning in the cold air. His gown and clothes were thoroughly soaked by the rain. As he reached the other side, another flash of lightning lit up the entire cathedral plaza. He heard footsteps behind him, but didn't bother to look back. He pushed himself faster, his feet searing with pain because of Eric's shoes.

He ran toward Notre Dame and prepared to cross in front of the cathedral. As he did, his feet slipped out from under him on the slick pavement, and he landed face first on the hard ground, the notebook flying from his hands. His chin hit the pavement hard and throbbed with agony. He struggled to get up, but a sharp dagger-like pain in his side dropped him to his knees. Trying to shake the cobwebs out of his head, he wondered if he'd broken some ribs. He focused his eyes in the dark, looking for the notebook. He had to have it back. It was too dark to see anything, and he crawled on his hands and knees in the direction where he thought the notebook had gone. He finally felt it and snapped it up close to his chest.

As Cade struggled to his feet, he felt a tremendous force from behind, knocking him back to the ground. He jumped up, ignoring the searing pain in his ribs. Before he could run far, however, Cade felt a bone-crushing pain in his shins and toppled over something. In the dark, he'd run into something very solid. Before he could even think what to do next, something heavy landed on him and knocked his breath out. He struggled to free himself to no avail.

"You little bastard," McCrady said, pushing Cade's head against the cold, wet stone. "You've caused enough trouble to last me several lifetimes," he added, between puffs of breath. "Now, you'll be a wonderful statistic – the first unsolved death of the new year." Foulheart gave a shrill, sinister laugh.

Cade squirmed, but couldn't free himself. The rain had slackened and the thunder was a distant rumble now. He was growing faint. He realized his only hope would be to toss the notebook into the Seine and distract McCrady. This would mean Cade would forever lose the chance to expose Foulheart's Clootie schemes and publish Soulbane's reports, but he had no choice. With a superhuman effort, he shoved McCrady to the side, sat up on his knees, and threw the book as far as he could.

"No! No! No!" screamed McCrady, who reached out, grabbing only air.

Between coughs, Cade gulped in huge amounts of air, his chest heaving.

"You've ruined me, Bryson. For that you die."

McCrady leapt on Cade and pinned him to the ground. Cade couldn't budge. His face was pressed against the cold, wet stone. Then Cade experienced something a thousand times worse: the most intense despair and hopelessness in his soul he'd ever known. It was intangible, yet as real as the pain in his ribs. Suicidal feelings welled up and he knew he could not hold out long against this powerful, evil feeling of despair. He recalled Eric telling him that it wasn't the physical harm, but the spiritual harm, that was so dangerous.

McCrady was ranting in some strange, incomprehensible language. Cade's despair continued to grow as he sensed this was the end. Unless … unless … the tape recorder! Eric had told him to use it if Foulheart discovered him. It was his last chance. He moved his right hand a bit and managed to place his fingers around the small recorder. McCrady, in his screaming rage, appeared not to notice. Cade pulled it out, switched on the device and turned the volume up as high as it would go.

After a short silence, Eric, his voice weak but recognizable, spoke, "Greetings, Foulheart, this is Soulbane." McCrady stopped screaming. "If you're listening to this, it means you've discovered Cade. I leave you this message as I prepare to join the Blessed Trinity in heaven. I've turned my spirit over to God and my persona as Majors is dying. I saved Bryson's daughter's life. Now, Foulheart, I have a special message for you."

The despair Cade was experiencing dissipated somewhat, and Eric's voice could be heard over the sounds of the dying storm. McCrady was eerily quiet. Eric's voice continued, "I want you to listen carefully to this, Foulheart. This is the word of God:

'Let the same mind be in you that was in Jesus Christ, who, though he was in the form of God, did not regard equality with God as something to be exploited, but emptied himself, taking the form of a slave, being born in human likeness. And being found in human form, he humbled himself and became obedient to the point of death – even death on a cross. Therefore God also highly exalted him and gave him the name that is above every name, so that at the name of Jesus every knee should bend, in heaven and on earth and under the earth, and every tongue should confess that Jesus Christ is Lord, to the glory of God the Father.'"

The recorder went silent. Cade braced himself for a fatal blow. His last thoughts went to Rachael and Sarah. He said a quick, silent prayer to God to protect them.

But instead of feeling a blow, Cade heard a wailing moan. The weight on him subsided. He jumped up, ready to run. As he did, the lights of Paris flickered, then returned to full illumination. He blinked several times as his eyes adjusted to the lights, and he saw then that a retreat was unnecessary. Before his eyes, McCrady had vanished, and only the large black gown was visible lying on the ground. Inspecting the gown more closely, he found nothing inside but black ashes – all that remained of Owen McCrady. Cade grimaced with pain and relief.

Realizing that he would elicit some unwanted questions if someone found him in this condition, Cade took a deep breath and stood, taking off his robe. His ribs throbbed with jolts of pain as he gathered up McCrady's robe, holding all the ashes inside it. He pondered the mystery of why Foulheart had left ashes, when Soulbane had not, wondering if Eric's repentance was the explanation. He walked to the parapet of the bridge and flung McCrady's robe out like airing a blanket. The ashes fluttered down slowly, likes leaves floating off trees in autumn. The swift river current carried the dark flecks away into oblivion.

EPILOGUE

If I climb up into Heaven, Thou art there,
If I go to Hell, Thou art there also.
If I take the wings of the morning
And remain in the uttermost parts of the sea,
Even there also shall Thy hand lead me;
And Thy right hand shall hold me.

— *139th Psalm*

"Quick, hide! They're coming," whispered Rachael, motioning with her hands for Cade to follow her.

Without a moment's hesitation, Cade and Rachael dashed into the adjoining room in Bridgett's cottage and eased the door shut. The curtains were drawn and it was dark inside the room. Cade listened intently and could make out the sound of the front door creaking open. He drew in a deep breath.

When the door shut with a thud, Cade put his hand on the doorknob and eased the bedroom door open. He peered through the crack, but could see nothing. Two figures came into view, and he pushed open the door and rushed out.

"Surprise!" he yelled.

Rachael called from behind him, "Happy Birthday, Sarah!"

Sarah's eyes widened, and she burst into a giggle. She turned to Bridgett Adams, who had just walked in with Sarah. "Look, Nana, they remembered my birthday!"

"Of course we did, sweetheart." Rachael stooped and gave her daughter a hug.

Cade swooped in and picked Sarah up in his arms. "Happy Birthday, my little princess."

"Thank you, Daddy," squealed Sarah with obvious delight.

Lauren walked in from hiding in the kitchen. "I think you all need to come in here." Cade carried Sarah into the kitchen, followed by Rachael and Bridgett. On the breakfast table was a cake with white icing and red roses, and eight candles.

"Goodie, goodie, a cake." Sarah clapped her hands. Everyone took turns hugging Sarah and wishing her Happy Birthday.

A few minutes later, there was a knock at the front door, and Bridgett went to answer it. She soon returned with Robert, Rose, and Clive, who were all smiles.

Cade put Sarah down and went over to greet his friends. "You're just in time. Welcome, and thanks for coming."

Rachael started lighting the candles. "Now, Sarah, make a wish before you blow out the candles."

The little girl closed her eyes tightly, as if in deep thought. She opened them and leaned toward the cake.

The assembled group sang, "Happy Birthday." Before the adults finished singing, Sarah puffed up her cheeks and ceremoniously blew out all the candles. Everyone clapped as she picked up a candle and licked the icing.

Rachael turned to Lauren. "Thanks for baking such a lovely cake for Sarah's birthday."

"Don't mention it," she replied, smiling. "After all, we have a lot to celebrate this January sixth – Sarah's birthday, Cade's return, and Twelfth Night."

"Yes," said Sarah, "my birthday's on the 'Piphany."

"That's right, sweetie," said Cade laughing.

Lauren cut the cake, while Rachael added a scoop of vanilla ice cream and handed a bowl of dessert to everyone.

As they stood in the kitchen eating cake and ice cream, Robert Thompson came over to Cade and put his arm around him. "Cade, I can't tell you how glad I am to be here with you and your family. I can only imagine what you've been through. I ... I ... " but nothing more came out. The old man's eyes glistened, and he smiled, giving Cade an extra tug around his shoulders.

Cade smiled weakly. "Yes, it's been quite an ordeal. Fortunately, we've heard the last of Foulheart. Bless you, Robert."

"I understand you almost had the Foulheart fellow's master plan."

"Yes, but I had to toss it into the river. What really kills me is I had to throw Soulbane's Reports away, too. All those years I had them and could have done something with them, and now they are lost forever."

Robert gestured toward Sarah, "Well, it's not the end of the world, is it? You're safe, and you have a beautiful wife and daughter. That's what matters."

"You're right, Robert, as usual."

Lauren walked over to them. "All the talk around Oxford is about the mysterious disappearance of Bodley's Librarian. Seems no one has an explanation, and the BBC has been snooping around. Yesterday, the gossip was that some 'irregularities' have been discovered at the library, but no one is saying yet just what they are."

Cade laughed. "You can be sure it will all get swept under the rug. We obviously can't divulge what really happened, or they'll lock us up and throw away the key."

"Not only Bodley's librarian," added Lauren. "The BBC is also reporting some strange disappearances of people all over the world – lab technicians, doctors, computer analysts, – just vanished into thin air without a trace. The one odd thing so far is that none of them had a family. They were well respected, but loners. There were some college professors, lawyers, politicians, and even, apparently, several priests. And Ian, of course, has disappeared."

At that moment, Bridgett said, "Oh, Cade, I almost forgot. Mr. Martin called the house this morning while you were taking a walk."

Cade's heart sank at the prospect, dreading that this glorious day was about to be ruined.

"What did he have to say?" he asked dejectedly.

"He said to tell you that a Mr. Pickering has been arrested along with some senators, and that all charges against you have been dropped. He wants to see you as soon as you get back about your partnership announcement."

Rachael ran over and hugged him. "Oh, Cade, that's marvelous."

But Cade stopped smiling, and Rachael asked, "What's wrong? Isn't that the best news you could hear?"

"I'm glad my name is cleared. But the only thing I'll see Harry about is to clean out my office." Cade gave a wry smile. He'd been willing to sacrifice his family and faith for this goal, and now that it was in his grasp, he was no longer interested.

"What presents did I get?" Sarah asked just then. The adults laughed.

"Now, Sarah, young lady, you *know* better than that," Rachael replied.

"You're right, Sarah," said her grandmother, not missing a beat. "What's a birthday without presents?"

Bridgett walked out of the kitchen and returned quickly with an armful of presents.

"Cool." Sarah tore open the wrapping of one of the presents.

Cade stood across from her, finishing his cake. This was one of the happiest moments he'd ever experienced. He looked over at Rachael and Sarah and felt himself the most blessed man in the world.

"I have another surprise today," Cade announced. "Rachael, close your eyes."

Rachael smiled impishly and closed her eyes tightly.

Cade added, "Now, don't peek."

Rachael made a mock frown on her face, but kept her eyes closed. Cade pulled out a box and walked behind Rachael. He lifted a pearl necklace carefully from the box. As he put it around her neck, Rachael's eyes opened, and she said excitedly, "Oh, Cade, are these really for me?"

"Merry Christmas and Happy New Year." Cade kissed her on the cheek after he'd fastened the clasp. Everyone else in the room clapped.

Rachael's fingers ran along the glittering pearls, and she smiled brightly. "You know, I'd forgotten all about Christmas presents! You shouldn't have, but I love them." She hugged Cade's neck, whispering in his ear, "I love you."

There was a knock at the door, and Lauren jumped up, saying, "That must be David ... I mean, Reverend Cooper." Her face turned red, and Cade and Rachael smiled at each other. Lauren added as she went to the door, "He said he'd try to make it."

Indeed, David Cooper came into the kitchen with Lauren. He held three bright red helium balloons and a small, wrapped present.

"How nice of you to bring some balloons for Sarah's birthday," said Rachael.

Sarah jumped up and ran to the vicar. "Oh, Mommy, they're not for me, they're for Uncle Eric."

Cade looked quickly at the adults, and everyone frowned except for the vicar, who kept smiling, as he held the balloons out to Sarah.

"What ... what do you mean, dear?" asked Rachael, a look of concern on her face.

"When Reverend Cooper came to see me the other day, I asked him to bring me some balloons, so that I could send a message to Uncle Eric."

"A message?" repeated Cade, profoundly puzzled.

"Yes. I'm going to tie a note to the balloons and let them go outside. Then, they'll float up to heaven and my note will get delivered to Uncle Eric. I want to tell him I love him."

Cade felt the lump in his throat and wondered what to say.

"What a splendid idea." Rachael stroked Sarah's head.

"Can you help me tie it?" Sarah looked up at the vicar.

"Of course I can," he said, bending down with the balloons.

Sarah ran over to a small bag and pulled something white out of it. Cade walked over, and she handed it to him. In her childish scrawl, she had written,

Dear Uncle Eric,

I miss you. Please tell God to take good care of you.

Love,

Sarah

Underneath, she had drawn a rainbow.

Cade stared at the note, his hand trembling and handed it to Rachael, who teared up as she read the note. Rachael handed it to Cooper, who tied the note on the end of the three strings.

"Let's send it off now." Sarah jumped up and down, clapping her hands.

"Put on your coat first, young lady," Rachael admonished with a grin.

Cade squinted as they walked into the bright afternoon sun. The bitter cold spell had finally passed, although it was still cool. The sky was clear and blue, and a soft wind fluttered through the village. Everyone assembled around Sarah.

"Here you go, Sarah," said Cooper handing her the balloons.

The little girl took the balloon strings in her hand, extended her arm and stood on tiptoe. She paused and released them. They rose quickly, the small white note spiraling upward behind them.

"Bye bye," Sarah yelled, waving. The balloons rose higher and higher, quickly becoming black dots in the sky. A current of air took them far down toward the horizon. In a few minutes, the balloons were invisible.

"They're gone," said Lauren, looking skyward and shading her eyes.

"I wonder how long it will take them to get to heaven?" Sarah asked.

Cade picked up Sarah in one arm, and put his other arm around Rachael. He looked up in the sky one last time. "Sarah, I wouldn't be surprised if Uncle Eric's already reading your note."

Sarah clapped her hands. She put them into her coat pockets and said, "Daddy I forgot. Uncle Eric said to give this to you."

She held out a piece of white paper. Cade, puzzled, put her down and took the paper from her. It was a crumpled, white envelope. He opened it and stared in astonishment at its contents.

"What is it?" Rachael asked.

"It's my computer disk. The one that I turned over to Ian at the Globe. Eric has given me back his reports."

"You're kidding?" Lauren now joined them.

Cade shook his head, gripping the disk tightly.

When the group returned to the cottage, Bridgett held up another present. "I've been meaning to ask what this present is that's been in my room."

"Oh," replied Rachael, "Neville Sterling brought that over on Christmas Eve. I guess in all the excitement, we forgot about it."

"I wonder what it could be?" inquired Lauren.

"Let me see, let me see," Sarah said, grabbing the present from her grandmother and sitting on the floor. Sarah tore off the wrapping to reveal a beautiful mahogany box.

"What's this?" the little girl asked.

Rachael stooped down toward the box. "Why, it's a music box." She opened the lid, and music played.

Sarah looked up wide-eyed. "Dr. Lauren, that's the same song you played for me on your flute!"

Cade's spine tingled as the music of Debussy's *Reverie* flowed softly from the box.

"You're right, Sarah," Lauren replied. She turned to Rachael and Cade, her face pale. "But, how did ... how could Neville have known? He brought the music box over here before I played this tune for Eric that night!"

Cade looked at Cooper. "That reminds me, David, I must say

good-bye to Neville before we leave for Atlanta tomorrow. I'm surprised I haven't seen him since I returned from Paris. In fact, I was hoping to invite him over for the party. Do you know how I can call him?"

"Neville?" said the vicar, shaking his head negatively. "I'd never seen him before Christmas Eve. I thought he was a friend of yours."

Cade stared at Cooper. "I only met him a week or so ago. I just assumed he lived here in the village."

Goose bumps ran up and down Cade's arms. He recalled Neville's words at the Bodleian that "people have entertained strangers unaware that they are angels." Without another word, he walked out the front door, looked up into the fading blue sky, and saluted toward heaven. "God be with ye, Neville."

THE END

ACKNOWLEDGMENTS

Many people have contributed to this book. First, my wife, Kelli, who has constantly encouraged me to pursue my dream of writing. Likewise, my sons, whom I love more than words can express, are a constant source of inspiration and joy. Also, the countless friends and strangers who read *The Soulbane Stratagem* and urged me to continue to write – especially those who requested a sequel.

To John Hunt I owe so much for his willingness to take a chance on an unknown author. I shall forever be indebted to him as a wonderful publisher, who truly changed my life for the better. My editor and friend, Colin Nutt, contributed a keen eye and excellent editorial judgment.

Several special friends have assisted with this book. I have no adequate way to express my heartfelt gratitude for their loving help, prayers, and encouragement. First, to those who carefully read drafts and provided many helpful comments: Paul Walker, Paul Zahl, Jeanette Sommers Wade, Steph Britt, Fran Cade, Hans Watford, and David Donaldson. Several others assisted in different ways, including Bruce Barbour, Michael and Margaret Comely, Jeanine Jones, Mary Ann Lucas, Nida Hammond, Sergio Stagno, Marilyn Meredith, Nancy Poynor, and Jay McDonald. Special thanks go to Ann and Gordon Rosen, and to Jerry Nelson, for their love; to Bradley Arant Rose & White LLP, an excellent law firm, for their support of my first book; and to Kenny Hartley for his wonderful design of Soulbane's website, www.soulbane.com.

Robert Fraley, who generously worked with me to get my first book published, died in a plane crash just before it was released. He was a man of faith and integrity, and a true friend. His widow, Dixie, is the epitome of grace.

I lost my best friend and father before this book was written. My Dad did get to read my first novel, however, and for that blessing, I shall be forever grateful. As shown by the dedication, I owe so much to my Mom and Dad, which I can only gratefully acknowledge, but never repay. I only hope that one day my sons will understand the depth of my love for them.

Finally, creative writing is a gift from God, and for that gift, I can only look toward heaven and salute with a grateful heart.

Philippians 1:3